The Candlemaker's Affair

Stephen Ross

Candlemakers Yard

www.candlemakersyard.com

Dedicated to Millicent, who has given me the space

to chase my dream and write this book.

Mi stima bo dushi.

Please donate to the Motor Neurone Disease Association,
Just Giving Fundraising page:
www.justgiving.com/page/candle-maker-1712138032164

Acknowledgements

Cover Artwork by Amy Smith of Two Lost Birds,
www.facebook.com/2lostbirds

Inside Front Cover Photo by Stephen Ross

Inside Back Cover Photo by Millicent Ross

Map & cover digital work by Jamie Whyte, see: **www.jamiewhyte.co.uk**

Editing and Proof Reading by Anne-Marie Hoppitt, BA (Hons), MA.
QLS Level 4 Proofreading and Editing.

Medical advisor: Mrs. Ann Devenish, RGN, RMN.

Police Advisor: Bob Connor

Somerset Advisors: Carol & Martin Barnes

Regional News: Kimberley Barber, Editor of the *Basingstoke Gazette*.

Contents Warning

Advisory 18+ only

Contains descriptions of sexual activity between consenting adults, foul language, threats of violence to people and animals, medical emergencies, death, misogyny, sexism, racism, gambling, prostitution, brothels, exploitation, smoking, courtroom trials and regional accents.

Please do not purchase or read this book if you might be adversely affected by reading about these subjects.

Introduction

This is not a sex book. Sex, or the lack thereof, is the fuel that powers this vehicle, but it is not the journey nor the destination. I wanted to create something to commemorate a fading generation, before they are consigned to life's scrap heap. This book will resonate with those fine, upstanding folks born in the twenty-five years after World War Two. They may now have silver in their hair, but they surely have gold in their hearts. They are the jam in the middle of the sandwich generation, probably still supporting their grown-up children, whilst caring for their elderly relatives. Their rocket may be high in the sky, but it is no longer in the ascendency. They may now work for a younger boss, someone whom they may even have hired themselves. They may have faced redundancy, possibly on more than one occasion. They may be wondering if their pension will be sufficient for a happy retirement, or will they have to downsize their home and tighten their belts? If they are lucky, they might still be in a loving and rewarding relationship. The passage of time can change married people, altering their relationship, possibly leading to the making of decisions which they may later come to regret. This book is about one such couple and the ramifications of when their boat was rocked. Weaving many background personal memories and anecdotes into this story made me laugh and cry in equal measure, as I let them flow to my keyboard. I hope that you have a similar experience as you read it.

This quote from Dan Snow inspired me to write this book:

'It is better not to have lived than to live and leave no trace of your existence behind.'

Contents

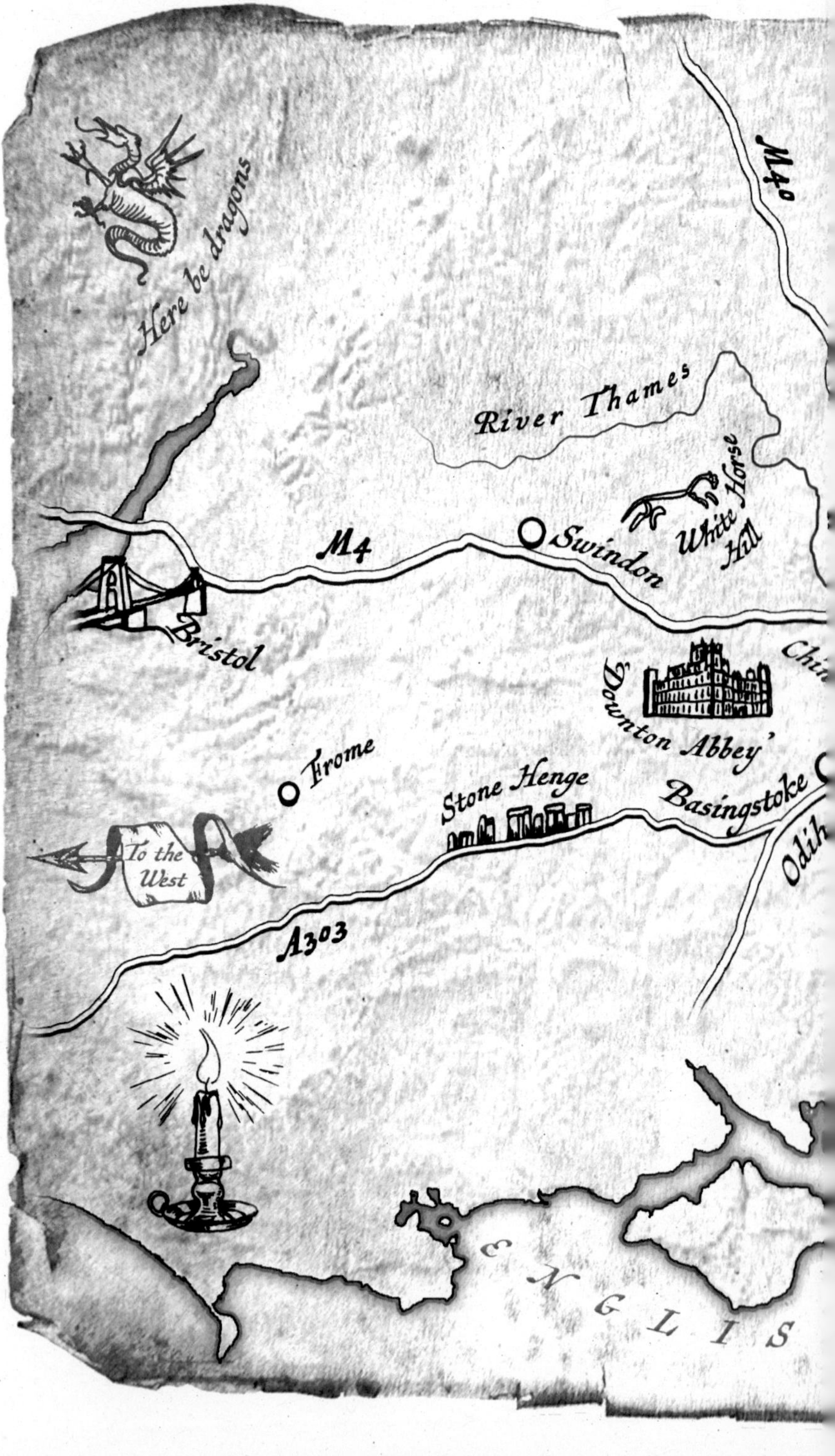
Here be dragons
M40
River Thames
White Horse Hill
M4
Swindon
Bristol
Chin
Downton Abbey'
Frome
Stone Henge
Basingstoke
Odih
To the West
A303
E N G L I S

Chapter 1

The Beginning of the End

7th March 2013

It was a dark and stormy night as Trevor got out of the car and trudged up his driveway, slowly inserted the door key in the lock and, as silently as he could, opened the door.

Ellen's voice came from above, 'Is that you Trevor?'

'Yes dear, sorry to wake you,' he said. *S**t!* he thought. In the porch, he shook the rain off his jacket, and came inside, shutting the door firmly behind him, hung his jacket on his peg and headed to the kitchen.

While making himself a mug of tea, Trevor's mind was distracted by thoughts of Jingfei and the argument they had got into earlier. She could be a real bitch when she was in a bad mood and sometimes it just needed one of the girls answering her back to set her off. The arguments were about money, they were always about money. Trevor knew that one of the girls was sending money home to support her family and another was still paying off the balance of her 'delivery charge', so he tried to see their situation from their perspective, but he had expenses to cover and Jingfei was still trying to clear her gambling debt to Mr. Doherty. Money had become a cause of friction between Trevor and Jingfei, and he hated friction, arguments, and all types of strife generally.

He had always tried to avoid it with Ellen, because she could hold a grudge and give him the silent treatment for much longer than made it worth his while to correct her when she was wrong. Sometimes he felt like Ellen had turned him into a eunuch, because he deferred to her so much in the name of conflict avoidance. At home he really felt like he had been turned into a 'Yes Dear' man, he gave in to her so much. Their relationship had worsened in the years since their two daughters went away to University, got themselves good jobs and then moved in with their respective partners. It had been a gradual process, like autumn tearing the leaves from a tree, no one incident was a milestone, just a slow descent down a depressing one-way path, a descent that Trevor could not see a way to reverse, nor did he really have any steam left in him, nor sufficient desire, to make the effort to do so.

Trevor and Ellen had met in the mid-1970s, when they were in their early twenties, and working in the City. She was working in the Marks and Spencer's, where Trevor used to go to buy his lunch. Trevor first noticed her auburn hair bouncing along behind her as she would scuttle back and forth carrying a tray of supplies to top up the shelves. He was sure that he had seen her smile at him, but he was, to say the least, a bit on the shy side and he was certainly not brave enough to make the first move and strike up a conversation with her. The only effort he really made was to dither over his choice of takeout lunch, in the hope of seeing her go by twice on her restocking route.

Ellen had noticed the gangly, well-dressed young man with a shock of blonde hair dawdling over his lunch choice on a few occasions, but she really was in too much of a tizz to pay him any mind. She knew that Miss Hawkins would be chivvying her up if her fridges were not kept as full as possible to satisfy the hunger of the lunchtime crowd. She certainly had no time for dawdling, *it's alright for these City folks to be frittering away their time,* she thought, *but some of us have got work to do here.*

Then one day she saw the gangly young man coming into the Food Hall, looking absolutely drenched and she suddenly realised that she had been so busy going back and forth restocking, that she hadn't noticed that it was raining cats and dogs out there. His shock of blonde hair had been replaced by a matted mop and he was not looking best pleased.

'Oh no, look at you moi luv,' she said, surprising him with her West Country accent. 'You must be soaked to the skin, you poor dear. I'll nip out the back 'n get you a towel.'

And before Trevor had a chance to say anything, she was gone.

She soon came back with a towel and an umbrella she'd borrowed from their Lost Property locker. ''Ere dry yur face with this, or you'll catch yur deaf o' cold. An' I've got a brolly, you can borrow to get yerself back to work.'

'Thank you,' he managed to splutter, 'but I don't want to take your umbrella, you'll need it yourself, later won't you?'

'No, I'll be fine,' she replied, 'you can come and walk me to the Tube after moi shift!'

And so, it began, slowly at first, as it was generally done in those days, it really was the man's prerogative to take the lead in these matters but Trevor would never have been described as a great leader, a taker of the first step, one to jump into things feet first, without a care for the outcome. No, Trevor was more of a thinker, one who takes things carefully and gives great deliberation to his actions and his work. *Who knows,* Trevor thought as he sipped his tea, *if Ellen hadn't had a heart of gold, if there hadn't been a downpour that day, things might have turned out differently, just like with the sliding doors of the tube train, in that film with Gwynnie.*

The rain was drumming on the conservatory roof as Trevor moved from the kitchen, sat down in his favourite cane chair and wrapped his hands around his mug of tea, *at least I can gain some warmth from that,* he thought. He had always considered himself to be a decent, honest and generous man, but it irked him greatly that these attributes were not shared by those closest him. Sometimes he felt that Ellen and Jingfei both took advantage of him in this respect, presuming that he would concede to their wishes or viewpoint. Tonight's argument with Jingfei was a case in point, she wanted to get a bigger place with a fourth bedroom, he knew that it would give them a bigger income and Jingfei knew a fifth girl that could work for them, but Trevor was well aware that the monthly rental of a four-bedroom house or flat in the same area would cost at least an additional £300 per month and bring with it more expenses and other issues. He knew that it would give them a net boost to their income, but

he had always wanted to err on the side of caution and keep as low a profile as possible in that business. This was what Jingfei refused to understand, that they were better off just sticking to paying back Mr. Doherty £2,000 per month, so she would be debt free before her birthday in August, rather than getting the bigger place and risking exposure in the process.

These thoughts did not help to brighten his mood. He finished his tea, put the mug in the dishwasher, turned the downstairs lights out and went upstairs hoping that Ellen had gone back to sleep. She hadn't. After taking a shower, Trevor found that she was still awake and lying in bed waiting for her daily debrief.

'How did it go at the Old Farts Club tonight then Trev?' she asked sweetly.

He knew that she didn't really want to know the answer to her question and that she had posed it just to use it as an opportunity to try to wind him up. She enjoyed calling it by that name, just to remind him that he was not a spring chicken anymore and that she had never really enjoyed going to their events, since she had become less outgoing following 'the change'. Whenever she deemed it worth her while to go to any of the events, it would always be at the end of long, drawn out and tortuous deal-making process, which Trevor knew, would ultimately end in 'success' for his side of the discussion, but it would not come easily, nor would it come without his agreement to sufficient purchases, promises made and general buttering up of his wife.

'Yeah, it was fine thanks love,' he lied. 'The usual crew were there, still practicing our parts for the next quarterly meeting,' he added, to pad out the lie a bit, just to give her some scintilla of supposed substance to make it seem that he really had been to an OFC meeting and to then let her move on to whatever was her 'Today's Special Issue'. He knew it must be coming his way, as she had waited up to this hour, she must really be waiting to impale him with something.

'Oh, that's good dear, so glad to hear that. Did you see that Dolly and Jack next door have got a new car in their driveway?'

'No, sorry Ellen, I didn't notice that,' Trevor said as he got in bed next to her, glad to finally know what this TSI was, 'it was chucking it down when I drove up, I got wet enough as it was, just dashing in from the car. I'll take a look in the morning.'

Ellen ignored that response, she wasn't going to let him get off so easily. 'Trev, don't you think that we should get a new car, we could get a nice one like Emma and Lee brought, that's a nice car, lovely colour and it's even got a guard sort of gate thing in the back for their dog.'

'We haven't got a dog Ellen,' said Trevor flatly.

'Oh, you know what I mean Trev, it's an Estate car, with plenty of room in the back for suitcases when we go away.'

'You don't like going away now Ellen, not like we used to anyway.'

'Yes I do Trev, it's just that we have to be around to keep an eye on Mum now, you know that Carol and Maria won't be able to spare time to check on her.'

'We don't need to get a new car Ellen, our one has only just had its first MOT, we've not even done 40,000 miles in it yet.'

'Trev, you know I never liked that grey colour you chose, you only picked it because the garage gave you good deal to get it out of their showroom. It never looked as nice as it did under their lights.'

Trevor liked the grey colour for its anonymity, it did not stand out at all at night and it was decidedly unmemorable in the daylight, that was exactly the way Trevor liked it to be.

He knew Ellen, like a dog with a bone, would need some kind of peace offering to make her drop the TSI, without losing face tonight, but he had no intention whatsoever of promising her a new car, his finances were stretched enough by having to maintain two households as it was.

'I'll go see Jack after work tomorrow love,' Trevor said, to try to fob her off, 'just to see if he got a good deal on it from somewhere.'

For Ellen, this reply really was lacking in sufficient commitment to satisfy her, but she decided that as it was later than she normally went to sleep, it was a big enough concession from Trevor to let him off the hook for now. After all she knew that she could return to the topic another time. She was happy at least that she scored a success by sowing the seed and getting it on Trevor's radar. 'OK love, say hi to Dolly and Jack for me, we really must have them round some-time soon, see if they're not doing anything on the weekend would you?'

Inwardly Trevor breathed a sigh of relief, he felt that he had ridden the TSI bronco like a pro, giving no ground, only a promise of a chat with Jack. He already knew that Dolly and Jack would be too busy to pop round this weekend. He would need to come up with a good enough reason for their absence, something which would not make Ellen smell a rat or want to pop over the road herself to double-check on his lie.

'OK love, will do, I'm ready for a little cuddle now, what about you Ellen?'

He already knew what her response would be, it was the same every time he asked for 'a little cuddle' these days, he just said it to ensure that their bedtime conversation was over for the night and that he could finally get some sleep. Jingfei really knew her job well and she had pretty well drained him earlier tonight.

He was beginning to realise that he was not as young as he used to be and that he might have to start cutting back on his visits to her, however unpalatable that might be to him. He would cross that bridge another time. He knew that he had to be delicate in his dealings with Jingfei, she had a volatility within her which had really shocked Trevor when he had seen it before, luckily not directed at him but at one of her customers, who'd foolishly tried to short-change her.

'Oh, don't be daft Trevor,' Ellen scorned him. 'You know it's too late for that!'

Yes, by quite a few years, thought Trevor, bitterly.

'Go to sleep yer silly bugger, it's late,' she said. With an air of finality she added, 'Sleep good love.'

'You too dear,' replied Trevor, glad to be able to finally draw a line under the tedious conversation and try to nod off at last.

This was the way it had been for some time now, since she had gone through 'the change'. But it wasn't really a matter of 'going through', as that would imply that there was a finite starting point and a finite ending point. A time when things were good, a time when things were not good, and then a time when things were good again. Their life together had been really good before that, they both continued working in the City; Ellen enjoyed her job at Marks and Spencer's, they were a good employer and she had a nice group of girls to work with, all of a similar age, outlook and aspirations. Before he'd met Ellen, Trevor had graduated from the Bartlett Faculty at University College London, with a good degree and was absolutely delighted to get an architectural assistant role in a firm where his Uncle Anthony worked. He loved working in the City, he loved the idea of working in the City, it was like the badges he'd earned in the Scouts, something to be proud of, to set him apart from his contemporaries at school who had not passed their A Levels and got a place at university. He even loved commuting by train, to him it was all part of the process of gaining the status and familial approval he so deeply craved.

They were married in 1979, but did not have a honeymoon, just an overnight stay in the Berystede Hotel in Ascot, where both sets of parents had clubbed together to pay for the wedding breakfast and evening party.

The main outward difference after the wedding, was that Ellen moved in to live with Trevor and his parents in Bracknell, while they saved up for a

deposit for a home of their own. Ellen however, was not as keen as Trevor on commuting, she had been happy staying in Wandsworth with her uncle Terry during the week and going home to Frome for the weekend. Her commute used to just be a 20-minute bus ride, rather than the hour and a quarter it took by train and bus from Bracknell. But that was insignificant compared to the joy that she felt at being Mrs Braithwaite. She repeated her new name to herself many times a day after they became man and wife, it sounded so posh compared to 'Smith', which she always thought of as being so common. She wanted to make sure that she could pronounce it in a comfortable and confident manner, to convey the impression that she had always been Mrs Braithwaite.

Ellen consciously started to try to shed her Somerset accent. Trevor had never mentioned it directly, but she was aware, as soon as she moved in with his parents, that people spoke differently in Royal Berkshire. Her parents noticed it when Trevor and Ellen visited them one Saturday, her Mum thought that she had gone 'all La-di-dah'. It hurt Ellen to think that her Mum thought that she had disowned her family. She had not intended to upset her family or deny her heritage, she just wanted to try to fit in better with Trevor's family, who had been so kind to her and invited her to live with them, under their roof. She also practiced her new signature until she felt that she had perfected it to the right level of style and sophistication, whilst still making sure that it would fit in the space on her new cheque book. It was longer than her previous signature, which she used to embellish with a swooping 'S' at the start of Smith. When she tried to repeat the trick with a stylish 'B', she soon realised that she would run out of space by the time she got to the second 'a'. She felt that it was not fair that she had to dial back on the flourish and she had always hated to compromise, even on small matters, but she finally managed to settle this inner turmoil and arrive at a suitable signature after many attempts.

By scrimping and saving Trevor and Ellen managed to save enough for the deposit on a house. Trevor had heard of a new housing estate being built near Basingstoke, where the houses were cheaper than Bracknell, but the commute into London would be longer and more expensive. This was to be the cause of their first argument. Trevor did not like the flats that they could afford in Bracknell, his architect's eye viewed them with disdain. They had been built in the 1950s and 1960s, to a tight budget, to house London's post-war overspill. Bracknell was one of the eight new towns built around London. Trevor's parents had moved to Bracknell when Trevor was three, they had seen the adverts, showing how lovely, green, new, clean and shiny Bracknell was. It was such a complete contrast to the East End of London that they left behind, which was still bomb damaged from the war, dirty, grimy, smoky and smelly. His parents knew that the East End was not a good, healthy place to bring up a child. They wanted more for him than they had had in the East End, even before the war, it was not a great place to live. It had great people and a real community spirit, but it was still the downwind side of London, fumes from the posh West End and the great smog regularly filled their lungs and brought them out in a fit of a racking cough. The council helped them with the move, as they were planning on bulldozing their row of back-to-back terraced council houses. A council van took their meagre belongings as well as Trevor and his mum along the old Bath Road, with his dad following along behind on his motorcycle and sidecar. It was a long bumpy journey, Trevor's mum had not realised just how much 'country' there was between London and Bracknell, but she loved the fresh air coming through the van's side window.

His parents soon made friends amongst their neighbours and through joining the congregation at the nearby Holy Trinity Church. So many of their new-found friends had also made the exodus from the East End, they rapidly found life comfortable in Bracknell, as they had much in common together. It used to quite amuse Trevor's mum to hear the old folks in the congregation, speaking in their rural accents, as it was such a contrast to the Cockney accents she had grown up with.

Reverend Norman Norgate, the kindly vicar of the Holy Trinity Church, realised that welcoming the new arrivals, with their coarse accents, would be the ideal way to breathe new life into his ageing congregation. He asked his wife, June, to start a 'Young Wives Club', a name which might be frowned upon in more modern times. June quickly found eager YWC members approaching her, after Norman included a piece about the YWC in the Church magazine and during his end of service notices. Trevor's mum was one of those. She headed up the knitting team, organising weekly Tuesday morning knitting sessions for novices and experts alike. Trevor hated those meetings, even though they only affected him during the school holidays and then only on one day a week, he hated them. He hated the fact that those women took his mum away from him; the holidays were the time when, being an only child, he deserved the full attention of his mum. He hated the fact that some of those women wore jeans with their unsightly protuberant bellies squeezing out over the top of the waistline. But most of all, he hated the fact that those women left an unpleasant aroma in his lounge after their weekly meetings. It wasn't just the assaults on his nasal cavities of the various perfumes they wore, there was an underlying smell emanating from the women that somehow worked its way straight into the distaste sensor of Trevor's brain and he hated that. Trevor was always keen to open the lounge windows after the meetings, a habit he took into later life. Ellen would call him 'Fresh Air Freddy' when he opened the windows, and especially on the cooler autumnal days, she would follow him around later, closing them slightly.

For Ellen, merely moving to Bracknell was a major change, she never really liked any kind of change and Bracknell was far more 'Towny' than she have ever known before, she really was a country girl at heart. When she first went there, she was disorientated by all the roundabouts and housing estates, she found it hard to get her bearings, but having moved in with Trevor's parents, she soon found that Trevor and she could take a bus to the Town Centre and Train Station, the route of which employed some clever short cuts to speed their journey. That sense of 'inside info' led Ellen to feel like a local and settle in. The thought of moving to another town and starting again just filled her with dread, she knew that she would have Trevor with her to help her settle in, but such things were somehow so much easier for Trevor. They had lived in Bracknell for four years now and it felt like home. Trevor had such a good sense of direction which meant that the unknown roads of Basingstoke would hold no fear for him. So, it was easy for Trevor to want to move from Bracknell to Basingstoke to get a nice house, but she was not keen and she let him know that every time the topic came up. Ellen really wanted to find a nice house in their budget in Bracknell, but it wasn't easy and it was causing a bit of stress between them.

Trevor, meanwhile, just couldn't wait to be free of his Mum's apron strings. He knew she meant well, but as a newlywed, he just wanted Ellen and him to start their lives as husband and wife, in a place of their own. At times it felt to Trevor like he was not married at all. It was as if the wedding simply hadn't happened and that here he was, still a young adult, under his parents' roof where they had simply rearranged the dining room chairs to accommodate a guest. Trevor's Mum always had a 'helpful' suggestion to chip into their conversations and she had already dropped a few hints about the 'patter of tiny feet'. At the moment, Ellen had taken these in good humour, as she knew how kind it was of Trevor's parents to accommodate them and how it gave them a chance to save up for a deposit, but Trevor just wanted to make the break as soon as possible, before any animosity crept into the extended Braithwaite household. He hated to upset his parents, he had always sought his Mum's approval; proudly reporting his good school grades, while forgetting to report the lesser grades. Even his choice of Scout badges reflected his Mum's view of what topics were important, like the First Aid, Collecting, Morse Code, Cycling and Cooking badges.

More importantly, as far as he was concerned, Trevor certainly found that his opportunities to exercise his conjugal rights were being severally restricted by the situation he now found himself in. Before their wedding,

Trevor and Ellen had been able to make use of the opportunities provided by Ellen's room at her Uncle Terry's flat. Terry had worked as a cleaner at the old Covent Garden Flower Market since the early 1960s, which meant that he would leave the flat just after 2pm and not get back until just before midnight. Fortuitously for Trevor and Ellen, this gave them plenty of time after work to enjoy each other's company and mutually learn what pleasures their bodies could offer them. In common with other teenagers, from about the age of about fourteen, Trevor had frequently felt the need to 'release the pressure' as he liked to refer to the act of self-pleasuring and he had gone on to develop a strong sex drive, in which Ellen was not shy about joining him. They used to joke about going to Uncle Terry's to play 'hide the sausage', it was one of their in-jokes they loved to share and snigger about. Not so now, living together in his parents' house.

Having a place of his own was also a matter of pride for him, it would be another string to his bow, another badge on his Scout's shirt sleeve, for as a junior architect, he craved the lifestyle and credibility that the fully-fledged architects had; a Sierra in the driveway and dinner parties with Prawn Cocktails, German wines and smart, witty, friends. Every time he showed Ellen a newspaper advert for the new houses going up in Basingstoke, they looked exactly like the houses they would see in the TV adverts showing dinner parties with happy people and after-dinner mints. For each advert Trevor showed her, Ellen would respond with comments about 'how nice Bracknell is' and why couldn't we 'wait a couple more years to save up a bigger deposit for a nice house here'. Trevor tried to explain to her about 'seeing the bigger picture' and 'making a life of our own', but he had the feeling that it was coming close to the time when he, as 'The Husband' and the main bread winner, would have to show her who wore the trousers in the relationship and make the decision to buy a house in Basingstoke, which would be suitable accommodation for the architect he intended to become.

He was sure he had an Ace up his sleeve, because he knew that Basingstoke was on the train route to visit Ellen's family in Frome and that would make it a quicker journey than from Bracknell, which involved a circuitous route and changing trains. One summer weekend in 1983 Trevor felt like it was now or never, he borrowed his dad's car and took Ellen for 'a nice drive in the country'. He decided to take the country route to Basingstoke rather than down the A30, as he wanted try to convey to Ellen just how lovely the area was. He feigned surprise when they came across the house builder's Show Home cum Sales Office, and he was confident that if he could only get Ellen inside, it would be a home-run. The thought of the double meaning made him smile.

As they pulled up Trevor said, 'Oh look Ellen, these houses are lovely, let's just quickly pop inside and take a look.'

She was immediately suspicious and on her guard, as soon as Trevor had started using his sweet-talking voice. 'No Trevor, you lied to me - tricked me into coming down here, I told you I wanted to live in Bracknell not Basingstoke! We're such a long way from anywhere here and they look so posh, we can't possibly afford one!'

Trevor was already out of the car and opening Ellen's door before she had a chance to finish her sentence. 'Come on love, we might as well pop in and have a look,' he said, 'What harm could it do, and anyway this is Chineham not Basingstoke.' Ellen was still wearing her best scowl as she reluctantly exited the car and Trevor guided her carefully, like he was carrying a tray of precious ornaments, up the driveway and into the Show Home.

Ellen was smitten as soon as she saw the kitchen, it was bright and airy and beautifully laid out with sparkly appliances and shiny work tops. She tried her best to keep her grumpy face on, but that was forgotten when she saw the rest of the house. 'Ooh Trev, its beautiful, are you sure we can afford one of these?' she said.

'Of course, love, I'm sure that I'll pass my next RIBA exam and that comes with a pay rise. It might be tough at first, but we can do it.' he replied, a little bit too quickly for her liking, just as if he had deliberately kept that bit of news back.

'Well don't think that I've forgiven you for being sneaky and bringing me down here on false pretences' she said, giving him a wagging finger, but with a twinkle in her eye.

However, this manifestation of Trevor's ability to manipulate her and lie to her was noted and filed away in the back of her mind. She was well aware that when some people heard her Somerset accent, they automatically presumed that they could get one over on her, but she was as sharp as a pin and had a sixth sense about who she could trust versus who she thought was shifty and not to be trusted. They soon decided to put down an off-plan deposit on a four-bed house in a small close and couldn't wait for their move in day.

Trevor's career progression went well and Ellen soon got used to the 15-minute bus ride from Chineham to Basingstoke and she was delighted to find that, even though the train journey into London was longer than it was from Bracknell, there were less stops and so it was quicker. Trevor was inwardly relieved to find that no one had tried to set up something like the dreaded 'Young Wives Club' in Chineham, so he was never troubled by female gatherings in their home. Also, with Ellen working, she never felt the need to socialise outside of their immediate environs. After two happy years in their new home, they decided that they should try to start a family and over the next two and a half years, they were blessed with the arrival of first Carol and then Maria. Ellen stopped work two months before Carol was born and threw herself into being a full-time housewife and mother. At first, she missed the buzz of working in the City, but having the girls and the house to look after gave her more than enough to contend with. The girls grew up fit and healthy, enjoyed being in the Brownies and then the Guides, had good friends, did well at school and were courteous, helpful and loving at home. Trevor and Ellen were rightly proud of their family and very happy in their home. Soon after they had moved into Loban Close, other new homes had been built to fill in the gap between Chineham and Basingstoke, but they had been lucky, getting one of the first houses on the estate, on a good-sized plot and then having nice neighbours move into the other houses in the close.

*

As Trevor got into his car the next morning, he looked around the Close and, now that the storm had passed, he thought that, all in all, it really wasn't such a bad place to live. He had made his life pretty good and he could keep it that way, just as long as he was like a ship at sea, keeping Ellen in her watertight compartment and Jingfei in hers. As he was waiting at the end of the Close for a gap in the traffic, so he could pull out, he waved to Gordon the postman, who was just starting his deliveries to Loban Close.

Chapter 2

The Workshop

March 2008

If Trevor tried to pinpoint an occasion when their marriage first started to go downhill, it would have to be after Carol started University in September 2004. Carol, being their firstborn, had a special place in their hearts, but Trevor sensed that for Ellen, returning to a quieter home after dropping her off at the Halls of Residence in Birmingham, was like her postpartum depression starting all over again. He knew that she would have to try to do something to shake it off. Ellen soon decided that Maria was more than old enough to look after herself, so when she saw a 'Help Wanted' sign in the window of the local Bakers shop, she went in and with her gift of the gab and Marks and Spencer's experience, was almost hired on the spot. Trevor was pleased that she was socialising again, as for too many years, while the girls were growing up, she had been a homebird and had become quite insular. She loved working on the counter at the Bakers, as it was a great source of local gossip and there was a never-ending stream of neighbours popping in for buns or cakes and a quick chat. She quickly became a great asset to the Bakers as her cheery, helpful manner was well received by the customers and was a boon to the sales figures. They didn't really need a second income now, Trevor had gained his architect's registration in 1982, so his salary had been more than enough for their needs for some years, but Trevor had been keen to try to keep Ellen out of the house for at least part of the week as she really was a great people person and besides, she had started putting on weight since she'd stopped work. Walking back and forth at the Bakers was really good for her fitness, just as if she was back at Marks and Spencer's again, moreover, she had regained her pre-child bearing self-confidence and it almost felt like she had pride in her 'status' as the neighbourhood focal point for chit-chat and gossip.

While at University, Carol met and fell in love with Mike, who was studying French and subsequently got a teaching position in Newbury. After Carol graduated, she'd got a Marketing Assistant position in Basingstoke, so they could live locally, a fact which delighted Ellen. Soon after Carol and Mike started their new jobs, they decided to get married. Trevor and Ellen helped them to purchase a terraced house in neighbouring Tadley and also helped with the redecoration of it, as it had, to quote the Estate Agent, 'room for improvement', a euphemism for old and neglected.

Unfortunately, in 2007, the Bakers closed down shortly after a supermarket was opened nearby. Ellen applied for a job there, but was not successful. Ellen felt discarded, as a lot of the vacancies were filled by young people from Basingstoke, which Ellen had come to consider to be a separate place where she didn't belong. She had grown content in Chineham, even though, to the untrained eye, they were inseparably joined together as one large town. Ellen started spending most of her time watching daytime television programmes such as Jerry Springer or the TV shopping channels. Trevor had noticed that there appeared to be an incoming tide of soft furnishings and glittery ornaments, he had tried to tell Ellen that the presenters on the TV shopping channels were not her friends, they were just appearing to be friendly in order to shift products to lonely people who probably didn't really need the tat that they were selling.

Ellen wouldn't have any of that, 'Oh Trev, I know that they are not my friends, but it is so nice to watch them, learn about new products and to have a bit of company during the day.'

'Ellen, you're trying to define your existence by avaricious consumption of useless items, we just don't need all this stuff you're buying!'

'But Trev, don't be like that, we've got lots of nice things around the house now, it cheers the place up a bit, makes it look nice when the family come round.'

'Ellen, if you're missing going out to work, perhaps you could do some voluntary work, Emma helps out in the charity shop in town, that gets her out a couple of days a week.'

Trevor didn't think that Ellen would ask Emma about doing voluntary work, but he knew that he needed to do something to try to help Ellen get her sparkle back.

Trevor wondered if it was the combination of the Bakers closing and the girls flying the nest, which had led to Ellen feeling a loss of direction and getting depression. Maybe it was the feeling of the generational changing of the guard, as Carol and Mike would become the young couple that they had once been, or maybe it was the onset of the menopause, but Ellen's mood had darkened during this time, as if somewhere deep inside her, a precious light had gone out. This was not something that he could easily deal with, his was a very practical world, a world of right angles and concrete, he made a design and then someone else would bring it into existence. If there was an issue, they would discuss it, solve it, job done, move on. Ellen's world was not like this and he had no idea about the right way to broach the topic with Ellen, to try to get her to see their GP about it. He could never get her to see their GP when she had minor ailments, so something as unspecific and ethereal as depression would be even harder to convince her of the need. He couldn't get to the bottom of her aversion to the GP's surgery, maybe it was a bit of a stiff upper lip attitude she had inherited from her parents who had experience of living through World War Two. Maybe it was that she had been brought up to respect the Doctor as a prominent member of the community, who's time was not to be frittered away lightly. What Trevor did know was that Ellen had gone off sex, leaving him to self-satisfy in the toilet, which was something that he was struggling to come to terms with.

Trevor had joined the OFC in 1985, when a colleague at work mentioned that it could be a good route to meet potential clients and make contacts at other Architect's practices, which could prove useful if he wanted to move into a larger practice. At first, he was somewhat bemused by the arcane terminology used and the courtroom like procedures, but he found the chaps he met there very friendly and welcoming, plus they had an excellent bar where they would retire, after the meetings, to discuss issues of the day and the like. This was the first time that Trevor had been able to socialise with men who were similar to himself, since he had left University. Living in a household of three women, he missed the banter and the company of men and certainly was not interested in a lot of the girls' conversations. He was not a football or boxing fan, or any other type of follower of male sports, where he might meet potential male friends. He had also lost touch with his friends from School and Scouts in Bracknell, when they moved to Chineham. Being able to get out of the house in the evenings gave Trevor a bit of variety from his previous life of: Work / Commute / TV / Bed / Repeat, and also an insight into how others lived and behaved, which he would not otherwise have had.

Soon after they moved into Loban Close, Trevor had decided that he needed to build a shed in their garden, where he could work on the home improvements and DIY projects they wanted to carry out to make their new house into a comfortable family home. After several years Trevor found that his shed had become overcrowded with 'non-core essentials' as he put it, or garden tools, chairs, etc. to the lay person. His solution was to use his 1999 Christmas Bonus to buy a large prefabricated workshop and have it erected at the side of their garden on a proper concrete base. With insulated walls, benches, multiple power sockets, windows and lights, it was a source of great pride to Trevor, he could really make this workshop his domain. Ellen and the girls knew that they were not welcome in there, if Trevor wanted a coffee or a tea, he would come into the kitchen and make it, his way, himself. His old shed had been demoted to storing garden tools and the lawnmower, which Trevor did not want to clutter up his workshop.

Now that he had a suitable workspace, he could give life to a dream that he had held back on for many years. He had long been fascinated by fire as a child, the idea that it had the power for good or bad, that it was something that had to be controlled to give benefit, that it linked us back to our prehistoric ancestors. His parents had always kept a box of candles in a drawer in the kitchen, in case of power cuts and Trevor had frequently 'tested' them, while his parents were out, just in case. He found an outlet for his fascination in the Scouts, where he could be relied upon to provide an excellent fire to cook food for his Patrol or get the camp fire burning nicely ready for the camaraderie of a great evening of 'Kumbaya' and 'The Quartermaster's Stores'. Trevor saw an advert in the *Basingstoke Gazette* for a candle supplies shop in nearby Odiham and decided to go over there one weekend. Ellen was left at home with the girls, so Trevor was free to explore the shop without the usual distractions. He was fascinated by the range of moulds, fragrance oils and different types of waxes and wicks available. He had soon piled up a basket full of supplies, ready to get him started on his new hobby.

It was only when he arrived home that he realised he had omitted to tell Ellen just how deep he was going to get into his new hobby.

'Trevor! What on earth is all this lot for? I thought that you were only going to get a few candles.'

'No love, I'm going to start making my own candles in my workshop. They'll be great for Christmas presents; you can get all kinds of nice scents for them.'

'Yes, but Trevor,' she said, as she was looking through all the bags and boxes piled up on the breakfast bar, 'you've got enough stuff here to start a factory, just how many candles are you planning on making?'

'Don't worry about it Ellen, it'll be fine, you'll love them when you see them,' said Trevor, already half way out the back door on the way to his workshop.

Trevor cleared off one of his benches and started laying out his purchases and getting himself set up to make his first batch of candles. It was only when he was in a quiet place like his workshop, that he noticed his tinnitus, most of the time he did not find it intrusive. So, usually, his first action upon entering his workshop was to switch on an old FM radio, which had been demoted from the house to his workshop. Most of the time he could not, if anyone had bothered to ask him, remember what song had just played. The radio was mostly on to provide a distraction for him, enabling him to concentrate on the task in hand. Today, however, was an exception, Classic FM were playing 'La Serenissima' by Rondo Veneziano. Its strong, repetitive driving beat and soaring violins made him feel like he had to work faster, which was an unusual feeling for Trevor, as he usually worked at a steady, measured, careful pace. *Steady on*, he thought, *don't want to spill the hot wax!*

Back in the house, Ellen was wondering if he had taken leave of his senses, she'd never seen Trevor get so engaged in something so random, so quickly. She remembered telling him about some lovely candle sets she had seen on a TV shopping programme recently, *well I never expected him to take off on it like a rocket, I'll just have to wait and see how it pans out* she thought.

Trevor meanwhile already had a batch of wax nicely melted in his pan and the moulds all prepared and standing like soldiers in a line, with their wicks proudly erect like their rifles. He switched the mini hob off and carefully poured the molten wax into the moulds, filling them to the brim, put the pan back down on the mini hob and felt pleased with himself. He did a quick tidy up of the bench, then headed back inside for a cup of tea.

Ellen was in the kitchen, preparing their dinner. 'How did it go love?' she asked, actually sounding like she was interested.

'Should be OK,' he replied, 'I've just got to wait for them to cool off and then we'll see.'

'OK,' she replied, 'dinner won't be long, you could check them after dinner Trev.'

When Trevor went out later, he was annoyed to find that the candles had shrunk back down in their moulds as they cooled, leaving the bottoms misshapen. He guessed that he would be able to top them up later, but the pot of wax had solidified, so he decided that it was better to come back to them tomorrow after some research. He locked up the workshop and went back inside, made himself a mug of tea and went upstairs to his study to switch his computer and modem on. Trevor never failed to smile when he heard the noise of the modem going through its handshaking routine, he was impressed that people could build something to make sense of that noise. Finally, he managed to get Ask Jeeves to open up, so he searched for candles in Basingstoke. Or so he thought, he was surprised to find that an advert for a Massage Parlour had popped up on the screen!

He rechecked what he had typed and realised that he had typed 'candies' instead of 'candles' and *'Candies'* was the name of a Massage Parlour on the Winchester Road in Basingstoke that he had no idea existed. He guessed that most big towns would have 'Massage Parlours', but he had never thought about it before, nor had he ever considered, if there were to be one in Basingstoke, where it might be. After getting that result, he forgot that he had intended to find out more about candle making that night.

Trevor's candle making did improve however, mostly by trial and error. That was one thing that Trevor liked about his new hobby, that if he didn't like the look of one, he could just melt it down and try again with minimal loss. *You can't do that with cakes,* Trevor chuckled to himself. He was soon adding details and decorations to the candles and would make up batches for Carol and Maria to wrap up in cellophane and sell at their Girl Guide or school fund-raising events, where his generosity was well received. He would make cinnamon scented candles for their Christmas sales and Easter Bunny shaped ones, and sometimes he would get requests for personalised birthday candles from neighbours or from Ellen's customers at the Bakers. To many people in Chineham, Trevor was only known for his candle making, and support for the school and the Guides. Some people might have thought that it was a strange hobby for an architect to have, but to Trevor it was a relaxation, he gained satisfaction by producing something quickly. As an architect, he worked to the beat of a different drum, some of his projects would be several years in the making, from initial discussions and sketches to client handover. Candle making almost gave him a sense of instant gratification, in great contrast to his normal workday.

It was a May evening in 2005 at the bar at the OFC, when Richard, an accountant at a Bank in the City, asked Trevor if he had considered a job move, as there might be a suitable position opening up for him at their Bank.

'No Rich, I haven't, I've been there for nearly 30 years now, I've built up a great team, we're working on some amazing projects and every day still holds my interest, so I've no real reason to look elsewhere,' Trevor replied.

'Well Trev, we're looking to expand our branch network and to bring the designs for them in-house, so we need the right person to head up that team, it could be a VERYY good move for you.' As Richard emphasised the 'VERYY' he rubbed the thumb and index finger of his right hand together to tempt Trevor even more. 'Well look Trev, have a think about it, if you want to pop in and have a chat with the Director, I can set that up for you.'

Trevor was not about to make a jump like that on a whim, he really had no reason to go job-hunting when he was about to turn 55 in a couple of months. They were OK for money at the moment; they weren't rolling in cash, but they had holidays in Spain, a new car every five years, nice meals out and good wine in the cupboard.

One weekend, Maria and Simon came round for Sunday Lunch. Ellen and Trevor had not seen much of them since they'd moved to Bromley after Simon got a job at a big insurer in the town. Trevor had seen that company's TV adverts and somehow, with a bit of a struggle, Trevor managed to resist the urge to make a quip about Simon going to work for a dog, he had guessed that it might not be well received by Simon and would probably only earn him a kick in the shin from Ellen, but still it gave him a chuckle inside. After Maria had graduated as a nurse, they'd been renting a flat in Hook, while Maria was working at the Basingstoke and North Hampshire Hospital and Simon was working at an Insurance Broker in Farnborough. Trevor liked Simon, he was a detail man too, Ellen thought that he was a bit dull, but Maria loved him and they had been engaged for six months. They were all happy when Maria managed to get a transfer to the PRU Hospital near Bromley around the same time as Simon's job change, it was just that the distance meant that they would see less of them.

'Dad, it's your 55th birthday in a couple of weeks, shall we book up a Tandoori or something?' asked Maria.

Trevor had not thought about doing anything special for the upcoming unwelcome anniversary, he was rather hoping that it could be glossed over instead.

'That sounds a nice idea darling,' he said, 'we should see if Carol and Mike are free.'

Ellen thought it was a good idea too. 'Yes Trev, you like that Tandoori near ASDA, we should book it up for the Friday night.'

After lunch, Maria was washing up the pots that she couldn't get to fit in the dishwasher and Trevor was drying them up, while Ellen and Simon were watching the football on TV in the Lounge.

'Dad,' said Maria, in a tone that immediately set warning bells ringing inside Trevor's head, he knew that he had heard that innocent word spoken in that manner before, 'we want to get married next year.'

'Oh, that will be lovely darling,' parried Trevor.

'Yes Dad, thanks, but we wondered if you would be able to help us to get a house in Bromley.'

'I'd love to help darling, but I'd have to check the numbers first,' said Trevor. 'We don't have as much spare cash as we had when Carol and Mike were married and we helped them to buy their house.'

'OK Dad,' replied Maria, a bit deflated, 'I understand, we'll think about how much we'd like to borrow and have a chat with you after your birthday.'

'OK darling, let's look at it then,' Trevor replied, already thinking that it might be a good time, after all, to follow up with Richard about the Bank role.

In late October, Trevor met Richard and Tim, his Director, for lunch in the Doggett's Coat and Badge pub on the south side of Blackfriars Bridge. Trevor had never been in there before, but to him the mere act of crossing the bridge into South London conveyed an air of shady dealings. Tim and Richard liked it for a similar reason, that they could be confident that none of their City colleagues would be in there to observe their meeting and set the rumour mill off and running. All three however, felt inwardly happy that they could look out of the riverside windows and keep an eye on the City, just to make sure that it was still OK, during their temporary absence. Tim was effusive on his plans to set up their own in-house design team for their projected branch expansion plan. At first Trevor was put off by Tim's no-nonsense manner and Yorkshire accent, but after short while, Trevor realised that underneath that 'man of the people' exterior, Tim was as sharp as a knife and very focussed on this project. He was also very good at asking the right kind of searching questions to see if Trevor had the mettle to head up the team, that Tim knew would be needed to reach the objectives he had in mind. After just less than two hours, Tim asked Trevor to meet him again in a couple of weeks, but at their London office, this time with another Director in place of Richard.

The second meeting went well, Trevor completely resisted the urge to ask about the two bowler-hatted gentlemen, that any television viewer would presume ran the bank, *this was not a time for levity,* he wisely decided. Trevor was impressed by their office; it was all very modern looking with glass walls and stainless steel everywhere. His own company's offices had been built in the early 1900s and were definitely more of an old school design, with some threadbare carpets, wood panelling with surface cabling, and paintings of dead architects to complete the look. He knew that joining the bank would definitely be a change of gear for him, he realised that he had become rather complacent where he was, but he felt that he could step up to the plate and make a good go of it if he was given the role. After just over two hours, he left the building with his head spinning. He would have to wait a couple more weeks before they would give him an 'aye or nay', but he certainly now realised just how important this expansion plan was to the bank and how the design department would be pivotal part of the overall cost control for the project. He was daunted by the opportunity and thrilled by the thought of the increased status and salary that it would bring, if he were to be successful.

In fact, it was not until the start of December, when Trevor received a call from Tim, informing him that he had been successful and asking him to come in to meet with HR and fully discuss terms and conditions. This put a lump in Trevor's throat, as he knew he would have to give in his notice where he had worked since leaving University. He knew that he would be facing a strained 3-month notice period of handing over the projects he had in his pipeline to other architects and to generally unwrap himself from a very comfortable safety blanket. His news was certainly met with surprise, not just because Trevor had come to be considered a pillar of the firm, but also that no-one had thought of him having the *cojones* to take on such a role.

When Trevor first mentioned that he was planning on making this move to Ellen, she was less than enthusiastic about the idea. She had become quite comfortable with the routine they had adopted, with Trevor commuting to the City every day and back home for dinner at 7pm. Now she realised that Trevor would be spending a lot of his time travelling around the country, designing the new branches for their network expansion. She didn't like change and she just felt that this would be unsettling for her, but she knew that Trevor was proud to have been given such a prestigious role and the higher salary would mean that they could comfortably help Maria and Simon with their house purchase. It was mid-March 2006 when Trevor proudly walked through the revolving glass doors of the bank and into his new life as a Bank Architect.

Chapter 3

Pandora's Box

March 2006

The first month at the bank just flew by for Trevor; in a whirlwind of learning the names of his new colleagues, a dizzying array of new acronyms to learn, getting his Security and IT clearances, agreeing a strategy plan with Tim and finding his way round the office. The big leap forward for Trevor was learning to use Revit architectural CAD software, in his previous role paper drawings were still used extensively, but this software just seemed to be light years ahead and greatly sped up the whole process. It seemed to him, that he had hardly had a chance to actually get started on any specific new design, as he had to get up to speed with all the minutiae of bank design. Trevor soon got the impression that he was now 'on the inside' looking out at the civvies who were not privy to some kind of secret, that they just wouldn't understand. There was nothing specific that he could point to, which might have created this atmosphere, it was more of a general presumption that the Bankers were a class apart from the hoi polloi.

For Trevor this was also a period of late evenings at work, taking work home at the weekend and generally trying to get to grips with his new role. He was pleased to be off for the Easter weekend, to get some downtime, have a dining room table full of family come over for Easter Sunday lunch and catch up with all the family news, which he had been missing out on recently due to the pressure of work. He had not seen much of his parents recently, their health had been declining, but he was glad that they managed to make the short drive down from Bracknell to join them for a family meal. Ellen's parents were also not very well and did not join them for lunch, they rarely travelled anywhere and the only time that they made the journey to Basingstoke was for Carol and Mike's wedding, when they stayed overnight and then quickly scurried back to the safety of Somerset the next morning.

By December, Trevor had managed to recruit a small team of architects and two Project Managers and was making great progress on Tim's strategic plan, which had now been updated to a more optimistic level. The new branches would expand the geographical reach of the bank across the country. By the summer of 2007 though, there were the first signs of the financial troubles to come, concerns were whispered about the Northern Rock and in September it had to be bailed out by the Bank of England. Before the end of September Trevor's branch expansion plan was frozen; only uncompleted branches would be finished off, new branches and refurbishments would be halted. 2008 started with optimism and high hopes that the worst was behind them, but it soon became an increasingly rocky year. Trevor and his team were trying to keep their projects moving forward as much as possible, while the size of their workload decreased.

The nails were put in the coffin for the bank in September of 2008, Trevor was devastated to hear that he would not be able to continue the branch expansion project. He and many of his colleagues were given redundancy packages, but that did nothing to brighten Trevor's mood, it was a bitter pill to swallow, it just seemed to completely devalue his work there and rob him of the esteem that he felt his position afforded him. Trevor decided that he hated the City and he hated the commute, he was determined that he would try to find his next job nearer to home.

Ellen was devastated too, when Trevor told her about his redundancy. She knew that things had been bad for a year now, but she thought that Trevor's job would be safe. It really came as a body blow to her. She had got used to Trevor being away on his site visits and his late evening working, for she knew just how much this job meant to him. Men have always seen themselves as defined by their jobs. It reveals their status to others, it is not just a matter of the salary, it defines their position in society, which is of primal importance to them. Like the pecking order of chickens in a coop, or which lion in the pride gets to eat first, men need their jobs for more than just money. Ellen knew that the redundancy would hit Trevor badly, she tried her best to keep a brave and cheerful face on for him, but she knew that they were heading for difficult times.

For Trevor, he just felt like the world that he had known for so long had suddenly been turned upside down, he could not understand how all his 26 years of hard work, all his hopes and ambitions, had been shattered by the actions of others a world away. In fact, it would be many years before researchers, journalists and lawmakers managed to piece together the complex tale of greed, risk-taking, poor oversight, fraud and blatant disregard for regulations which was at the core of what came to be known as 'The Great Recession'. Just like a squashed hedgehog in the middle of the road, Trevor had no idea what kind of juggernaut had just run him over, he just knew that he was hurting and he was down for the count. He was not in a rush to get another job; his redundancy package would keep them going for a while, he could take some time out to lick his wounds. Thankfully, he had been overpaying his mortgage for some years and had finally paid it off in 2004. They were debt free; their car was only two years old; they were both now aged 58. So, it was not quite time to retire to a bungalow on the South Coast just yet.

Trying to put a positive spin on his situation, he thought he could now afford to reassess their situation, get a better work-life balance, try to get a better relationship with Ellen, start afresh. This was something that he had been glossing over for too long now, all the trips away, late nights at the office or OFC, were ways he had used to avoid facing the fact that since Ellen had gone off sex, they had drifted apart. They were living together but apart in the same house; he had not directly broached the subject with Ellen, their conversations were now limited to non-confrontational, mundane issues, like news from the girls, their parents' health or the shopping list. Physical contact was limited to a peck on the cheek on departure from or return to the house and the occasional stroke. Trevor had seen readers' letters in the Sunday supplement advice columns, where 'Aunt Margaret' recommended that the correspondent take their spouse to special couples counselling sessions, but he could not imagine a way that he could get Ellen to agree to that. Whenever he had tried to get her to see the GP about her weight gain, which he thought could lead to Diabetes, she was reluctant, to say the least. She did not like talking about personal things like that, even to a GP, so he doubted that she would talk to a GP or a counsellor about her loss of libido or menopause symptoms. Even he found it hard to talk to her about that subject, he had tried a couple of years ago, but he realised that she was in denial and had brushed him off.

After a week or so of moping around the house, he decided that he now had more time to spend making candles. It was a hobby that had, in time become rather forgotten about, especially since the girls left the Guides and Ellen left the Bakers, without those outlets to drive demand, it had seemed a bit pointless to keep making them. But now, in the lead up to Christmas, he had an idea to take a selection of them to the local craft centre and see if he could get them sold there. It didn't take him long to make a nice selection of samples, all wrapped up in cellophane for maximum appeal. He put them in a box and drove to the craft centre on a midweek day, when he thought that it would be quieter there, compared to the weekends when they usually visited. He was right, it was a damp day and there were very few cars in the car park, as he walked into the courtyard, which the shops and café were arranged around, he could only see a couple of people having coffee in the café, and all the shops looked empty apart from the staff. He went into *Pandora's Box*, the gift shop he knew, from his previous trips with Ellen, would be the most likely outlet for his candles. As he entered, the chap behind the till smiled at him in recognition of a familiar face, Trevor returned the smile and walked up to the till, the box he was carrying drawing interest from the man. Trevor didn't know his name, but he guessed that it wasn't Pandora.

'Good morning,' said Trevor.

'Morning, how are you?' replied the man.

'Good thanks, how about yourself?' said Trevor.

'Yes, fine thanks, what can I do for you?' the man said, trying to peer into the box.

'I'm Trevor,' said Trevor offering his hand.

'Phil,' replied the man, shaking Trevor's hand. 'What can I do for you Trevor?'

'I've got some samples of my candles to show you Phil, I just wondered if there might be an opportunity to sell them, through your shop?'

'Let's have a look at them then Trevor,' said Phil, opening up the box.

Impressed by Trevor's work, Phil paid for the box of samples and gave Trevor suggestions for other designs which he thought would be good sellers.

Trevor drove straight from the craft centre to the candle supplies shop in Odiham. As he was driving, one of his favourite songs from the late '70s came on the radio, it was 'Galaxy of Love' by the Crown Heights Affair. Listening to it, took Trevor's mind straight back to their wedding reception, it had been a big hit at the time and was a great floor filler when it was played by the DJ. His enjoyment of it, however, was now tempered by the sadness about the gulf that now existed between Ellen and him, he wished that he could find a way back to their former happiness. When he arrived at the candle supplies shop, he stocked up with all the materials he would need to get production rolling. Making candles that might sell was only a small achievement, but it put a spring in Trevor's step which hadn't been there for a while.

Even Ellen noticed, when he arrived home. 'Cor you're chirpy, what's up?' she asked.

'I've just sold a box of my candles to the craft centre dear,' said Trevor proudly.

'Oh well done you! I'm pleased for you,' she said, glad to hear that he was a bit happier.

'Yes, I've just stocked up and I'm going to deliver another box to them on Tuesday and we'll see how that goes,' said Trevor, giving Ellen a triumphant peck on the cheek.

Over the coming weeks, leading up to Christmas, Trevor was making one or two deliveries a week to Phil. Trevor got on well with him, they had a similar sense of humour and were of a similar age, with Phil merely a few years younger than Trevor. Whenever Trevor made his deliveries, he would sit and chat to Phil and drink Phil's percolated coffee, which he rapidly acquired a taste for.

'Yeah Trev, it's better than the stuff they sell in the café over there for four quid,' Phil commented.

'I think I'll see if I can buy one of these aluminium percolators online Phil,' said Trevor. 'I hadn't seen them before, but they do make nice coffee.'

'Yeah,' said Phil, 'my wife got me into them, it's one of the best things that I have left from her, bitch!' Phil spat the last word out, 'She divorced me five years ago now, went off with her Salsa dance teacher.'

'Oh, I'm sorry to hear that Phil,' said Trevor, 'that must have been tough on you, do you have any kids?'

'No, thankfully not Trev, that definitely would have made it even harder.'

After Christmas, the trade at the craft centre pretty much dried up, but Trevor still popped in to chat with Phil. Many of the other shops closed for January, most of the shop owners took their holidays at this time of year; some went skiing and some went to the Caribbean for a bit of winter warmth. But Phil kept the gift shop open because there were still a few regular customers popping in for Birthday cards and presents. Chinese New Year and Burn's Night would not bring him much business, but he said he would do better in February with Valentine's Day. One day their conversation turned to sex or the lack thereof, Phil seemed surprised to hear that Trevor had been living in a sexless marriage for so long, that he could not imagine himself being in that situation.

Phil revealed that a month after his wife Pandora left him, he had visited a massage parlour in the Winchester Road.

'Was it called *Candies,* by any chance Phil?' asked Trevor

'Oh, you know it then Trev, you ole rogue!' smirked Phil

'Only from an internet search Phil, not from experience,' rebutted Trevor quickly. 'And an accidental one at that.'

'Hey, I'm not judging mate, I'm in no position to judge.'

Trevor explained that he had mistyped candles into the search bar and then discovered that there was a massage parlour in Basingstoke, that he had previously never known about.

Phil promptly went on to give Trevor a detailed review of what was on offer at *Candies,* including some vital dos and don'ts.

Trevor was in a quandary, it was one thing for a divorced man to visit a massage parlour, but it was something completely different for a married man to do so. He could imagine how embarrassed and upset Ellen would be, how shocked Carol and Maria would be, if they found out. The potential impact on his family worried him greatly. But still the seed had been sown in Trevor's mind. Trevor knew he had turned into a Male, Pale, Stale, Yesterday's man, but inside of him, a flicker of the old Trevor still burned.

Trevor had not been actively looking for a job, but one day Phil mentioned that the Kitchen Showroom next door was looking for a new designer as their previous one had returned to Australia when his work permit ran out. Trevor popped into their showroom and was impressed with the range on display, these were not cheap Swedish chipboard units, they looked really good. Phil had told him to ask for Barry, but when Trevor looked around, there was only one man in there, so he walked up to him.

'Barry?'

'Yes, hello, can I help you?'

'I'm Trevor, friend of Phil's next door.'

'Hi Trevor, friend of Phil, how's it going?' Barry said with a smile.

'Good, thanks Barry,' replied Trevor, 'Phil mentioned that you might be in need of a designer?'

'Well, he's correct there Trevor, have you got experience?'

'Not exactly, but I've been an architect for 36 years, so I might have the skills you need.'

'Well Trevor, it sounds like you've got more experience than I need, why would you want to work here?'

'For all those 36 years, I've been working in the City and I'm just about fed up with that rat race, it's time for a change.'

Barry nodded. 'Come in the back.'

Barry showed Trevor the CAD package they used for the kitchen designs, it was so similar to the Revit software which Trevor had learnt at the Bank, that he was able to demonstrate a few shortcuts to Barry and make a quick 3D view of a couple of cupboards to impress Barry. In less than an hour Trevor found himself with a new job and even better still, it was locally based.

Trevor found he'd soon got the hang of his new job. Now he was based in the showroom most days, helping people who had arrived with pencil sketches of their kitchens, to visualise how their new kitchen could look, by making a beautiful 3D image. It was more of a sales role than he had ever had before, but he loved it, mostly because the pressure had been dialled back from his previous roles. Naturally, the salary was also sizeably reduced, but without the cost of commuting and including the mileage allowance, he was still earning enough to get by. Some evenings or weekends would see him out on customer visits; measuring up kitchens, drafting outline plans on his laptop and generally finding parts of Basingstoke and the wider hinterland that he never realised existed, despite having lived in the area for over 25 years.

*

One evening, he had a call at home from his Mum, *this is unusual,* he thought, *it's normally us that call them, not the other way around.*

'Trevor darling, it's your dad, he's been coughing up blood, they've taken him to the Royal Berks by ambulance.'

Trevor quickly explained to Ellen, that he was going to pick up his Mum and take her to the hospital. Ellen went as white as a sheet, but she managed to give him some pound coins for the car park, before he dashed out of the door. Trevor's journey to Bracknell to collect his Mum and then onwards to Reading, was a bit of a blur, luckily the rush hour traffic, which Reading was notorious for, had subsided and he even managed to find a parking space in the car park, which would never happen in daylight hours. Inside the hospital, the reception desk was empty, but Trevor used the enquiries phone to find out from the switchboard which ward his dad had been taken to. Trevor felt like he was back in the Scouts, on one of his Orienteering courses as they tried to find their way through the three-dimensional maze that was the Royal Berkshire Hospital, and they were both out of breath by the time they arrived at the Ward Sister's desk.

Strangely all Trevor could think of, was that asking for the 'Ward Sister' was probably not the right PC term for the position nowadays, but he couldn't focus enough to work out what the right job title would be, he just asked if they could see Leslie Braithwaite. They were shown into a smaller 6-bed room off the main Ward corridor. Trevor could see his dad in the bed furthest from the door, near the window. He was sitting almost upright, asleep, snoring quietly.

The Staff Nurse explained that they had given him something to let him rest. His Mum stroked her husband's hair, wiped her tears and put the pyjamas and toiletries in the bedside cabinet, while Trevor tried to find out from the Staff Nurse what had happened and what was going to happen to his dad. He didn't get any further information other than it would be Doctor's rounds at 10am, so they might get some answers then. They sat with Dad for a little longer, then they decided that they should go home and return in the morning. When Trevor dropped his Mum off, he gave her a hug, to try to calm her, but she was still shaking silently, so he walked her inside and made them both a cup of tea, before heading home, which he reached just after midnight.

Trevor was up early the next morning, drove to Bracknell, collected his Mum and they both walked to the Train station and caught the train into Reading. They arrived on the ward just before 10am, Dad was awake, but looked ashen and unkempt, Mum fussed around him, tidied him up and plumped up his pillows, it was like a squaddie getting his bed squared away, ready for the Corporal's morning inspection, almost as if a tidy looking patient would automatically be granted better health. The Doctor was not the one who had seen Dad yesterday, but the Junior Doctor had been there, so he was able to bring the Doctor up to speed. The Doctor requested a slew of tests to be carried out the same day. So began their ordeal; tests, medicines, chemotherapy, illness, good days, bad days, specialists and multiple trips to the RBH, until eventually the Small-Cell Lung Cancer took Dad away from them at the start of December 2009.

Trevor and Ellen had made sure that Trevor's Mum came to live with them after Dad died, she was completely drained, an empty shell and not in any state to look after herself at home all alone now. It took a couple of weeks to convince her to make the move, but they managed to achieve the move just before Christmas. In the New Year, they put her house on the market and were pleasantly surprised at just how much the house prices had risen in Bracknell since they'd moved away. Trevor was glad that they had set up Enduring Powers of Attorney for his Mum and Dad a few years ago. Previously, Ellen's parents had not been keen to do this, but now they finally agreed to get the newer Lasting Powers of Attorney set up.

The house sold just after Easter, and they had used some of the money to build a self-contained, single floor, Granny annexe, which Trevor had designed, on the other side of their house to Trevor's workshop. On occasions Trevor had cursed the size of their plot, particularly when the grass needed cutting, but now he was pleased to be able to have his Mum close at hand, but with her own privacy when she wanted it and able to join them at meal times. Ellen started taking her to the local church on Sundays and also to the Bridge Club sessions in the church hall on Wednesday evenings, she enjoyed meeting people of her own age and many of them were in similar situations. Trevor invested the rest of the money in ISAs and Funds, which had slowly started to regain some of their pre-crash value. Trevor didn't know which ISAs and Funds to select for Mum's investment, but one of the chaps from the OFC took her on as a client, promising good returns and low rates of charges. Mum was soon feeling at home, especially once she was able to move into her Granny annexe before Christmas 2010.

Trevor's work for the Kitchen Showroom had taken a hit during the second half of 2009, due to all the time off and travelling involved in helping his parents during his dad's illness. Barry had been exceptionally considerate in giving Trevor the leeway to arrange his workload as best he could around all his conflicting duties. At times the pressure had built to the point where it felt like Trevor was back at the Bank again, but he managed to juggle all the balls and stay on top of things. Sadly, the same could not be said for supplying candles to Phil. Trevor went to see him in the New Year and they had a coffee and a long chat together. Phil was upset to have missed some of the Christmas sales, he had brought in alternative candles to fill the gap, but these did not have the personalisation that Trevor used to put on them. He asked Trevor to get him stocked up in time for Valentine's Day and Trevor promised that he would get on to it straight away.

*

One cold February evening in 2010, while out on a visit to measure up for a customer's kitchen, Trevor realised that this house, was just along the Winchester Road from the massage parlour. After completing the survey, he left his car outside their house and, as casually as possible, sauntered along the road, until he was almost opposite *Candies*. He could feel his heart pumping for no real reason; he wasn't really about to be savaged by a sabre-toothed tiger, but it was that same caveman fight-or-flight instinct causing the adrenaline surge in his body. He was in a quandary, one side of his brain told him that this was wrong, that this was danger, the other side was saying that it was just a common business transaction that he was contemplating, something that has happened for thousands of years and will continue to happen for thousands of years to come.

Initially the building looked like a regular shop front, in a row of terraced shops with flats on the floors above, the difference with *Candies*, was that the shop window was completely blacked out, giving no clue to the trade being carried on inside. The other shops had security grills pulled down in front of illuminated display windows. *Candies* was the opposite, there was no security grill, the dark shop door was shut, but accessible, and there were a pair of small spotlights attempting to illuminate the board above the shop window where the word 'Candies' and a mobile phone number were painted in purple paint against the black background. Trevor figured that this was why he had never noticed the place before, it was not meant to be noticed; it did not stand out at all, anyone driving past it, during the day or night, would probably not consciously register the place, they might indeed just sub-consciously file it away as just another closed down shop. Trevor could see that two of the windows on the upper floors had their curtains drawn and lights on, but apart from that, there were no signs of activity or occupation. Trevor scanned the passers-by, none of them were paying any attention to *Candies,* there was a Kebab shop, a few doors along, which had a few people hanging around; and on Trevor's side of the road there was a late-night convenience shop open, with vegetables piled up on boxes in front of it. There was quite a bit of traffic around, this was a busy road at any time of day; and the few parking spaces available were all taken. Trevor tried to see if there were any CCTV cameras around, but decided that he had better come back in the daylight to check properly. He could feel that his heart rate had slowed somewhat and his face did not feel so flushed now, but his mind was racing as he headed back to his car.

The following week he returned to the customer's house to show them the kitchen plans he had drawn up, but this time he had arranged to go on a Saturday afternoon, as he knew there would be a lot more people in the area. He tried to not rush the presentation too much, but it was very shortly after they agreed to proceed that Trevor was flying out the front door, and around the corner to where he had parked this time, his heart rate rising all the time. The parking space he previously used was occupied, but Trevor had decided, even before he'd left home, that he was going to park in one of the side streets. As a person who had little adventure in their life, today was making him feel like one of those Private Detectives he'd seen in those old American films. He chuckled to himself, *maybe I should have worn a long mac with a turned-up collar, fedora and dark glasses,* but that definitely would have made him stand out in the 'mean' streets of downtown Basingstoke! He dumped the design files in his car, locked it and walked along the Winchester Road checking for CCTV cameras and coming to a stop outside a charity shop, just along from the convenience shop he'd seen the other night. It was a bit further away from *Candies,* but he decided that it was a better location to observe from. He noted the CCTV cameras by the traffic lights, outside the pub and near the junction with Sarum Hill. He didn't see anyone going in or out of *Candies* during the time that he was there and wondered if there might be a rear entrance to the place. He walked around the block, and found a likely alleyway, but couldn't actually find a rear entrance to it. Phil hadn't mentioned a rear entrance, but he didn't want to bring up the topic again with Phil, for fear of raising suspicion of what he was planning to do. He went back to his car, sat down and thought for a bit, before driving home.

One evening in the following week, Trevor told Ellen that he had to pop out to do a kitchen survey and would see her later. He found a parking space in the side road off the Winchester Road, parked up and walked along to the charity shop, where he stood with his back to the window for a couple of minutes, looking around and checking, but he could see nothing untoward. He crossed the road, walked up to *Candies* and tried the door, it was open and in he walked.

Chapter 4

Through the Black Door

February 2010

Trevor was pleasantly surprised to see how well it was decorated inside. Phil had told him a lot about the place and the girls, but Trevor was still expecting to encounter a dingy, scruffy place, instead it looked like a nicely presented lounge, with rose coloured walls, three modern two-seater settees, a picture of a lake-land scene on the wall, two large mirrors, soft lighting and background music playing gently. An Oriental lady walked out of a doorway from the rear of the building, but Trevor couldn't see beyond her, as it was darker in there and a bead curtain had fallen back into place as she walked towards Trevor.

'Hi, how are you, Honey?' she said in a pleasant but well-practised manner.

'Fine thanks,' said Trevor, but the first word was barely audible, as his throat had dried up. Trevor managed to ask for a petite young lady, as he was certain that he did not want anyone that would remind him of Ellen.

The Madam went into the back and returned with three women dressed in thigh length negligees and high heels for Trevor to choose between. Trevor chose a blonde called Velna and gave the madam £150. Velna led Trevor through the bead curtain and up a narrow staircase to a first-floor room. It was small, with a bed, two bedside cupboards, a chair and had missed out on the redecoration that the downstairs had received. Trevor had not been this nervous for decades, although Velna tried to put him at ease, but he was somehow put off by her Eastern European accent. She slipped out of the negligee and helped him off with his shirt and vest, only then did she manage to get Trevor to lie back and relax.

As Trevor was driving home, his head was spinning with so many mixed emotions that he was having trouble concentrating on his driving. He nearly pulled out in front of a car on a roundabout, until the sound of its horn blasting at him, promptly refocused his attention. Feelings of Guilt, Elation, Satisfaction, Fear and a strange sense of Fulfilment, almost akin to fitting the last piece in a jigsaw puzzle. They were all competing inside his head. It was as if a mystery, one he had been wondering about for some time, had now been solved.

When Trevor arrived home, Ellen was on the phone to her Mum, so he just gave her a quick wave as he slipped upstairs to have a shower. As the water played over him, it almost felt like a spiritual cleansing, washing his sins away, but he knew that the feelings of guilt and fear of exposure would take more than soap and water to assuage. Trevor rationalised his infidelity by likening his situation to that of President and Mrs Clinton, if the wife wasn't 'putting out' then the husband would seek satisfaction elsewhere and that didn't work out... too bad. With the Clintons, even Monica Lewinsky managed to bank a couple of million dollars out of it! Trevor dried himself, put on his pyjamas, dressing gown and slippers and went into his study to switch his computer on. As it was booting up, he went over the events of the evening in his mind, even just thinking about them made his heart rate rise, he knew then that he would be going back there soon.

'Hi Trev, how did it go tonight dear?' Ellen's voice brought him back down to earth with a bump, he'd been so deep in his thoughts that he hadn't heard her come up the stairs.

'Yes, good thanks love, I was just going to put my layout onto the computer, while it's fresh in my mind.' He knew, then, at that point, that lying to Ellen was going to be something that he would have to get used to. 'How's your Mum doing Ellen?' he asked her, just to set her off on a tangent, one he knew he could now let her rabbit on about for a while and it would only require the odd 'Hmm', 'OK' or 'Oh dear' from him to keep her going, while he tried to focus on a survey that he'd been to earlier in the day. It was lucky that he had done his usual detailed drawings of the kitchen, for this afternoon seemed to be a lifetime away.

It was a couple of weeks later that Trevor decided he needed to return to *Candies*. When he walked in, he was greeted by 'Madam Chang', as Velna had called her. 'Hello Mr Keith, how are you?'

Trevor had told Velna that his name was Keith and had not given a surname and only paid in cash. 'Good, thanks Madam Chang, and you?'

'Yes, very good thank you Mr Keith, have you had a shave now?'

Trevor realised that in this house of secrets, there were no secrets. Velna had asked him if he wanted 'a shave' and at first, he hadn't cottoned on to her meaning, but then the penny had dropped.

'Yes, Madam Chang, I have had a shave now.' Trevor was still finding it a bit itchy down there, but at least he had no worries about Ellen finding out, as they hadn't seen each other in a state of undress for several years now. 'Is Velna in tonight, Madam Chang?' Trevor asked.

'No Mr Keith, sorry, but I have a very nice lady, that I think you will like, her name is Suzy, you just wait there Mr Keith, I'll be right back,' she said as she disappeared behind the bead curtain.

Madam Chang returned with a slightly built Chinese lady, with beautiful flowing dark hair, wearing a black camisole, high heels and a demure smile, Trevor guessed that she was in her mid-forties, a bit older than Velna, but there was something about her demeanour that interested Trevor, she gave off the required level of subservience for her role, but there was an air of confidence in her smile and in the way she moved. 'Hello Mr Keith,' she said, 'my name is Suzy.'

'Hello Suzy,' said Trevor.

He paid Madam Chang and Suzy lead him by the hand through the bead curtain, up the staircase and into a different first-floor room.

Trevor was not as nervous now, as he was last time with Velna. Suzy's calm but confident manner quickly put him at ease, as she slid out of her camisole and helped him off with his shirt, he had decided to give the vest a miss this time, thinking that it did nothing to enhance his appearance.

When his time was up, he felt better than he had done in years, there was almost a spring in his step as he walked back to his car. He still had the feelings of guilt and fear of exposure, but the way that Suzy had treated him and had quickly learnt how to turn him on, made him feel that taking this course of action had been justified and long overdue, after all he was only making up for the fact that he could not get this satisfaction or these feelings at home.

The next time that Trevor wanted to go *Candies*, he decided to go to a phone box near the craft centre and ring up first, to check if Suzy was going to be available later. Madam Chang recognised his voice and said that Suzy would be available for him at 9pm, she almost sounded pleased that Trevor had phoned up, perhaps she believed that she now had a new regular customer. As Trevor walked along the Winchester Road towards *Candies*, he realised that he had now overcome most of the nervousness that had dominated his first visit. Although guilt and fear were still nagging at the back of his brain, he had now mostly resolved his internal conflict and could open the door to *Candies* without his hand shaking. Madam Chang greeted him with a smile as he entered, took his money and went to get Suzy. She also looked pleased to see him, as she led him upstairs. When his time was up, and he was about to go down the narrow staircase, when Madam Chang stopped him.

'Mr Keith, perhaps you would like to use the rear door instead tonight? it's just down here.'

She took Trevor to the rear of the house, where a fire exit door led out onto a steel staircase. She flicked a switch next to the door and lights illuminated a rear courtyard, leading to a black door onto the alleyway that he had previously unsuccessfully explored. At the door, she showed him the intercom switch, which he could ring the next time he visited.

'This door is for our VIP customers Mr Keith, it is much better for you, to come in this way, no?'

'Yes, thank you Madam Chang,' said Trevor, surprised that he had not noticed it last time, but then it was only a small metal plate with a flush button and a few speaker holes in it. Trevor made his way back to the car, feeling like he had gained some form of promotion or entitlement, as if the door to another world had opened up to him, it put a smile on his face, something that hadn't been there for a while now.

Over the coming months, Trevor opened up a bit to Suzy during his visits; explaining that his wife loved him, that she would not be without him, but that she gone off sex around three years ago; that he would not leave her, but that he visited Suzy to fill that gap in his life. He had still not told her his real name, nor anything about his home or the rest of his family, but to Trevor, their conversations were becoming an important part of their time together. Suzy in turn revealed that her 'contract' to Madam Chang's brother, who had paid for her journey to the UK, would not finish until at least Easter next year. Trevor had never considered what her backstory might be, in the same way that when eating spare ribs at a BBQ, you would not wonder about the pig having been penned up in a shed. He had never thought about what might drive women to work as prostitutes. His eyes were opened up to the sad tale behind her demure smile.

In Suzy's case, she said she had been working on her neighbour's farm until her father was trampled and killed by their bullock and overnight Suzy became the main breadwinner for her mother and her two Aunts that lived with them. She could not earn enough money to support them all merely by working on the farm, they were only just getting by when her father was working on the farm as well.

Madam Chang's brother, who lived in the next village, promised that he could get Suzy a good job in a restaurant in London, if Suzy promised to repay his costs. Suzy had been daunted by the thoughts of such an upheaval, but staying at home would have a meant a life of grinding poverty for her and her family and a new life in London had sounded so glamourous to her. She had been driven overland to Vietnam, flown to Turkey and then smuggled, by lorry, via Germany to London. She only worked for a fortnight in the Chinatown restaurant, before deciding that the hours were too long and the wages too small, such that after paying for her lodgings and repaying her fare, there was not enough to send home to support her family. One of the other girls working in the restaurant told Suzy that previously another girl had left the restaurant to work for Madam Chang in order to make more money. At first Suzy had been horrified at the thought of working as a prostitute, but she soon came to the realisation that with the poor wages in the restaurant, it would take her nearly ten years to repay her fare, especially if she wanted to keep sending money home. It took her another month to get the move to Basingstoke arranged between the Changs and the restaurant, but once Suzy was at *Candies*, she found that while Madam Chang was very strict with the girls, she made Suzy as welcome as she could, with a shared room on the top floor and a wardrobe of suitable outfits for her new work. It took Suzy a while to get used to her new life at *Candies,* but the other girls helped her with hints and advice on how to deal with the different sorts of clients that she might encounter and what things to try, to keep them happy.

Trevor was deeply moved by Suzy's story; he could not believe just how lucky he was to have been born in England and it truly put his redundancy from the bank into perspective. Life in the UK was accompanied by so many luxuries, which its inhabitants presumed were their God-given rights. From the Magna Carta to the NHS, basic rights and necessities were taken for granted, which was not the case for the rest of the world. He had been given a good redundancy package and was now able to get a better work-life balance and afford the luxury of Suzy's occasional company. It troubled him slightly to realise that here he was, using her to satisfy his basic need for sex, when she had suffered so much; from the separation from her family to the tortures of her journey to get here. He wasn't really trying to assuage his guilt, by trying to justify his actions as carrying out some form of charity work, but he was changing his perspective and he realised that by funding the trade in sex workers and creating the demand, he was as much the cause of their suffering as the people traffickers were in the first place. The seed of an idea had been planted in his head, he knew that, like Michael Jackson, he was not going to 'Heal the World', but he could try to *'Make it a better place'* at least.

One day, just before Christmas, Trevor asked Suzy what she planned do when she managed to finish paying Madam Chang's brother back.

'I would like to have my own place, like this but better for the girls,' she replied.

Trevor had never thought of that before, but it made sense of a sort. It was a business that she was experienced in, she could make more money running a brothel, than by working for someone else. Her illegal status meant she couldn't just join the world of taxpayers and get a regular 9-5 job. At that moment Trevor also realised that she would need help from someone with legitimate status to fulfil her dream, had she realised this?

'Could you run a brothel on your own Suzy?' he asked.

'Yes of course I could!' she said indignantly.

Trevor decided to drop the topic, he hadn't come here for an argument. 'OK, that'll be great then,' he said to try to draw a line under it.

'What do you mean Keith?'

'Well, how will you get a place?' he asked.

'I could rent a flat Keith,' she replied, more hesitantly.

'Suzy, to be able to rent a flat, any Landlord or Estate Agent will want references, identity documents, credit history, employment status, etc. how will you get those?'

'Well, how could I get those then Keith?'

'I don't think that you could get them Suzy, unless you knew someone who could forge them for you, which would be expensive,' replied Trevor, unenthusiastically.

'Keith, could you rent it for me?'

Her forthrightness surprised him, even though the idea had already crossed his mind. Part of him had great reservations about the idea, but he was beginning to realise that it would be the best way to proceed, as without his help, she wouldn't be able to go-ahead, without getting herself in deep with someone unsavoury.

In the New Year, Trevor started making enquiries at local Estate Agents about renting an unfurnished flat in the town centre. He arranged to meet Suzy on her 'days off' in a quiet car park, a little way down the Winchester Road from *Candies*. They would sit in the back seat of Trevor's car, the rear windows had a dark tint which made it very hard to see in from the outside, and he showed her the pictures of the flats which he had downloaded onto his laptop. Suzy had kept Madam Chang informed of her plans to branch out on her own, when her debt was paid. She knew that with Basingstoke not being a large town Madam Chang would have found out anyway, sooner or later, and she did not want to make an enemy of Madam Chang, because she had always treated Suzy and the other girls well and had given Suzy a good example of how to run a successful brothel.

Madam Chang knew that Suzy had worked hard for her over the past five years and had earned her freedom, it was a shame that Suzy was not going to stay with here. She had got some good regular customers, but it was inevitable with the girls they brought over; they always thought that the grass was greener outside *Candies*, yet most of them came back to her after a while, when they encountered the reality that lay outside her door.

In March, they found a suitable flat that they could both agree on, on the 10th floor of the Alencon Heights tower block. Very near to the train and bus stations, the Shopping Centre, car park, and cash machines, so it was very central, easy for out-of-town visitors to find, it had a secure door video link entry system and the tower block was very anonymous, so they shouldn't have any nosy neighbours. It was quite a recently built block of flats, with a Mini-Supermarket occupying the ground floor. The flat had been decorated and fitted out well, in the modern style; with a reception room and three bedrooms, one of which was ensuite, with a large walk-in shower. One of the bedrooms was very small, but Suzy said she already knew exactly how she was going to use that room. Trevor had borrowed money from his Mum's ISA account for the deposit, but he was confident that he would be able to pay it back, once their new business was up and running. Money had been tight for a couple of years once Trevor's redundancy money had run out, although his income from doing the kitchen designs was reasonable and covered their basic outgoings. Trevor was still selling candles to Phil, but that was what used to be called 'pin money', it gave them some cash in hand. Trevor's Mum had been doing her bit by contributing her pension money to the Braithwaite household income, but it was really the amounts that Trevor had been spending on Suzy that had cleaned out most of their savings. He was now glad that Ellen had never taken an interest in their finances, just as long as her credit card was not declined by the TV Shopping channels, she was happy. Trevor was quite literally banking on this new venture to get his finances back on an even keel.

It was just before Easter that Trevor signed the paperwork, paying a month's rental in advance plus another month's rental as a deposit. He collected the keys and started getting the flat furnished, mostly with bargain priced furniture, beds and appliances from a charity furniture warehouse. Trevor had got the details of a 'Men and Van' outfit from the

Basingstoke Gazette and, for some extra cash, they were happy to bring all of Trevor's purchases up to the flat and set them up for him. Trevor tried to get most of the heavy lifting work done before Easter, he knew that Ellen was expecting him to be home over the Easter weekend, because they had both sets of their daughters and sons-in-law visiting, as well as his Mum to look after. He knew that between trying to get the flat ready for business as well as playing happy families, it would make it a very busy time for him, but for once he knew that he was going to have keep the peace on the home front and just let Suzy get on with sorting out the soft furnishings, curtains, bedding and the like over Easter.

On Maundy Thursday 2011, when Trevor brought Suzy to the flat, she was surprised to see how much work Trevor and the van men had done in getting it ready, as she had only seen it when it was empty, during their viewing. Trevor explained that he was going to have to leave her to put all the finishing touches to the place over Easter, as he would not be able to get back until afterwards. Suzy was so excited with the flat, she kept going round bouncing on the unmade beds, checking the kitchen cupboards and appliances, admiring the view. He had prepared a speech about new beginnings etc. for her, but forgot most of it when she insisted on celebrating the opening of their new business in the main bedroom. Later, after they'd had a shower together, Trevor gave her the £600 he had put aside for the soft furnishings, curtains and bedding, etc. She could easily walk into the Shopping Centre and get everything that she needed there over the weekend. Just before he left, he remembered some of the things that he wanted to tell her earlier, before she had distracted him.

'Suzy, can you please come and sit down here for a bit?'

'Yes of course, Keith,' she said as she sat next to him on the settee.

'Suzy, if we are going to succeed in this business, then we must be honest and open with each other.' She nodded, letting him carry on. 'My name is Trevor not Keith, Trevor Braithwaite in fact.'

'Thank you, Trevor,' she replied with a sweet smile, 'I guessed that Keith was not your real name, but it didn't matter and yes, I agree, we must be totally honest and open between ourselves. I know how lying to your wife has been eating you up for so long.' Trevor smiled back at her, but before he had a chance to speak, she continued, 'And my name is not Suzy, Madam Chang got that name from an old book, my real name is Jingfei Liu.'

Trevor leaned forward and kissed her. 'Hello Jingfei Liu, how nice to meet you.'

'Hello Trevor Braithwaite, nice to meet you too,' she replied with a tear welling up in her eye.

It was at this point that Trevor knew that his feelings for her were running deeper than he had realised and that this was definitely much more than just a business partnership.

Chapter 5

Into the Dragon's Den

April 2011

Good Friday was warmer than the usual Easter weather, Trevor still remembered when he was a Scout in the early 1960s, they were at an Easter camp at Gilwell Park and it snowed, barely enough to make a couple of snowballs, but enough to stick in his mind, in a place labelled Easter Memories.

He was out cutting the front and rear lawns, for Trevor, it was always a battle of wills between him, the lawn and the weather. There was some kind on unwritten law that he had, something along the lines of 'Thou shalt not cut thy lawn until Easter is passed'. He had no idea why he had developed this; it was probably just based on a reluctance to concede that his coming weekends would involve some commitment to helping Ellen look after the garden, rather than his usual habit of making candles or just general pottering in his workshop. To Trevor, this warm weather was clear, but unscientific, evidence that Global Warming was real. It felt like every year it was getting harder for him to win the battle of wills and this year was the worst. He had shamefully cracked a month early, but at least he could blame the late arrival of Easter this year on the vagaries of the lunar cycle, he was well versed in dealing with those, having lived with Ellen and the girls for so many years.

Trevor's Mum was helping Ellen with tidying the flower borders, Ellen was getting more and more concerned about her, as she had been showing increasing signs of memory loss recently. Mum was 85, so it could reasonably be expected, but Ellen was convinced that she was showing the signs of Dementia. Ellen was alert to this because her own parents were suffering from Dementia. Ellen had tried to get Mum to visit their GP to get a Dementia check arranged, but Mum kept making excuses to put it off.

As they were all in the back garden, Ellen motioned to Trevor to look at his Mum, who was standing in front of a tall rose bush, with secateurs in hand, but she was motionless.

Trevor went over to her. 'You alright Mum?' he said.

She gave a little jump, as if his words had made her spirit crash-land, back into her body. 'Yes, fine thanks love,' she replied. They had noticed how Mum had been calling them 'love' recently rather than using their names, like she used to do, Ellen was convinced that this was a sign of Dementia, a defence mechanism, a way to cover up the fact that it would have taken her a couple of seconds to remember their names.

'It's a bit warm today, Mum, would you like to come inside for a cool drink of lemon barley water?' Trevor asked, knowing that lemon barley water was a link back to Mum's past, that she would not resist.

'Ooh, yes please Trevor, that would be lovely, thanks,' she replied, slipping her arm through Trevor's and walking back to the house with him and Ellen following along behind them.

As they all sat down at the kitchen table drinking their cold drinks, Trevor decided that it was up to him to force the issue. 'Mum, we think that we will have to make an appointment at the GP's for you next week, you know that you are forgetting more and more things now.'

'Yes Trevor, but it's just old age, you know, we all get it,' she replied.

'Yes, but Mum, its best that we get it checked, just to be on the safe side,' Trevor insisted, 'Ellen will go with you, because I'll be at work, but you could have a coffee in the Precinct Café afterwards, that'll be nice, you like having a coffee there don't you Mum?' Trevor added, trying to sweeten the deal.

'Oh, OK then Trevor, if you think it's necessary,' she finally conceded.

Ellen decided it was time to lighten the mood, 'Come on Mum, you've had your tea break, those roses won't deadhead themselves,' she said with a smile, giving Mum a hand up.

His Mum chuckled, 'Yes you're right there Ellen, let's get on with them!' she said, whilst trying to put a cheerful face on, as they both sauntered out to the garden.

Trevor finished off the lawn and put the lawnmower away, his mind drifting off to visions of Jingfei going round the shops, collecting huge bags of cushions, curtains and sheets.

*

Jingfei was indeed enjoying a bit of freedom, the like of which she had not known for a long time. She had never explored the Shopping Centre before and certainly not with a wad of cash burning a hole in her purse. To any passer-by, she made a strange sight, wearing dark glasses inside the shops, as she tried to avoid the embarrassment of seeing any of her former clients. She brought the bed sheets in one shop, then quickly realised that if she also purchased the pillows she needed, she would not be able to carry everything, without help. Instead, she did some basic food shopping, then went outside to the taxi rank and took a taxi back the few hundred yards to the flat.

Once back in the flat she realised just how spartan it looked compared to the displays she had just been admiring in the Shopping Centre and she knew that it would take her most of the weekend to get the flat ready for business. She made herself a sandwich and a cup of tea, then headed back to the Shopping Centre.

This time Jingfei went in via a different entrance, one she had spotted from the taxi earlier and which was nearer to the flat. Only once inside the Shopping Centre, did she notice a horse race being shown on a television in a betting shop and was immediately drawn to it. It reminded her of her late father, who used to bet on horse races and would insist that he could spot the winner as they walked around the parade ring. She never knew how successful her father was with his betting, as she could only remember a few times when he came home from their nearest town with cash for her mother. There were more occasions, she remembered, when he came home drunk and a bad argument with her mother ensued.

She went inside the betting shop to get a better view of the television. There were a few men in there, but she was the only woman. At the far end of the shop was a glass screen, behind which a bored looking cashier glanced up when he heard the door open, then give her a second look, as he didn't get many female customers in and certainly none wearing dark glasses. Jingfei stood in front of the television, which had now changed to the preamble of another race. As she watched the horses being paraded around, she was trying to look for one with good movement or a shiny coat, like her father used to believe were the signs of a winning horse. She took a sharp intake of breath, when she saw a chestnut horse with a lovely shiny coat, but it was the horse's name that really attracted her, it was 'Tianma' a famous horse from Chinese mythology. To Jingfei this was really auspicious, she knew that she must put a bet on that horse, Trevor would be so pleased when she could show him her winnings. She moved her dark glasses up onto the top of her head and walked towards the cashier.

*

At home Trevor knew that he would have to wait until after Easter to call the GP and get an appointment for Mum, he remembered hearing that the GPs got surges of calls of that nature, after Bank Holidays and other occasions for family gatherings. At times like those, younger family members might notice the degradation in the health of their elder family members, but Trevor felt embarrassed because he had not picked up on it earlier, given that Mum was living with them, but also because he had become blinkered to his family while he was so engrossed with Jingfei and the flat. Ellen and Mum continued pottering in the garden and later Trevor had Mum help him make candles in the workshop, which she enjoyed. The next day Trevor took Mum with him to the craft centre to deliver his latest batch of candles to Phil. She enjoyed looking round the shops in the craft centre and seeing the Kitchen Showroom where Trevor was based.

It was a lively household on the Easter Sunday when Carol and Mike and Maria and Simon came round for lunch. Mum was in fine form, telling the family stories about Trevor as a young lad, scrumping and letting off bangers in the street, which he'd saved from Fireworks Night. *It is strange how the mind works,* thought Trevor, her memories of events, music and films from the past were still intact, while recent events were already getting hazy. Later when Trevor told the girls that Nan would be seeing the GP about her declining health, they both agreed that they too had noticed the difference in her recently. This made Trevor feel even more guilty; he had not only been cheating and lying to Ellen, he had let his Mum down by misappropriating her money and ended up ignoring her health, just so he could satisfy his own primal needs. To think he had originally blamed Ellen for making him go to *Candies,* but he now realised that he could not pin all of this guilt on her.

Despite his guilt, Trevor was itching to get back to the flat to see what progress Jingfei had made in his absence. He wasn't able to use his usual reasons for being out of the house in the evening, as he knew that Ellen would know that the OFC would be shut and no one would expect to have a kitchen survey carried out on Easter Sunday or Monday evening. So, it was not until the Tuesday morning that he managed to go and see Jingfei and the flat.

Jingfei was pleased to see him, but the flat was still looking a bit spartan, he thought that she would have got more bedding, curtains and soft furnishings, but she said that it was more expensive than they thought that it would be. He would have to make a trip to one of the out-of-town warehouses to pick up some more items himself, he decided, plus he needed to get her some food basics and other things. It suddenly dawned on him that he must have been wearing rose-tinted spectacles before, when they were making their plans for this venture. It was now as if he was running two households with all the associated errands and duties. He hoped that it would soon settle down, but right now, it was more work and expense than he had considered.

Jingfei had got in touch with two girls who had previously worked at *Candies*, but who wanted to come and work for her. They would be arriving on Thursday she said, so Trevor and Jingfei were working hard to get everything ready to start work on Friday, which would be a Bank Holiday courtesy of Prince William's nuptials. Trevor had placed adverts in the *Basingstoke Gazette, Hampshire Chronicle* and the Newbury and Reading weekly papers, which came out every Thursday, so they only had a couple of days to get the finishing touches completed.

Chun Hu and Qi Qi Yan arrived on Thursday afternoon and Jingfei went to meet them at the train station; they were very impressed by the flat, apparently the brothel where they had been working in East London was a bit shabby and not in a good area. Jingfei agreed with the girls that Chun Hu would be called Meiling and Qi Qi Yan would be called Bai-yu, they also agreed how much they would charge the customers and how it would be split between them.

Trevor was happy for Jingfei to take charge of that side, he knew that he needed £500 per week to cover the costs of the Flat Rental, Newspaper Adverts, Utilities and Council Tax, so as long as he got more than that, he would be happy. For Trevor, Friday would be a normal working day, so he was able to keep in touch with Jingfei by text, she said that her mobile phone had been very busy since the papers came out and the girls were already booked up for the weekend. Trevor decided that for now he would reduce the number of papers he ran the adverts in, but keep an eye on the bookings in case he needed to reverse that decision later.

When off duty Chun Hu and Qi Qi Yan had been sleeping in the small third bedroom, but after a couple of weeks and in response to customer demand, Jingfei decided that the time had come to implement her original idea for the room. She contacted Violetta; a large Romanian girl with specialist skills, who used to work at *Candies*, but had fallen out with Madam Chang over her earnings. Jingfei had kept in touch with her and knew that she was now working at a Fish and Chip shop in Odiham, where her brusque and heavily accented 'Wha U Wan?' was renowned for greeting and intimidating customers in equal measure. Violetta came to visit Jingfei one Monday afternoon to have a look at the small third bedroom and discuss financial terms and what equipment she would require, if she were to take on the room. The discussions went well and she was interested, but Jingfei told her that she would have to check with her partner before giving Violetta the go-ahead. Trevor tried not to visit the flat much, now that it was in business, but he did do so on occasions, as he still had to satisfy his needs and his relationship with Jingfei had gone from strength to strength since she left *Candies* and was now managing her own girls. Trevor was impressed when her heard her idea, she presented it very much as a business plan, just like they did on *Dragons' Den* or *The Apprentice*. So much so, Trevor felt compelled to ask her if she had been watching those TV programmes, to which she replied that she had and that she thought that she had learned a lot from them. Trevor's admiration and respect for Jingfei grew, he told her that he would start making the necessary arrangements and order the equipment that Violetta wanted and let Jingfei get back in touch with her to sort a starting date.

It was just over a week later when Phil called Trevor to let him know that a large box had arrived for him and that it was taking up space in his small storeroom. When Trevor went to collect it one Saturday morning, a couple of days later, Phil was curious about it.

'I didn't know you had a dog, Trevor?'

Trevor realised that the box had been clearly marked 'Large Dog Cage', he hadn't considered that when he asked Phil to take it in for him, explaining that it was going to be part of a surprise for Ellen. 'No Phil, we haven't got the dog yet, I had to get this first. Would it be OK to get another box delivered here, it won't be anywhere near as big as this I promise.'

'Yeah, that will be OK Trev, Mum's the word,' Phil said, tapping the side of his nose conspiratorially.

Phil gave Trevor a hand to get it in his car, which proved useful as it took a bit of a struggle to get it in, making Trevor worry about how he would manage to get it out, in the underground car park of the Alencon Heights tower block.

When he got there, Trevor did indeed find that it was difficult for him to get it out and then drag it to the lift, even though he had stopped as close to the lift as he could. He then moved his car to his allocated parking space and walked back to the lift, becoming somewhat annoyed to find some nosy hipster giving his box a close inspection whilst waiting for the lift to arrive.

'You're not allowed to have pets in these flats you know chum,' said the hipster.

'Yes, I know,' said Trevor 'I've just got to store it for a friend until he gets back from holiday next week.' Trevor hated being called 'Chum', it sounded more like dog food rather than a greeting. The lift arrived and at least the hipster had the decency to help Trevor get the box into the lift and then out of the lift, when it arrived at the 10th floor.

'Thanks,' said Trevor noticing that the hipster had pressed the button for the Penthouse floor.

'You're welcome chum!' replied the hipster. 'Hope it doesn't bark too much!' he added as the lift door closed.

Trevor swore under his breath.

Trevor had already moved Chun Hu and Qi Qi Yan into a three-bed family room at the Travel Inn hotel around the corner from the flat. He had negotiated a good rate for a long term stay and paid for a month in advance when he'd booked it, telling the receptionist that their house had been flooded out. This was the savvy part of Jingfei's plan, the girls could stay there for £50 per night, while Violetta would be paying them £170 per night to rent the small third bedroom, which she would be operating on a sort of freelance subcontractor basis.

It took Trevor most of the rest of the morning to clear out the small third bedroom. At least the bed came apart easily enough, he would take that to the dump later. He laid a clear tarpaulin over the carpet, as he had been asked to do and he then started to fit the soundproofing panels to the walls, they had decided that ceiling did not need soundproofing as it was a thick concrete slab. By now Jingfei had woken up and made him tea and a sandwich for his lunch, then helped him to assemble the dog cage on top of the tarpaulin. They decided that the room would be ready for business as soon as the other box of equipment arrived.

When Ellen and Mum attended their GP appointment, Ellen reported, the GP asked the surgery nurse to run some blood tests and referred them to the Carlton Centre, a local NHS clinic specialising in Dementia patients, for an assessment. Their appointment there took a couple of weeks to come through, but when it did, Trevor went with them. They were seen by a specialist nurse called John, who had a lovely manner and had clearly been very well trained in dealing with elderly people with memory issues. After their introductions, John soon put Mum at ease and they chatted for a while about how she was feeling, if she had any hobbies etc. and what she enjoyed doing, he then said that he would carry out a 'cognitive assessment test' on Mum. This involved a series of visual, numerical and language questions, after which John said that he thought that Mum did have the symptoms of Dementia and would give her a prescription for Donepezil, to try to slow the advance of the symptoms. They left the clinic in a mixed mood; it was good to have a diagnosis to confirm their belief that Mum was suffering from Dementia but it was bad to realise that she was on a downward slope, without a way back up out of the mist that was already occluding her mind. They tried to put a brave face on, but there was no denying the reality of the situation, they would need to keep a closer eye on Mum from now on and try to make as much as they could of the remaining time that they had with her, while she was still cognisant.

It was just after the Spring Bank Holiday, when Trevor received a call from Phil to say that the other box had arrived. Trevor picked it up the next time that he went to the Kitchen Showroom and took it round to the flat, the next morning. He left the box for Jingfei and Violetta to unpack and finish the room off.

Violetta decided that she would be known as Mistress Drac, as she had been called that when she worked for Madam Chang, as it would make it easier to attract some of her old clients. Trevor had been asked to bring a box of his larger candles to the flat, he thought that they were going to be used to add some atmosphere to the flat, but he would find out later that Violetta needed them for another reason. They agreed on the wording for a separate advert for Mistress Drac, Trevor knew that the advert would have to be placed in a specialist BDSM magazine, rather than the usual local press. He had already brought a separate mobile phone, so Jingfei could answer those calls appropriately, they would now be ready for business in a couple of days.

Later in the afternoon, Trevor received a call from the landlord's agent, asking to visit the flat, Trevor asked if there was a problem, but the agent was not giving anything away. They agreed to set up the visit for the Friday morning. Trevor arrived there early, to try to tidy it up as much as possible, Jingfei had not been happy about having to wake up so early, but she knew that it was the least worst option. When the agent arrived, he asked to see in all the rooms, Trevor had already covered the dog cage with a large black sheet and put his laptop and two monitors on top of it.

When the agent queried why there were soundproof panels on the wall, Trevor explained that he did voice-over work for documentaries and that this was his office and recording studio. This seemed to satisfy the agent and he was also happy with the other rooms. As the agent was leaving, Trevor pressed him about the reason for the visit, he replied that he was investigating a report of a pet being kept in one of the 10th floor flats, but it must have related to one of the other flats on this floor.

After their meeting in the lift, Trevor had thought that the hipster might have reported him, but now he was certain that he had. He told Jingfei that they would have to be extra careful in future, or as they used to say in the Second World War 'The Walls Have Ears!'. That expression required a little bit of an explanation from Trevor, as she had not heard it before, but having grown up in China, she soon understood the meaning and agreed that they would need to be more careful, as the flats were not as anonymous as they previously thought.

It only took a few weeks of having the three girls working, for Trevor to realise that he had a problem. They were taking in more cash than he could comfortably deal with, even though he was paying as many bills as he could with cash and he had opened a savings account to repay the loan from his Mum. Whilst driving around the region doing his kitchen surveys, he would pay the cash in at different bank branches, to try to avoid suspicion. He would pay for any shopping or supplies that Jingfei needed with cash and the Hotel was happy to receive cash in advance for their room. He even took to making monthly overpayments into Carol and Maria's mortgages of £500 each, which was the maximum allowable. He was in effect using the profits from the flat to reduce the capital amount owed on Carol and Maria's mortgages. He could only think of doing this as a win-win situation and all would be well and good as long as he could keep Ellen and Jingfei apart.

*

Jingfei was also enjoying her new-found wealth; she had never had this much spare cash burning a hole in her pocket. She was sending more money home to her mother than ever before, at first her mother was curious about what had brought about this change of fortune, but Jingfei wrote to her mother, saying that she was now running her own restaurant, something mother was happy to know and after all, it did have a ring of truth to it. She had also found that she much preferred being a Madam than being a working girl, now she only had Trevor to keep happy and that was easy, as she knew exactly what he liked and what she had to say and do to keep him exactly where she wanted him to be. He was now like a well-trained dog, sweet, obedient, he would run errands for her when she needed and was useful for acting as the legitimising glue that kept the flat and her new life all together.

She was a little bit ashamed to realise that deep down she despised him for being a weak man, one who was not strong enough to stand up to his wife and demand that she should submit to the will of her husband; but Jingfei could also quickly put that thought to the back of her mind, because she knew that her current good fortune was based on Trevor's weakness towards his wife. So, she had no reason at all to rock that boat. All things considered, she just couldn't believe her luck, she had really landed on her feet now, this was the role that she should have had from the start, it was exactly what she deserved.

*

One sunny weekend in August, Trevor took a couple of days off from his surveys, to take Ellen and his Mum to see Ellen's parents.

Mum Smith had a broad smile over her face as she greeted her daughter at the front door, 'Alright, me babber?'

Ellen's face lit up with a great big smile and she hugged and kissed her Mum. Dad Smith had stayed inside as he was not as mobile as his wife.

Trevor and Ellen had been aware for a while that Mum and Dad Smith were in declining health, but it came as a shock to see just how bad they were, and how much they had declined since they last came to Frome at

Easter. It looked like they had both continued to gain weight, which concerned Ellen, as it would not help their mobility or health and could lead to diabetes. Mum Smith normally took great pride in keeping her home 'spick 'n' span' as she like to say, so it was a shock for Ellen to see the kitchen untidy, with dirty dishes in the sink and an overflowing rubbish bin. Even Trevor noticed that the carpet needed a good vacuuming, which, after a few initial pleasantries, he promptly got stuck into. Mum Braithwaite was happy to sit and chat with Mum and Dad Smith, but even she gave the sofa a few swipes with her hand before taking a seat. Ellen decided that the kitchen needed her attention first, and so it took them just over an hour of tidying, to be able to feel comfortable enough to make a cup of tea for everyone. Ellen gently tried to steer the conversation around to getting some occasional carer visits to help them with their needs around the bungalow, but Dad Smith was having none of it.

'We dun't need no 'elp, we do get a bit betwaddled now 'n' then, but we're OK, right!' was his response to their concerns.

Mum Smith didn't seem quite so convinced, but she didn't say anything in front of her husband. After their cup of tea, Ellen went with her Mum to tidy up in the bedroom and change the bed sheets. There they managed to snatch a whispered conversation, away from Dad.

'It would be nice if we could have a bit of 'elp, Ellen luv', Mum said, with a tear welling in her eye.

'Don't worry Mum, we'll get something sorted.' Ellen carried the old bed sheets to the utility room and Mum brought their dirty laundry. When Ellen had loaded and started the washing machine, she gave her Mum a long hug, they both had tears in their eyes.

Trevor had emptied the rubbish bag and suggested that they all go to the local Beefeater for lunch. As expected, only Dad Smith was less than enthusiastic, but Ellen dragged him off to the bedroom to find the new clothes they had brought him for Christmas. They were in the wardrobe, untouched since they had been placed there eight months earlier. Ellen soon had him looking presentable and they all went outside to try and squeeze into Trevor's car.

Lunch went well, apart from Dad Smith spending too much time admiring the waitress's legs. Ellen had to help him cut up his chicken and roast potatoes, but they all managed to polish off their plates and give great consideration to the dessert menu that the waiter brought. Ellen was pleased that Dad had shown sufficient restraint to not mention that the waitress had been replaced by a waiter, she had noticed him looking around, but he had kept his silence. The lunch had lifted their spirits a bit and the drive back to the bungalow was filled with their usual family banter, unlike the journey to the restaurant. As soon as they got back Trevor got the lawnmower out and started cutting the rear lawn, Dad Smith decided that the football on the TV required his undivided attention, while the ladies decided to tidy up the front garden. When Trevor finished cutting the grass, he hung the washing out and went back inside to join Dad Smith watching the football.

At half time, Dad Smith said quietly to Trevor, 'Yer know Trev, I think that it would 'elp Mum keep this place ship-shape 'n' Brissol Fashion, if we had an 'elper pop in now and then.'

Trevor held Dad Smith's hand. 'Well I'll get something arranged then, shall I?'

Dad Smith nodded and gave Trevor a little smile. Trevor made a mental note not to use the word 'carer' to Dad Smith again, that would be an easy concession to make. Inside, Trevor was brought to point of tears, it was a hard thing for a proud man like Dad Smith to admit, but he was glad that he had managed to get those words out of him, it would have been too painful a process to get them the help they needed, without Dad's consent. After Full-time, Trevor made a cup of tea for everyone, while Ellen made some sandwiches for her parents to eat later that evening, after they had left. On the journey home, Trevor told Ellen that her that Dad had requested 'an 'elper'.

Ellen smiled, that news seemed to calm her a bit.

On the Monday, Ellen rang Dr Oyebanji, her parents' GP and was pleasantly surprised to get a call back from him, within the hour, so she was able to discuss her parents' needs. Dr Oyebanji assured her that he would get the District Nurse to pay them a visit to make an initial assessment. Ellen thanked him, but was at pains to point out the use of the word 'helper' not 'carer'. Dr Oyebanji fully understood and agreed, he was well versed with dealing with proud people.

Trevor contacted the Vicar at their local church, where Mum and Dad Smith had attended regularly for many years, to ask if he was aware of a suitable person who could do a bit of regular paid gardening work for them. The Vicar had someone in mind and would get them to call Trevor.

Trevor and Ellen vowed to pop down at least every fortnight to keep a better eye on them, they both felt a bit guilty at not having visited them more often. Ellen had phoned her Mum at least once a week, but now she realised that sometimes you needed to make the effort to go and see people, to really see how they were coping, not just take their word for it during a phone conversation. Later that evening, Ellen rang her Mum to let her know what was being arranged for them, she could hear her Mum weeping gently at the other end of the line, which caused her too to have a cry. Ellen knew that they already had the Lasting Powers of Attorney in place for her parents, and now she knew that the time when they might be needed, was getting nearer. It is tough when the child becomes the parent, but it is a debt from our childhood which many are pleased to repay, but not one that everyone gets to chance to do so.

*

Meanwhile, Jingfei was oblivious to Trevor's visit to Frome, she was enjoying being able to bet on more horse races than ever before. She would get up, just after midday and pop down to the betting shop in the Shopping Centre to place her bets. They had got used to seeing her in there now, she was not drawing the attention that she used to, when she first started going. She had not seen any other women there, but she didn't mind, she knew that she still stood out from the usual crowd of scruffy men in there, but she had developed an aloof aura as a form of defence shield long ago, for dealing with these sorts of situations. On one occasion there, while she was standing in front of a TV monitor, studying the horses in the parade ring, a man sidled up to her. She tried to ignore him at first, as she sensed that he wanted to strike up a conversation. She noticed that he was not scruffy like the other customers in the shop, but he smelt of smoke and she hated that, she was just about to head to the counter to place her bet when he spoke.

'I wouldn't bet on dat one if oi were you darlin.'

That got her back up straight away. 'I'm not your darling' she said firmly, looking him in the eye. He was quite a bit taller than her, not as tall as Trevor, but his eyes were the most piercing light blue she had ever seen.

'Oh, don't be loike dat, I'm just trying to save you wasting yer money on dat ole nag,' he replied, his Irish accent coming through clearly to her now.

'OK,' she said, 'which one should I bet on then?'

'Put an each-way on Golden Arrow,' he said pointing to the monitor, where a shiny light Chestnut horse was putting on a lively display as he was being walked around the parade ring, 'dat'll put a smile on yer lovely face.'

For a split second, she was in two minds, should she punch him in the goolies for his cheek or take his advice. She decided on the latter course of action, turned and walked towards the cashier, placed her bet, then moved over to the coffee machine, took a coffee and returned to the monitor, standing next to him, but still trying to convey her displeasure at his intrusion. She sipped her coffee as the horses lined up at the starting gate, she was still not convinced that Golden Arrow was a good horse to bet on, as he did not look like the winning horses that her father had told her to look out for, but then again, since she had been betting using her father's tips, she had mostly lost. This was a fact that upset her, she felt that somehow, she was letting her father down, if she was honest, it was also one of the reasons why she had kept her betting from Trevor. Then the horses were off and running; there were only six in the field, so it was easy for her to keep an eye on Golden Arrow, that and the fact that he hadn't had a good start and was lagging behind the pack by a couple of lengths. She put her coffee down, feeling despondent, but she soon noticed that after the first jump, her horse was gaining on the others. A jockey was unseated at the next jump and after the last jump, Golden Arrow was closing fast on the leading horse. She was jumping up and down with excitement, clutching the Irishman's arm, as the horses neared the winning line. As they crossed the line, Golden Arrow was just a head behind the winner. She squealed and clapped her hands excitedly, causing the more seasoned punters to smirk at her, but she didn't care; she almost wanted to kiss the Irishman, but decided against it. Instead, she thanked him and went to get her winnings, she was about to walk straight out of the betting shop, when he stopped her.

'Is dat all you got?' he asked, 'dat's not much you know, you should have put a proper bet on darlin,' he continued. Before she had a chance to respond, he said, 'ders's a pub round the corner, let's go for a quick drink an oi'll tell you how to have a proper bet on the gee-gees!'

She was intrigued to hear more and fascinated by his confident and jovial manner. 'Oh, I can't, I've got a lot on today,' she said unconvincingly.

'Oh, it won't take long to have one drink, just one drink. Doherty's the name by the way.'   .

Jingfei didn't respond with a name, but she nodded her approval and followed him out of the betting shop.

He led her to the King's Arms, where they sat outside in the beer garden; at one of the tables, so he could smoke; it was a warm summer's day and there were quite a few people drinking there, but none as incongruous as the large man talking to the petite oriental lady wearing dark glasses.

She still always wore her dark glasses, when out and about in the daylight, for fear of potentially causing an embarrassment to one of her customers, even though she did not recollect ever seeing any of them, she still preferred to take this minor precaution.

Mr Doherty, meanwhile, told her that he used to be a horse trainer near Dundalk, but omitted to tell her that he had been fired after an insider betting scandal involving some rather nasty people from north of the border. He bragged about his betting successes, based on being able to read horses and successfully predict winners by studying their form and watching them closely in the parade ring. His claims made Jingfei curious, so she gave him her £130 winnings from Golden Arrow, to see what he could make of that. After another drink, they were ready to go, he gave her his phone number and told her to call him in the evening. As she was about to leave, he suddenly said, 'You didn't tell me yer name.'

'It's Suzy,' she said, not quite ready to fully trust him yet.

Chapter 6

The Little Red Book

September 2011

Trevor had got into the habit of collecting the post from the flat at least once a week. The rear of the mailboxes could be accessed just inside the entrance lobby, between the main door and the lift. Mostly their mailbox would be stuffed with junk mail and flyers, but Trevor knew that the utility bills and other important post for the flat would be delivered here. The landlord had thoughtfully placed a recycle box near the mailboxes to try to collect the junk mail, rather than have the tenants distribute it over the lobby floor. Trevor stood by the recycle box, flicking his junk mail into it, when he came across a hand-written note 'PLEASE TELL YOUR VISITORS TO RING YOUR BELL – NOT MINE!!!'. Strangely, the first thought that came into Trevor's mind was the use of a hyphen between 'bell' and 'not', *or was it a dash,* he wondered, he had never really got to grips with grammar; with his architect's-technical-mathematical background, he kept thinking of the hyphen as a minus sign, which, in this case made a bit of a mess of the sentence. After he'd got that thought out of the way, he was aware and concerned that the flat had now become visible, in what was meant to be an anonymous tower block. This was not what he wanted. He would have to tell Jingfei firmly to instruct their customers carefully when they called up, to be sure to ring the right bell in future. He knew that it would be the first-time visitors, not the regulars, causing the trouble, he had put the name 'Salome' beside the flat's doorbell, but perhaps that was too subtle for some of their customers, and he knew that it didn't help the clients when they were buzzing the keypad at the main entrance door.

*

Jingfei was annoyed to hear from Trevor about the note and she promised to be more insistent when new customers called up in future. However, she was thinking more about placing her bets with Mr Doherty. After a couple of weeks of getting her some good returns on the bets he placed for her, he had told her about his 'office', which was located at the rear of a car repair garage, in one of the back roads in South View, a short walk behind the Train Station. Here he ran what was known in the tabloids as an 'illegal gambling den', but what he preferred to call his 'Private Club', which made it sound grander than it was. Really it comprised of a small roulette table, a card table, a small bar, a dirty toilet and a TV screen.

True, it was a Private Club in the sense that you only got in by personal invitation and the entry 'donation' was a flat rate of £40 to cover the 'free' drinks, but the main money spinner for Mr Doherty was his little red book, in which he wrote down the bets that he happily took from his customers on anything they wanted to bet on. From football, rugby, cricket, boxing matches, horse or greyhound races, elections, he would take a bet on anything and he mostly won, but that fact did not stop his punters from coming back and trying to win their money back from him, which they seldom did. He was assisted by Magda, who ran the bar and kept the punters drinks topped up, Agne on the roulette table, and Billy and George, who during the daytime carried out dubious repairs on cars, but whose main role was to be on the door and keep an eye out for trouble, both inside and outside the club.

Jingfei felt most comfortable on the roulette table; perhaps it was the chance of instant gratification that attracted her to it, the summary justice it dealt out, win or lose, fly or die and the knowledge that if you lose, you could be only a spin away from a big win. Either way, Jingfei was spending more of her afternoons there, rather than in the flat, where she was meant to be tidying up and getting it ready for the evening's business.

Most of the time that she was there, Jingfei would be the only female punter, some afternoons a Nigerian woman might also be there, but otherwise Jingfei stood out in the club. She occasionally received some unwanted attention from one of the punters, but had perfected her skill of staring daggers at them and giving them a swift brush off, sometimes dosed with few choice expletives. Once, she had recognised one of her old customers from *Candies,* she gave him a nod of acknowledgement, but he immediately looked away and then left soon afterwards.

By now, she had picked her favourite spot to stand at the roulette table, from where she could keep an eye on the comings and goings in the room as well as on the roulette wheel. She had recently started to reduce the amount of money that she sent home, as she was now spending more on the roulette wheel than she had ever intended to. That was not as a result of a conscious decision, she certainly enjoyed getting a high from gambling, but she just did not realise that it was gaining a hold on her in a way that might, in some circles, be referred to as 'Chasing the Dragon'. Each unsuccessful bet would be followed by a larger one to try to win back the previous loss, this hopeless system was rapidly becoming a self-destructive gradual downhill slide, the reality of which she tried to ignore. Occasionally she would run out of cash before she felt that she had had her fill of gambling for the day, but with a few strokes of his pen in his little red book, Mr Doherty would lend her a stack of chips, to keep her at the roulette table for a little longer.

*

Trevor was not aware that Jingfei was building up a betting debt, but he had noticed that the flat was not being kept as tidy or as fragrant as it used to be. Men are alleged to be not as perceptive to mess in their living space as women, but Trevor had been trained well by Ellen, who had high standards and had always taken great pride in keeping their house neat and tidy. Trevor had got into the habit of visiting the flat around lunchtime on Thursdays, so he could climb into bed with Jingfei before she got up for the day and have his 'Conjugal Visit', as he jokingly called it. He would also collect the cash from the week, so he could distribute it to the hotel, banks and building societies. On one Thursday, he noticed a lot of dirty crockery in the kitchen sink and the dishwasher had not been emptied.

This to him, indicated that the kitchen hadn't been tidied the day before. Additionally, the lounge was a shambles, cushions in various places, empty glasses and full ashtrays on the coffee table.

When he asked Jingfei about it, she became angry and said that she had not been feeling well yesterday, but she would tidy up later. He was surprised about how angry she was about it; he didn't think that he had asked the question in an accusatorial manner, he just guessed that she was being overly defensive about it, to cover a loss of face. Trevor decided that he really should leave the running of the flat to Jingfei, because, after all, they had decided to set it up mainly as a benefit to her and to let her send more money home to her mother. He was happy that the cash that he was getting was covering all their bills, and actually leaving him more left over than he had anticipated, when they first discussed the plan.

This situation continued for a year in this manner, with Trevor still oblivious to the debt mountain that Jingfei was running up at Mr Doherty's club. That was, until one Thursday lunchtime, as he was walking towards the entrance door to their tower block, when he was approached by a heavyset man, who spoke to him brusquely in an Irish accent, 'Listen pal, yer girlfriend owes me twenty-foive grand and I want it back!'

Trevor was taken aback, not only by the man's sudden approach and his malevolent manner, but also by the all-pervasive smell of smoke that surrounded him like an aura.

Before Trevor had a chance to stutter any kind of rebuttal, the man continued, 'You'd better cough up the dosh pal, or I'll send the boys round to stuff yer cat down yer throat!' said the man, jabbing his forefinger forcefully into Trevor's sternum. The man was shorter than Trevor, but he was wide enough to convince Trevor that any sort of physical retaliation on his part, would not be advisable. Trevor briefly considered that he should tell this man that he did not have a cat, but then thought better of it.

'What on earth are you talking about, Mr??' Trevor managed to spurt out, with his pulse racing and his breath not coming easily.

'Doherty's the name pal, and don't play innocent with me, when are yer going to gimme moi money?'

'Well, I'm sorry Mr Doherty, but I really have no idea what you are talking about,' said Trevor, trying to regain his composure.

'Suzy, the little Chinese whore, she's yer girlfriend roight!'

It was definitely more of a statement than a question and, to Trevor, it let a small amount of light filter through the fog of confusion swirling in his mind. 'Yes', said Trevor cautiously.

'Well listen pal, yer might not know dis, but she's been playing the wheel at moi club for a couple of years now,' Mr Doherty continued, now in a slightly less aggressive manner. 'An she's run up quite a tab, yes quite a tab indeed she has.'

Trevor noticed that there was definitely a hint of a sardonic smile in Mr Doherty's face, as if he quite enjoyed playing cat and mouse.

'Now listen, oim a reasonable sort of man yer know Keith, an oi don't expect it all back roight away,' Mr Doherty continued.

Trevor's mind side-tracked to wondering how this thug he had just met apparently knew he could be called Keith, without being accused of misidentification.

'Now Keith, oi tink dat you should go and have a little chat with our Suzy, an' put a few missing pieces in your jigsaw puzzle.' Mr Doherty said. Inwardly, Trevor agreed with him – 'After all, we're both businessmen Keith, oim sure we can come to some kind of an arrangement to get moi money back, without needing to get nasty.'

Trevor felt the subtext in his sentence and quite agreed with Mr Doherty, that nasty was not the best way to go. Thoughts and questions were still racing round his head, but he was at least getting his breath back now.

'Tell Suzy to come an' see me on Monday, so we can sort sometin' out, she's been a bit shy recently, it'll be good to catch up, she knows where to find me.'

With that Mr Doherty turned and walked off, without even waiting for any kind of response from Trevor. It was clear that Mr Doherty felt that he had delivered his message and that further discussion was not necessary.

Trevor was relieved to see his back and resumed his journey up to the flat. He was pleased to have a few moments in the lift to try to settle his composure. Inside he was fuming, but he knew that the coming confrontation with Jingfei would not be easy and that if both of them turned the heat up, it would get bitter, very quickly, which would not be the best route to finding a resolution.

She was still asleep when he went in the bedroom and sat on the end of the bed; she felt the movement and woke up, bleary eyed. 'Hi Trevor, how are you?'

'I've had better days,' said Trevor flatly, 'I've just met Mr Doherty outside the building.'

Jingfei sat bolt upright, her eyes suddenly wide open and scanning his face, trying to see what was coming next.

'He asked me for £25,000,' said Trevor, as her mouth fell open and her eyes widened.

'Trevor, I can explain,' she stammered.

'That would be good Jingfei,' he replied, trying to be as calm as possible.

'Oh Trevor, please forgive me, I've been betting more than I should have. I don't know why, I just got wrapped up in it and borrowed the money from Mr Doherty,' she pleaded.

'OK, yes, but how could you let it build up to £25,000?' he asked, barely managing to moderate his voice now.

'I just don't know Trevor; I suppose that I kept believing that my luck would change and I could bring it back around,' she said weakly.

'Jingfei, you had plenty of cash, you didn't need to borrow any money from Mr Doherty, or did you gamble all of that as well?'

'No, I still send money home to Mother.' She omitted to mention that what she sent home, was less than she used to send. 'But Trevor, the £25,000 is not all betting money, Mr Doherty adds interest charges as well you know.'

'OK, yes I believe you, I'm sure he would add interest charges Jingfei,' replied Trevor calmly. 'He doesn't look like someone who would be running a charity.'

'Oh no Trevor, are you OK, did he get violent?' she asked, partly in concern and partly to try to deflect the conversation.

'Yes, I'm OK thanks, but I was a bit shook up by it all,' he replied, giving her an inch this time for her concern. 'He doesn't know our real names, he called you Suzy and called me Keith.'

'Yes,' said Jingfei, 'I never really trusted him enough to tell him my real name, but I don't know how he knew that I live here and how he knew to call you Keith'. They were to find out later, that the punter who recognised Jingfei at Mr Doherty's club, told Mr Doherty that he knew Suzy from *Candies*. Then Mr Doherty went to *Candies* looking for Suzy, where Madam Chang told him that Suzy had set up her own brothel with Keith in the Alencon Heights tower block. Mr Doherty had then had Billy keep an eye on the place and he had noticed which intercom button was the one that got the most use in the evenings and from that had spotted Trevor emptying the mailbox on Thursday lunchtimes.

Jingfei got dressed and they started to discuss how they were going to pay off the £25,000. They decided that if Jingfei stopped betting completely and if Trevor only took enough money to cover the bills, they could pay back Mr Doherty £2,000 per month and be clear of the debt in 18 months. They would go together, to see him on Monday and see if he would accept the deal. Trevor was calm but insistent, when he made Jingfei write and sign a statement, swearing that she would stop betting and save as much money as she could to contribute to the repayment schedule. It was just like a business contract, because even though their relationship was complicated by love, it was still, at its heart, a business relationship. Trevor, now feeling that his vital signs were now returning to normal, made Oolong tea for the both of them and tried to get Jingfei to open up about the reasons for her gambling habit, it wasn't easy; she responded with a mix of embarrassment and self-defence.

'Maybe I was trying to prove to myself that I could be better than my father, I'm not sure Trevor,' she said glumly, 'I just liked getting out of here, doing something for me, on my own. You know that I'm so grateful that you got me out of *Candies* and got the flat for me Trevor, but it just seemed like I was like a swallow being moved from one cage to another!' She could feel tears running down her cheeks as she realised that she had never put her innermost feelings into words before and had certainly never shared them with anyone else.

She clung tightly on to Trevor as if she was afraid now that her guard was down. The feng-shui symbology of her revelation was lost on Trevor, but he knew that had never seen her so vulnerable before. He had never thought of the flat as being like a cage for her, but deep down he knew that she was right, he had moved her from one cage to another, no matter how well meaning he had been. It had also been a move with financial benefits to him, but at the expense of Jingfei, Violetta, Chun Hu and Qi Qi Yan. He had the advantage of having a life outside of these four walls, a job, other tasks and family to fill his day and other thoughts to occupy his mind, but to these women, it must just be like being a cog in a machine, stuck in a relentless routine with only one day off a week and no light at the end of the tunnel.

Trevor comforted himself with the knowledge that none of the girls were enslaved by debt to him, they could leave whenever they pleased, so their staying intimated that they were happy enough where they were. Qi Qi Yan was still paying off the balance of her 'delivery charge', but that was a common situation for these girls to be in, it was the arrangement that she had signed up to, in order to escape the rural drudgery back home. At some point she would be debt free and be able to increase the amount of money she regularly sent home, just like Chun Hu and Jingfei were doing. He also knew that he couldn't just start playing happy families with Jingfei just to keep her happy, he would have to be firm but kind with her, get her clear of Mr Doherty - and make sure she stayed clear of him, once her debt was paid off. Yes, they would go together, to see him on Monday and check if he would accept their repayment terms. He was not looking forward to meeting Mr Doherty again, but at least this time he would not be caught by surprise.

Jingfei also felt apprehensive about the proposed meeting on Monday, as she had been avoiding Mr Doherty's club for some time now. She had started paying him back, but he was getting more and more impatient and had threatened her, but she had no idea that he had found out about the flat and she was deeply shocked when Trevor told her how Mr Doherty had threatened him. She had never imagined that Trevor would find out about her betting debt, especially in that manner, she promised Trevor that she would stop betting and had been happy to sign the statement, as she knew that it was only a piece of paper, but it had the power to reassure Trevor and get him to contribute to paying her debt off, so she considered that to be a win for her. Sometimes, she really did despise Trevor's weaknesses, but if she could use them to her advantage, then more fool him. She knew that all men were weak, they were guided by their dicks not their brains and could be so easily manipulated, so if she could benefit from that knowledge, then she was obviously smarter than them.

Trevor was glad to have the weekend at home with Ellen and Mum, to take his mind off the coming Monday. The mundane domestic conversations were a relaxing contrast, he even managed to spend time with Mum, tidying the garden, clearing up the leaves and making candles. It was 18 months since Mum had got her Dementia diagnosis, she did not appear to have deteriorated too much, but it was a hard thing to determine, when you are so close to a sufferer on a continual basis.

It was a bit like an ant climbing a statue, you need to take a few steps back to get a proper view. They would get a better idea, in six months' time, at their next annual assessment, at the last one John had not scored Mum any different from her first test and she had kept taking the medication prescribed for her in the meantime. They all knew that Mum would not get better, they were really just trying to keep her as comfortable and involved in the household daily goings-on as possible and make the most of their time together while they could. It was at times like these that Trevor realised how strange it was that Ellen and he were now taking on the parent role for her, it felt like payback for when Mum had raised Trevor. This helped him put his other troubles into a new perspective, it didn't make him look forward to Monday, he just knew that he would get through it and life would continue on its path regardless.

On Monday afternoon, Trevor parked in their parking space under the tower block and caught the lift up to the flat as usual. When he entered, he was surprised to see Jingfei dressed better than he had ever seen her dressed before. He realised he was now being made privy to another side of her life that he, up until last week, had not known existed. It annoyed him; he could not believe that she had been so stupid as to have run up such a huge debt at an illegal gambling den and unnecessarily exposed their business.

An irony in this situation, that brought a wry smile to his face, was the fact that his illegal operation was now financing another illegal operation in some strange kind of circular money-flow model, from which the tax man had been excluded. It had never really crystallised in his mind before, the fact that he was running an illegal operation - it was just a way of helping Jingfei earn enough money to make a life for herself and support her family back home. There was no grand, long term plans laid down, they just wanted to make sure that they could cover their costs.

They walked separately to Mr Doherty's club, Jingfei taking the lead, and Trevor following along fifty yards behind, as nonchalantly as he could. Trevor was not familiar with the area north of the railway station, the kitchen clients that he visited, were mostly in the nicer areas of Basingstoke. It made him think of those old American films featuring the white-trash kid who grew up on the wrong side of the tracks and was probably destined to be no good. *It was strange how a railway line or a river could be so divisive to a town,* Trevor thought.

His musings were cut short as he realised that they had arrived. Jingfei walked into a car repair garage, and waited just inside the shutter doors to let Trevor catch up. He could feel his heartbeat rise and his palms starting to sweat as he entered the garage. It looked quite gloomy and scruffy, certainly not the sort of garage that he would choose to service his car, but then they were not here for that. Jingfei led him to the rear of the garage, where there was a small office and a corridor, with a large man standing by a door at the end.

'Hi George, we're not staying long today,' Jingfei said, as casually as she could, to the man.

'Hi Suzy, yes Mr Doherty's expecting you,' said George, opening the door and moving to one side to let them both pass through.

Trevor was surprised to see that, beyond the door, the club was larger and better decorated than he expected after seeing the garage. Jingfei walked up to Mr Doherty, who was sitting on his usual bar stool, chatting to a girl behind the bar and keeping an eye on proceedings.

'Hi Suzy, Keith, good to see yer both,' he said, with the smirk of a 'cat who got the cream' on his face.

Jingfei and Trevor both managed to respond with a nod and a tight smile.

They discussed repaying Jingfei's debt and Trevor was pleasantly surprised when Mr Doherty accepted their offer of £2,000 per month, the deal was probably swayed by Trevor bringing him an envelope of £50 notes as their first instalment.

'Are you gonna have little go on the wheel then Suzy?' Mr Doherty asked, just as they were about to leave.

'No, I'm giving it a rest for a while, thanks,' she replied curtly.

'OK, no worries, oi'll see yer next month,' he said, as they were already halfway to the door.

They walked, separately, back to the flat, where Jingfei made them Oolong tea. Once seated, Trevor looked her square in the eye and made her promise that she would never go back to Mr Doherty's club and that she wouldn't go to the betting shop either. Trevor did his best to maintain a kind but firm tone with her, but he knew that he had to make it clear to her, that she had let him down badly. He had sympathy for her situation, knowing that her life was not fulfilling or varied and that apart from Trevor and the girls, she had no other company or social circle, but that was not something that he could help with. He was not prepared to risk his happy family life further, just to make her life better. She had the life that she chose at *Candies,* and he had rescued her from that, but he was certainly not a believer in the fake Chinese proverb about saving someone's life making you responsible for them for ever. He had kitchen surveys scheduled for the rest of the afternoon, so he didn't really have time for his conjugal visit, in truth, he wasn't really in the mood, he was still simmering, and wanted to get out and get some fresh air, so he made his excuses and left.

*

Jingfei was pleased that Trevor left quickly, she didn't like it when he was angry with her, it just wasn't fair. This was her business, she and the girls were the ones earning the money, she should be allowed to spend the money how she liked. Trevor wasn't as strict as Madam Chang, but otherwise he was almost the same, as far as she was concerned. She knew that the money she was now going to pay him, would only cover the expenses for the flat, so he was the one that was losing out by helping her repay her gambling debts, but to her, instead of eliciting sympathy, it just reiterated how weak he was.

That was the one thing that had surprised her the most, when she arrived in England, just how weak and malleable the men were compared to the men back home. She had soon realised that this was something that she could take advantage of and she had no guilt about doing so. She would however, try to keep her promise to Trevor to stop betting; it annoyed her to have to admit that she had run up such a large debt, it felt like she had failed on three fronts.

One, she should have won at Roulette, she was sure that she had devised a good system, but it had kept letting her down. Two, she should have been able to control her losses, she knew that it was a weakness she had inherited from her father, he too was never able to walk away from a losing streak. Three, she should have been able to keep her gambling a secret from Trevor, she had known that he would disapprove of it and how she spent her money, although it should have been none of his business anyway. To Jingfei, the fact that she had not been able to control these things, represented an annoying loss of face, redemption of which would be her incentive to repay the debt as quickly as possible and go back to sending more money home to her Mother.

*

Trevor found he calmed down over the course of the rest of the afternoon, the kitchen surveys were a dose of structured normality that he could control and focus on, taking his mind off Jingfei and her debt. He assured himself that he had got his message across to her and that she really would stop betting now.

When he arrived home, he soon found the normality of everyday conversation with Mum and Ellen a banal distraction and a comfort. He wished he could discuss his worries about Jingfei's debt with someone, but he had no one who was close enough that he could trust with such a secret. He had always liked to keep his life in watertight compartments, he had kept the news of his redundancy from the Bank in 2008 away from his friends at the OFC for more than nine months. It was only when Richard had mentioned that his sister had brought a house in Alton, near Basingstoke, which needed a kitchen upgrade, that Trevor revealed his new occupation and volunteered to do a survey and get her a discount, if she wanted to go ahead with it. Richard, it turned out, was not surprised to hear about Trevor's redundancy, he knew a lot of the Banks had suffered badly in the financial crash, but he was surprised that Trevor had kept it from him and the other chaps at the OFC. They had always thought of themselves as a tight knit group of like-minded fellows, who could be trusted to discuss each-other's dalliances, family problems and concerns, over a beer in a fraternally lips-sealed manner, as part of a male mutual support network. That cast Trevor in a different light in Richard's mind, and he wondered what other secrets Trevor had going on behind that serious exterior.

From Trevor's point of view, he instantly realised that, in trying to help Richard's sister, he had broken the OFC omerta of 'no secrets between us' and had unintentionally cracked open one of his watertight compartments. It was no big deal, it was just a redundancy, it was not an aspersion on his architectural skills, he was just collateral damage from a global financial meltdown, but it had hit Trevor hard and made him feel that his rocket was no longer in the ascendency. That was the reason why Trevor had not revealed his redundancy to the OFC, he did not like to be the source of bad news, especially when it looked like he had slipped down a rung on the social ladder. His accidental revelation made him feel that he was being reappraised by his friends at the OFC. They were still as amiable to him as before, but the atmosphere just felt different after that. Perhaps he was being oversensitive, but he knew that, in future, he would need to be more careful to avoid such slip-ups and from then onwards he had determined to keep the different aspects of his life separate from each other. This was particularly applicable to Jingfei, hence the position that he found himself in now, without anyone that he could confide in and discuss the situation.

The next day, after he had completed his afternoon surveys, he popped into ASDA on his way back to the Kitchen Showroom. He knew that ASDA's

World Foods aisle was the place that he could buy Phil's favourite brand of ready-ground filter coffee powder. At least at Phil's he knew that he could unwind, drink some percolated coffee and chew the cud. If Trevor was from a younger generation, he might have called it 'chillin' but either way he enjoyed Phil's company. Their conversations usually ranged from the interminable motorway roadworks, the useless local council, immigration, politics and Reading Football Club, the latter Trevor was not really interested in, but he had picked up some background matter on the subject, for it was one of Phil's favourite topics of conversation.

Today however was different, after Phil had thanked Trevor for his pack of coffee and brewed them a fresh pot, he said to Trevor,

'Hey, 'ave you heard about *Candies*?'

'*Candies*? Oh, that place, no, what?' said Trevor.

'Been shut down! It was raided by the Border Force!' Phil said, 'Peter, who comes in here, said he saw some girls being led out to a van the other day. It's a bloody shame, those girls knew just what I liked, now I'll have to find another place.'

'Oh.' Trevor said with pretended disinterest. Much as he would have liked to help a friend out, to mention his side business to Phil would be too great a risk of exposure to take. Watertight compartments only work if you keep them shut tight.

Trevor had often wondered how Madam Chang had survived so long in a high street location without being raided, he had always presumed that she had some powerful friends who knew how to grease the right wheels. Trevor later found out, from one the chaps at the OFC, that there had been a big shake up in the Border Force after Home Secretary Theresa May, demerged it from the UK Border Agency in March 2012. The Border Force now came under direct ministerial control and it appeared that the new broom had decided to make its presence known and show that the Border Force was to be taken seriously now. This naturally concerned Trevor, he feared for Jingfei, the girls and his own hide, not necessarily in that order. They should be a bit safer because his business was operating from an anonymous flat, not on a high street, but he had no intention of closing down or *being* closed down right now. Jingfei still had a large debt outstanding to Mr Doherty and even though he was getting by with his reduced weekly cash injection from the business, he longed for the days when the loan would be repaid.

On Thursday, Trevor made his usual visit to Jingfei, determined to try to appear as nonchalant as possible, but that fell away as soon as he walked through the door.

Jingfei was all over him 'Oh Mr Trevor!' - He knew straightaway just how stressed she was, as she had never used the term 'Mr' with him since they started their business - 'Madam Chang's been arrested!' she cried as if a family member had just died, 'Border Force gonna come for me Mr Trevor!' Tears welled in her eyes.

'No, they're not Jingfei,' Trevor tried to assert, 'We're not on their radar, we've been careful to keep a low profile.' She did not look convinced, so Trevor continued, 'Madam Chang was too high profile, there's been a change at the Border Force, they have to show results and high street massage parlours are an easy target for them. We just need to keep being careful and not stand out Jingfei.'

She seemed slightly pacified, but not totally.

'What we gonna do Trevor?' she begged.

'Nothing different Jingfei, we can just keep on as we are. We've not had any trouble here, no one has made any complaints about us, we just keep things going along smoothly and pay off Mr Doherty.' Trevor saw that she was calming down now, she wiped her eyes and pulled his head down to kiss him on the lips. Their conjugal visit was fired by a new passion, it was as if the scent of danger had lit a passion in her, or as if she had realised just how much she depended on Trevor and how she needed to keep him happy.

Chapter 7

A Change is Gonna Come

February 2013

Christmas 2012 and New Year 2013 passed uneventfully for Trevor and Jingfei, the middle of February ushered in the Chinese New Year, which this year was the Year of the Snake. This, Jingfei said, signified tenacity and cleverness, while also being associated with the element of fire. In the larger Chinese astrological cycle, this particular year was also associated with the element of water, which made 2013 the Year of the Water Snake. Jingfei and the girls were aware that this combination of the water and fire elements might signify turmoil in the months ahead, but old superstitions were not something that people of their generation paid much attention to. Trevor meanwhile was feeling good, money was coming in nicely, they had picked up a couple of new regular customers from Madam Chang's, who Jingfei had carefully vetted before giving out their address. She was still being extra cautious, and most of their customers were now regulars. Trevor was happy that Jingfei's debt was being paid off, he had taken to dropping the money off at Mr Doherty's club himself, to keep an eye on the balance still owing. Trevor, with his usual eye for detail, had been quite religious about keeping a track of all the money he received from Jingfei. He had created a spreadsheet even before they started renting the flat, which now showed a rather large figure, and on it he had also kept a track, of all their outgoings, as well as the money paid to Mr Doherty.

One day just after Chinese New Year, Chun Hu asked Jingfei if her friend Lan Fang could come to work with them. They figured that if they reorganised their rota for days off, Lan Fang could be used to keep all three rooms earning on longer hours, all week, and boosting their income.

Trevor thought that it was a good idea when Jingfei asked him about taking on Lan Fang. He didn't think that it would be an issue at the Travel Inn, as he had been using the same three bed family room for nearly two years now and there had never been any problems. There still would not be more than three girls resting in there at any one time, and the Hotel knew that they were getting paid regularly and promptly, so much so they had even had the decency to freeze the room rate. Although that might have been in light of increased competition from a rival hotel, which had opened nearby recently.

Lan Fang was so desperate to start work, that she arrived the day after Valentine's Day. Chun Hu met her at the station and took her straight to the Travel Inn, so she could unpack before going to meet Jingfei at the flat in the afternoon. Jingfei welcomed her and made them both a cup of Oolong tea, they discussed the working and financial arrangements and decided that Lan Fang would start work that evening. Lan Fang said that she had already one client who would like to visit her in the flat, Jingfei was concerned about this, because it was unusual, but Lan Fang convinced her that he was OK and would be no trouble, so Jingfei relented and let Lan Fang arrange for him to pay her a visit on the weekend. Lan Fang said that this client knew her as Lijuang, so Jingfei said that she should keep on using that name to save any confusion. Jingfei showed Lan Fang the bedrooms that she would be using and also showed her Violetta's room, just to prevent her being curious. Lan Fang was not fazed by Violetta's room, but she was pleased when Jingfei showed her into the larger bedroom, because Jingfei had left an Orchid fragrance reed diffuser in there, giving the room a lovely ambience.

'Oh Jingfei, that is so sweet of you, to think of that!' she said as she gave Jingfei a big hug.

'Yes, I guessed that, because of your name, you might like Orchid fragrance,' smiled Jingfei, glad that this little touch had been appreciated.

Lan Fang settled in quickly and got on well with the other girls. The Friday night and Saturday night were busy, but on Sunday night, when Lan Fang had arranged for her client, Nick, to visit, he had trouble getting in. He phoned Jingfei from outside the tower block, complaining that he couldn't get past the outer door.

'Sir the flat number is 1002.'

This time, when he keyed that into the entry pad, it buzzed a picture up to the video link inside the flat OK and so she released the outer door lock to let him in.

'Got given the wrong flat number, they said it was 0102,' Nick said when he arrived at the flat, 'miserable old woman there wouldn't let me in.'

'Sir please do not make that mistake again,' Jingfei warned him sternly, 'we do not want any trouble with our neighbours.'

She knew that they had previously had a bit of trouble with clients buzzing the wrong flat, but that was shortly after they had moved in and, as far as she knew, they had not had any trouble since. Jingfei knew that none of Violetta's customers would be causing any trouble, as they were so well trained, Violetta even made them kneel, hooded, in the lounge, while waiting for her attention.

*

Over the winter Ellen had noticed further decline in her parents' health. Trevor and she had managed to keep their promise to visit them at least every fortnight, although it did not prove as easy as she hoped, because Trevor had to balance it in between carrying out his surveys and he often had evening meetings at the OFC to attend.

Also, it meant needing a day when Carol could come over and sit with Trevor's Mum, as she too was getting worse. She had now been taking Donepezil for nearly two years, they were sure this had slowed the rate of increase of Mum's dementia symptoms, but they knew it was not a cure. Ellen thought that it was a bit like putting a jet in a holding pattern over an airport, you can do that for a while, but it does not prevent the pull of gravity. Dr Oyebanji, Ellen's parents GP, had done a sterling job of arranging 'elpers', they were now coming every Monday, Wednesday and Friday and the District Nurse visited once a month. Ellen often managed to coincide their visits to the District Nurse's visits, so they could have a catch-up chat outside afterwards. The District Nurse agreed that it would be best to keep her Mum and Dad at home for as long as possible. They had now been diagnosed with arthritis, and hypertension on top of the dementia which had been eating away at them for more than two years. The slowing effects of Donepezil were beginning to lose the battle against the incoming tide of dementia for Ellen's parents, and she knew that they could not stay at home for much longer.

*

After two weeks of having four girls working, Jingfei found herself pleased with how things were working out and wished that she had thought of it earlier. She wanted to keep the time-off rota system going, it was something that she had decided was needed when she and Trevor had started their business. When she had worked in London and at Madam Chang's, she didn't have nearly so much time off as her girls, and had sometimes got quite fed up with her lot. So, she had decided that when she had her own place, she would be a better Madam to her girls. Of course, such kindness came at a cost to her business, but she felt that, overall, trying to keep the girls happy would help them to work better and retain more regular customers, which would in turn reap rewards. She started to wonder if she should ask Trevor about getting a bigger flat or, even better, a detached house, somewhere she wouldn't have any neighbour problems. She determined that she would suggest it to Trevor when she saw him on Thursday. She knew that when she wanted to get Trevor to do something, she had to approach him with idea the right way at the right time and make him think that it really was his great idea in the first place. She had known him for long enough now, to know exactly how to manipulate him to get what she wanted. By September her debt to Mr Doherty would be paid off and that would be a good time to make the move, in which case she would need Trevor to give notice on this flat soon and then they could start looking for somewhere better to match her plans.

*

When Trevor arrived on Thursday afternoon, he immediately sensed that something was up. The flat was looking particularly clean and tidy and there was a pleasant aroma around the place. He knew that Jingfei must have made a special effort in preparing for his arrival; so, just like in *Star Trek*, when the Klingons suddenly materialise in front of the USS Enterprise, he mentally put his shields up. She made them both a cup of Oolong tea and they sat in the lounge to sip it. After a few pleasantries, Trevor sensed her tense up and take a deep breath.

'Trevor, look at this lovely detached house for rent in South View.'

So that was it, he thought!

She continued, 'Look it's got 4 bedrooms, 3 bathrooms, big driveway and a joined on double garage for Violetta.'

'They call that an Integral Garage Jingfei,' corrected Trevor, playing for time.

'OK Integral Garage for Violetta, but just look at it Trevor,' - she waved an Estate Agent's glossy A4 brochure at him - 'It's only £1,600 per month, and we could convert the other garage into a bedroom for the girls, so we wouldn't need the Travel Inn anymore.'

Trevor was curious, but tried not to show it. He glanced at the brochure, it did indeed look good, the location was still quite central and she did have a point, saving £1,500 per month from the Travel Inn and putting that into their business would make sense. He could feel the shields coming down, he hated it when she had a good idea. *She must have been watching* Homes under the Hammer *now as well as* Dragons' Den, that thought made a smile slip free from his lips.

'Yes, it's not bad Jingfei,' he said grudgingly.

'I knew you'd like it, Trevor!' she said triumphantly, while stroking his thigh.

'It needs a lot of redecoration,' he parried.

'Yeah, we can do that together Trevor, let's go take a look.'

'OK,' said Trevor, 'I'll call the estate agent and find out when we can get to see it,' Her face lit up, like a child unwrapping a Christmas present. Oh, she still had that magic inside her that had first attracted him to her. She led him by the hand to the bedroom for his reward.

On Saturday morning Trevor's Mum was late getting up for breakfast. Ever since she started living with them, she had got into the habit of washing and dressing herself every morning and coming into the kitchen to make herself a cup of Earl Grey tea. She would sit at the small kitchen table in the corner, watch Lorraine on TV and sip her tea, waiting for Ellen to come down and make breakfast for the two of them. She had found herself a good strategic position in the kitchen, she could keep an eye on the comings and goings, see the TV, and not be in the way of through traffic, but able to watch Ellen as she cooked. Mum was very sensitive to letting Ellen keep charge in the kitchen, she knew that it would cause friction between them, if she started to take over. It was like the hierarchy in a pride of lions in their territory, Mum knew that she was no longer the Lead Female and that this was not her territory, but she still wanted to be involved, to peel the carrots when Ellen tasked her so to do and be company for her daughter-in-law Ellen.

Despite Trevor getting up early every day of the week, he still could not have a lie-in on the weekends. He would usually get up around half past seven, come downstairs, make himself a mug of tea and go back upstairs to his study to switch his computer and check his overnight emails. So, this day he was surprised, when he came back downstairs, not to see Mum sat in her corner. It was now just gone half past eight and Mum was usually in her sentry box by now. At the other end of the kitchen extension

was the door to Mum's Granny Annexe. Trevor opened the door and found it unusually quiet inside. She usually had her old transistor radio, or wireless as she preferred to call it, on by now. Trevor walked to her bedroom door and knocked.

'Mum, you alright?' he called, there was no reply.

His heart beat a little faster. He opened the door gently, the bedroom was still in darkness, which was definitely unusual for Mum at this time of the morning, she, like him, was an early riser. Trevor moved to the window and cracked open the curtains a little bit, to let a shaft of light in, which illuminated her motionless body on the floor by the side of the bed.

Trevor got down on his knees by her side and repeated, 'Mum, you alright?' a bit more urgently this time. He rested the back of his hand on her cheek, it was very pale and cool to his touch, but not cold. She murmured something unintelligible.

'It's Trevor Mum, you alright? Did you have a fall?'

Again, she only managed to mumble something.

Trevor's heart was racing now. 'I'll be right back Mum,' he said as headed to the door, stopping abruptly, turning around, he grabbed a pillow from the bed and slid it under her head, then pulled a blanket off the bed and put it over her, before heading to the door again and walked briskly through the kitchen to the hallway. He grabbed the cordless phone off the hall table and dialled 999 for an ambulance. Ellen heard him on the phone and came downstairs to see what was going on. Trevor, still talking on the phone to the ambulance service, led Ellen through to Mum's bedroom. She was still as he had left her. The ambulance operator said that an ambulance was already on its way to them, but asked Trevor to check her breathing in the meantime. It was shallow but steady, Mum could still not say anything.

Ellen had tears running down her cheeks. 'Mum, we're here, we love you Mum,' was all she could get out, as they both knelt by Mum's side. It seemed like ages, but it was only 15 minutes before the ambulance arrived, Trevor ushered the paramedic technician through the house and into Mum's bedroom.

'What's the patient's name please?' she asked.

'Shirley,' replied Trevor.

'Hello Shirley, my name's Mary, I'm just going to check your blood pressure, if that's OK,' said the paramedic. She worked like a well-oiled machine, gently talking to Mum and Trevor whilst carrying out the basic tests. Her colleague found his own way through the house and stood back a bit while keeping up a dialogue with Mary.

The paramedics decided that they needed to take Mum into the Basingstoke and North Hampshire Hospital, Trevor told Ellen to go with Mum and he would follow in his car. Trevor let them go ahead while he called Carol and Maria to let them know what was happening, locked up the house, checked that his car was OK for fuel and headed out to the Hospital. As he was driving, an old tune from the 1960s came on the radio, 'A Change is Gonna Come' by Sam Cooke. He thought that it referred to the Civil Rights movement of that era, but two lines from it resonated with him today. *'I'm afraid to die, 'cause I don't know what's up there, beyond the sky.'* And *'There have been times that I thought I couldn't last for long, now I think I can carry on.'* He knew that there was no need to rush, not that he was someone who didn't care about the speed limits, but ambulance queues outside the Hospital were well documented in the local press, as were the parking problems. However, this time of day on a weekend morning was apparently contrary to the usual situation, for when he arrived, he was able to find a parking space without too much trouble. When he got into Accident and Emergency and asked for Mum, they had already been told to wait in a 'Cubicle'. Trevor hated the usage of that word in the Hospital context. Due to the shape of the bed, it was more of a rectangular shape than a cube and it didn't have any form of wall, only curtains which flapped open as the Doctors whizzed by. Also, to his mind cubicles were those awful rabbit hutches they use to sub-divide modern, open plan offices, where people talked loudly on phones, oblivious to their neighbour two feet away.

Mum was still not coherent, and they had put a drip into the back of her wrist, but she felt a bit warmer and some colour had returned to her cheeks.

Ellen was pleased to see him. 'Oh Trevor, so glad you made it luv, I was so worried,' she whispered, a hint of her long-buried Somerset accent slipping out due to the stress.

A nurse came to carry out more tests and informed them that a Doctor would be along to see them shortly. They didn't know if Mum could hear them, but they tried to chat to her anyway, just in case. They told her where she was, that they were waiting for the Doctor and that they both loved her very much. Rather surprisingly a Doctor did indeed arrive after about 10 minutes, he spoke quite softly and explained that he thought that Mum might have had a stroke, but they would need to carry out more tests and keep her in for observation for a couple of days. He was very careful to include Mum in the conversation, even though she was unresponsive, and Trevor appreciated that consideration.

Ellen wanted to go home to get some clothes and toiletries for Mum, which Trevor hadn't thought about when he had left home. Ellen wouldn't drive home on her own. Although she had passed her driving test many years ago and always used to do the lion's share of the taxi duties when the girls were growing up, but since then she started relying on Trevor to take her out to go food shopping and the odd doctors or dentist visits. She mostly stayed at home now, especially since Mum had moved in with them. So, it was Trevor and Ellen who returned home to collect a bag of Mum's clothes and toiletries.

While Ellen was packing a bag for Mum, Trevor rang Carol and Maria to give them an update on Mum's condition. When they arrived back at Mum's bedside, she was still not coherent, then a Nurse came to say that

the Doctor wanted to talk with them. He looked in on them about 15 minutes later, to report that he did not believe that Mum had had a stroke, but she did have a urinary tract infection. They would need to keep her in to give her antibiotics and carry out observations on her for a couple of days but that he expected her to be much better by Monday. A nurse and a porter arrived to take Mum up to the F2 Ward, Trevor gathered her belongings and they trooped along behind the trolley. Mum was put into an eight-bed room off the main Ward corridor, Trevor realised that this was clearly the elderly ladies ward and Mum's arrival appeared to be the highlight of the day for the other patients in the all-female side-ward.

It was a great relief to Trevor and Ellen, to get Mum out of the A&E and into a 'proper' ward, a bit like reaching Base Camp on Everest, but without the snow. They stayed for the rest of the afternoon, but Mum was sleeping most of the time. When the ward staff came round with the evening meal, the nurse recommended they go home and pop back tomorrow, she promised to call them if there was a change in Mum's condition. They felt better knowing that Mum was in good hands now.

On the Sunday morning, when they arrived back at the hospital around 10am, Mum was lying on her bed, very still with her eyes closed. When Trevor gently stroked the back of her hand, she opened her eyes halfway and mumbled something that they couldn't understand, but they were pleased that she was showing a sign of improvement. They tried to keep a conversation flowing, keeping to general topics, Mum would occasionally make an inaudible response, but kept nodding off. By 1pm, they decided to head back home and return tomorrow. Once they were home, Trevor made them both a mug of Earl Grey tea and they sat in the lounge, lost in their own thoughts for a while.

Hospitals depressed Trevor, they reminded him of the time he spent in the Royal Berkshire Hospital, three years ago, with his Dad during his final days. Trevor thought, *We need times like these to appreciate what we have and make the most of the time we with our families.* Trevor and Ellen

both knew that they were moving into a new stage in their lives. Some people called it the 'Sandwich Generation' when people in their 40s and 50s are looking after their grown children and their parents at the same time, with little time to attend to their own needs.

Well, to Trevor's mind, he and Ellen were a bit older than that and were now moving out of the jam and into the upper slice of the sandwich, with all three remaining parents in ill health, they were heading to a time of change. *At least the girls are settled, we don't need to worry about the lower slice at the moment,* he thought. *We might even be able to come through this stage in our lives and have some time for us to travel a bit and do things together for a change.*

He leant over and gave Ellen a kiss on her cheek. 'I love you old girl.'

'What suddenly brought that on Trev?' Ellen said, feigning a suspicious look. 'I ain't got no money you know!' she joked back. It was another of their old in-jokes and one of those things that are sometimes used between couples to strengthen their bond.

Trevor was aware that he had not made enough of an effort to be a good husband to Ellen since she had lost interest in sex. Sometimes it made him feel guilty, that he hadn't done more, but then he knew that those feelings of guilt would disappear when he was with Jingfei and he didn't want to give her up.

When they visited Mum on Monday, she was awake when they walked in to the side-ward, she looked up and smiled when they approached the bed.

'Hello Mum, how are you today then?' asked Trevor.

'Trevor?' she asked a little bit unsure.

'Yes Mum' said Trevor 'and Ellen.'

Mum looked at Ellen. 'Ellen, hello,' said Mum, a little bit clearer now.

The longer they stayed and chatted with Mum the more lucid she became, like one of those infernal low-energy bulbs warming up. In the side-ward, there was a sense of anticipation in the air, as the time for Doctor's rounds approached. The ward staff fussed around, tidying bed sheets, patients, flowers and IV poles, even the patients looked brighter as the hour approached. The Doctor breezed in, accompanied by a phalanx of Junior Doctors and Students. Each patient in turn was spoken about and discussed by the team, in a manner that made Trevor imagine visitors to a museum discussing the thirteenth trilobite that they had seen that morning. When it was Mum's turn, one of the Junior Doctors, deftly picked the clipboard out of the pouch at the bottom of her bed flicked through a couple of the pages of her notes, 'Mrs Braithwaite, UTI...' and the rest was lost on Trevor and Ellen, but there was a lot of 'umming' between the medical staff and deference to the Doctor, until the Junior Doctor with the clipboard asked Trevor, 'Are you the son?'

Somehow Trevor resisted the temptation to give her a sarky response about being the moon, instead settling for, 'Yes, I am.'

'Good,' replied the Junior Doctor. 'Well, we'd like to keep Mrs Braithwaite in for at least another night, just to keep an eye on her, but she has made good progress.'

Trevor tried to reply with a 'Thank you,' but as he was saying it, the group were already moving on to the next bed.

Trevor and Ellen told Mum the good news that she might be able to come home tomorrow, whilst trying to overhear what ailments were afflicting the other patients in the side-ward. They gave Mum the copy of *Woman's Weekly* that they had purchased in the hospital shop, on their way in earlier, so she would have something to look at, if she was able. By 12pm they decided that it was time to head back home and return tomorrow.

On the Tuesday, they took some of Mum's nice clothes and shoes in for her, they knew that if she was well enough to come home, then she would want to look her best, for even in a sick ward there is a social hierarchy. On the way into the ward, they checked at the ward reception desk with the Sister in Charge, who confirmed that Mum had already been given the all clear to go home. When they went into Mum's side ward, Mum was sitting up in bed, looking around, a well-thumbed copy of *Woman's Weekly* lying on her bedside table. 'Ooh you're here,' she said, smiling at them. 'Did you hear, they said that I can go home,' she continued, beaming.

Blimey, Trevor thought, *it's not quite Lazarus of Bethany, but it's flipping close!* 'Yeah, that's great Mum!' he said. 'We've brought some clothes in for you, let's get you dressed to go,' he added as he pulled the curtains around her bed, making sure that he was on the outside and Ellen was on the inside. 'I'll just wait out here Mum,' he said as he left to wander up and down the main ward corridor for a little while. He went back to the ward reception desk, to let them know that they were going to take Mum home. The nurse there said she would call for a porter to bring a wheelchair to take Mum to the Car Park, 'Trust policy,' she said.

Trevor nodded and smiled at her; he had expected nothing less. He wandered back to Mum's side-ward, where the curtains were still drawn around Mum's bed. He went back out to the corridor, he had spied a noticeboard there earlier, where he thought that he might find something to occupy his mind for a few moments.

Mum was soon ready, so she sat in the visitor chair beside her bed, showing off her graduation outfit to the rest of the ward. Ellen perched on the bed, but Trevor could see that she wasn't comfortable, due to the bed's height. Trevor, meanwhile, kept watch in the corridor for the arrival of the porter. Trevor could not think of hospital porters without thinking of the Jimmy Savile revelations, he knew that this was wrong, it was just the way that his neurons had been wired by the recent news. Just the same way that you know that B follows A, hospital porters and Jimmy Savile had become inextricably linked in his mind. He was sure that he was not alone in this, at which point in his musings, the porter arrived in the corridor; Trevor gave him a little wave and the porter responded with a nod and headed towards Trevor. Mum was happy to get in the wheelchair and she gave a little smile to the remaining occupants of the side-ward as she was whisked regally out.

As soon as he could reasonably do so, after they arrived home, Trevor made his excuses and drove to the Kitchen Showroom, to catch up with

Barry and see what was happening about the surveys which had had to be re-scheduled during his absence. Trevor noticed that the list now included two afternoon surveys for Thursday 7th March, encroaching on his Jingfei time.

Barry apologised, 'Yeah, sorry about that Trev, I know you like your Thursday afternoons off to take your Mum out, but that's the only time that I could get them rescheduled to, from last weekend. The customers were already a bit miffed, that we had to let them down on the weekend.'

Trevor bit his tongue; he knew he had dropped Barry in it at short notice. 'OK Barry, no worries, I'll get them done.'

He didn't like it, but he knew that he would just have to fit a quick visit to Jingfei, later than usual on Thursday afternoon, to pick up the cash. He left the Kitchen Showroom and headed out to his first survey and to try to catch up on his backlog.

Trevor managed to get his Thursday surveys finished by 7.30pm in the evening, but his last survey was out in Newbury and then on his drive back from there, the A339 was blocked at Kingsclere. When he got to front of the queue, he asked the workmen on the traffic lights, what the holdup was all about. They said that they were doing some filming for *Downton Abbey* at the entrance to Kingsclere Castle and they had permission to halt the traffic, when they were shooting, to stop the modern traffic being in shot. Trevor was not at all happy, as he had promised Jingfei that he would be there just after 7pm. As it was, he finally arrived just after 8pm, but she was already worried about him.

'Oh Trevor, I thought that you had had an accident or something,' she whispered to him, her moist eyes revealing her concern.

'No, I'm fine, it was just roadworks on the road from Newbury,' he whispered back, omitting the bit about *Downton Abbey*, he knew she was not a fan of the series, she thought that it was all about class separation and stuffy old rich people.

It was unusual for Trevor to be in the flat when there were clients there, but he knew that he needed to pick up the cash. Jingfei told him that there was only someone in with Qi Qi Yan and someone else in with Violetta, and her room was soundproofed, so they didn't have to worry about that. They went into Jingfei's bedroom and locked the door. He did not know then, but this would be the last time that they would share a bed together.

It was nearly an hour later, while Trevor was still trying to get his breath back, that Jingfei pulled the brochure for the detached house out of one of the cupboard drawers. *In wartime,* Trevor thought, *such manoeuvres might have been called deception, lull the opposing force into false sense of security and then hit them hard when they are least expecting it.*

'Trevor, when are we going to see this house?' she asked sweetly.

He knew that she had him on the ropes. 'Sorry Jingfei, I didn't get round to calling the agent.' As soon as the words left his lips, he knew he was in trouble.

'But Trevor, it's been a week since we decided to go and see it, you said you would call them, why didn't you?' her tone was less sweet now.

He didn't want to tell her about the trouble that he had been having with Mum, that was a different watertight compartment. In truth, the house had slipped his mind until he was waiting in the queue at Highclere. He knew the topic would come up tonight, because Jingfei had less balls to juggle in life than he did and she could devote some of her time to

preparing conversations such as these. He was still not yet fully recovered from his earlier exertions, so the best that he could come up with was the plaintive, 'I'm sorry Jingfei, I just forgot about it.'

The argument that ensued was worse than any other argument that they had had before. She thought that he wasn't supporting her as much as he should. He thought that they should be more wary about making a move into a stable residential neighbourhood like that, where the curtain twitchers would be keeping a wary eye on every visitor. The beauty of the tower block was the anonymity it offered to them and their clients.

She wanted to get yet another girl in to increase their turnover and would need another room for her. He could see her point of view completely and her idea certainly had a lot of merit; but it was the increased risk of exposure that worried him. When he reminded her of Madam Chang's fate, Jingfei just dismissed that as 'Nasty old woman who got what she deserved', which surprised Trevor, as he hadn't realised that there was so much bad blood between them, or maybe it was just Jingfei's bad mood. Either way he suddenly realised that he hadn't eaten yet this evening. He decided that he needed to get out of the flat. He picked up the money that he originally came for, let Jingfei check there were no clients in the hallway, kissed her goodbye and made his way down to the underground car park.

As he pulled out of the car park, he was surprised to see just how stormy it had become while he had been inside. He had his wipers on the fastest setting in order to keep the windscreen clear enough to see out. He had never used the fastest setting on his wipers. *That must be for monsoon time* he mused to himself.

On the way home he stopped at the McDonalds and had a Quarter Pounder meal. There were a few teenagers supping milkshakes in there, but otherwise it was quiet, being too late for the family dinner customers and too early for the after-pub crew. He was still mulling over the argument with Jingfei, to say that he was conflicted would have been an understatement, but deep down his concerns of exposure were foremost.

He mentally prepared his cover story for tonight, Ellen would be happy to believe that he had been at the OFC, hence the need to have a meal before going home. He had no need to rush his meal, the later he got home, the better to minimise Ellen's questioning. If asked, he could say that he didn't stay on for a beer with the chaps, because he wanted to see how Mum was, even though he already knew that she had thankfully made a full recovery. When he got back into the car, he changed the radio channel to Classic FM. 'Moonlight Sonata' was playing as he pulled out of

McDonalds car park, it was a favourite tune of his, but tonight the weather was not looking anything like moonlight shining peacefully upon Lake Lucerne. That contrast made him smile. As he pulled into their driveway, he was pleased to see that their bedroom light was off, *that's a result,* he thought, as he turned his jacket collar up to try to keep the rain off his neck, on his walk to the front door.

I hope Ellen's already asleep, thought Trevor, as he put his key in the door lock, *I really don't want to be confronted by another one of her TSI's!*

Chapter 8

Another Sliding Door Moment

8th March 2013

It was a busy Friday for Trevor, but at least he was able to clear off the last of his backlog of surveys. He hadn't had time to get to the bank to pay in the cash that Jingfei had given him yesterday, but he frequently used the fuse compartment under his steering wheel as an overnight safe deposit box, so he tucked the envelope of banknotes in there for now and replaced the cover plate. When he arrived home in the late afternoon, Mum was having a cup of tea in the lounge with Ellen, he went over to give them both a kiss on the cheek. He sat with them for a while, hearing about how their day had been. Mum was back to her normal self now, much to the relief of Trevor and Ellen. It had been a bit of a scare for them all; although it was only a week ago, it seemed longer and it had been a stressful time for them.

Ellen got up to start making dinner, Trevor followed her into the kitchen to see if he could help with the dinner. On the breakfast bar was the post, which as usual was mostly leaflets and junk mail.

'Ooh yeah, I meant to tell you Trevor, it looks like you've got a speeding ticket, there's a letter from Hampshire Police for you, with a Winchester postmark.'

He knew Ellen was trying to wind him up, just as he knew that he hadn't got a speeding ticket, but he did wonder why he would have received a letter from Hampshire Police.

He took the letter and a bill upstairs to his study, to switch his computer on. As it was booting up, he opened the Police letter, he could feel his pulse quickening. There was a single A4 sheet of paper inside, signed by a Detective Constable Barnes, saying that they obtained his contact details from his Landlord and that they had received reports that he had been allowing an anti-social nuisance to continue in the Alencon Heights tower block.

Trevor had never been so shocked, an icy chill swept down his spine. The letter went on to state that operating a brothel was an illegal activity and that it should cease immediately. Trevor thought that he was going to vomit, he dashed to the toilet and was indeed sick. He had always put thoughts of exposure to the back of his mind. The potential for police involvement or being arrested was something that he – perhaps rather naively now – never thought would happen to him. His mind was racing, he was in two minds about going to tell Jingfei immediately or wait until tomorrow. He knew that if he waited until tomorrow, he would not be able prevent Ellen from noticing his discomfort overnight, for he would not be able to sleep tonight. He needed to invent a credible story to get him out of the house ASAP. The best that he could come up with was that Barry had just called him to say that there had been a break-in at the Kitchen Showroom, and he had to dash out to help him tidy up and secure the building. Ellen was understandably shocked and surprised, but promised to put a meal for him in the microwave, ready for his return. The thought of food nearly made Trevor sick again, but instead he was out of the door and in the car, before he felt guilt about lying to Ellen.

As he drove, he started to wonder how he could contain this news, he needed to keep his watertight compartments sealed. He never liked feeling out of control and this was beginning to feel like being as far out of control as he could ever be.

When Trevor arrived at the flat, Jingfei was surprised to see him, he had never before turned up unannounced, during their business hours. The girls were watching TV in the lounge.

'Trevor what are you doing here?' Jingfei asked, 'The first customer is due in a half-an-hour.'

Trevor took her into the bathroom to talk to her. 'Jingfei, we have to close down immediately, we have been reported to the police!'

'What do you mean Trevor?' her voice trembled.

'One of the neighbours must have reported us, because the bloody idiot punters keep ringing the wrong bloody bell Jingfei!' His hand was shaking as he showed her the letter from the police.

She didn't understand all of the letter, but she understood enough of it, which, combined with seeing Trevor so afraid and upset as he was, convinced her that they needed to act immediately.

As soon as they left the bathroom the girls realised that there was something wrong from the look on Jingfei's face. She told them that they were going to have to close up tonight and that the girls should collect any of their belongings and go back to the hotel straightaway. Chun Hu asked what was going on, then she started crying when Jingfei replied that they had been reported to the police. Violetta was angry and cursed something which they didn't understand. Jingfei told the girls to stay at the Hotel until she called them and that she would text the clients that they were expecting tonight, to tell them that they were closed. Trevor told Jingfei that he would see if the detached house in South View was still available for rent, so they could move there ASAP.

Trevor didn't think that there was much more he could do in the flat that night. The girls had gone and Jingfei had sent the text messages, it suddenly seemed unusually quiet in the flat. Jingfei made them both a cup of Oolong tea and they sat together for a while on the sofa sipping their cups, occasionally chatting as casually as possible about moving into the South View house, as if it was a certainty. They were trying to put a positive spin on the situation that they had suddenly found themselves in, but there was an unspoken undercurrent of tension and concern about the police involvement. While the tea was easing it, it was not erasing it. Trevor thought that closing the flat down and preventing further complaints from the neighbours, might be enough to prevent any further police action.

After all, whoever had heard of the police giving anyone advance warning of an impending police raid and especially giving that warning by post! Was manpower really in such short supply in Plodville that they had to use Postman Pat to do their work! The absurdity of the situation was dawning on him, he would normally have found this sort of story highly amusing, but right now he was in no mood to chuckle about it. It would have been different, of course, if he was looking into someone else's life, that would be funny. Perhaps more so in the funny-peculiar sense of the word, but he could just visualise himself, holding court in the bar at the OFC, keeping the chaps in hysterics, as he milked the story for all it was worth! He suddenly realised that, if this got out then *he* would be the focus of their merriment at his expense and his gloom sunk to a new depth. He did not dare to share this thought with Jingfei, as he still wanted to try to keep her in a separate compartment from his home life. He then realised he had better prepare a good story for Ellen and head home. He told Jingfei that he would let her know what the Estate Agent knew about the South View house tomorrow, which partially pacified her and then kissed her goodbye.

When he arrived home, Mum had already retired to her annexe, but Ellen was watching the Shopping Channel on TV, and was eager to know what the situation was at the Kitchen Showroom. Whilst microwaving and eating his dinner, Trevor rolled out his carefully prepared story, which was met with multiple gasps of 'Oh no!' and 'Gosh!' from Ellen. Inwardly, Trevor was saddened by continually lying to Ellen, but he saw no alternative, he had got himself into this situation and he was desperately hoping that he would be able to keep it going. After a while Ellen's interest tailed off and she returned her attention to the TV, Trevor put his plate and cutlery in the dishwasher, set it running and headed upstairs to his study. He was itching to see if the South View house was still available for rent. Sometimes he felt like he needed a crank handle on the side of his computer, to speed up its wake up and webpage loading. Eventually he managed to get to the right webpage and was pleased to find that the house was still available for rent. He made a note of the Estate Agent's phone number so he could call them in the morning, as he knew that they would be open on a Saturday.

The next morning, straight after breakfast, Trevor made his excuses about still having surveys to carry out and left the house. He drove to the nearby Tesco, parked in their car park, called the Estate Agent and managed to set up a viewing for 2pm that day. He then went into the store's coffee shop and sat and nursed a latte for half an hour. If anyone who knew Trevor had seen him there, they would have been quite surprised to see him whiling away some time in a coffee shop. Trevor had never been known for idleness, he always had things to do, 'fish to fry', places to go, etc. but today, he just felt that he needed to have a moment or two for a spot of reflection, or 'Astral Projection' as Jingfei had once called it with the help of Google Translate.

The need to virtually step outside of our shell and give a bystander's view of one's situation, is something innate in us, but often overlooked as a means of obtaining a sanity check.

Trevor was still very concerned about the letter from the police. Should he just jack it all in, give notice on the flat rental contract, walk away from their business and let Jingfei sort out her debt herself? He felt that this could be another one of those 'sliding doors' moments. There was a lot going for the finish it now option, before he committed to renting the South View house, he doubted that there would be a better opportunity for making a hasty exit. Returning to the moment with a bump, he stirred the froth into the last of his latte and made his mind up, as he downed the dregs in one gulp.

Trevor took a slow drive to the flat, he had no reason to rush, and the Saturday shopping rush hour was well underway in the town centre now. When he arrived in the underground car park of the Alencon Heights tower block, he spent an inordinate amount of time getting his car neatly reverse parked and centrally aligned in their allocated parking space and walked to the lift. He had prepared his speech on the journey from Tesco and the voice inside his head gave it one final run through on the journey up to the 10th floor. Jingfei was already up when he let himself in, after their initial pleasantries, Trevor was just about to start his speech, when she blurted out, 'Trevor, did you get a viewing arranged for us to see the South View house?'

'Yes, I did Jingfei, but…'

'Oh great!' she exclaimed, her face beaming a great big smile, 'When can we go then?'

'Well, that's what I wanted to talk to you about, come sit down here,' he patted the sofa, as he sat down.

Before she could sit down, the intercom buzzed, instantly changing her smile to a frown. 'We're not expecting anyone Trevor, I've already cancelled all the appointments,' she said as she turned and headed to the intercom. 'Hello, who's there?' she said in a well-practised manner, looking at the little video screen showing a man wearing a suit and tie, which she knew was not how most of their visitors dressed.

'It's the Police, can we come up and have a word with you?' Jingfei's face turned ashen, she turned to Trevor, who had overheard the exchange and also looked pallid.

'You'll have to let them in Jingfei,' he managed to stutter.

Jingfei pressed the door release button and said '10th floor,' flatly into the intercom.

Trevor quickly glanced around the lounge, operating on some kind of autopilot, looking for any contraband that he needed to stash out the way in the two minutes he knew it would take the Police to cross the lobby and come up in the lift. He could find nothing that jumped out to him as requiring immediate concealment, so instead he straightened the cushions on the sofa, for an instinct deep inside him believed that the Police would never arrest anyone with a tidy sofa! At a later stage, when he had more time to reflect on it, Trevor realised that he must have been in shock at this point and had indeed acted on an instinct, one he must have learnt from his Mum 'Quick! Visitors are coming! Plump the cushions!' He supposed that in medieval times, when an Englishman's home was his castle, the cry of 'Enemy horsemen are coming!' would have been met with 'Archers to the Battlements!' Now it was met with 'Plump the cushions!' instead.

Trevor opened their entrance door and waited half in the doorway and half in the corridor, ready to direct the Police to their flat. He'd seen those TV programmes where the Police gain entry to houses using their 'Big Red Key' and he didn't want damage like that to be done to the flat! A couple of seconds later the lift arrived with a *bing!* alert and a smartly dressed couple stepped out, glanced around, saw Trevor beckoning them and walked towards him.

'Mr. Braithwaite?' said the man.

'Yes,' said Trevor.

'I'm Detective Constable Kevin Barnes and this is Detective Constable Anita Dorey,' he said, showing Trevor his warrant card and motioning to his colleague, who nodded an acknowledgement whilst showing her warrant card.

Trevor nodded back, noticing that DC Dorey was pulling a small, wheeled suitcase.

'We have a search warrant to search this flat in connection with an investigation into an offence, which we believe may have been committed.' DC Barnes waved an official looking sheet of paper at Trevor, which he took hold of.

'Can we come in?' said DC Barnes, already shifting his weight forward before Trevor managed to get an 'OK' out.

Trevor motioned them to come in, directing them down the short hallway to the lounge and shutting the entrance door behind them. Jingfei was standing at the kitchen door, her face still very pale.

'Hello, my name is Detective Constable Kevin Barnes, can I ask for your name?' said DC Barnes walking up to Jingfei, showing her his warrant card.

'My name is Jingfei Liu,' she replied shakily.

'Miss Liu, this is Detective Constable Anita Dorey,' DC Barnes said, pointing to DC Dorey, who also showed Jingfei her warrant card.

He then turned to Trevor, whose hands were shaking as he was scanning the search warrant and finding that the word 'prostitution' kept being repeated.

'Are there any other occupants in the flat Mr Braithwaite?'

'No,' said Trevor, thankful that Jingfei had told the girls to stay at the Hotel. Trevor's head was spinning, he had only opened the warning letter from DC Barnes yesterday and now, on a Saturday, they were here! He had never heard of police procedures being carried out like this. His first instinct was to complain to DC Barnes, but he decided better of it.

'Mr. Braithwaite, Miss Liu, we are going to carry out a search of these premises in connection with an investigation into offences of causing, inciting or controlling prostitution for gain, or trafficking for sexual exploitation,' said DC Barnes. 'Would you both kindly take a seat on this sofa, while we carry out the search,' he added, pointing to opposite ends of the sofa.

DC Dorey lifted her suitcase onto one of the lounge chairs and opened it up, passed a pair of nitrile gloves to DC Barnes and put her own pair on. So began an extensive search of the flat, they worked their way round methodically, taking multiple photos of the rooms, the contents, everything. Trevor and Jingfei's phones and the contents of their pockets were put into evidence bags. The same with the contents of the bedrooms, the bedside cabinets, condoms, lubricants, wet wipes, underwear, etc. The contents of Violetta's dungeon were of particular interest. All the evidence bags were carefully labelled, logged and lined up in the hallway. They even, triumphantly, found a stash of banknotes, which Jingfei had tucked away in the bottom of a Bran Flakes box in a kitchen cupboard. Trevor presumed that she had chosen a Bran Flakes box for use as a safe, because she knew that no-one else would go near it. DC Dorey counted the cash, announced that there was £3,290 in the cereal box and sealed it in an evidence bag. There was not much documentation in the flat, Trevor had been careful to keep all of that at home, but they took the Estate Agent's glossy A4 brochure of the South View house and some other brochures, which Jingfei had collected.

Thinking about the documentation, made a thought suddenly hit Trevor between the eyes, they would want to search his home as well! He could feel his heart racing, he would not be able to prevent that, nor keep the reason for their search from Ellen and Mum! He thought that his mood yesterday, had been at an all-time low, but now he was feeling even worse, he could feel sweat rising on his forehead. He had to get to the toilet without delay! He jumped up and blurted out 'Toilet!' to DC Dorey, who had no chance to stop him before he was crashing through the toilet door and retching loudly until he was empty. He had not dared to deviate from his trajectory to explain to the Police Officers that he was not disposing of evidence or something else incriminating, only that he was completely and utterly focussed on reaching the toilet bowl before his ability to retain his breakfast was lost.

Trevor rinsed his mouth in the sink and returned to his seat on the sofa, smiling weakly to DC Dorey as he passed her. She looked back at him blankly and in that moment, he realised that as a potential criminal, he had now been demoted from being treated civilly, as an upright citizen, to being treated with disdain and suspicion. For Trevor, who had always considered himself to be a gentle, kind, considerate soul, this change would take some getting used to, but he would get used to it and it would change him. It was a lesson for Trevor, to realise that his actions had consequences and these were not only restricted to the realms of crime and punishment, they would also affect his family, others and his future. He had started the business with Jingfei to help her and also to help him stay with Ellen, but it had become something much more than that. It became something that had taken over so much of his life, causing him to lie constantly to Ellen, Mum and others that he cared about. As he sat desolately on the other end of the sofa to Jingfei, he realised that he had never felt so alone or so apprehensive about what the future held for him. It was a wake-up call that he had somehow denied the existence of, for so long, one that he had thought would never come, but now it had and he knew that everything was about to change for him. He made a decision and stood up.

'Excuse me officer,' he said to DC Barnes, 'I have an admission to make...'

DC Barnes abruptly stopped Trevor, by raising his hand, 'Hold on a moment Mr Braithwaite, please sit down, I will have to caution you first.' And so, DC Barnes said those famous words that Trevor had heard many times on TV programmes, but had never expected to be hearing them first hand himself. 'You do not have to say anything. But it may harm your defence if you do not mention, when questioned, something which you later rely on in court. Anything you do say may be given in evidence.' DC Barnes got his notebook and pencil out ready to receive Trevor's confession.

On hearing those words, Trevor's blood ran cold, the seriousness of his situation filled his head with a multitude of thoughts. After a brief pause and a deep breath Trevor resumed, 'I've rented this flat at 1002 Alencon Heights for two years. I am married, but Jingfei is my mistress and she lives here. Whilst I've rented this flat, I've placed adverts in the papers allowing this flat to be used as a brothel, where prostitutes operate from.' He took a deep breath and flopped back into the sofa, a weight had been lifted from him, he could breathe easier now. Jingfei and the Police Officers looked at him in disbelief.

'Mr Braithwaite,' said DC Barnes, breaking the silence, 'Thank you for saying that, I will finish writing it down in my pocket notebook,' which he duly did and asked Trevor to countersign and date it.

The search took nearly three hours, inwardly part of Trevor admired their thoroughness and detailed record taking. His admiration, however, was somewhat diminished by his realisation that each evidence bag tagged and every byte of data recorded, was to their benefit and his detriment. It was mid-afternoon when DC Barnes declared that they had finished their search and wanted to take them to Basingstoke Police Station for questioning.

DC Barnes asked Trevor to stand and said to him, 'Trevor Braithwaite, I am arresting you on suspicion of causing, inciting or controlling prostitution for gain, or trafficking for sexual exploitation. You have already been cautioned that you do not have to say anything. But it may harm your defence if you do not mention, when questioned, something which you later rely on in court. Anything you do say may be given in evidence.'

Trevor felt weak at the knees, but all he could utter was a pained 'Oww.' Hearing the policeman repeating those words, did not sit any easier with Trevor, than the first time he had heard them. It was still a shocker to him. DC Dorey then did the same to Jingfei, who appeared more stoic than Trevor, but still could not stop a tear slipping from her eye.

DC Barnes made some calls and arranged for a Police patrol car to come and collect them. Trevor, made the mistake of asking if he could get his jacket from his car. This would prove to be an expensive jacket. DC Barnes said that he would take Trevor to his car for his jacket, so they walked to the lift, leaving DC Dorey looking after Jingfei. Once in the underground car park, Trevor showed DC Barnes where his car was located. Trevor opened the car, retrieved his jacket and suddenly realised that now he had shown them his car, they would be bound to come back with another search warrant for it. That would let them find the envelope of cash in the fuse compartment and so he decided that it would probably be best to declare it now to DC Barnes.

'DC Barnes, there is an envelope of cash in the fuse compartment,' said Trevor, pointing to the fuse compartment cover plate.

DC Barnes opened the cover plate, reached in and pulled out the envelope of cash, opened the envelope and quickly flicked through the notes. 'How much do you think there is here Trevor?'

'I think that there is about £2,500 in there officer,' replied Trevor, who hadn't had a chance to count it, but he knew that £2,500 was about average amount that he would collect from Jingfei every week.

'We cannot discuss this anymore at the moment Trevor, we'll come back to it when we are in the station,' said DC Barnes as he put the envelope into his jacket pocket. 'We'll take it upstairs for now.' DC Barnes took the car key, locked Trevor's car and escorted him back up to the flat.

*

Once back in the flat, DC Dorey counted the cash in the envelope from the car, declared it to be £2,870 in total and sealed it in a separate evidence bag.

DC Barnes' phone rang, after a short conversation, he said that the patrol car was waiting for Trevor and Jingfei in underground car park. He let Trevor go round the flat, checking that everything was switched off etc., Trevor and Jingfei were allowed to take their jackets, wallet/purse and door keys, but nothing else. They went down in the lift with DC Barnes and they were put in the back of the patrol car and driven off to Basingstoke Police Station.

Once they were gone, a PC, who had arrived in the patrol car, was told to stay beside the lift door while DC Barnes went up to the main lobby and outside the building, to move his car from the Visitor parking space near the main entrance, down to the underground car park, where he parked near to the lift door, under the watchful eye of the PC. DC Barnes then went back up to the flat to start collecting all the evidence bags, with DC Dorey carrying them from the flat to the lift door and DC Barnes taking them down in the lift and transferring them to their car, which the PC was still keeping guard over. On one of the lift journeys down, he was joined by an elderly lady, who couldn't stop looking at him and the selection of plastic evidence bags spread across the floor of the lift. It looked to DC Barnes like she wanted to ask about the evidence bags, but somehow, she managed to resist the temptation to ask her question, limiting their conversation, with typically British reserve, to a salutary 'Good Afternoon' which was reciprocated by DC Barnes. The lady got out on the ground floor, leaving DC Barnes to carry on to the underground car park. When they finished removing all the evidence bags the Detective Constables closed up the flat and made one last trip down in the lift. They loaded the last of the evidence bags into the boot and the ones that wouldn't fit in the boot, were loaded on the back seat of their car. DC Barnes gave Trevor's car keys to the PC and asked him to wait for the recovery truck to come and collect Trevor's car. The PC looked a bit miffed as he realised that he was going to have to walk back to the Station.

Chapter 9

Change Point

9th March 2013

It was only a short journey from the flat, around the outside of the Shopping Centre, to the police station on London Road, a route Trevor knew well from carrying out his kitchen surveys. Thinking of that pained him greatly, he doubted that Barry would want someone with a criminal record going round to his client's houses. He had known that it was a job which really was below him, but he had kept doing it, almost to spite the City, which he still hated for throwing him out of a career that he loved and deserved. He was only 62 now, that was too young to retire, but he would be lucky to get any kind of employment after this. The fear of exposure that he had kept at the back of his mind for so long had now come home to roost. He kicked himself for not making the decision to close it all down earlier, but he had been lured into Jingfei's dream of expansion. It was not until this morning that he had finally made that decision and by then it was too late, the Police had already obtained a search warrant and their fate was sealed. Everything was going to change, after this he would be lucky to be able to make a few pounds selling his candles.

He knew that he had let so many people down, he was going to have so much explaining to do and worst of all, he would be an object of ridicule to so many of his contemporaries. His gloom sunk to a nadir, how could he have done this to Ellen and his family? He imagined the terrible conversations to come.

Trevor and Jingfei didn't talk during the short journey, they just held hands while they were both thinking their own thoughts.

*

Jingfei tried to hide her tears and keep a stoic look upon her face. Inside, however, she was fuming, it had all been going so well, Lan Fang had settled in quickly and was popular, they were about to move to a lovely house and she would soon be clear of her debt to Mr Doherty. She knew that, back home, such police trouble could be avoided by keeping a few local officials on side with bottles of whisky, favours and some cash. It gave her a glimmer of a bitter smile to realise that the thing she disliked about England was that it wasn't as corrupt as back home. Thinking of home focussed her, she knew that she would be deported as soon as they confirmed her illegal residence status. This was not something that she wanted to happen, she had become quite accustomed to her life in England, she had, eventually, got used to the weather, she had money in her purse, respect from the girls, a business to run here and she was able to support her family back home. These were important things to her and she did not want to lose them, but she was slowly resigning herself to her fate, knowing that it had been good while it had lasted.

*

Trevor had only ever driven past the Police Station before, he had never had cause to step inside, but now he and Jingfei were led around to the rear entrance, through a couple of swipe access doors and into the custody suite. They were asked if they wanted to call their solicitors, but never previously having need of this type of solicitor, they did not have one that they could call. The Custody Sergeant said that duty solicitors would be appointed for them. They were ushered into separate interview rooms; DC Barnes went in with Trevor and DC Dorey went in with Jingfei.

DC Barnes explained to Trevor that he and Jingfei would have to wait in the interview rooms until their solicitors arrived, during which time he and DC Dorey would be booking in the evidence bags. Trevor was brought a cup of tea, he thought about asking to call Ellen and let her know where he was, but then decided that that would not be a good idea, there was nothing useful that she could do, she would only get stressed about it. Besides it would be better if Trevor could break the news to her in person.

As he nursed his tea, he remembered learning something. Popular western belief was that the Chinese word for crisis *'weiji'* is made up of the characters for danger and opportunity, but in reality, the second character *'ji'* is only part of the word for opportunity. On its own its meaning, Jingfei had said, was more like 'change point'. One of President J.F. Kennedy's speech writers is believed to be the source of this error, but none the less, the idea that from crisis comes opportunity has passed into popular western wisdom, presumably because it makes for a gung-ho anecdote, and who would want to let the truth get in the way of a good anecdote.

Today was a certainly a change point. A day in which all he had worked for, all he had built up, was about to be turned upside down. His relationships with his family and friends would be badly affected, he felt most worried about how Ellen and Mum would react. He knew that Ellen would not worry about his whereabouts as long as he was home by dinner time, she was quite used to him working long days on the weekends – it was easier for him to get appointments for his surveys then.

After an hour, Trevor's duty solicitor entered the interview room and introduced herself as Caroline Moore. Trevor was immediately drawn to the cut of her dark brown pencil skirt. *Not what I imagined a solicitor to be wearing, but it certainly suits her,* he thought, *nice light brown bob, none too shabby!* Caroline explained that DC Barnes had already given her some outline details and told her that Trevor had made an admission, but she wanted to hear Trevor's account before he was interviewed under caution. Trevor asked her about Jingfei, but she replied that she only knew that Jingfei was in another interview room and that a different duty solicitor had been assigned to look after her. Trevor was not exactly mollified by this news, but it was nothing more or less than he expected, soon after his arrest he realised that they would be treated differently and separately and that he might not see Jingfei again. Whilst waiting for his solicitor to arrive, Trevor had decided that he wanted to get out of this awful situation as soon as possible and that the easiest way to do that would be to make a full confession and plead guilty. He explained this to Caroline, who asked him to slow down a bit to let her make detailed notes about the case.

When Caroline had got sufficient details from Trevor, DC Barnes joined them in the interview room and announced that he will be recording the interview. He unwrapped two new cassette tapes, loaded them both into the tape recorder and started it running. Trevor was surprised to see cassette tapes still being used, they reminded him of the 1980s, he wondered how Her Majesty's Inspectorate of Constabulary had managed to ignore advancements in technology and stick with good old cassette tapes. DC Barnes abruptly brought Trevor back from his musings, telling him about the recording process; pointing out the indicator showing that the recording equipment was activated and recording. He explained that the interview was being audibly recorded, gave his name and rank and asked Trevor and Caroline to identify themselves. DC Barnes then stated the date, time of commencement and place of the interview. He reminded Trevor that he was still under caution as he had already been arrested on suspicion of 'causing, inciting or controlling prostitution for gain' and that he had also been given the PACE warning.

The reality of his situation was really hitting home to Trevor, but he knew that nothing less than continuing with his full confession would be the best way for him to proceed. He was not some kind of arch-criminal, he had managed to get himself into this situation by trying to keep his marriage and that had led him to trying to help Jingfei. A lightbulb lit up in Trevor's head! *Have I been used by Jingfei?* He wondered why he had never thought of that before. Had he been wearing pink blinkers all this time? He wasn't sure, he guessed that it might have been a two-way street, either way, he now had to face up to his situation and Jingfei would have to take her own chances.

It took almost two hours for Trevor to complete his outpourings, giving

DC Barnes far more information than he might have expected. DC Barnes warned Trevor that he would be following up on some aspects of Trevor's confession and that he probably would have to attend a second interview, at a later date, to go over some of the details. Trevor had declined to identify Mr Doherty and his club as the cause of Jingfei's debt, he had decided that Mr Doherty was Jingfei's problem and exposing him would gain Trevor nothing apart from an uncomfortable retribution. Trevor was more concerned about what was happening to the girls staying at the Travel Inn. The room rental costs had come up under questioning by DC Barnes regarding Trevor's expenses, so he presumed that DC Barnes would soon be visiting the hotel. Trevor, however, felt a moral obligation to the girls, to keep them out of trouble as much as possible.

After the interview was concluded, Trevor was taken back to the Custody Sergeant's desk and released on bail, pending further investigation. He was ordered to keep in touch with the Probation Service, and report to his local Police Station every week. Trevor was mightily relieved to leave the Police Station and get some fresh air at last, it was something that he had gained a new-found respect for, even though he had only been inside the Police Station for a couple of hours. The stifling atmosphere, the clanging of the metal doors, the mental stress of revealing his secrets, the loss of freedom of movement and freedom of control, even for such a short period of time, had combined to give Trevor a taster of how his future might look and it disturbed him. He walked around the corner to the taxi rank and took a taxi to the Travel Inn. On the journey there, he could not resist checking behind him to see if he was being followed, he felt stupid doing that, but he couldn't resist the desire to do so. He didn't think that they were being followed, but none the less got the taxi to drop him off at the Shopping Centre. He could walk through there to the hotel. He decided that, if he was being followed, there was no need to make it any easier for the police.

At the hotel's front desk, he told the receptionist that he wanted to cancel the room. She was surprised to hear this, as Trevor had now become their longest 'resident', but she was also savvy enough to know not to ask if there was a reason for the cancellation. Trevor used his credit card to settle the bill and made his way to the room, once again checking around him while he waited for the lift to arrive. The girls were pleased to see him, they had been concerned after not being able to get any reply from Jingfei's phone. Trevor's eyes widened at that, he suddenly realised that with Jingfei's and his phones being held by the police, the police would have access to their clients' phone numbers. He told the girls that he and Jingfei had been arrested and that they all had to leave the hotel immediately, as the police might be on their way there; that they should switch off their phones and dump the SIM cards, somewhere away from the hotel. The girls, immediately realising the urgency, packed quickly and they all left by the rear emergency exit. Trevor felt obliged to give them some money, but he only had some change in his wallet, all the banknotes had been taken as evidence. The girls didn't seem to mind as they said they had their own cash in their purses. They said a brief goodbye and they all split up and went their own way. As it was now after 6pm, Trevor decided that he had better get home before Ellen started to worry about his whereabouts.

He walked to the train station, stopping on the way to buy a new mobile phone, with his credit card, from a phone shop. He then took a taxi from the rank outside the train station to home. He had a little bit of time during the journey to try to work out how he was going to break the news to Ellen. He knew that there would not be an easy way to do it, but he had never been a believer in the 'Blurt it all out' method of bad news distribution. His preferred approach would be more along the lines of drip feeding the news a bit at a time, but that plan was thwarted as soon as he walked through the door and Ellen started speaking.

'Hi Trev, where's the car? Why did you come home by taxi luv? Did you have an accident? Are you OK? You're as white as a sheet Trevor, what's happened?'

Ellen's ability to fire multiple questions at him like a gatling gun had previously amused him, but in his present mood, it just irked him, *more loss of control,* he thought, *I must be in control of this narrative!* 'I'm fine love, don't worry...' he managed to get out before Ellen responded.

'Oh, good Trevor, now come and have your dinner, it's late and you know that Mum doesn't like to be having her dinner too late. You can tell us what you've been up to over dinner.'

This was definitely not going Trevor's way, he had hoped that he would be able to give Mum a potted version, after Ellen had been given most of the details. He certainly had no intention of giving Ellen EVERY detail on the first run through. Trevor's mind was still trying to keep his watertight compartments secure, something along the lines of Nero's violin playing during the burning of Rome.

He slipped into autopilot, laying the dinner table and pouring drinks of squash for Mum, Ellen and himself. Ellen brought the laden dinner plates in from the kitchen, while Trevor went to collect Mum from her annexe.

As soon as they had got Mum seated at the dinner table, Ellen asked, 'So come on now Trevor, tell us what happened to the car?'

So, there it was, he's standing at the crossroads wondering which way to go.

'It's at a garage for inspection,' was the best that he could come up with to try to answer the question, as succinctly as possible, without really lying or opening the full can of worms. 'Did you have a good day, Ellen?' he quickly asked, trying to distract her.

'No!' she replied. 'They delivered that dress that I ordered last week and it's too small! Can you believe it, I ordered the right size and it is marked as size 22, but it's never a size 22! Now I'm going to have to take it to the Post Office on Monday to send it back for a refund!'

'Don't worry about that love,' Trevor interjected 'I can drop it off at the

Post Office for you on Monday.' he said, trying to be as helpful as possible, thus keeping her off the scent. He had noticed how Ellen's weight had been steadily creeping up in the six years since she stopped working at the Bakers. He presumed that it was a combination of the lack of exercise and motivation that her job there had provided, together with the onset of the menopause and the sedentary TV-shopping lifestyle that she had drifted into since stopping work. Trevor, on the other hand, was proud that he could still fit into the 34' waist trousers that he wore to his first interview on leaving University. He didn't actually wear them, he just kept them as a memento, as a big game hunter would keep an animal's head on the wall, as a reminder of great times in days of yore. Even he was once a dashing young man, setting out on the world. *How had it come to this?* he wondered. Here he was trying to maintain the same external appearance, but inside he had changed, become self-centred, lying to Ellen, a criminal in-waiting, about to bring shame and humiliation on himself and those he cared about most.

Luckily for him, Ellen soon moved off the car topic, somewhat helped by Mum enjoying Ellen's pie so much, it took her mind down Memory Lane, reminiscing about the pies she used to cook at home.

'Les used to love my Steak and Kidney pie, Ellen,' mused Mum, 'I used to have a little china blackbird to put in the middle of the pie dish, to hold the pastry up and let the steam out,' she continued. 'Trevor always liked to have the corner slice of the pie, where the thickest part of the crust was.'

Trevor smiled, even though he had heard Mum talk about her pies many times before.

'Trevor used to call it Four and Twenty Blackbird pie!' Mum chuckled, hitting her punchline triumphantly. 'Les and Trevor always used to josh me about that. I wonder what happened to the blackbird?'

'I don't know Mum,' said Ellen, remembering the extensive search for it when they moved Mum in to live with them. 'It must have got lost in the move Mum,' she offered kindly, knowing full well that in the weeks after Trevor's Dad died, his Mum had made a daily routine of taking trinkets, keepsakes and clothes to her local charity shop. It might have been a way for her to have some company during those dark days, or it might have been that she was in some elongated form of shock, either way Ellen and

Trevor knew that there were quite a few ornaments, trinkets etc. that had not made the journey to Chineham with her.

Trevor and Mum cleared the table, while Ellen settled down to watch the news on TV. As Trevor was loading the dishwasher, Mum sidled up to him,

'Are you alright Trevor? You seemed a bit quiet tonight darling.'

Trevor realised that the dementia had not dimmed Mum's powers of perception. 'No I'm fine thanks Mum, it's just that I've had a bit of a busy day today.'

Somehow lying to his Mum was a greater sin than lying to Ellen, he could feel his face flush. Trevor scratched the back of his neck, too late realising it was a sign that Mum had seen many times before, when he was a teenager and had received a bad school report and was trying to hide it or just hoping that it would go away.

'Is there anything that I can do to help Trevor?' she asked sweetly.

He was never surprised at the depth of love that his Mum could show, she had always seemed to have bottomless well of love and care for family and friends. He was pleased that the dementia had not robbed her of that wonderful facet of her character. All he could do was to turn and give her a big all-encompassing hug. 'I love you Mum,' he said, as he bent down and gently kissed her forehead.

They both had tears in their eyes. Mum wasn't sure why Trevor was being like this, but she treasured shared moments of love like these, as did Trevor, who was feeling worse now that it was dawning on him just how much damage the coming revelations would do to the family.

Trevor set the dishwasher running and washed up the pots that wouldn't go in the dishwasher, while his Mum dried the pots. After this nightly ritual was complete Mum retired to her annexe to watch *Emmerdale* and/or 'Corrie', which Trevor and Ellen had never considered to be suitable for their consumption. Instead, Trevor would normally sit with Ellen and make comments about the TV news and small chit-chat about the clients that Trevor had met that day. Today of course, had not been a normal day, the events of which were weighing heavily on Trevor's mind, he was still undecided about how to break it to Ellen. When he was made redundant from the bank, it had taken him a couple of sessions such as this to break the news to Ellen. Ellen had to be 'handled', she had metamorphosed into a 'glass half empty' person since the Bakers had closed down all those years ago. Whenever there was bad news of any kind, no matter how inconsequential, Trevor knew that he had to find some way to sugar coat it, to try to prevent Ellen seeing her downside of any event. The 'darts of doom' as Trevor liked to inwardly refer to her innate ability, her desire, to focus on the worst of any occasion, used to irritate Trevor. He had always preferred to see his glass half full, but he had learned that managing the input Ellen received, was the best way to minimise her negativity and reduce the wear on his patience. That was his plan this time, but he just couldn't work out how to tell her what had happened in easily digestible chunks, especially whilst maintaining some kind of positive spin.

'Ellen,' said Trevor, during a particularly dreary news item, 'I've got to tell you about the car.'

Ellen's ears pricked up, she was immediately suspicious, Trevor only ever called her by her name when there was something serious that he had to tell her. 'What about the car Trevor?' she asked, the hairs on the back of her neck rising.

Trevor realised that he had alerted her to incoming bad news by the way she had called him Trevor, not her usual 'Trev', but he decided that he needed to keep going now. 'The Police have impounded it…' was all he managed to get out before she interrupted him.

'You've not been parking on the double yellows again have you Trev?'

'No,' he replied, 'they're going to search it.'

'Search it Trev? What on earth do you mean search it? You've not been dealing drugs, have you?' her voice was rising up an octave as she started to wind herself up.

This is not going well, thought Trevor, and there was insufficient sugar coating available for the coming revelations. 'No of course not, they've impounded it so they can search it for cash and evidence,' he mumbled, but Ellen heard him clearly enough.

'Evidence of what Trev? What on earth have you been up to?' she asked, sounding genuinely concerned now.

Over the course of the next hour, Trevor slowly rolled out the whole story to Ellen, trying to give her a broad outline, while missing out the more salacious details. At various points of the narrative, she responded with sobs of 'No Trevor, how could you?' - 'What are we going to do now?' - 'Will you go to jail?' - 'I'm sure they'll come for the house!' and a few more repeats of 'No Trevor, how could you?' Trevor did not labour his point to Ellen, about her loss of libido being the catalyst for his actions, but he knew that he wanted to make her understand how he had got into his present situation. This really was more a case of him trying to partially cleanse his soul, rather than him trying to pass the blame onto Ellen, he knew that he could not reasonably do that. The old proverb 'a problem shared is a problem halved' came to his mind as he unconsciously scratched the back of his neck again.

That was an act which did not go unnoticed by Ellen. Her mind was in turmoil, how had Trevor been leading a double life for the past three years? How he had been lying so bare-facedly to her, Mum and the girls. The girls! *How was she going to be able to explain this to them?* And her parents would be mortified. It would be a big local story, she knew that it would all come out, was there anymore that he wasn't telling her? She would be a laughing stock, it was so unfair, how could Trevor do this to her? She felt so overwhelmed by it all, the potential consequences, she could not stop the tears from rolling down her cheeks, she didn't really want to stop them, indeed she wanted Trevor to know how much he had upset her and now her tears were her weapon of choice.

Trevor, feeling guilty at seeing Ellen's tears, got up and went to the kitchen to make them both a mug of hot chocolate. It was a token gesture, but it would give Ellen a chance to re-run his words through her mind and gather her thoughts. Ellen was a slow burner, she would process the night's revelations and would come back with more questions over the coming days, but first she would give him the silent treatment for a day or two, maybe it would even extend to three in this instance. Trevor carried the chocolate drinks into the lounge and they sat on the sofa, deep in their thoughts, supping the drinks.

'Do you love her?' Ellen asked bluntly.

'No of course not Ellen,' Trevor lied, 'it was just lust and business' he continued, somehow resisting the urge to scratch the back of his neck this time.

'But Trev, you carried on making love to that woman for three years!' Her voice rising, 'You cannot tell me that you didn't have feelings for her during all that time together!'

Ellen's ability to cut through the chaff of all the worries that Trevor had going round in his head and get to the nub of the issue – at least as far as she was concerned – both impressed and annoyed Trevor. He knew that he was the one that was going to bear the responsibility for his actions. He knew that he had let Ellen down and that her feelings would be rightly hurt, but as far as he was concerned that was just collateral damage and

she would be okay. She had set him off on this path and they were now at this point because of that. It was a selfish viewpoint and one that Ellen would not comprehend, so he knew that he would have to find a way to pacify her.

'Well, yeah, I suppose I did have feelings for her in the early days, but that must have been infatuation, when I got to know her more, I realised that she didn't have your warm heart or caring nature. I think that to her, it was just business, I really was just another punter.' Trevor felt that he had dealt well with that question.

Ellen finished her chocolate, stood up and bluntly said, 'I'll make up the bed in the spare room for you Trev,' and walked off upstairs.

Trevor was slightly taken aback by the coldness of her statement, but decided to only say, 'OK love,' in response, he was simply happy that a line had been drawn under the awkward conversation for the time being.

Trevor watched the TV for a bit longer, or rather the TV was on and Trevor was sitting in front of it. His mind, however, was on other matters the noise of the TV was merely enough to prevent Trevor sitting in the non-silence of his tinnitus. He played out various scenarios in his mind, what might happen to him and those around him in the coming weeks and what actions he should take to mitigate the downsides. He approached this dilemma in the same methodical manner he used to approach architectural projects. Cause and Effect, Client Demands versus Budgets, Inputs and Outputs, 'If that happens, then I will have to do this'. He knew that there would be many variables in the coming months, for him to predict and determine what he should do in response to. His main priority would be to do whatever he could to minimise any jail time, he was not a young man and he knew that jail would not be a good place for him. He also wanted to minimise the adverse effects for his family, but that would be difficult as it would be largely out of his hands. Still mulling these things over in his mind, his switched the TV off, emptied the dishwasher, went upstairs and had a shower. As he headed to the spare bedroom, he could

hear Ellen sobbing quietly in their bedroom.

'Night love,' he said gently as he passed their bedroom door, but received no response.

It was strange to be sleeping in the spare bedroom and it took a while for him to get to sleep. It was not just the feel of the unfamiliar bed, he had Jingfei in his mind, wondering what sort of unpleasant place she was being kept in and what the future held for her. He knew that he still cared for her, they had been a part of each other's lives for three years now, but in his heart, he knew that his attitude towards her was changing. He presumed that she would be shipped back to China and that he would be the one with his feet to the fire for this. But still, he was sad that her dream had died, a dream he had come to share. It reminded him of how he felt when he was made redundant from the bank. Something bad had happened to him due to external forces beyond his control, and it left a bitter taste in his mouth. Now that a maelstrom was heading directly his way, he would have to dial back his concern for Jingfei to allow him to concentrate on getting the least worst outcome for himself.

Chapter 10

Another Door Slams

9th March 2013

After arriving at the Police Station, DC Dorey had ushered Jingfei into a separate interview room from Trevor, brought her a plastic cup of water and told her to wait there while the evidence was being booked in. After an hour and a half, DC Dorey returned with Jingfei's duty solicitor, who introduced herself as Rebecca Hawkins. Rebecca asked Jingfei if she wanted to have a translator present, which Jingfei declined, so DC Dorey left the interview room. Rebecca sat down opposite Jingfei and asked her about her residency status. Jingfei had known that this would be one of the first things that would come up and she had already decided that saying anything other than the truth would not be beneficial to her outcome in the long run. Jingfei admitted that she had entered the UK illegally and had also worked in the UK illegally. Rebecca said that Jingfei would need the assistance of an immigration specialist, as she understood that the Police were intending to contact the Border Force, who might in turn consider that an administrative removal would be appropriate for her. This was what Jingfei thought would happen to her, as it had for some of the girls who were working at *Candies* when Madam Chang had been raided by the Border Force. Rebecca also promised to contact the local Citizens Advice Bureau, who might be able to advise Jingfei for free. Rebecca stepped out of the interview room to check with DC Dorey about what the Police intended to do. After a short while, DC Dorey and Rebecca returned to the interview room. DC Dorey announced that she will be recording their interview and she unwrapped two new cassette tapes, loaded them both into the tape recorder and started it running. She informed Jingfei that she was being interviewed on suspicion of being an immigration overstayer and the focus of the interview stayed on that topic. This surprised Jingfei, as she thought that she would also be facing prostitution charges, but she didn't query the omission with DC Dorey, perhaps the Police were just happy to be able to pass her along to the Border Force and out of their jurisdiction.

When the interview was completed, DC Dorey took Jingfei back to the Custody Sergeant's desk and she was formally arrested on suspicion of being an immigration overstayer. DC Dorey then took Jingfei to a cell to await the arrival of the Border Force agents. It was only when DC Dorey had closed the cell door that Jingfei allowed herself to shed a tear. She had, up to that point, maintained her composure, despite the whole gamut of emotions surging through her. It had always been in her nature to maintain an aloof veneer of toughness, but underneath, she had been badly shaken by the arrest. Mostly she felt anger at having her business destroyed, she had worked hard at getting Trevor suckered in and setting up the girls in the flat. Secondly, she knew that she would soon be on a one-way ticket back home. Her family would be pleased to see her for a little while, until they realised that she had not come back home for a short visit. The loss of income to the family, that she had been supporting for so long, would be a bitter blow to her elders. Worse still was that the loss of face would do substantial damage to her family's reputation, which had been boosted considerably by them having a rich daughter, with a good job, sending money home to support the family.

After about an hour, the Custody Sergeant opened Jingfei's cell door and told her that the Border Force agents would not be able to come until the next day. He offered to get her a takeaway meal; she declined the Chinese option, as she had never been able to accept the English version of Chinese food. She had not minded the Chinese food they served in the Chinatown restaurant she worked in years ago, but even that was not the same as her Mum's home cooking. She resisted the temptation to tell the Custody Sergeant exactly what she thought about the taste of the English 'Chinese food' and instead demurely accepted his second menu choice; a Burger and Chips. She felt no anger towards the Custody Sergeant, he was just doing his job, he seemed to be fair and not judgemental towards her.

The only anger she felt was towards the neighbour who had reported her and to those idiot punters that kept pressing the wrong call button. They were the real reason she found herself in jail. Deep down, she knew that this perception was not entirely correct, but it served her current purpose to put the blame on others. It gave strength to her veneer, thereby denying her own culpability for her criminal actions.

A little while later a PC delivered her burger, chips and a waxed paper cup of soft drink. The burger was barely warm, but nonetheless Jingfei thanked him. A very short time ago, if someone had given her such a burger, she would have given them a tongue lashing, but now she was adjusting to her new reality. She was no longer a businesswoman, a woman with a flat, money and employees. She was now an illegal alien, unwanted in this country, something to be got rid of. The thought of her drop in status made her want to weep. That realisation stuck in her craw more than the burger. She wondered about what had happened to the girls. Had Trevor been released? If he had, would he go to the Travel Inn to warn them? What if he was followed to the hotel by the police? She worried about the futures for the girls; Violetta was smart and her skills would be in demand at other suitable establishments. She did not imagine for one second that Violetta would go back to the Fish and Chip shop in Odiham. She was more worried about Lan Fang, Qi Qi Yan and Chun Hu. They were lovely girls, but they needed someone to always look out for them, to stop them being used. That thought made her chuckle inside. She of course had been using them, but working for her was different. She had looked out for them, cared for them, made sure that they had something to eat, gave them time off, kept them in a nice hotel. Jingfei felt sad for the girls, as she realised that it would be a tough time for them, until they found a new place of work. She was sure that no Madam would treat them as well as she did. *Hopefully,* she thought, *they will not get caught by the Border Force, they have managed to survive so far in the underground economy, and they must have saved up a bit of cash to tide them over until they could find a new employer.*

Jingfei tried to sleep, but Saturday night in the police cells is never a quiet time; drunks swearing, metal doors slamming and prisoners denying their guilt loudly, all part of the cacophony that kept waking her. In the occasional quiet spell, her own thoughts would prevent her from going back to sleep. She kept pondering her future, searching for a hope to cling to, or a way to navigate to a good outcome, none came to her. She knew that the future for her was bleak and she could not find any glimmers of hope to help raise her spirits and get back to sleep. Another door slammed somewhere, she swore to herself, and a tear rolled out of the corner of her eye onto her grubby pillow.

Somehow, without realising it, she did manage to get to sleep, for she was startled awake by the unlocking of her door in the morning. A different PC brought her a cup of tea and news that Border Force agents would be coming later in the morning to interview her. Jingfei was not sure what annoyed her more at that moment, the fact that she had been woken after struggling for so long to get to sleep or that, as per the English default, they had put milk in her tea. She decided to put on a brave face and drink the tea. She remembered Trevor telling her once about how, in the olden days in England, they used to put petty criminals in wooden stocks on the village green and throw rotten vegetables, or worse at them. Perhaps milk in tea was the modern equivalent of that, well milk in tea was probably preferable to a face full of rotten vegetables.

A little while later a WPC brought a towel and wash bag and took her to the Ladies toilet, so she could freshen up. The WPC would not leave her unattended in the toilet area, but at least Jingfei could shut the cubicle door. She had refused to use the metal toilet in her cell, she still had standards and pride, so she was very ready to use the white porcelain toilet. She felt better after a flannel wash.

When the WPC took her back to her cell, someone had put a pair of grey jogging trousers and a grey sweatshirt on her bed. She was somewhat pleased to have some clean clothes, but looked at the offering with great disdain. She decided to put them on, and again the thought of rotten vegetables came to mind. After making her bed, there was nothing else to do apart from await the arrival of the Border Force agents.

She did not know how long it was until they arrived, but it felt like a long time before her cell door was opened and the same WPC from her ablution trip led her to an interview room and departed. Her solicitor, Rebecca Hawkins, was already there along with a woman she introduced as Susan Brown, her immigration specialist. DCs Dorey and Barnes were absent, much to Jingfei's surprise. Also in the interview room were a male and a female Border Force agent, who said their names, but they did so too quickly for Jingfei to catch. Jingfei was not that bothered about trying to remember their names. She was now sensing that she was being pushed into the start of a long production line, probably containing many such functionaries which would ultimately result in her being spat out into a grim cell in China. At that moment she realised just how much, and in such a short time, her spirit had already been squashed by the machine that she was now inside.

The Border Force agents wanted Jingfei to detail every part of her timeline starting with her journey from home to London, where she worked in London and then on to her time in Basingstoke. She tried to decide what delicate information about her employers she could leave out and what she had to give up. She knew that she was on a one-way ticket back home, but there was no need to invite unnecessary retribution from those who had helped her in the past, after all she might need their help in the future, if she were to try to return to the UK. The agents were pressing her for details of names, places and dates, all of which she gave vague replies to, feigned forgetfulness about, or supplied fictitious Chinese sounding names along the lines of 'Fred Bloggs' and 'Aunt Sally'. Very little of the interview covered her work as a Madam in Basingstoke, which, Jingfei realised, tallied with the absence of the DCs in this interview. The police were indeed washing their hands of her, happy to pass the problem on to Border Force agents. In that instant she knew that Trevor was going to be carrying the can for the brothel. The police would not be getting extra points for having her locked up as well as Trevor, she just would not be worth the extra paperwork to them. After all, following a jail stay at the Taxpayer's expense, she would still only end up being deported, they might as well get rid of her sooner rather than later and save the public purse.

After an hour and a half, the Border Force agents announced that they were concluding the interview and that, because they believed that she was a flight risk, she would be transferred to the Yarl's Wood detention centre to await a voluntary deportation.

Jingfei said that she would not challenge the 'Voluntary Deportation' order, because she knew (and Susan Brown had stated as such) that she had no valid grounds to do so. Her solicitor and her immigration specialist had not had much involvement in the interview and had little advice for her at the end of it. However, they said that they would be keeping in touch with her during her time at the detention centre, which was of little consolation to her. The male Border Force agent left the room and came back about ten minutes later, saying that they were not able to transfer her today as it was a Sunday, but they would get her transfer arranged for tomorrow, so she would have to spend another night in a police cell. At that moment, she was annoyed to be delayed, because her mind was still stuck in her usual 'Quick, quick, quick, business, business, business' mindset. Yet she was no longer the hard businesswoman, she was now an illegal immigrant, an object to be moved around at the will of the state.

Jingfei was taken back to her cell to spend the rest of the day and night. She was frustrated and bored in equal measures, having never had so much free time on her hands. Even in the flat, when the girls were working, she was always busy, taking calls, making bookings, tidying rooms, washing and tumbling bed sheets, making drinks or food for the girls. She had set up a strict schedule for herself, to ensure the business ran smoothly, the punters were satisfied and the place always looked classier than *Candies* had. She took pride in her work and likened herself to being a Captain at the helm of the ship or a Conductor guiding her orchestra through a symphony. But all that was gone now, the ship had run aground and the orchestra had left, she was alone to face a gloomy future. Tears crept down her face and each one annoyed her further, she was losing face. She would concede to shedding a tear or two in her cell, when she was on her own, but from now, outside her cell, would be the place for her stern face or as Trevor used to put it 'A stiff upper lip'. That phrase had amused her when she first heard it from him, she expected that Trevor was needing his stiffest upper lip right now. She suddenly realised how little she had thought about Trevor since they had been arrested, this surprised her, but she soon realised that she had switched to operating in 'Practical Mode'. She was in worse trouble than him, he was not the one being deported, he would not be sent back to work in the fields, on a farm that could not support them. She had no feelings of guilt for how she had got Trevor into the situation that he now found himself in. He could no longer help her, so she had no need of him, he had served his purpose well. She would have liked it to have continued longer, she saw the move into the South View house as a great leap forward, a boost to her status, but now it was not to be. She thought about the money that she still owed to Mr Doherty, but decided that she was clear of that now, the Border Force agents had seen to that. Mr Doherty could go and chase Trevor for it, but her removal from the UK would get her off that hook. In her Practical Mode, she was her only priority.

*

Sunday was a bleak day for Trevor, he had slept badly and woke early. He walked to the local shops to get his usual Sunday newspaper, as was his habit of many years. While in the paper shop, he glanced at the *Basingstoke Gazette*, half expecting to see his face splattered over the front page, but of course it wasn't. *It might be at some point in the near future*, he thought glumly, but not today. He knew that the local rags would be overjoyed to be able to splash such a salacious story over their pages, no more 'Cat stuck up a tree' stories for them for a little while. *It would only be a matter of time*, he thought, *before it all comes out and that will be bound to turn Ellen positively volcanic!*

The shame of it, the thought of having people laughing at her behind her back, would all be too much for her. There would be a rocky time to come for him at home. Back home with his paper, he made himself a mug of tea, sat down at the breakfast bar and tried to read some of the stories in the paper, but he couldn't focus on them. His mind kept wandering off on multiple threads, he needed a car, it would be ages before the police released his car, if at all, they may just sell it off if they decide that it formed part of his ill-gotten gains!

They were bound to search the house for evidence of the money trail, his computer will be seized for sure.

What will he tell Barry at the Kitchen Showroom, for surely the truth will come out soon enough? Once the story got out, Barry would have to let him go, he would not want his business to be associated with a pimp!

He had to stop the rental on the flat as soon as possible, then that would only leave the duration of the notice period to pay the rent for.

Where will he get money from now?

Is that what I am now, wondered Trevor, *a pimp?*

For some reason, his mind visualised filling in an online car insurance form, one where they ask for your profession.

I probably can't continue to use 'Architect' as I have done for many years; even though making kitchen drawings might not truly fit under the 'Architect' heading. He doubted that 'Pimp' would be on the drop-down list and probably 'Criminal' wouldn't be on there either.

He finished his tea and decided that the first thing that he really needed to do would be to limit the amount of evidence the police would find, when they inevitably knocked on his door. He was halfway up the stairs to his study, when he saw Ellen emerging from her bedroom.

'Morning love,' he said as breezily as he could.

'Humph,' was all he got in reply as she headed to the toilet.

Trevor had expected nothing less, but still it stung him, to realise just how much he had hurt and betrayed Ellen. Saying nothing more in reply, Trevor went into his study, switched his computer on and sent an email to the landlord of the flat, giving him the three months' notice that he was vacating the flat. He did the same for the Council Tax and Utilities for the flat. He then started moving files off the computer and on to a memory stick. He searched through his emails, deleting any that he thought might be of interest to the police. There weren't that many, he had always tried to do as much of his and Jingfei's business as he could verbally, precisely to limit the audit trail.

In the bottom drawer of his desk was a locked tin box in which he kept his 'rainy day' money; money that he had siphoned off from the takings, which had not been paid into the girl's mortgage accounts, or used to pay his bills. Well, a 'rainy day' had finally arrived, and he hoped that it would not get much 'rainier' than it was at the moment. He counted - just over £6,700 - divided it up into envelopes of £500. The odd amount left over he put into his wallet, just in case he was searched, he would let the police find that and then they hopefully would be satisfied that they had all his cash.

Trevor heard a car pull up outside the house, got up and looked out of the window and immediately felt the blood drain. It was a police patrol car. He hadn't finished his tidying up; they had come sooner than he expected! And on a Sunday as well! The indignant voice inside Trevor's head cried, *'Have these people no respect for the Sabbath?'* leaving him with a wry smile on his face.

He breathed a sigh of relief however, when he saw that there that there was only one occupant in the car, and that was a uniformed PC, who was now walking up the driveway. Trevor shut the study door and flew down the stairs, trying to get to the front door before Ellen had a chance to get involved. Trevor opened the front door half a second after the PC had rung the bell. *Close but no cigar,* thought Trevor.

The PC jumped slightly, clearly surprised by Trevor's appearance before he had barely taken his finger off the doorbell.

'Who's that at the door Trev?' Ellen shouted down the stairs.

That annoyed Trevor. He had never worked out how Ellen had developed a sixth sense, for knowing when to 'offer input' and when to ignore something happening in Trevor's realm. She could usually be relied upon to 'offer input' when it was least required and the input would usually be designed to inflict the maximum damage to Trevor's ego. The concept of BTFO was not known to Ellen.

He quickly smiled at the PC, to acknowledge his presence, held up his index finger to indicate 'wait a second' and turned to reply to Ellen. He had a short list of reply options, but quickly decided that calling out, 'It's the Police, for me dear,' was the most diplomatic and brief one he could muster in that instant, but sad that he couldn't come up with a better answer, one which would also discourage her from attending the door in person.

'Good morning,' said Trevor as he turned back to face the PC. 'Can I help you officer?' By which time of speaking Ellen had also appeared, in her dressing gown, just behind Trevor.

'Are you Trevor Braithwaite?' said the PC, at which point Trevor noticed the number on his shoulder epaulette was 1829.

'Yes officer,' replied Trevor, resisting the temptation to simply offer his wrists for cuffing.

'Sorry to trouble you, but do you have a second key for your car sir?' responded PC 1829. 'The other key broke in the lock.'

'Oh, for God's sake Trevor!' yelled Ellen from behind Trevor's back, as she stormed off towards the kitchen. The PC did not appear to be too disturbed by Ellen's outburst, he had clearly seen worse in some of the nether regions of Basingstoke.

'Yes officer, just a second please, I'll get it,' said Trevor. Trevor went to the coat cupboard in the hallway, opened the metal key box inside the cupboard and pulled out his spare car key and gave it to the PC.

'We'll be moving your car to the station today for inspection, someone will contact you when you can collect it,' said the PC, turning to return to his patrol car. Clearly he had decided to make himself scarce and let Trevor face the music on his own.

Trevor breathed a quick sigh of relief; the feeling was short lived. He may have got rid of the PC, but he now had the wrath of Ellen to face. Trevor headed to the kitchen, knowing that he would have to offer a *mea culpa* to start the process off. He knew that he would never get forgiveness, nor did he actually deserve that, but he had to make a start at clearing the air between them.

Ellen was standing by the kitchen sink, staring out of the window. Trevor walked up behind and tried to snuggle her around her waist from behind, as was their way, but she brushed his hands away brusquely.

'I'm so very sorry Ellen, I've been a fool, you don't deserve all this grief I'm bringing down on you,' said Trevor.

Ellen spun round. 'What do you mean you're sorry Trevor? You're not sorry for me! You're just sorry you got caught with your pants down, that's all!' she spat out, her face flushing to red. 'How could you have got involved in all that Trevor? What on earth made you want to become a pimp?'

Trevor guided Ellen to the kitchen table, so they could both sit down, in the hope that it might calm Ellen down a bit. They talked for about half an hour, until Mum came in for her breakfast, at which point they reverted to an uneasy 'Happy Families in Autopilot mode'. Trevor did not know how best to break the news to his Mum, it would all come out sooner or later, but right now Trevor knew that he had to concentrate on trying to mend fences with Ellen and finish preparing his study for the inevitable coming police investigation. Ellen cooked Sunday breakfast, which was eaten in the dining room *'comme d'habitude'*, after which Trevor loaded the dishwasher and cleaned the kitchen, while Mum retired to her annexe.

Mum had stopped going to church on Sundays since she moved to Chineham, she had been to the church near them soon after she arrived, but didn't like it. 'Too modern,' she said, 'got no character' and she didn't like the vicar or the service, 'too happy-clappy'. Ellen had been disappointed as Mum had been a stalwart of the church in Bracknell and had gained a wide circle of friends through her connection to the church. Ellen thought that Mum could have made new friends through the church in Chineham, but as the dementia progressed, she realised that it just wasn't going to happen.

When Trevor finished tidying the kitchen, he went to sit in the lounge with Ellen, who, to Trevor's surprise, promptly turned the TV showing the Shopping Channel off. This signalled to Trevor that she was ready for a proper discussion, she would normally leave it on whenever Trevor came to talk to her. To Trevor's relief, she had dialled the anger back a bit and was now apparently ready for a proper conversation about what had happened and what might happen in the coming weeks and months. She was worried about Trevor having to go to jail, about losing the house and what the effect would be on Mum and their family. Trevor tried to pacify her as much as possible, but there were so many unknowns that he couldn't answer everything she put to him, never mind to her satisfaction. Trevor decided then that he really needed to get back to tidying up his study, hiding the cash and all those other things that he needed to do, to prepare for a police search of the house.

Time to use his special trick to escape further questioning. 'Like a cup of tea love?' he asked in his sweetest voice as he rose to his feet.

'No thanks Trev,' replied Ellen, who was already too deep in her own thoughts to notice that Trevor was making strides towards the door.

Trevor made his tea then headed upstairs, deliberately avoiding looking into the lounge as he passed. He then started to find places to hide the envelopes of cash; at the back the desk drawers, behind some books on a shelf, behind the bath side panel, in the loft and in his workshop. Better not to put any under the mattresses as they might be discovered by Ellen or the police. He flipped through the files in his filing cabinet, separating them into three piles, which he mentally named 'Hide,' 'Shred' and 'For Plod'. He put the 'For Plod' files back in the filing cabinet, but right at the back of the bottom drawer. After feeding the 'Shred' files to his shredder, he put the 'Hide' files in a small suitcase, put that inside another suitcase, which was in the loft. Being a good citizen at heart, he emptied his shredder bin into his paper recycling box. He then went back to checking his computer for any other files that he needed to move to the memory stick. He copied the spreadsheet that he used to track the finances for the business on to the memory stick. He decided that he had better leave the spreadsheet on the computer, he knew that the police would expect to find something like that, at the very least. Finally satisfied, he emptied the computer recycle bin and hid the memory stick in a pair of socks, which he in turn stuffed into a shoe at the very back of his wardrobe.

Trevor went downstairs and, leaning into the lounge doorway, said, 'Ellen, I am just going to go out to buy a small car, so I can get around, until I can get my own one back.' He knew that she would not be happy to have an expense like that, when their future finances were uncertain, 'I need to get mobile again, I've got so many surveys to finish off for Barry.'

Ellen had a sceptical look on her face, 'Where's the money for that going to come from then Trev?'

'Don't worry,' he said. 'I'll put it on the credit card for now.'

She did not look convinced, but surely, she knew that they could not be without a car for very long.

Trevor called the local taxi firm to come and pick him up and while he was waiting, he looked through the car adverts in the *Basingstoke Gazette*.

There were a couple of likely garages on the nearby A30, they should have something suitable, so he decided to start his search there. A short while later, the taxi pulled up outside. Trevor gave Ellen a quick peck on the cheek, to which she did not resist, and went out to the taxi.

*

Ellen carried on watching the Shopping Channel for another hour or so, until she was surprised by the landline phone ringing. She had always had a fear of the house phone ringing, it was one of her 'darts of doom' triggers, as Trevor thought of them as. She picked it up gingerly, 'Hello?'

It was one of her parents' carers or 'elpers' as her dad preferred to call them. Her dad had collapsed in the garden and had been taken to Frome Hospital, the carer was going to stay at home with Mum, but could they go to be with her dad in hospital?

Ellen replied that of course they would go, but as soon as she put the phone down, she was thrown into a panic, how was she going to do that? Trevor could not have possibly brought a car by now, Maria and Simon were all the way over in Bromley, and Carol and Mike were visiting Mike's parents in Nottingham today, so they wouldn't be back until late.

Ellen rang Trevor's mobile phone. As soon as he answered, she blurted 'Trev, did you get a car yet?'

'We just doing the paperwork and insurance on it, what's the matter Ellen?' replied Trevor, somewhat surprised to get a call on his new phone, but more so by the hurried tone in Ellen's voice.

'Dad's collapsed in the garden, we've got to go to the hospital Trev, he's on his own in there.'

Chapter 11

Into each life, some rain must fall

(Henry Wadsworth Longfellow)

10th March 2013

The journey to Frome Hospital from Chineham took them just over an hour and a half. The Ford Focus that Trevor had brought was not very comfortable and it smelt of cigarette smoke, which Ellen would normally complain about, but she had too much else on her mind to do so. It had still taken Trevor around an hour to get home after Ellen's phone call, as he had to convince the garage to let him have the car straight away, without preparing it. That delay gave Ellen enough time to pack an overnight bag for each of them, she did not know how long they would be away, but she did not want to leave without any form of preparation. Ellen had phoned Carol to ask her to look after Trevor's mum while they were away. She had then told Trevor's mum that they had to go to her parents and that she had left a ready meal in the fridge for her and that Carol would be around later and wouldn't that be nice. Ellen knew that, due to her dementia, it didn't pay to give Trevor's mum too much detail at one time, but she would be alright until Carol arrived.

Trevor managed to arrange the insurance and vehicle tax on his phone and the payment for the car required extra security checks before it was approved. All that time, Trevor was trying to get things moving along as quickly as possible, to get home as soon as he could, to gain maximum 'Brownie' Points from Ellen. He knew he needed to make as many as he could from this 'opportunity'.

Ellen would be in emotional turmoil and therefore there was no reason why he should not make a start on his rehabilitation in her eyes.

When they arrived at the main hospital reception, they were told that Ellen's dad had already been transferred to the Bristol Royal Infirmary. Ellen knew that it meant that Dad's injury must be serious. They drove to Ellen's parents' house to pick up a bag of essentials for her dad and see how Mum and the carer were coping.

Much to Trevor's relief, Ellen's focus was now on her parents, he knew that the topic of his arrest would be a major TSI for Ellen in the coming weeks, probably months, but in the meantime, he was just happy to have a task in hand to supersede his misdemeanours. When they arrived, Lisa the carer let them in. Mum was sitting in her chair watching the TV.

'Florence, it's your daughter Ellen come to see you,' Lisa said to Mum.

Ellen kissed her mum, then knelt beside her and stroked her hand.

'Hello love, are you alright?' Mum asked Ellen,

'Yes Mum, we're fine, Trevor's here too,' Ellen replied.

'Where's Edgar, I haven't seen him for ages?' asked Mum.

'Dad's in hospital mum, we're just on our way to see him,' Ellen replied, realising that her mum's dementia had deteriorated since they last saw her in February. Ellen went upstairs to pack a bag for her dad, while Trevor checked with Lisa about overnight care cover for Mum.

'My shift is ending soon,' said Lisa, 'but a night nurse will be arriving soon to take over.'

Trevor thanked Lisa and sat next to his mother-in-law and tried to make a light conversation about the TV programme, but it soon became clear to Trevor that her mind wasn't engaged in the TV.

'Where's Edgar?' she repeated.

'He'll be back soon Mum,' was the best that Trevor could offer her. When Ellen came back downstairs, they made their excuses, kissed Mum goodbye and headed off to Bristol.

It had already turned dark when they left Frome, which did not please Trevor, he was driving a car that he was not fully used to, on winding A-roads which required his full concentration and a light drizzle had just started, which showed him that he needed to get new wiper blades as soon as possible.

Ellen was running through all the injuries that her dad might have suffered and when she tired of that topic, she started going through various possibilities of what was best to do for her mum. As usual when Ellen was hypothesizing out loud, he would respond with various forms of 'uh-huh' or 'OK love' which were just enough to convince her that he was still engaged in the mostly one-sided conversation, but he would not issue a detailed responses which might make her absorb his reply and try to start a full conversation on that topic. He was present in the car and eager to help Ellen's dad in any way he could, but his mind was still focussing on what he should be doing to mitigate the damage coming his way following his arrest. He knew that, for cashflow reasons, he would have to keep working for Barry, providing Barry wanted him to. He suddenly realised that he had not thought about Jingfei and what was happening to her. He felt no guilt for the situation that she was in, she knew that leading the life she did was risky and that it could come crashing down at any moment. He realised what a fool he had been to go into business with her, it would have been fine if he had just kept his involvement at the punter level. Was it his greed that that had driven him to change to being a pimp? He didn't like that word; he didn't really think that he was a pimp, he was more of a facilitator, helping an entrepreneur run her business.

'What's that Trev?' asked Ellen, suddenly interrupting his thoughts.

He hadn't realised that he had smirked out loud at the thought of declaring himself to be a facilitator, loud enough for Ellen to hear. 'Nothing love, it's just a tickle in my throat, that's all,' he replied, as convincingly as he could.

He decided that he had better concentrate on his driving now that he was coming into the southern Bristol suburbs, where the roads were always busy, Sunday night or not.

Trevor dropped Ellen off at the Upper Maudlin Street entrance, while he went to look for a space in the adjacent NCP car park. He phoned her when he got back to the main entrance.

She sounded terrified. 'He's in the Emergency Department Trev, he's fractured his hip!'

Trevor made his way up to the 2nd floor Emergency Department and was directed to a cubicle by one of the nurses, where Ellen was sitting next to her dad, who was lying, asleep in bed with an oxygen mask on his face and leads connecting him to a heart monitor.

'Mr Smith has been given pain relief and is now comfortably resting,' the nurse told them. Ellen was just about to ask him what would happen next, when the nurse interjected, 'I will get a doctor to come and answer your questions, as soon as possible. Excuse me please,' he said, turning and stepping away before he had even finished saying the word 'please'.

It was busy in there, as Trevor expected that it would be, probably the same in any big hospital in any big city, any night of the week he thought. He glanced around and spied a spare chair in the only cubicle where the curtains were not drawn closed. He walked purposefully over to the cubicle, grabbed the chair and whisked it back to 'their' cubicle, walking with a nonchalant air to dissuade anyone who might have had the temerity to query his purloining of the chair. He put the chair next to Ellen and sat down.

'Don't for one moment think that I have forgiven you Trevor,' she said in a low voice, 'we'll talk more about that whore later!'

Trevor could almost taste the venom in her voice as she spat the word 'whore'. He had been put on notice of that which was to come.

It was almost midnight before a doctor came to see them.

'Hello is it Mr Smith?' she said to Trevor from the other side of Edgar's bed.

'No, Braithwaite,' he replied, 'Mr Smith is my father-in-law,' Trevor said, motioning to Ellen's dad, 'and this is my wife Ellen, his daughter'.

'Apologies.' The doctor looked at them both. 'My name is Ann Peters. Mr Smith is very ill, a fractured hip is a major injury for anyone, but for a person of his age, it is a very serious injury,' she continued. 'He also has hypertension and there is evidence of heart disease on his ECG. We'll soon have him moved up to the OTU where we will monitor him carefully overnight. He will need a thorough assessment by the cardiology and medical teams prior to surgery for his hip fracture. Unfortunately, I cannot tell you how long this will take, but he will be a priority case.'

'What is an OTU?' asked Trevor.

'Apologies,' Doctor Peters said again, 'we get used to having so many acronyms here. OTU is the Orthopaedic Trauma Unit'.

Trevor nodded.

'What surgery?' asked Ellen, her voice faltering.

'That will be up to the consultant to decide,' replied Doctor Peters.

'Oh gosh!' said Ellen, through a sharp intake of breath.

'We've made him comfortable for now, so I would recommend that you go home and get some rest, then pop back in the morning,' Doctor Peters suggested.

'We live in Basingstoke,' replied Trevor.

'Oh, I see, well perhaps you could get a hotel room, there is a hotel next to the nearby Cabot Circus Shopping Centre,' offered Doctor Peters. Ellen glanced at Trevor.

'Thank you doctor,' said Trevor, 'I think we'll get Dad settled in the OTU first,' he continued.

'As you wish, I'll get a porter arranged as soon as possible,' Doctor Peters replied.

Trevor wondered to himself if it might likely be light by the time 'as soon as possible' came?

.

To Trevor's surprise, a porter and a nurse arrived in less than 10 minutes and skilfully prepared Dad's bed to be moved. Ellen gathered his clothes and scant belongings, she and Trevor followed along in procession down the corridors, behind the bed and the monitor stands, towards the trolley lift. There was a short wait for the lift to come and take them up to the 6th floor, but they were soon being guided to a bed space in a small side ward in the OTU department. They introduced themselves to the reception nurse, Trevor gave the nurse his mobile number and they said that they would be back in the morning. Trevor led the way back to the NCP car park and they drove the short journey to the Cabot Circus Shopping Centre car park, which was adjacent to the Hotel. They made their way round to the hotel reception, pressed the reception bell to rouse the duty manager and asked for a room for a couple of nights. They explained the fact that Ellen's dad was in the Bristol Royal Infirmary, so they couldn't give an exact departure date. The duty manager said that it would not a problem at all, as they frequently had patients' families staying there, but they only had Twin-bedded rooms available.

Ellen interjected, 'That will be perfect!'

Ever alert, Trevor immediately wondered if the hospital staff were on some sort of a commission deal with the hotel, but he quickly dismissed the thought as pure cynicism.

The room was nice, with a more modern design and furnishings than Trevor had seen at the Basingstoke Travel Inn. Luckily, he just managed to bite his tongue, in time to prevent that scintilla of information being said aloud to Ellen. She would have jumped on that snippet straightaway, to find out how come he knew what the rooms in the Basingstoke Travel Inn looked like, whether she was distracted about her father or not.

*

They prepared for bed in a strained manner. Ellen would have preferred a room of her own, but decided that that would have been churlish. She would have to put up with unwanted proximity to Trevor, because they were both there to help her father.

She didn't sleep well, she had too much going around in her mind, it had been a dizzying couple of days for her, she just felt that her world was being turned upside down and shaken around, as if she was in a giant snow globe. This was totally contrary to her normal, peaceful, daily routine; housework, caring for Trevor's mum and looking out for bargains on TV. Her main worry now, was naturally her dad, but she was also concerned about her mum being left with the carer. At least, when she had phoned Carol earlier, she was pleased to hear that Trevor's mum was happily chatting with her granddaughter, a rare treat for both of them. These worries, however, did not put Trevor's arrest out of her mind, she was still seething about that. *How could he have done that? How could he have done such a thing, to lie, straight faced to her for so long? To sleep with that woman and then come home, kiss me and share my bed!* She had never before thought that anyone, especially Trevor, could ever disrespect her so much, she felt dirty, hurt and abused. She hated Trevor for what he had done and now to compound her hurt, she had to share a room with him. It made her skin crawl.

*

Trevor, on the other hand, found he was feeling confident that, Ellen had put his arrest behind her, for the time being, focussing instead on her dad. It was sad that her dad was very ill, but in Trevor's mind, the timing was fortuitous, as it was distracting Ellen from his misdemeanours and gaining him Brownie Points to boot.

He slept well and, in the morning, they both went down to the basement restaurant for breakfast. Trevor tucked into the buffet, Ellen could only manage a Danish pastry and a cup of tea. As they were about to leave the hotel, the receptionist called them over to validate their parking ticket. Trevor thanked her for reminding them, Ellen almost burst into tears. A simple act of kindness like that, in her time of stress, had set off her emotional rollercoaster. Trevor was confused and put one arm around Ellen's waist to comfort her. She pushed it away and strode towards the front door. Trevor caught up with her and they walked side by side, without touching or holding hands.

Walking back to the car, Trevor was amazed to see that last night, without noticing, they must have walked right past a short, incongruous row of four old brick terraced houses and an old pub, all squeezed in between the concrete forms of the Hotel and the Cabot Circus car park. It was rather like in the cartoon film *UP!* Trevor thought. The pub was called The Phoenix and it struck Trevor that here was a complete contradiction to the phoenix rising from the ashes of mythology. Here was something old that had somehow been preserved in amongst all these new buildings. There was a street name sign nearby, which looked like it was meant to read Tucker Street, except it had been carefully renamed to something vulgar by a graffiti artist with two dabs of paint. They drove in silence to the hospital, where Trevor dropped Ellen at the main entrance again and then he went off to park the car. When he got back to the hospital, Ellen was waiting for him by the lifts, which they took up to the 6th floor OTU. They introduced themselves to the current reception nurse, who reported that the consultant would be doing rounds at 10am, so they would know more after that, but at the moment Ellen's dad was awake but still on pain medication.

They went to his side ward and saw that he was lying flat on his back and snoring loudly. Trevor was surprised to see that there were two visitor chairs already there, both on one side of the bed. Ellen sat nearest to her dad's head and gently stroked the back of his hand. Trevor was about to sit down when his new phone rang, he hadn't set the ring tone to his

favourite *'Für Elise'* yet, so it took him a second or two to realise that it was his phone that was ringing. He swore under his breath and motioned to Ellen that he was going to take it in the hallway.

It was Carol; the police had arrived at their house with a search warrant and that they wanted Trevor to be present during the search. Trevor realised that he hadn't told Carol about his arrest, so he gave her a few key points and said that he was on his way home from Bristol. Carol pacified the police by telling them that her grandfather had had a fall and was in hospital in Bristol. Trevor went back into the ward and told Ellen about the police waiting for him at home, so he had to leave straight away. She was not at all happy, but soon realised that Trevor had no option, she knew she could get a taxi back to the hotel if she needed to. Trevor promised that he would be back as soon as possible, once he had finished with the police. Once out of the car park, it didn't take Trevor long to get onto the motorway. While heading home, alone at last in the car, he had a chance to mull over the events of the last few days. He was more focussed on his own situation, rather than worrying about Edgar's fractured hip. He had to do whatever he could to keep out of jail and to minimise the amount of money that the police would seize under POCA, the Proceeds of Crime Act. Trevor remembered that when the Act went through Parliament in the early 2000s, he had thought that it was a good thing to be able to get the ill-gotten gains back from lowlifes like drug dealers, bank robbers and the like. But now here he was, probably included in such crooked company. He was confident that he had hidden most of his cash in safe places and that the carefully selected files that he had left on his computer were incriminating, but not too incriminating. He couldn't think of anything else left at home, that the police would be interested in. They had taken so much evidence from the flat, they surely had enough now to build their case. Thinking of the year 2000 made Trevor remember singing along, with the girls, in the 1980s, to the song Disco 2000 by Pulp. *'Let's all meet up in the Year 2000, won't it be strange when we're all fully grown.'* He remembered thinking at the time, that there would be change of Millennia coming, and what would it bring? Thirteen years on and it seemed to Trevor that it had brought trouble.

It took Trevor just under two hours to get home. When he pulled up, he saw, much to his annoyance, that the police had parked on his driveway.

He quickly decided that arguing about it with them would be counter-productive, so he parked on the road instead. Inside he found DCs Barnes and Dorey drinking tea and chatting cosily with Mum and Carol in the lounge. Somewhat surprised to find this scene and on autopilot sociable mode, he walked up to them and shook their hands, as if they were old colleagues. He gave Mum and Carol greeting kisses and sat down on the spare chair, which was his least comfortable chair and was usually only occupied by Mum's current knitting. After a few pleasantries and updates to Mum and Carol on Edgar's health, Trevor started to rack his brain about what would be the best way to separate the police from his family.

DC Dorey was apparently ahead of him. 'Trevor, could we go up to your study?' she said, surprising Trevor by using his first name.

'Yes, of course,' he replied, thankful for an out. 'We won't be long Mum,' Trevor said as he and the DCs headed up the stairs.

In his study, Trevor immediately noticed the absence of his PC, some signs of disturbances to the desk and to his bookshelf.

'Mr. Braithwaite,' DC Dorey said, swiftly moving from social mode to business mode, 'here is a copy of our search warrant, allowing us to search your house, with or without you being present,' she said, passing it to Trevor. 'We have taken your computer for investigation; would you kindly write the password down?' she continued, while passing her notebook to Trevor, he duly complied.

'We have also taken three envelopes of cash, totalling £1,500, from your desk. We believe that the money may be the proceeds of crime and it will be kept as evidence pending further enquires,' announced DC Barnes, with the slightest hint of a smug smile on his lips.

It took Trevor a lot of will power to keep his best poker face on.

'We have also taken some files from your filing cabinet,' said DC Dorey.

'Here is a list of the items we have taken as evidence,' said DC Barnes, handing Trevor a sheet of paper.

Trevor's neck was getting sore from constantly turning from one officer to the other as they talked, so he was most relieved when DC Dorey announced that they had completed their search and that they would contact him in due course. Soon afterwards they left, reversing out of the driveway and leaving tyre marks on Trevor's lawn, much to his chagrin.

Trevor brought a suitcase down from the loft and, anticipating a longer stay in Bristol, packed some more clothes for him and Ellen. He then went downstairs to check with Carol, that she would be able to look after Mum for a bit longer. She said that she could, but she would need to go home to collect some clothes for herself, so Trevor let her borrow his car. As it was lunchtime, he decided to go to the kitchen to make a sandwich and a cup of tea for Mum and himself. Trevor hadn't had a chance to figure out what the police had told Mum and Carol about the reason for their search, but, importantly to Trevor, it didn't seem like they had revealed anything that was detrimental to Trevor's standing in his mother's eyes. Carol, however, would be a different matter, her compliance would not remain unconditional, Trevor had seen that she had given him a quizzical look when he went up to the study with the two officers. He knew that she had her suspicions, but being a kind soul, she had realised that her beloved parents needed her to step in and look after her grandmother, while they were looking after her Mum's parents. It transpired Mum was concerned about the police visit, but she was sure that 'her Trevor' would sort things out and it would all be back to normal soon.

Trevor and his Mum finished their lunch and Trevor tidied up the kitchen,

leaving Mum to have her usual 'fiesta', as she loved to joke about her afternoon nap. Trevor went out to his workshop to check if the police had been snooping around in there. Seeing that the keys had been left in the workshop door instead of hanging up inside the kitchen, revealed that they had indeed been in the workshop. He could see that his storage drawers had not been fully shut and his boxes of candle moulds had been moved, but they had missed the envelopes of cash which he had put under his stack of scrap wood pieces. This cheered him up a bit, so he locked the workshop and went back inside the house. He didn't have long to wait before Carol returned, carrying a small suitcase.

'Come on Dad,' she said. 'What on earth is going on?' she continued before he had a chance to give her the 60% truth he had prepared, 'And I don't mean about Grandad Edgar!' she insisted. 'The Police, what on earth were they doing here with a search warrant? They gave Nan such a fright this morning!'

Lying to Carol would be harder, for Trevor, than lying to Ellen. He had always admired the way that Carol, embodied the ideals she learnt in the Guides, now here he was defiling those. He knew that eventually the whole story would come out and, because Carol lived and worked locally, she would soon be embroiled in the maelstrom of social media gossip and unwanted media attention, which was sure to ensue. For now, however, he just wanted to lay out the bare bones of the story to his family, minimise his embarrassment and try to retain some shreds of dignity. *At least Maria would be spared all the furore,* he thought, *with her and Simon living over Bromley.* A little Basingstoke tittle-tattle wouldn't reach over there, surely.

Trevor started reeling out a similar version of the story he had given Ellen, to Carol. She had different questions for him to Ellen's, but there was still a lot of 'Oh Dad! How could you?' interspersed with, 'And you carried on with that secret life for so long, lying to us all.'

Trevor was finally saved from further discomfort when his phone rang. It was Ellen, 'Trev, you gotta get back here now please, Dad's taken a turn for the worse!'

Trevor told Carol that he had to dash back to Bristol, he really had no wish to continue the conversation with Carol and was glad to have an excuse to escape. He gave Carol a quick peck on the cheek, her response was cold and muted, but he thanked her for continuing to look after his Mum, grabbed the suitcase and headed out of the door. In the car he was able to have a bit of time for himself, some thinking space, an opportunity to consider his options. *What would be the police's next move? Was there some flash, young Police accountant, right at this very moment, forensically examining the accounts on his computer trying to work out just how much they could squeeze out of him under POCA!* Suddenly, into his mind, popped *'POCA-Hunters'*. That gave him a wry smile, he was now being hunted by Pocahunters! His smile dropped, *how would Jingfei cope with life back in rural China?* A place she had worked so hard to escape. He felt guilty for not thinking about her more, but he had been so swamped with his own problems, that he had put her issues to the back of his mind.

The traffic on the motorway was worse on the journey back over to Bristol, as it was now the afternoon rush hour, and all the commuters were escaping London. Finally, he reached the quieter stretch of the M4, between Newbury and Swindon, which, being at the middle of Southern England, had nobody really trying to dash to it or away from it. After that point, he began the downhill run to Bristol, where the worse of the traffic was now on the other side of the motorway, heading away from Bristol to the leafy hinterland to the east of Bristol. However, once he was off the motorway, he ran into the Bristol evening traffic, where everyone is trying to get everywhere and all at the same time. He had heard his phone ring a few times during his journey, but because he hadn't linked it to the car's audio system yet, it wouldn't automatically switch to handsfree, so he had just ignored it. At least the hospital car park had plenty of spaces for him

to choose from, he had already determined the best part of the car park to park. Not up too many of those awful corkscrew levels and then he knew which were his preferred spaces near to the lifts. He was soon back in the OTU, striding towards the small side ward, where he had left Ellen and Edgar that morning. He was totally surprised to find that Edgar's bed was empty and neatly made up; Ellen was nowhere to be seen. Trevor checked his phone and saw that the five missed calls were from Ellen. He walked to the reception desk, which he had just bypassed, and saw that there was a different nurse, to the two that he had met before, on duty.

'Hello,' he said, 'I'm Mr Smith's son-in-law, do you know where he is?'

A flicker passed over her face. 'One moment please,' she said, rising from her chair and walking to a little office behind the reception desk. A Staff Nurse stepped out of the office and approached Trevor.

'Hello, is it Mr Braithwaite?' she asked.

'Yes,' said Trevor, with a note of caution in the tone of his short response.

The Staff Nurse nodded. 'Could I have a word with you, please Mr Braithwaite?' she said, motioning Trevor to follow her into her office.

The sense of foreboding increased on Trevor, as he walked around the reception desk and into the Staff Nurse's office. 'Please have a seat Mr Braithwaite,' she said, pointing to a chair at the corner of her desk. She closed the door gently and sat down. 'Mr Braithwaite,' she began, 'Mr Smith suffered a cardiac arrest this afternoon and although we commenced resuscitation immediately, we were unable to save him,' she said it in gentle, well-practised tones. 'I am so sorry for your loss, Mr Braithwaite,' she continued, leaving a short pause for Trevor to absorb the news. 'Mrs Braithwaite is waiting for you in The Sanctuary, on the Lower Ground floor. Would you like me ask one of the nurses to show you the way there?' she added, by way of drawing a line under the conversation, one-sided such as it was.

'No, I'll be fine, thank you,' said Trevor. 'Thank you for caring for my father-in-law,' he added with difficulty. He had always liked Edgar and they both got on well, once Ellen's parents had come round to accepting that their precious daughter would be marrying someone 'from the big smoke', as they regarded anywhere east of Swindon. Edgar was a no-nonsense, practical man, who could turn his hand to anything requiring hard manual work and attention to detail. Trevor found it hard to believe that Edgar had gone, he knew that Ellen and Florence would both be devastated. As he made his way down to The Sanctuary, Trevor wondered if Florence's dementia might partially shield her from the loss of her husband, it was a terrible disease, but it might have a minor benefit for her in these circumstances.

When Trevor stepped out of the lift on the Lower Ground floor, he immediately noticed that the atmosphere down there was totally different to the busy OTU floor he had just left. The OTU was well lit and always a hive of activity, and just like a real hive, every worker there knew their assigned tasks and diligently went about their difficult work with an air of efficiency and competency. He saw a sign directing him to The Sanctuary and made his way along the quiet corridor, with its walls painted in muted pastel colours. The air was filled with the scents of cleaning fluids, mixed with other smells that Trevor could not determine. Pushing open The Sanctuary door, Trevor saw through the dimmed lighting that there were clusters of armchairs around low tables, only two of which were occupied. Trevor walked up to the table where Ellen was sitting, deep in conversation with an elderly lady. They had arranged two of the armchairs to allow them to face each other and they were both holding each other's hands, resting them on their knees. The unknown woman gave Trevor a suspicious look as he entered their space.

'Trev,' exclaimed Ellen as she stood up to nuzzle into Trevor's grasp, 'I missed you so,' said Ellen, wiping away a tear. Ellen looked down at the seated woman, saying, 'Joan, this is my husband, Trevor.' And then to Trevor, 'Trevor, this is Joan, one of the Sanctuary volunteers.'

They both greeted each other and Trevor sat down on one of the spare armchairs, allowing Ellen and Joan to resume their previous positions.

Turning to Trevor, Ellen said 'They'll have to do a postmortem on Dad, Trev,' - Trevor nodded - 'It was awful, the machines started beeping, people were rushing in, then they whisked me out of the room, it was awful Trev. I needed you there with me! You didn't answer my calls!'

Both Ellen and Joan looked at Trevor, looking for a suitable response, all he could come up with was, 'I'm sorry Ellen, I was driving on the motorway, I couldn't answer the phone.' He knew that they were expecting more, but he didn't have anything better to offer them, and certainly nothing that would bring Edgar back for Ellen. Trevor realised that letting Ellen vent her spleen at him would help her work through her emotions at this time of raw hurt. It would take her a long time, but she would get there.

'Joan says that she will help us through the paperwork and all that Trev,' Ellen said to Trevor while smiling at Joan.

'Yes, it will take a couple of days Mr Braithwaite,' Joan said to Trevor, 'but Ellen's given me your mobile number, I'll pass it on to the support team so we can keep you informed,' she continued.

Trevor thanked Joan.

Ellen looked at Trevor, 'I've gotta tell Mum face to face Trev, please take me home now.'

They both thanked Joan and made their excuses and headed to the car park. It was only after Ellen had sat down in the car, that she let out a wail and cried, she had held it all back for too long. Trevor just sat and waited, comforting her as best he could, while taking her stinging rebukes for not being present when she needed him. After a few minutes, she apologised and said that she was ready to go, so they drove to the hotel to collect their things and settle the bill. Trevor was pleased to see that it was dry on the journey back from Bristol to Frome, as he still hadn't brought new wiper blades for the car. He knew that there was a petrol garage on the

main road near to Frome, so he could fill up the car and get some wipers there. As he pulled into the garage, Ellen's phone rang, but he got out of the car anyway and started filling the tank. He walked into the garage and found the wipers he needed and paid for them and the fuel at the cashier. Walking back to the car, he could see that Ellen was gesticulating wildly for him to hurry up.

As he opened the car door Ellen shouted, 'Trev, Lisa the carer says that Mum's taken a funny turn, she's called the ambulance.'

Trevor threw the wipers on to the back seat and headed straight to Ellen's parents' house.

When they arrived, they could see the ambulance, with its flashing blue lights, outside Ellen's parents' house, partially blocking the narrow road. Trevor parked down the road a bit from the ambulance, to try to prevent adding to the traffic holdup which had already formed. He and Ellen made a dash for the house, which left Ellen quite out of breath by the time they made it through the front door.

In the lounge, the scene before her made Ellen scream, Mum was flat out on her back, on the floor, with a female paramedic giving her chest compressions. A male paramedic was intubating her with an Ambu bag attached to a tube which had been inserted into her windpipe. A defibrillator was connected to the pads on Mum's chest, to try to detect Mum's pulse. Lisa announced to the paramedics that Ellen was their patient's daughter, they nodded in response, while trying to concentrate on their tasks. The lounge floor had multiple opened plastic bags scattered around Ellen's mum, Trevor knew that they were from the electrode pads and needles, etc. that the paramedics were using on her. He was having a bad feeling about this.

The female paramedic said to Ellen, 'The Doctor's on his way,' as she changed places with the male paramedic, so that she could take over the intubation.

Ellen asked, 'Is there anything that we can do?'

Both paramedics, glanced up, with sorrowful looks on their faces, solemnly shook their heads and returned their attentions to Ellen's mum. Trevor motioned Ellen to sit on the settee with him, where he held her with both arms, while she gently sobbed on his chest. Tears filled Trevor's eyes too.

Dr Oyebanji arrived about ten minutes after Trevor and Ellen, he surveyed the scene as he introduced himself to the room and then knelt down to have a hushed conversation with the paramedics. With the defibrillator switched off, the doctor checked for a pulse and after a few moments, gave a nod to the paramedics, he placed his right hand on the male paramedic's shoulder to indicate his work was over and then placed his left hand on the back of the female paramedic's uppermost most hand, to let her stop too. He stood up and faced Trevor and Ellen.

'I'm ever so sorry, but there is nothing else left that we can do for Mrs Smith.' He glanced at his watch and spoke to Ellen, 'I presume that you must be Ellen? I'm Doctor Oyebanji, I've been your mother's GP for a couple of years now.'

'Hello doctor,' Ellen managed to get out before her sobs overtook her. She remembered that she had spoken to Dr Oyebanji a while ago to get Mum and Dad's helpers arranged.

'So, you must be Trevor then,' the GP said to Trevor, 'Your mother-in-law always spoke highly of you.'

'Thank you doctor,' said Trevor, trying to stifle his surprise at this announcement.

'Yes, Florence frequently told me how proud she was that her daughter had married someone big in the City!' the doctor announced.

That almost made Trevor choke! He didn't realise that his in-laws still thought that he was a City architect, and there was no point in trying to correct that error now. 'Thank you doctor,' was all he was able to say before returning to comfort Ellen.

'Would you excuse me for a moment, I just have to go to my car,' Dr Oyebanji said, nodding to the paramedics, who started clearing all their equipment and detritus away, as he left.

It was suddenly quiet in the lounge as the paramedics worked smoothly and methodically and had cleared almost all of their equipment before Dr

Oyebanji returned, carrying an A4 sized folder and clipboard. Lisa brought a bed sheet to put over Florence and offered everyone a cup of tea, which only Trevor and Ellen accepted. Dr Oyebanji sat on an armchair and started taking details from the paramedics and completing his paperwork. After a short while, he thanked the paramedics for their hard work and let them leave.

'Ellen,' Dr Oyebanji said, looking up from his clipboard, 'Do you know if your mother wanted to have the Co-Op handle her funeral arrangements?'

This started Ellen crying loudly. Trevor realised that they hadn't even had a chance to start making the arrangements for Edgar's funeral. Trevor told the GP that Edgar had just died in Bristol and that they were on the way to tell Florence. Dr Oyebanji said that he would have to ask the coroner to schedule a postmortem for Florence, and in the meantime, he would call the local Co-Op funeral directors to collect Florence and take her to the Frome hospital mortuary, pending the postmortem. He briefly stepped into the hallway to make the call and then returned to the lounge to continue his paperwork.

Trevor sipped his tea, while Ellen left hers on a side table untouched. After a little while she asked, 'What do you think it was Doctor?'

'Sorry Ellen, I don't know,' he replied, 'that is why we will have to have a postmortem, to find out.'

'She was a good mother to me,' Ellen said in a low voice.

'And you were a good daughter to her Ellen,' said Trevor.

Ellen, feeling like she was on an emotional tightrope, was just about to give Trevor both barrels, when she realised that doing so in front of the GP would not be a good idea. She knew that there would be time enough for that later.

Dr Oyebanji finished his paperwork and they all sat in quiet contemplation while awaiting the arrival of the funeral directors, which didn't take long.

They brought a trolley into the house, but only as far as the hallway, having decided that they would not be able to turn it through ninety degrees to get from the hallway into the lounge. Trevor and Ellen went into the kitchen while the funeral directors put Florence into a bariatric bag, then carried her out of the lounge and put her on their trolley. After they had covered her with an ornately embroidered, deep burgundy removal sheet, they looked towards Trevor and Ellen, in the kitchen, to see if they wanted to join Florence in the hallway, which they did. Trevor and Ellen gently laid their hands on the removal sheet and bowed their heads in unison with the funeral directors, while Dr Oyebanji looked on solemnly from the lounge door. The funeral directors wheeled Florence out of the front door and down the footpath to the back of their van, which they had parked in the space vacated by the ambulance. Trevor, standing on the doorstep with Ellen, wondered why funeral directors called their vans 'Private Ambulances', everyone knew that it wasn't an ambulance, it was not going to be rushing anywhere. He decided that it must be part of a common psyche to want to cloak the practicalities of death in comfortable words, lest it intrudes into our daily lives, too rudely, too soon.

Trevor and Ellen walked back inside, Dr Oyebanji said that he was leaving, but he would be in touch with them about the postmortem and that the funeral directors would contact them when the funeral could proceed. Trevor and Ellen feeling drained just went to sit in the lounge for a while. Lisa came into the lounge to say that she would have to leave now, but had tidied things up in the kitchen. Trevor and Ellen thanked her for her kindness and for looking after Florence and Edgar so well.

When she had gone, Trevor went into the kitchen and made them a fresh cup of tea, as Ellen still hadn't touched the previous one, which was stone cold by now. Trevor took the teas into the lounge, Eleen was still sat frozen in the same position he had left her, he put her tea down on the side table nearest her, located the TV remote control and switched it on. Trevor hated the sound of silence; his tinnitus had been getting worse since he stopped working in the City and he liked to at least have a radio on to distract him from the whistling in his ears. He sometimes wondered if it was just that when he was working in the City, there was so much activity and noise going on all the time, that he hadn't realised tinnitus was creeping up on him. Having the TV on also saved him from the aura of silence that was emanating from Ellen. He knew better than to be complacent about her silence, she was processing the day's events and no doubt still seething about his arrest, a tsunami would come soon enough. Time for a distraction of his own.

'Ellen, I don't fancy driving home tonight, if I go and get us some fish and chips, shall we stay here over tonight?'

Ellen's face changed from blank to quizzical.

'Yeah, good idea Trev,' she said after a couple of seconds, 'I'll go and make up the spare beds for us, while you're out.'

Trevor knew how to get to the nearby fish and chip shop which Florence and Edgar were regular customers of. While they were preparing his order, he sat in the car and linked his new phone to the car's audio system, then fitted the new wiper blades he had brought earlier. When he got back to the house, Ellen had prepared two trays, so they could eat their fish and chips off them, in front of the TV, just like her parents used to. This amused Trevor, as they would never do this at home. There, the dining room was where the dining was done and the lounge was where the lounging was done!

He figured that this was Ellen's way of commemorating the passing of her parents, by emulating one of their little pleasures. They watched a couple of programmes, then decided that it was time for bed. Ellen had made up the single bed in the box room for Trevor and she knew that the double bed in the guest room was always kept ready for the times when her and Trevor used to visit. The conversations between them had been kept to a minimum all evening, she was feeling too tired to start anything off with Trevor and he had felt no reason to give her an opening for spleen venting. It felt a bit like two rival lions circling each other in a cage, Trevor trying to be as helpful as possible and keep a low profile. While Ellen, knowing that Trevor still deserved a real good earful, was mindful that she needed his help to clear up all the loose ends that had suddenly landed in her lap. Trevor was glad to have a shower to cleanse himself from the day's stresses and then to get into bed to wrap himself in a duvet, to metaphorically isolate himself for at least a night, from all his trials and tribulations.

Chapter 12

The Lid Blows Off

12th March 2013

In the morning, they had a quick tidy of the house, then drove to the nearby Little Chef restaurant for an Olympic Breakfast each. When the girls were young, a mid-journey stop at a Little Chef would be a special holiday treat. Those days were gone now, but Trevor knew that the nostalgia of it would bring a little smile to Ellen's lips. As in the days of yore, neither of them could polish the whole plate off, but they made a good go of it. The rest of the journey back to Chineham passed peacefully enough for Trevor's liking. Ellen started talking about selling her parents' house, the thought of which cheered Trevor greatly, but he knew that he dared not show too much enthusiasm for the topic, *helpful assistance, but not a greedy hurry would be the correct approach,* he decided. Ellen was concerned about what to do with all her parents belongings, there were only a couple of nostalgic items there that she wanted to take to Chineham. She decided that they should get a clearance company in to clear the rest of the contents. She knew that they already had too much of Trevor's parents' furniture and belongings, or 'Old Tat!' as she preferred to call it. They had taken more than they really wanted, just to ensure that they would be able to furnish his Mum's annexe with familiar items to help her settle in comfortably, but Ellen hated most of it. She wondered if, one day, Maria and Carol would take the same view on the contents of their home.

Trevor's Mum and Carol were pleased to see them back and very sad to hear about the closely timed passings of Florence and Edgar.

'Oh my gosh,' said Carol. 'That must have been so traumatic for you both, to have all of that in a couple of days!'

'Yes, it was awful,' said Ellen, with a deep intake of breath. She was glad to be home, the last few days had felt like she had been doing at least two Triathlon events at once. *This was not how my life was meant to be!* she thought indignantly. She wanted to go back to when Trevor was working in the City and the girls were young. Things were easier then, she could take the girls to school, have a nice bit of 'me' time, keep the house clean and tidy, watch a bit of telly, money wasn't tight and she'd had only the four of them to concentrate on. It was all getting too complicated now, looking after Trevor's Mum, Trevor's arrest and all his shenanigans! Now funerals to plan for her own parents, clearing and selling of their house, all that travel back and forth! It was all getting a bit much for her, she hoped that she would soon be able to see the light at the end of the tunnel! Carol made a pot of tea and they all sat around the kitchen table, reminiscing about the good times they had had with Florence and Edgar, as a way of taking the edge off their grief.

*

The previous day had seen Jingfei woken by the Custody Sergeant with a cup of tea and a ham sandwich, for which she was grateful. Her gratefulness surprised her, it made her realise just how quickly she had adjusted her standards, in a downwards direction, since her arrest. In the flat she took pride in usually making noodles or congee for breakfast, or occasionally, when necessary, Bran Flakes. Trying to keep hold of her cultural norms was very important to Jingfei, she had managed it well in the flat, but she had no chance of doing that now that control of her life had been taken out of her hands. After a little while a WPC, a different one to yesterday, took her to the Ladies toilet area. When the WPC returned her to her cell, she was disappointed to see that there were no fresh clothes laid out for her. It certainly looked to her like they were getting ready to be free of their unwanted guest. Without her phone, she had lost track of time, but a short while later the cell door opened and the WPC told her that a Border Force agent had arrived to take her to

Yarl's Wood. And so, without much ceremony, although she was not expecting any, Jingfei was taken back to the Custody Sergeant's desk and released into the custody of the female Border Force agent. She was taken down to the Police Station car park, where a large white van was waiting. This surprised her as she was expecting a car. A waiting officer opened a side door on the van and the Border Force agent guided her up some steps and inside the van, where there were individual metal cells on each side of the van, with a narrow corridor running the length of the van. She was put in a cell about halfway down the van and the Border Force agent locked the door.

The journey to Yarl's Wood took hours, not just because it was a long way but because the van had speed limit restrictions and also because the van had four more 'passengers' to pick up at other points en route. Jingfei quickly had no idea where she was, where the stops were or how much longer it would be before they arrived. She learned later that the cells in the van were known as sweat boxes, and not without justification. She only had a small square window to look out of, and all of these factors combined to make her feel quite nauseous. She nearly did bring her ham sandwich up, when the aroma of another passenger's vomiting crept through the door of her cell, but somehow, she managed to keep it down. This was just as well, as the unfortunate person who was the source of the foul smell, was on the receiving end of much abuse and cursing from the other passengers, who all sounded like they were women of varying nationalities, but combined together into a sisterhood of vengeance which was promised to be delivered when they were inside Yarl's Wood. Jingfei was reminded of the *Bad Girls* TV series she used to watch, where the inmates had an innate need for a pecking order and no one wanted to be at the bottom of that. She had guessed that such a thing would exist in Yarl's Wood, but she was surprised to find that it could exist in a van, where all the occupants were separated in cells, had never met and only had their voices as weapons. It made her determined to put on a hard façade as soon as they got out of the van and inside Yarl's Wood.

*

Oblivious to Jingfei's troubles, Trevor got on with adjusting to his new normal. He had been ordered to keep in touch with the Probation Service, by reporting to Basingstoke Police Station every Wednesday, which he duly did. He knew he had to break the news of his arrest to Barry at the Kitchen Showroom, as soon as possible, for surely the truth would come out soon enough. Trevor presumed that Barry would have to let him go, as he would not want his business to be associated with a pimp! Barry, however, took it surprisingly well.

'Wow Trev! You're a bit of a dark horse aren't you!' Barry said, with a slight tinge of admiration in his voice. 'Well, I certainly can't do without you mate; we've been getting some great installation work out of your surveys and they've all been trouble free. Even online, there's been a lot of satisfied customers, leaving positive reviews for us and all the installers are very happy with the quality of your work. I mean, you haven't been found guilty of a crime yet, and the charges that you're facing are not exactly contrary to kitchen design, so to let you go, would be like shooting myself in the foot.'

Hearing this cheered Trevor up no end. 'Thanks Barry, I really appreciate that.'

'Listen,' said Barry, 'I've got some more survey request forms for you to crack on with.' He handed the wad of forms to Trevor.

'Thanks again Barry, I appreciate your support,' said Trevor. He walked out, a little bit happier, knowing that a reliable income would come in very handy in the coming weeks and months.

Trevor's immediate concerns were, in sequence order; the postmortems of Ellen's parents, followed by their funerals and sale of their house, which was the main target in the front of his mind. He knew the house sale would provide funds to cover his court costs and the amount that he anticipated the Pocahunters would be looking to claw back from him.

The only fly in that ointment would be that the house sale might take a while to go through and when it did, it would be Ellen who would be the beneficiary, not him. He would need to work on Ellen like never before. He held no misconceptions that it would be easy for him to work his way back into her good books, let alone to get her to divert her inheritance to pay for his misdeeds. So, he was pleased when, a week later, Ellen received the results of her parents' postmortems. When he saw the two brown envelopes arrive, both addressed to Ellen, he was sure that it was the postmortem results, as she never normally had post addressed to her only. It took all his willpower to resist the temptation to rip open the envelopes, but he knew that to get back in her good books, he had to play the long game. He left them on the breakfast bar, placed as casually as he could manage, but in a prominent position, guaranteed to catch her eye when she came downstairs.

He was just tidying up the kitchen after his breakfast, when Ellen came in. Trevor feigned surprise at seeing her, even though he had heard her less than gentle footsteps on the stairs.

'Oh, hello love,' he said sweetly, 'like a cuppa?'

'Oh yes please Trev, thanks,' she replied as she breezed past the letters, towards the door to Trevor's Mum's annexe. 'Mum not up yet?' she said redundantly.

It was always guaranteed to annoy Trevor, when she did that, *of course Mum is not up yet, do you see her here? Do you think that she is outside changing the oil in my car maybe FFS!* Trevor thought, but had long ago learnt to bite his tongue on such occasions, particularly now, knowing that it would make the chances of him getting hold of Ellen's inheritance disappear off into the far distance.

Ellen went into Mum's annexe and brought Mum back with her. 'Here, sit down Mum, Trevor will make us a nice cup of tea,' Ellen said, guiding Mum to her seat at the kitchen table.

Trevor did as he was told and also made toast and marmalade for them both too. *Buttering them up,* he thought with a smile, as he buttered their toast. Trevor had surveys to do, so he made his excuses and left them chatting at the kitchen table. Walking out to the car, he was fuming that Ellen hadn't even looked at the letters. He guessed that she had seen them and presumed that she had deliberately ignored them, as her way of hiding from bad news. He was sure she understood, that either opening the letters or leaving them on the breakfast bar would not change the fact that her parents had died. It was just an ostrich's reaction, to bury her head in the sand, trying to delay the receipt of the news. He would see if they were opened, when he returned after doing his surveys, there was nothing to be gained by trying to push Ellen right now.

After finishing his surveys, Trevor went to the flat, to start cleaning and emptying it out. He felt strange being in there on his own. It was so quiet in there without Jingfei, but he could still smell her perfume. He knew that his feelings for her ran deep, but he hadn't expected her arrest to affect him so much. He would have to block those emotions out now and crack on with the process of exiting the flat. He used bin bags for the smaller items, towels, sheets, crockery and food etc., so he could take them down to the dumpster in the underground car park. He phoned the same 'Men and Van' chaps who had previously helped him to get the flat furnished. Luckily, they were still in business and agreed to come on Monday to take all the bulky items to a nearby hospice furniture store which had told Trevor that they would be grateful to receive his donations. He decided that it would be best to strip out Violetta's dungeon before the van guys arrived on Monday, because the other bedrooms easily passed for regular bedrooms. He started by dismantling the dog cage and dragging it piece by piece into the lounge, after that exertion he could only sit down and rest. This made him realise that he was not getting any younger, he would be 63 years old this year, and right now, he was feeling every one of those years. At least pulling all the soundproofing panels off the walls, was easy enough, he was tall enough to not need to use a set of steps to reach the higher panels. Unfortunately, there were lots of double-sided sticky tape pads left stuck to the walls, as well as the restraint fixings. He decided to leave Violetta's tarpaulin down for now until he had cleaned and repaired the walls. He was glad then that she had asked to have a clear tarpaulin put down, as it had saved a lot of wax drips and other substances from sticking to the carpets.

After depositing the bin bags in the dumpster, he headed home, keen to find out if Ellen had opened her envelopes yet. He was not surprised to see them in exactly the same place he had left them this morning.

'Ellen, these letters are addressed to you,' he said as casually as he could, as he walked into the kitchen, where she was stirring a pot on the hob.

'Yeah, I know Trev,' she replied, 'but I just can't face them right now, could you open them for me please love.'

Trevor swept them off the breakfast bar and sat down at the kitchen table to read them. Edgar's postmortem revealed that he had died of hypertensive heart disease with left ventricular hypertrophy and a secondary cause of coronary artery disease. Trevor had to go upstairs, switch his computer on and search the internet for a translation. 'Sudden heart attack, with pre-existing cardiovascular disease,' he announced to Ellen, when he was back in the kitchen. 'I suppose it could have hit him any time,' he added, in the absence of an immediate response. Trevor could see that Ellen had gone pale, he went to cuddle her, switched the hob off and guided her to her seat at the kitchen table and sat her down. 'He had ticking timebomb inside him love,' he said gently to her, adding 'I'll make you a cup of tea.' As he headed to the kettle, she picked up the letter and looked at it, eyes un-seeing. She was still staring blankly at it when Trevor brought the tea over.

'Thanks love,' she managed to get out as Trevor sat down next to her and opened the other envelope.

Trevor didn't need to search the internet for a translation for Florence's cause of death, it was given as a ruptured intracranial aneurysm. He remembered that phrase from when a colleague at the bank keeled over at his desk one day. Their first aider had tried to resuscitate him until a paramedic arrived, but neither of them could help him, despite trying for more than an hour. The dreadful scene had returned to Trevor's mind when Florence died, so he was not overly surprised to see confirmation of his suspicions. He tried to relay that information to Ellen as gently as he could, but he knew that, given it was her mother, there would be no way to stem the tears. 'There was nothing that the paramedics could do for her, love,' he said softly while holding her tenderly. She could be a real pain to him sometimes, but it was at times like these, that the depth of their love for each other shone through. Both the letters confirmed that the bodies could now be released to the funeral directors. Trevor decided to call them in the morning to arrange collection of the bodies and to start making arrangements for a joint funeral.

In the morning, after calling the funeral directors, Trevor called Mr Hooper, the Basingstoke solicitor he had used to draft Florence and Edgars Lasting Powers of Attorney forms. Trevor had decided that he should change the ownership of their own house, one hundred percent into Ellen's name, to keep the Pocahunters from forcing him to sell that. He also asked Mr Hooper to change their mirror wills to make their daughters the next in line for inheritance of their estate. Mr Hooper, quite rightly, queried what was driving Trevor's decisions, to which Trevor felt compelled to tell him a potted version of the truth. Mr Hooper was not happy about making the changes, but said that he would make a start on the work. He also offered Trevor the contact details of a colleague who could defend Trevor and was most surprised when Trevor said that he would be pleading guilty and that he had already asked Caroline Moore, the duty solicitor who was present at his arrest, to represent him in court. Mr Hooper tried to dissuade Trevor, from that course of action, but Trevor was adamant he wanted to continue down that route. He wanted the court case finished as soon as possible, to let him try to rebuild his relationship with Ellen, without further ado.

He had a few surveys to do over the weekend, so he decided to put some tools and plaster filler in his car so he could also go the flat and finish removing the restraint fixings and double-sided tape. He also found time to fill the holes and give the walls a quick coat of paint. He took a quick look around the flat and decided that he did not need to paint anymore of it, the landlord would probably expect that it would need redecoration before it would be rented out again.

Monday came and Trevor was there, nice and early, to let the van men in to do the removals. They told Trevor that the charity shop wouldn't take the mattresses and two of the chipboard dressing tables, so they would have to take those to the council dump instead. That involved extra mileage and therefore extra cost. Trevor suspected that they might be scamming him, but he agreed to the extra charges - he just wanted to be clear of the flat. This part of his life was over now, he had to make a new future for Ellen and him. It would be different; it would probably not be what he wanted, but he would have to make the best of it he could. As soon as the van men finished and left, Trevor decided that he had a last opportunity to self-satisfy in the flat, so he went to the toilet and did so. It was not something that he was proud of, but he could not resist the urges. Once the flat was gone, it would not be easy for him to find a bit of personal space at home, with Ellen and Mum always fluttering around. He hadn't thought that this downside of losing Jingfei would arise so soon, but it was another part of his new normal that he was just going to have to adapt to.

Trevor and Ellen decided to hold a joint funeral for Ellen's parents near Frome, to make it easier for their local friends and neighbours to attend. They managed to get a slot booked at the beautiful Semington crematorium on the Wednesday after Easter. Carol wanted to attend her grandparents' funeral. Fortunately, as it would be the Easter school holidays, her husband, Mike, offered to look after Trevor's Mum for that day. Trevor and Ellen decided that they should go down to Frome before Easter and stay for a couple of days in the nearby Travel Inn, whilst clearing out the house. Trevor arranged for a local clearance company to clear his in-laws' house. There were a few small nostalgic items that Ellen had already decided that she wanted to keep, but it really was a very small amount of memorabilia that she wanted to take, and certainly nothing that wouldn't fit in the car. While they were in Frome, Trevor took Ellen into her parents' solicitor's office to collect their wills, so Trevor could take them back to Basingstoke and ask Mr Hooper to get the Probate process started. The house clearance went well, the company that Trevor had asked to do the work, just took it all without a quibble. Trevor had no idea if it was just taken to the local dump or if some of the better items, of which there were a few, would end up in a second-hand shop. He was just glad that they had done the work that he had asked them to, without an extra charge.

Being in her parents' empty house saddened Ellen greatly, this was the place where she had grown up and she had many happy memories of that time and of this area. But now she had made new memories in Basingstoke, and with her parents gone, she no longer had any ties to her home-town of Frome. She felt like she had been cut adrift in a life raft with Trevor, and he had done his best to sink it! She was worried about the outcome of the trial, how would she cope on her own with Trevor's mum, if they locked Trevor up? She feared the adverse local publicity she would get. She was sure that people would be laughing at her behind her back, or she would get funny looks when she went out shopping. Sometimes her anger at Trevor, and his selfish actions, boiled up inside her and she felt like screaming out loud at him, but instead, for the time being, she would keep it all bottled up inside her. She needed Trevor to help her sort out the funeral and the sale of her parents' house. She decided that when that was sold, she would put the money into the new bank account she had opened recently in her name. *Keep it away from Trevor, that would teach him*! For the first time in a long while a little smile crept over her face.

They returned home on the morning of Maundy Thursday, and after dropping Ellen and their bags at home, Trevor headed to Basingstoke Police Station. He had to apologise for not attending his Probation appointment the day before, but his excuse about having to attend to his in-laws funeral arrangements was accepted, much to his relief. Before he left, he gave them his new phone number. He went home and sat down at the kitchen table with Ellen to plan the funeral service. The funeral directors had already emailed Trevor a suggested outline order of service, so after choosing music for the beginning and the end of the service, they discussed what Trevor should include in his eulogy. Trevor had volunteered for this duty, as there was only Ellen who knew them better, but she knew that she would not be able to hold herself together well enough to get through it without breaking down. Trevor, incorrectly, took this delegation as a sign that Ellen was beginning to thaw.

Trevor and Ellen spent Good Friday and the Saturday working their way through their own long list of overdue domestic chores. They had been so busy recently that they hadn't had time to look after their home and their own lives. They invited Carol & Mike and Maria & Simon to have a family Easter Sunday lunch with them and Mum, as they had not had a chance to all get together for such a long time. On such occasions, Trevor was usually tasked with peeling potatoes, preparing vegetables and laying the table. Ellen and Trevor had always had this division of labour between them, she would do the cooking and he would carry out all the ancillary tasks, to ensure that Ellen could focus on her cooking. Trevor had spent the last couple of days generally giving Ellen a wide berth, whilst doing whatever he could to help around the house, and being as sweet as he could towards her. He was confident that his tactics were working, she was being quite amenable towards him, they had even shared a joke about a TV programme they had watched the night before. All was going well, the guests were all seated at the dining table, Ellen was dishing up in the kitchen and Trevor was going round the table, filling five glasses with his favourite Châteauneuf-du-Pape red wine or orange squash for Mum and Maria.

Suddenly, the was a loud crash in the kitchen, quickly followed by a scream and a stream of swear words, coming from Ellen at the top of her voice. Trevor, swiftly deciding that an audience would not be required, motioned to his family to stay seated, while he would go and investigate.

'What's the matter love? What can I do?' he asked as he entered the kitchen. Ellen was sitting at the kitchen table, sobbing. A metal cooking tray was upside down in the middle of the floor, a large Yorkshire pudding on the floor in the corner partially under one of the kitchen cupboards.

'You'd rather be with her, wouldn't you!' Ellen hissed at Trevor, 'You're here, but you're not here! You're thinking of her! I can see it in your face! Don't lie to me Trevor.' More sobs followed.

Trevor proffered his handkerchief to wipe away her tears, but she pushed it away.

'You make me so angry Trevor, what is to become of us, if they put you in jail?'

'We'll be alright love, I'm sure they won't send me to jail,' Trevor said, while trying to cuddle her, but again she pushed him away.

'How do you know that Trev, just how the f**k do you know that?'

Trevor had never seen her like this before, she was inconsolable and she would certainly never normally swear out loud like that. Maria appeared in the kitchen door, sidled up to her Mum and put her arm around Ellen, who sobbed louder, as if the comfort of her daughter allowed her to release more built-up pressure.

'You dish up Trevor! I'm going to have lie down upstairs,' said Ellen, with steady finality, as she rose to her feet and walked off, down the hallway, supported by Maria.

Trevor put the Yorkshire pudding in the bin and the cooking tray in the sink, used some kitchen roll to wipe the greasy floor and surveyed the plates laid out on the breakfast bar. They were all fully loaded, apart from peas, which he distributed in a rather slapdash manner. He picked two plates up and carefully carried them into the dining room, to be greeted by four expectant faces, silently staring at him.

'Mum's not well, she's gone to have a lie down.' That was the best explanation that he could come up with, as he gave a plate to his Mum, who looked at him quizzically as he put the other one in front of Carol.

'Dad?' said Carol, stretching the short word into a longer question.

'Yorkshire pudding's off,' said Trevor, ignoring his daughter. 'Sorry, it took a tumble.'

Simon stood up and headed to the kitchen, returning with two more plates of food, one of which he passed to Mike, he put the other one where Maria had been sitting. Trevor returned to the kitchen and came back with a saucepan of gravy and a ladle, which he put in the middle of the table. Carol looked at the saucepan in surprise, she knew that her Mum would never do such a thing, after all, they had gravy boats for that. Simon, in the meantime, had gone back to the kitchen again and returned with the last two plates, one of which he put in front of Trevor's carver chair at the head of the table, the other in front of his own seat. Trevor went back to the kitchen to wrap the last plate in clingfilm and put it in the microwave in case Ellen wanted it later.

Maria came in and sat down where Mike had put her dinner. 'Dad, Mum burnt her arm, I gave her a bag of frozen peas to cool it down. She is sure that you will be going to jail, why are you so sure that you won't be?'

Trevor had always admired her way of getting things done, no faffing around, 'let's get things sorted'. But this interrogation, by his own offspring, in front of his nearest and dearest, was utterly humiliating.

'I'm sixty-two Maria,' he said, 'I'm sure no judge will send someone of that age to jail, it's not like I shot someone, or robbed a bank, is it?' he paused to catch his breath. In the absence of a reply from his family, he continued, 'I pleaded guilty at the first opportunity, I've given them all the evidence and cash I had from it, I've done my best to make their job easy, so I am convinced that any judge with a modicum of compassion, would show leniency towards me.' He could see that Maria and Carol did not look convinced.

Trevor's Mum had tears in her eyes. 'What's all this about you going to jail Trevor, I don't understand?'

'No, it's fine Mum, I won't be going to jail, Ellen's just got herself all worked up and slipped with the Yorkshire pudding, there's nothing to worry about,' Trevor said unconvincingly.

'I'm tired, I can't take any more of this, I'm going to have a lie down,' Trevor's Mum said as she got up from the table, having barely touched her lunch, and headed out of the dining room.

'Love you Mum,' was all Trevor could say as she walked past him, without receiving acknowledgment. Trevor started picking at his food, the others followed.

Carol took up the attack. 'Why did you do it Dad?' she asked, 'You've really hurt Mum, you know.'

'I know that it was wrong to get involved with her.' Trevor said, having decided that using Jingfei's name at home would not help his situation. *Better not mention the name of the beast!* he thought. 'But I was just so miserable, when your mother started having her troubles.'

'You can't blame it on Mum,' Maria snapped back, 'you've broken her heart you know?'

'I know darling,' replied Trevor, 'I don't know how I am going to make it up to her.'

'I am sure that it will take a while Dad,' Maria said, more calmly now. 'But you have to try, she needs you, and you need her.'

Simon and Mike had clearly decided that it was their place to keep quiet and enjoy the food. Butting in to their in-laws' problems would not be very tactful, given that it was their host who was on the receiving end of the roasting over the coals, so efficiently provided by their wives.

Trevor managed to get a few more mouthfuls down, before deciding that he really should go up and say something to Ellen. He wasn't sure of what he could say to start to bridge the gap between them, but he knew that he had to try to make a start. *Maybe now that Ellen has vented a bit of steam,* he thought, *she might be more amenable to some more apologising?* 'I'm going to go up and see Mum,' he announced, as he pushed his chair back, stood up and walked upstairs.

Chapter 13

What Happens in The Earl Haig...

31st March 2013

Ellen was lying on her bed, still holding the bag of frozen peas that Maria had given her, to her arm. Trevor could see that her eyes were red and she had been crying, but was now dry of eye.

'I'm so sorry love, it was a terrible thing to do, I just don't know how I can apologise enough to you,' Trevor began.

'Sorry I made a scene down there Trevor,' said Ellen softly.

Trevor was more than surprised to hear an apology from Ellen, but thought, *No, I must not try to capitalise on this achievement too soon!* 'You shouldn't apologise Ellen, it's me, I owe you, Mum and the kids a thousand apologies.' *Was that too OTT?* he wondered.

'I just sort of exploded Trev,' Ellen continued, 'It was like someone else had taken me over. That hot Yorkshire pudding pan burnt my arm, as I was carrying it from the oven to the breakfast bar, and it just dropped as I screamed.'

Trevor gently removed the bag of frozen peas, looked at the red welt on her arm, 'I'll go and get some Germolene,' he said heading to the bathroom cabinet. He returned with cream and a roll of bandage, which he proceeded to apply gently on Ellen's burn. 'It looks like the peas kept the burn from swelling too much love,' he said as he tended to her wound, Scout First Aid knowledge had still stayed with him. 'I'm sure it will be better tomorrow.' Then he added, 'You know that I'll do whatever it takes to make it up to you Ellen.'

'I don't even know how to make a start on that list Trevor,' she said with sadness in her voice. 'It just feels like the last few years have been one big lie.'

She's right, thought Trevor, *Why was I so stupid to think that I could get away with having an affair for so long?* 'I know you're right love,' he said to her gently, 'maybe we should go to couples counselling.' *Fat lot of good that will do,* he thought, mentally crossing his fingers, *Oh God, I hope that she will say no to that s**t.*

'Are you out of your mind Trevor?' Ellen said decisively. 'Why on Earth would we pay someone to listen to me slagging you off, when I can do it at home for free!'

That's more like my Ellen, he thought, *thank you Lord.* 'Shall I warm up your lunch and bring it up for you Ellen?' he said, knowing full well that she hated eating in the bedroom.

'No, that's alright Trev,' she said, 'I must go downstairs and see the kids.'

Yes, Trevor thought, *no matter how old and bold your offspring are, you still see them as your kids.*

Trevor made a show of helping her sit up and get up out of bed,

'Oh do stop fussing Trevor, it's only a burn, not an amputation,' she said in mock admonishment. *No reason why I shouldn't milk this for what it is worth, while I can,* she thought. *There's no way that I am going to let him off lightly, after what he's done to me and the family!*

She smiled gently to Trevor.

Great, she's coming round, this is going to be easier than I thought, he mistakenly presumed. He moved to the side, to give her some space to get out of the bedroom door, then tidied the bed sheets, to make it look presentable again. With Ellen in the lead, they headed downstairs. As they were going down the stairs, they could see that Carol, Mike, Maria and

Simon were sitting in the lounge. Ellen went in, while Trevor headed to the kitchen, tidying up the kitchen, after mealtimes, was his duty. He was surprised to see that the kids had already cleared up the kitchen, and, he presumed, thrown the rest of his lunch in the food recycle bin.

Trevor walked to the lounge, 'Anyone want some Lemon Meringue Pie?' he asked and received five *yeses* in response. Back in the kitchen, Trevor switched the kettle on to make tea and coffee for his guests and pulled the shop brought Lemon Meringue Pie out of the fridge. *A few years ago, Trevor thought, Ellen or Mum would have made a Lemon Meringue pie from scratch, but nowadays it is just not worth the hassle. Lots of things have gone that way, it's a shame really. What do we do with all the time we save?* He wondered. The kettle switching off brought him back from his ruminating to reality. He dished up six portions of pie onto plates, put them on a tray with cake forks and took the tray into the lounge, putting it down on the coffee table. 'Who wants tea or coffee?' he asked, taking a quick count of the order. 'Simon, could you pass these plates round for me? Thanks,' he said as he headed back to the kitchen, returning shortly with the teas and coffees, which he passed round, before sitting down in his favourite armchair and taking a mouthful of pie.

'Mum, Dad,' Maria said, breaking the silence, 'we have some news.' That got the attention of the assembled company. 'We're expecting a baby in September!' she proudly announced. Ellen leapt up out of her chair, walked over to Maria, who stood up to receive a hearty hug from her mum.

'Oh, that's beautiful darling,' Ellen said, tears again running down her cheeks.

Trevor went over to Simon and gave him a manly hug, clumsily combined with a firm handshake. Trevor had never really figured out how to make that movement work properly. He knew that it was the right thing to do, he just didn't get that many opportunities to practice it. 'Congratulations, my good man,' he said, again he was even a bit clumsy with his phrasing.

Maybe it was the shock of suddenly finding out that he was to become a grandfather, or maybe it was because his mind was still in turmoil over how to turn things around with Ellen. *This bit of good news is just what I need to distract Ellen,* he thought, now with a genuine smile on his face.

Trevor and Ellen swapped places to congratulate the other proud parent-to-be, then sat down, so that Carol and Mike could congratulate them as well. Trevor was somewhat pleased that the conversation about babies had lightened the mood in the room. He knew that he was not off the hook with Ellen by any means, but having something good for her to focus on, would do him no harm.

'I wondered why you wanted squash instead of the old CNDP with your lunch,' said Trevor, like a proud Hercule Poirot calling out the murderer. Maria smiled sweetly at her dad, apparently happy to let him have a moment of pride, after grilling him so much earlier.

The conversation turned to the funeral on Wednesday, Maria and Simon were taking the day off work and would drive there on their own. Carol and Mike would come early to Trevor and Ellen's house and Carol would go in their car with them. Mike had decided that he would take 'Nan Braithwaite' to the local Milestones Museum, where she could reminisce about the old days in the replica streets and shops. All the preparations having been made, Maria and Simon decided that they should head back home to Bromley. Once again, as they were leaving, there was more love and best wishes all around, which pleased Trevor no end, as it kept the heat off him for a bit longer. Carol and Mike didn't stay long after that. Carol wanted to give her parents some space to work things out between themselves and motioned to Mike that it was time to go.

After they left, Trevor cleared the plates and cups from the lounge, loaded the dishwasher and set it going. As he walked back to the lounge, he half expected to find Ellen watching the Shopping Channel, but not this time, the TV was off.

'Come sit with me a bit Trev,' she said gently.

He knew that he couldn't refuse, but he still felt like a Christian entering the Roman Colosseum. For a split-second he thought about starting a conversation about the new baby, but decided better of it, this was not a time for more distraction techniques, so he just sat and waited for Ellen to say her piece.

'Trevor, you cannot imagine just how deeply you have hurt me,' she started, 'I should divorce you and take you to the cleaners, no judge on this planet would give you any compassion then!'

Ouch, that hurt! thought Trevor, *she must have overheard the conversation in the dining room earlier.* He decided to hold his peace for the time being and let Ellen get as much as she wanted off her chest.

'You have treated me with total disrespect and disregard,' she continued, 'you were only thinking of your own primal urges! You didn't give a s**t about how it might affect Mum, me and the girls. Maria and Simon might be out of the limelight, living over in Bromley, when this all comes out, but Carol and Mike are well-known locally and will be laughing stocks, because of your selfish actions!' her voice was rising steadily as she made her way through her condemnation, so much so, she was almost out of breath by the end.

Trevor let her catch her breath and waited to see what would follow, he sensed that she had more ammo ready.

'Will they try to make us sell the house to pay any fines Trevor?' she asked, her voice back down a few decibels.

At that point Trevor realised that he had been so busy, he hadn't told her about asking the solicitor to put the house in her name, to keep the Pocahunters at bay. Nor had he told her that, sooner or later, there probably would be Pocahunters circling, like vultures over a carcass. *Softly, softly catchee monkey,* he thought. He would leave the Pocahunters conversation for a later date.

'No love, they won't make us sell the house,' he said, pleased, at last, to have some good news to come back with. 'I'm sorry, I forgot to tell you I have already asked the solicitor to put the house one-hundred percent in your name.'

'You did what Trev?' she exclaimed. 'What the f**k did you do that for! You just can't stop going around behind my back! They're going to be coming after me now then!'

'No, no!' Trevor interjected. 'It's OK love, you'll be fine. It's just a way to keep the house away from them. If I don't own it, they cannot make me sell it,' he added hurriedly.

'Are you sure Trev?' she asked, in a slightly more moderate tone now. 'But why didn't you tell me when you did that?'

'Yeah, I'm sorry about that Ellen, we were just so busy with your parents' house, the postmortems and all that, it just slipped my mind.' He knew that he was telling the complete truth, for a change, but he could see from her face that she was not totally convinced that his plan would work, but at least she was giving him a hopeful look. On the absence of a quick follow up question, he decided that he should give her a bit of time to process her thoughts, so he stared at the TV. Being switched off, it allowed him to see her reflection, she looked frozen in time. He would bide his time, and just wait for the next rally.

*

Ellen was busy trying to figure out why, for all those years, she had not thought that anything was wrong? *Was I blind?* she wondered. *Was I stupid? How did I not notice all his absences?* 'Did you ever go to the OFC meetings then, Trev?'

'Yes, of course I did love, but just not as many times as I said that I did,' he replied honestly. 'And also some of the times when I said that I was doing surveys in the evening, I would finish the survey quickly and then-'

'Stop!' she said abruptly, 'I don't need to hear all the gory details, if you don't mind!'

He was surprised and relieved that she had called a halt to his explanation

I suppose she didn't want me to rub her nose in it anymore, he thought. 'Shall warm up your lunch love? You must be hungry by now?' He asked in his most considerate tone.

'Yes, please Trev,' she replied, in a distant voice, clearly still deep in thought.

Trevor was pleased to get out of the lounge and let her keep mulling things over. He knew it wasn't over, she would come back soon enough, with another question. He switched the microwave oven on and laid a place for Ellen at the kitchen table. Knowing that Ellen preferred a white wine, he poured her a glass from the bottle in the fridge door. He looked around, trying to see what else he could do to claim a Brownie Point or two. Nothing sprung to mind, and at that moment, the microwave went 'Ping!' He walked to the lounge, leaned in the doorway and said 'Popty Ping!' the Welsh slang phrase for microwave, it was another one of their *'in-jokes', throwing all caution to the wind,* he thought. He was pulling out all the stops to try to win her back.

As Trevor peeled the clingfilm off the plate, Ellen sat down at the place that Trevor had set for her and took a sip of the wine. Trevor set the plate in front of her and she started eating.

'Where's all the money gone Trevor?'

WOW!, thought Trevor, *she's taken a leaf out of Maria's 'direct to the point' book*!

'Well,' Trevor began, knowing that this would not be an easy conversation, 'I have some cash here that the Police missed, I have been over-paying the girls mortgages every month-'

'What!' she interrupted him, 'You've gone behind their backs, putting your illegal money into their homes! What on earth were you thinking of? Were you trying to get their homes sequestrated?'

'No, of course not,' he replied, more than a little bit surprised by her use of that word. It was the right word for the job, but certainly not one from her standard vocabulary. 'Don't worry, their homes are safe, the police won't have found anything relating to those payments on my computer or in my files. I just paid the cash in using the paying in slips at the building society branch counters. I didn't even need to tell the girls; they might not even notice when they see their annual mortgage statements.'

'But Trev,' Ellen replied 'That is so risky, are you sure that the police won't find out?'

'Yes, I'm sure.' said Trevor. 'The rest of the money, I used to supplement our income from the kitchen surveys, pay off our household bills and so on. We needed that income and now we will miss it, it won't be easy, we might have to see what we can cut back on,' *Now is as good a time as any to sow the seeds in her mind,* 'We have a lot of charges coming on the credit card every month, we'll need to look closely at those for starters.'

'Yeah, but Trev,' Ellen replied defensively, her eyes avoiding Trevor's gaze, 'the things that I get from the Shopping Channel are all on easy-pay, so that lets me spread the cost out.'

'Of course, love,' said Trevor gently, the faint scent of a minor victory in his nose. 'But the charges still do add up each month. Perhaps, if, next time you see something nice on there, you could think if we really need it?'

'OK Trev, I'll try to be more careful. But it will be easier after we sell Mum and Dad's house, won't it Trev?' she replied, pleased with herself for realising that, after all, she had the solution to their problems.

Trevor smiled sweetly at his wife. 'Yes, that will help greatly love, thanks for thinking of that.' Inside he was gloating, *Talk about slam dunk, that couldn't have gone better, I've cracked the door open, a glimmer of light is shining through, now I won't have to worry about how to pay the Pocahunters, when the time comes!*

Trevor saw that Ellen had almost finished her lunch, 'Would you like a tea or a coffee love?' he asked as he stood up. *This is not a time for complacency,* he reminded himself, *she still has more anger to release, it is bound to come out in the coming days, but at least, I've got her on the right track now.*

'Coffee please Trev,' she replied.

Trevor made coffee for both of them and then said to Ellen, 'I'm going to take mine upstairs love, I need to work on my eulogy for the funeral, and check the other details for Wednesday.'

'OK love,' she replied, 'I'll go and see how Mum is and see if she wants a cuppa.' She took her coffee into Mum's annexe.

Trevor made his way to his study, to switch his work laptop on, he hated using it at home, but he was not about to buy a new computer, he would rather wait until he got his own back from the police. He spent an hour or so, writing and re-writing his eulogy and when he was happy with it, he printed it off, ready for Wednesday. He had then started to look for a place to hold a wake, when he remembered that Edgar's local, The Earl Haig, served food, had a function room and was not too posh, so it might not be too pricey. He gave them a call and in less than ten minutes had it all arranged.

After firing off a couple of emails to the florist and the funeral directors, he started looking for estate agents in Frome. This was the real focus of his attention at the moment; *How much is it worth? How quickly will it sell? Will the sale price leave us with some change after the Pocahunters have taken their pound of flesh?*

He found a similar house which had sold for just under £210K a year ago, so he took that as a baseline price, *I will have to get a painter and decorator in to tart it up,* he thought, *there is no point in trying to sell it looking like it does at the moment. And it will need new carpets and vinyl flooring, that would definitely help to shift it quickly, at a good price.*

He suddenly felt that he was being a bit cutthroat, focussing on selling Flo and Edgar's house, before they were even in the ground. However, that feeling quickly passed, when he calculated that £210K should leave him with a good amount of change. Ever the pragmatist, Trevor knew that saving his own bacon was the best thing to focus on right now. Using his favourite online search engine, Trevor chose two estate agents in Frome; one was part of a national chain, the other a local company with good reviews. He called them both, mainly to check that they were working on the Easter weekend. Satisfied with their responses he set up appointments to meet them after the wake. *Might as well make the most of my time down there,* he thought, *in a true Boy Scout manner.*

Feeling that he had done enough organising for now, he shut the laptop down and went downstairs. Ellen and Mum were in the lounge watching *Easter Parade* on the TV. *I cannot think, how many times they've watched this!* thought Trevor *It's repeated every bleeping Easter!* Deciding that feigning interest in it would earn him some more much-needed Brownie Points, he sat down and put his most attentive face on.

'You see Trev,' Ellen announced during one particularly energetic dance routine, 'if you'd had lessons, I'm sure we could have danced like that!'

Not in a million years of lessons, thought Trevor, as he smiled sweetly at Ellen. She had, in her younger days, been a good dancer. *Those days are long gone now,* thought Trevor. He was saved from further wincing, by his phone ringing, 'It's Barry,' he announced as he stood up and walked to the kitchen to take the call.

'Sorry to call you on your day off Trev,' said Barry. 'Could you fit another survey in tomorrow morning, it's in Bordon, so your second survey will put you quite close? The only other day they could make, is on Wednesday, but then you're off for your in-laws' funerals.'

'Yes, I can do that Barry, no worries,' Trevor replied, knowing that he owed Barry some favours for being so flexible with Trevor's recent absences and for not minding about his arrest. 'Just text me the details, I'll go there after my second survey.'

Trevor realised he had been so distracted by trying to keep Ellen sweet, that he hadn't prepared for the surveys scheduled for tomorrow. *Oh well, I will just have to miss the rest of* Easter Parade, he thought as he headed, cheerfully, back up to his study.

The surveys on Monday all went well. Trevor had momentarily wondered if the last-minute additional appointment was an April Fools trick, but it wasn't. Tuesday's appointments also went without a hitch and Trevor was able to process all the drawings on Tuesday evening, so that Barry could send the quotes out while Trevor was at the funeral on Wednesday. Trevor had an early start on Wednesday morning, he took the car to the local car wash for a good inside and outside clean up. It was the first time that he had had it done since he brought the car and he hoped that a professional inside clean would rid the car of its cigarette smell. When he returned home, Carol and Mike had already arrived and were chatting with Mum and Ellen in the lounge. Trevor made tea for them all, while they were drinking that Trevor said to his Mum, 'Mum, Mike is going to take you out for a bit of a treat today.'

'Oh, that is nice of you Michael,' said Mum, always preferring to use people's full name, rather than the diminutive version.

It must be a generational thing, thought Trevor, *people of the older generation, seem to have more respect for one another, than is common nowadays.*

'I don't like funerals, I've been to too many,' Mum continued, 'they just seem to make everyone sad and it's a nonsense about giving the departed a good sendoff, they've already gone.' Mum's bluntness and not very Christian attitudes surprised Trevor, but he put it down to her increasing dementia symptoms.

'We'll be going soon Mum,' said Trevor. 'Don't worry, we will be back tonight.'

'Don't you worry about me Trevor,' Mum replied 'I'll be just fine, if I've got young Michael to look after me.' Mum said, giving Mike a theatrically sized wink, causing a light chuckle in the room.

It's nice to know that Mum has still got her sense of humour, thought Trevor. After a last-minute check that they had gathered everything they needed, Trevor, Carol and Ellen set off in the now shiny and sweet smelling Focus.

'Glad they managed to get rid of that cigarette smell Trev,' said Ellen.

'Yes, me too,' replied Trevor. He half expected Ellen and or Carol to get back to the topic of his arrest during the journey to Frome, but they didn't. The conversation mostly revolved around their memories of times spent with Flo and Edgar and the stories they had heard about Edgar's younger days, as a teenager during the Second World War, and during his National Service after the war.

When they arrived at Ellen's parents' house, they saw that Maria and Simon were waiting in their car, which was parked just along the road from two traffic cones that had been placed in the road in front of the house. Trevor parked behind Maria and Simon's car. They all got out of the cars, greeted each other and walked up the footpath to the house. Before they could get to the front door, they heard a voice call out, 'Coo-eee Ellen.'

They looked around but couldn't see anyone.

'Over here,' came the voice again.

Then Ellen remembered Gareth, the 'enthusiastic' neighbour.

'Hi Gareth,' she shouted in the general direction of the neighbour's fence. *I remember how Mum and Dad used to chuckle about their neighbour Gareth,* thought Ellen, *they knew that he was well meaning, and always keen to help them with any odd jobs around the house or garden,* but sometimes *'he could be a little bit too keen',* they had told Ellen.

'I'll pop round,' replied the voice from behind the fence.

Ellen knew that there was no need for a reply, *he'll be halfway here by now anyway,* she thought.

'Hello,' said a shortish man with a ginger beard and a thinning ginger pate, bounding his way up the footpath. 'It's been such a long time since we last met, and it is so sad to be meeting now, in such awful circumstances.' He continued, barely stopping for breath. 'I'm Gareth, from next door,' he added, somewhat unnecessarily, as he proffered his hand to each of the visitors. 'You must be Trevor the architect-' he said as he shook Trevor's hand. Trevor smiled and nodded in return. '-I rescued those cones, you know, after they were left here when they resurfaced the road a few years ago. I knew that they would come in handy one day!' he announced proudly. 'I wanted to save a space for the hearses, it would be very unseemly to have them driving round the block looking for a space, wouldn't it?'

'Hello Gareth,' said Ellen, *how does he manage to get so many words out without taking a breath*, she wondered. 'It's so good to see you again, Mum and Dad often spoke about how much help you used to give them.' *I'd better leave out the over-exuberant bit,* thought Ellen. 'How have you been keeping Gareth?'

'Oh, fine thanks Ellen, but it was such a shock to all of us in the road, when we saw the ambulances here, for two days in a row! It must have been awful for you both.'

Ellen had heard from her Mum and Dad that Gareth was the man with his finger on the pulse of the road. Ellen's dad was convinced that he must have set up covert cameras to enable him to regale them, with such detail, of all the comings and goings in the road. 'Will you be able to join us at the funeral Gareth?' Ellen asked, out of politeness. *I'm sure that Gareth wouldn't want to miss out on such an important event for the road.*

'Yes, I will, thank you Ellen. I saw the obituary notices in the *Frome Times*, so I told the neighbours about it, because I am sure that they would not wish to miss their opportunity to pay their last respects to Flo and Edgar,' Gareth said, finally taking a deep breath.

Trevor thought, *I am most impressed at Gareth's ability to fire out so many words with just one lungful, he must have trained as a freediver or something! It certainly looks like what he lacks in stature, he makes up for in enthusiasm!*

'Glad you can join us Gareth, it means a lot to us,' said Trevor, *there goes the food budget* he thought, *the nosey git has invited half the bleeping neighbourhood!*

Ellen, keen to get on, said, 'Well Gareth, we look forward to seeing you and the other neighbours later, we've just a few things to sort out before the hearses arrive.'

'Of course,' he said, 'I'll leave you to it, see you all later.' He turned and headed back down the footpath.

Trevor unlocked the front door and he, Ellen and Carol went inside.

'It feels so strange being here, it looking so empty and Nana and Gramps not here,' said Carol, her eyes moistening. Maria linked elbows with her for mutual comfort.

Trevor immediately noticed the smell inside the house. *It might have been acceptable when Flo and Edgar were living here,* he thought, *but I've definitely got to get the carpets replaced, after I get it redecorated throughout. There is no way that we will make top dollar on this place until it is really presentable.*

Trevor had brought his tape measure and notepad along, so he could make a floorplan sketch, to take to the carpet store on the retail park, after the wake. He knew that they would want to do their own survey later, but at least having his own floorplan would enable him to get a ballpark figure for the work. *Oh gosh,* he thought, *I'm going to have to let the carpet people, the decorators and the estate agents get access for all this work. I'll be buggered if I'm going to keep popping back and forth to let them in and out! I'll have to ask Gareth to hold a door key, I'm sure he won't mind, I bet he'll love being involved in all that!*

Simon volunteered to help Trevor measure up. While they were doing that, Ellen, Maria and Carol worked their way around the house, checking that all the cupboards and fitted wardrobes had been emptied. They were pleased to find that the clearance company had done a very thorough job, both inside the house and also in Edgar's shed.

Trevor and Simon were just finishing measuring in the bedrooms when Ellen called up the stairs, 'Trevor, the hearses are here.'

Carol dashed outside to move Gareth's cones to let the hearses park. It turned out that the cones had not been needed, as there were not many other cars parked in the road. Carol put the cones in Gareth's front garden, at which moment Gareth opened his front door.

'Thanks Carol,' he shouted, 'Glad they came in handy!'

Carol was about to put him right, but decided better of it, so she shouted back, 'Thanks Gareth,' and gave him a thumbs up. Trevor, Maria and Ellen came out to inspect the hearses, checking the beautiful flower wreaths they had ordered and the 'MUM' and 'DAD' displays.

'They're nice,' said Ellen, *but I really wanted 'MOTHER' and 'FATHER', that would have been much posher,* she thought *but Trevor said that would be too expensive, for just a couple of hours in the limelight, then to be dumped in a skip round the back of the crematorium. He can be so mean sometimes. I will make sure that I mention this, when he comes crawling for my inheritance, he deserves to squirm a bit for what he has done!*

Ellen was still wrapped up in her thoughts, when one of the undertakers, a stern looking lady with tied back hair, came up to her. 'Hello, is it Mrs Braithwaite?'

'Yes,' said Ellen.

'Hello Mrs Braithwaite, my name is Maggie, I'll be your funeral director today. I'll be in your father's car with Derek driving, and in your mother's car is Adrian and John. Should you have any queries or concerns, please come to me as soon as possible, or just ask any of my colleagues. We want to give your parents the send-off they deserve.'

'Thank you, Maggie,' Ellen said, 'and this is my husband Trevor and my daughters Maria and Carol.' They greeted each other.

'I understand that you will be driving to Semington in your own car?' Maggie said to Ellen.

'Yes, that is correct,' said Ellen, *Trevor even wanted to scrimp on the flipping funeral car for us, the closest relatives, it's so disrespectful!*

Trevor joined in. 'I think that there will be a few of the neighbours following along.'

'Don't worry Mr Braithwaite, we won't go fast,' said Maggie with the slightest hint of a smile passing her lips.

Trevor looked up and down the road and could see that Gareth and a few of the other neighbours were dressed in sombre outfits and standing beside their cars, waiting for the off. *This is like a dark humoured version of the start of a Le Mans 24-hour race* he thought, supressing a smile.

'I think that we are all ready to go then,' Trevor said to Maggie.

Maggie nodded agreement and headed back to her hearse. Trevor went back to the house to collect his floorplans and tape measure, then locked the front door and they all got in their cars. That was the signal that the neighbours were waiting for, they also got into their cars and waited for Maggie to lead the hearse on the start of Edgar's and Flo's final journey. She solemnly walked in front of the hearse for about forty metres from the house, then stopped, moved to the side to allow the hearse to come alongside her, nodded stiffly to Edgar's coffin, got in the hearse and the procession started to drive off to the crematorium. The service went well, though the chapel was not even half full, without the neighbours, it would just been the Braithwaites and a couple of Edgar's drinking buddies from The Earl Haig.

After the service they all headed to the Earl Haig for the wake. Trevor was surprised to see that the function room was quite full, he was sure that there were more people in there than were at the funeral. *Got a bunch of freeloaders here!* he thought, *Glad I didn't make it free bar, or we would have been swamped!*

Gareth sidled up to him. 'Lovely service Trevor,' he said, 'glad we had a good turnout from the road, it would have been a bit quiet in there otherwise.' Trevor nodded in agreement to Gareth.

Gareth continued, 'You know Trevor, if there is anything that I can do to help you out with the house, just give me a buzz,' he said passing Trevor a business card. 'My number's on there.'

'Thanks Gareth, I appreciate your offer,' replied Trevor, 'I'll tell you what, I do need to get the place redecorated and new carpet put down, if I gave you a door key, could I ask them to contact you for access?'

'Yeah, that will be no problem at all, I'm mostly working from home now anyway,' Gareth replied.

'Thanks Gareth,' said Trevor.

Ellen recognised some of the neighbours, so she and Carol went over to chat to them, while Maria and Simon went over to look at the condolence cards which had been put on a side table, near the log fire. Trevor made his way to the bar, to try to introduce himself to Hannah the landlady whom he had booked the event with. The barman went to get Hannah for him and soon returned, followed by a flustered looking lady.

'Hello Trevor,' she said, 'Nice to finally meet you, I think that I will need to make some more sandwiches and sausage rolls. We've had more of Edgar's friends turn up than we expected!'

'OK Hannah,' replied Trevor 'but no more after that please.'

At that moment Gareth appeared next to Trevor, with a man who looked familiar to Trevor. 'This is Sid from Number 23 Trevor,' Gareth announced, 'He's a decorator, he could give you a quote for doing up Flo and Edgar's house.'

'Thanks Gareth,' said Trevor, then turning to Sid, 'you were at the service, weren't you Sid?'

'Yes, I was Trevor,' replied Sid, 'I did a little outside painting for Edgar last year, lovely couple, we will miss them so.'

'Great,' said Trevor, 'I'm going to give Gareth a door key, so he can let you in, when you are ready to take a look at the work. It really needs a top to bottom tart up. Here's my mobile number, so you can give me a price.' Trevor wrote his number on a scrap of paper he had in his pocket and gave it to Sid.

Trevor made his way to the buffet table, which was certainly looking a bit depleted. Realising that he hadn't eaten since his early breakfast, he put a few morsels on his plate, just as Hannah appeared with replenishments.

'Thanks Hannah,' he said.

'You're welcome,' she replied, as she turned and headed back behind the bar.

The buffet table had suddenly become popular, so Trevor quickly grabbed couple of the fresh sandwiches and headed over to where his family were huddling. 'If you want some food, you had better get a move on,' he said nodding in the direction of the buffet table. Carol, Maria and Simon heeded his advice, leaving him and Ellen to sit down at an empty table and be alone together for the first time this day. *I'll play a safety shot,* he thought. 'The Vicar did a nice service; don't you think love?' he asked Ellen.

'Trevor,' she began softly, 'I am so glad that my parents didn't hear about your disgusting, shameful shenanigans, before they passed!'

Wow! That came out of left field, he thought.

Before he could come up with a suitable reply, she continued, 'Just look at all these friends and neighbours of theirs, people they have known for years. They would have been laughing at Mum and Dad now, instead of mourning their loss. I'm torn Trevor, of course it was a tragedy to lose them so quickly and I may never get over that loss. But I am at least happy that they didn't have to live to see their highly regarded architect son-in-law, get jailed for running a *brothel!*' She said that last word loud enough for a couple at a nearby table to turn their heads towards Trevor and Ellen.

'Keep your voice down a bit love, this is not the place for that discussion,' Trevor said trying to calm Ellen down a bit.

'Why not Trevor?' She replied in an even louder voice, 'Why the f**k not, they are all going to hear about it soon enough, you know, you dirty old bastard!' she spat that last word out and by now, the room had quietened down and Ellen was now the focus of their attention.

'Maybe, we should go love?' said Trevor desperately trying to salvage what he could of the situation.

Maria came over and hugged her mother, 'Come on Mum, it's been a stressful day,' she said gently to Ellen, 'Let's go and get a bit of fresh air.' She motioned to Trevor for the car keys, which he passed to her.

'Can you please get Carol and tell her, we're going,' Trevor said to Simon, who nodded in reply. Trevor went to the bar, to settle the bill with Hannah.

'Going already my love?' said Hannah with a mischievous smile on her face.

S**t, thought Trevor, *if she heard that, then all the rest of this lot must have heard it too, or they will hear an elaborated version of it, as soon as we leave!*

'Yes,' said Trevor. 'We've got some errands to do now and a long journey home as well, so we had better be going.' He added truthfully, but it came across a bit lame, *And I've got no intention of providing anymore entertainment for you lot.* After paying the bill on his credit card, he tried to say goodbye to Gareth, who clearly was miffed that he had been deprived of valuable information to entertain his neighbours for months to come.

'Ellen alright then Trevor?' he asked, apparently trying to feign ignorance of the scene he had just witnessed.

'No, sorry Gareth, she's very upset,' said Trevor, trying to close the conversation down as soon as possible, 'it's been a tough time for her, losing both parents like that. We'll get her home, so she can rest. Thanks for your offer of help with the house Gareth, we really appreciate it. I'd better go see to her right away,' he said, turning on his heels and ignoring Gareth's follow up questions. As he walked out the door, he could hear the conversation level rise again. *Well, that will definitely keep them gossiping for a while,* he thought as the door closed behind him.

Chapter 14

The Fire and The Faith

31st March 2013

As he walked to the car, Trevor thought, *Ellen used to hardly ever swear, but now she has sworn out loud at home and now in the pub! I knew that this was not going to be easy, but I never thought that it would be this hard!*

He could see Ellen standing near the car, surrounded by Carol, Maria and Simon. 'Mum wants to go home Dad,' said Maria.

'Yes of course,' said Trevor, 'I've just got to go to the carpet warehouse and then get a key cut for Gareth.'

'Mum wants to go home *now* Dad!' said Carol.

'We can drop you home Mum, we're going up the M3,' said Simon.

'Thanks Simon, that's very kind of you,' said Ellen.

'Can I also come with you?' Carol asked Simon.

'Yes, of course you can Sis,' said Maria.

Trevor had never felt so alone. 'I'll see you later,' he said to their backs, as they got into Simon's car. As they pulled away, it was only Simon who looked at Trevor and gave him a quick wave. All Trevor could muster in return was a hand slightly raised and a forlorn smile.

The saleslady at the carpet warehouse was pleasantly surprised to see such a detailed floorplan. 'Oh it makes a nice change to have a plan like this to work from Mr Braithwaite,' she said to Trevor, 'and you're sure that you want to stay with that mottled grey from the Swanage range?' she asked, while thinking, *Tight fisted git! I'm not going to get much commission on that cheap s**t!*

'Yes, that will be fine thanks,' said Trevor, 'it will be nice and hardwearing,' *Not that I care how long it lasts,* he thought, *it's just got to look good in the Estate Agent's pictures.*

'And you're sure that you want to stay with the basic underlay?' *I'm not going down without a fight,* 'The Belgrave underlay will make it so much nicer to walk on.'

'Yes, the basic will be fine thanks,' said Trevor, feeling like a broken record.

'OK,' she said, 'and we've already got the vinyl flooring to go in the bathroom, kitchen and entrance hall. So, I'll just add the door joining strips, carpet gripper strips and of course the take up and disposal of the existing flooring, so we can see what the total comes to.'

Probably a lot more than I wanted it to come to, thought Trevor, as he gave her a slightly resigned smile. He then gave her Gareth's phone number to arrange access for their surveyor to double-check Trevor's floorplans. He really couldn't get out of there quick enough. As soon as she finished the quote and he had paid a deposit, Trevor said, 'Thanks very much, as soon as we are nearly finished with the decorating, I'll give you call to arrange a fitting day.'

'Thank you' said the saleslady, somewhat surprised by his hurried exit. *He is clearly not from round these parts,* she thought.

Trevor had spotted one of those key-cutting Portakabins near the entrance to the retail park, so he drove over there to get a spare door key cut for Gareth. He then headed back to Flo and Edgar's house, where he found the Estate Agent from the local company, already waiting outside for him. It didn't take Trevor long to show him around the house and garden.

The agent wanted to take photos.

'No,' said Trevor, 'let's hold off that until after we have redecorated and got the new carpets down.' The Agent agreed and as he was leaving, the other Estate Agent from the national chain arrived. As she passed the local Agent on the footpath, Trevor could see them exchanging looks of disdain and distrust. *Makes me think of rival lions sizing each other up on the African savannah,* he thought with a smile.

The new arrival appeared to be pleased on seeing Trevor smile at her.

'Hello Mr Braithwaite, so nice to meet you, I'm Shelly,' she said unleashing a well-rehearsed greeting smile.

Trevor reciprocated and ushered her inside. *Hmm, she's definitely a looker and her perfume makes such a pleasant change in here,* he thought. He took his time showing her around, explaining that he was about to get the house fully redecorated and new flooring fitted.

'Yes, Mr Braithwaite.' Shelly said, 'Just let me know when the refurbishment had been completed and I'll pop back and get the photos done.'

'Would you like to take a picture of the floorplans that I prepared?' Trevor offered, 'So you can make a start on the sales brochure?'

'Do you want us to market this property for you then Mr Braithwaite?' Shelly asked coyly.

'Er yes, er, I suppose so,' said Trevor, more than a little bit flustered, *S**t, I'm sure I've gone red!*

Shelly pretended not to notice Trevor's discomfort; she was accustomed to having that effect on older men. 'That will be great then Mr Braithwaite, thank you,' she said. 'Do you mind if I call you Trevor?' she asked, gently sliding a multipart form out of the leather folder she was carrying. 'Shall we get a few details down then Trevor?' *Men are such suckers!* she thought.

Somehow Trevor managed to resist spluttering, as a double entendre rattled through his mind. 'Yes, let's get going Shelly,' was the best he could come out with, as he sat, breathing through his nose and watching her start filling in the Instruction Agreement.

Shelly didn't take long to finish completing her form and to get Trevor to sign it, *no point in hanging around once the fish has been landed!* she thought. 'Thank you for your time, Trevor, it was nice to meet you,' she said, as she offered Trevor a limp lettuce of a handshake.

Trevor held her hand for a split second longer than maybe he should have. 'Nice to meet you too Shelly, I'll be in touch when we are ready to get the photos taken.'

She had already turned her back and started walking away, before Trevor had finished his reply, but he was quite happy just to watch her waggle her way down the footpath.

Time for a bathroom visit, thought Trevor, checking the lingering fragrance on his hand.

When he was finished, he checked that the house was all locked up and went next door to give Gareth the door key. *I hope he is still at The Earl Haig,* thought Trevor, but Gareth opened his front door before Trevor was halfway up his driveway.

'Hi Trevor, how's Ellen?' Gareth asked, but before Trevor had a chance to reply, Gareth continued, 'She seemed very upset at The Earl Haig.'

'Yes, she was,' Trevor replied, in his most-polite manner, *if it weren't for the fact that I need favours from this guy, I would have told him to BTFO!* thought Trevor. 'She's gone home with Carol and Maria, it's all been a bit too much for her recently, she needs to get some rest.' Trevor continued. Hoping to put a line under that topic, he thrust the door key towards Gareth. 'Here's the spare key I promised you Gareth.'

'Thanks Trevor,' replied Gareth, before turning to the subject that he really wanted to quiz Trevor about. 'That was a nice bit of totty you had in there just now, you ole rogue Trevor!'

Trevor could feel his face turning red and he couldn't resist the urge to scratch the back of his neck, 'No!' replied Trevor, realising too late he was slightly overdoing the indignity level, 'She was an Estate Agent, we're going to put the house on the market, when it's been done up.'

'Yeah, I guessed that you would, but either way, she was quite easy on the eyes though weren't she!' Gareth said with a smirk spreading across his face, as he noticed Trevor's face turn red. *Who'd a thought it, Trevor the posh City architect, is an old letch!* thought Gareth, *Sid's gonna wet himself when he hears this!*

'Oh, I gave your number to the flooring people, as well Gareth,' Trevor said, trying to get the conversation back on his track and make a quick exit. 'I know that you said it would be OK Gareth.'

'Yeah, no problem at all,' Gareth replied.

'Listen I've really got to head home, gonna see how Ellen is,' said Trevor, trying to get out of further intrusive questioning from Gareth.

'Ok, give her my love,' said Gareth, disappointed that his game was cut short.

'Thanks, see you,' said Trevor, turning around to get to his car as quickly as possible. *I'm glad to be out of here, I wonder if they are all as nosey as Gareth down here?*

Trevor got in his car and started on his journey home; the silence of the journey gave him time to think about how to deal with Ellen. *Maybe she needs some counselling*, he thought, then he remembered her very negative response, that last time he suggested that they should go to couples counselling. *Maybe I could ask Carol to suggest it to Ellen, she might be more amenable if her daughter suggested it? Gotta be worth a try, she's too much of a loose cannon at the moment.*

The radio started playing Celine Dion's, 'Think Twice', *'Baby, think twice for the sake of our love, for the memory, For the fire and the faith that was you and me.'*

"For the fire and the faith that was you and me," thought Trevor, *I have so broken that faith, but was that because Ellen put out the fire? It is not really fair of me, to pin the blame on Ellen for the trouble that I am in now, but she was the catalyst, without doubt. Anyway, I cannot tell her that I blame her, I need her onside, to get her inheritance, I know that I will need that to feed the Pocahunters.*

He kept mulling things over on the rest of the journey and it was dark by the time he got home. Carol and Mike's car was parked on the road outside, so he could park on his driveway. He had correctly guessed that Maria and Simon would head home, after dropping Ellen and Carol off. The family were gathered in the lounge, Mum was pleased to see him.

'Oh Trevor,' she said, 'so glad you made it home OK; we were so worried, we saw on the news that there was an accident on the motorway!'

'No, I was fine Mum, I came on the A303 instead and there were no problems on that route,' replied Trevor.

'I had such a lovely day at the Milestones Museum today with Michael, he was so kind, showing me round there, it is lovely, you and Ellen should go there sometime Trevor,' Mum said, showing more sparkle than Trevor had seen for a long time.

'So glad you had a good day Mum,' said Trevor smiling at his Mum. 'Your journey home OK love?' he said to Ellen in an effort to break the ice and re-establish a line of communication.

'Yeah, it was fine Trev,' Ellen replied flatly.

'Mum says that you both should go to couples counselling' said Maria, in her straight to the point manner.

Maria and Carol must have worked on Ellen during the car journey home, bless them, thought Trevor as he noticed Mike shifting uncomfortably on the sofa. *Poor chap, looks like he's sitting astride the continental divide and can't make up his mind about which side he wants to be on.*

'I agree,' said Trevor, 'I'll do a web search tomorrow, to see if I can find somewhere local we can go.' Trevor thought, *I had better not say that when it was my idea the other day, she flatly refused. There is no point in rubbing her nose in it.* Inside he knew that he could proud of his magnanimity.

'What do you want couples counselling for?' said Mum, 'Me and Les never had that!'

'I've let Ellen and all of you down badly, Mum,' said Trevor, Mum looked surprised, but before she could raise a question, Trevor continued, 'I've been having an affair, for three years now, and I have been arrested.'

'Arrested Trevor?' Mum asked, her voice up an octave from normal, 'You don't get arrested for having an affair. Shame on you Trevor Braithwaite!'

His Mum's words cut right through him, she had not used that tone of voice, nor his surname since he was a teenager and had let Wendy-next-door's bike tyres down. 'No Mum, you're right, I was arrested for running a brothel,' Trevor continued, by way of a less than illuminative reply.

'Is this some kind of a joke Trevor?' said Mum, 'If it is, then it's not funny, it's giving me palpitations. Is this what upset poor Ellen so much on Sunday?'

'No, sorry Mum,' replied Trevor, 'It is not a joke, I wish that it were, but it is real, there will be a court case, I just don't know when at the moment.'

Ellen and Carol were watching this exchange between Mother and Son, Ellen was enjoying it more than Carol, *about time she knew the truth about her lying, cheating Son!* thought Ellen.

'Is this why the Police were round a couple of weeks ago?' asked Mum.

'Yes Mum,' replied Trevor, 'they were collecting evidence.' *I shouldn't have kept it from her, I thought that I was trying to protect her, but I was really just trying to have a couple more days in her good books, now it's worse, much worse. I have been so selfish, and now I've really hurt Mum, as well as Ellen.*

'But what were you doing in a brothel Trevor, no hang on, you said "running" a brothel, I don't understand what on earth is going on, are you a Pimp?!'

Trevor's Mum put so much venom in the word 'Pimp', that Ellen thought, *Shirley's teeth are about to fly out!*

'Yes, I suppose that I was Mum, but I've closed it down now' Trevor said defensively.

'Well don't think for one moment, that that makes it all OK now then,' Mum replied. 'I still don't understand how you came to be running a brothel, Trevor?'

'He wasn't actually running it Mum,' Ellen said, as she thought, *I'll give you chapter and verse Shirley, on your sainted son, then you will really know what he is like underneath that prim and proper exterior!* 'He was just fronting it for his girlfriend, while getting free nookie on the side as a bonus!'

Mum's jaw literally dropped. Carol and Mike strained to keep a straight face, Ellen felt like the cat that got the cream, Trevor just bowed his head and shook it slowly side to side.

'Is that true Trevor?' said Mum, with tears in her eyes, 'How could you do those things Trevor? Let us all down like that, it's dreadful!'

That response from his Mum stung Trevor deeply, 'dreadful' was just about the worst word in his Mum's vocabulary, he couldn't even remember when he had last heard her use it. 'Sorry Mum, I just sort of slipped into it.' It was a lame response, but it was the best he could come up with.

'Shoulda kept your trousers on, then you might not have *slipped*,' she replied, with an amount of sarcasm sufficient to make Ellen and Carol raise their eyebrows. They had never heard her talk to anyone like that before, especially not 'her Trevor'. Up 'til now, Trevor's Mum had always conveyed the impression that Trevor could walk on water, if he chose so to do.

Mike did not quite manage to hide the smirk that passed over his face when he heard Trevor's Mum response.

'I'm off to bed,' Mum said with finality, 'I can't take any more of this, I'm sure I'm going to have nightmares tonight.' She walked over to Mike and said, 'Thank you for a lovely day, Michael, I did so enjoy it.'

'You're welcome, Nan, good night.' Mike replied, with new-found respect for his wife's grandmother.

'Anyone else wanna kick a man while he's down?' asked Trevor pitifully.

'Don't you, for one moment, think that you've been let off the hook, after a little telling off from Mummy!' Ellen said, sarcastically, having decided it was her turn to take up the cudgels. 'How can I ever trust you again? You've brazenly lived a lie for the past three years, that is over a thousand days! Every one of those thousand mornings you've woken up and thought "what lies shall I tell to my nearest and dearest today?" I know that you used to treat me as an idiot sometimes and twist me round your little finger to get your own way, but I had no idea at all about just how two-faced and devious you could be! All just to get a bit of pussy! You disgust me, Trevor Braithwaite!'

For a little while, nobody said anything. Then Carol said to Mike, 'We'd best be off now.'

Mike nodded in agreement, thinking, *there is only so much humiliation-watching a decent minded chap can take.*

They stood up and said their goodbyes. Normally at this point they would discuss when they would next get together, but tonight, without a word being said, they skipped that little ritual. Trevor waved them goodbye at the door, feeling like a marooned sailor mournfully staring at the departing rowboat that had just abandoned him on a desert island. He knew that he was going to have to make a serious start on the healing process with Ellen, *that's going to be a mountain to climb,* he thought, *but even the journey of a thousand miles begins with one step.*

So, he made that first step into the lounge, where Ellen had switched the TV on to the Shopping Channel, with the volume down low. 'Like a cup of tea love?' he said, with metaphorically crossed fingers.

'Yes Trev, and a slice of the cake on the breakfast bar,' Ellen replied, much to Trevor's relief. *That's not entirely a good sign, she deliberately missed out the 'please,' but at least she doesn't want to start another round now,* he thought.

Trevor was getting quite used to sleeping in the spare bedroom now and, without discussion, they had developed a special bathroom-access routine. Working in a manner similar to the male and female weather-house dolls, they would access the common areas of the landing and the bathroom, without seeing their opposite half. Trevor, in his never-ending quest for Brownie Points, would patiently wait in his room to let Ellen go first, and only when he heard her door close, would he dare to venture out to complete his ablutions.

When Trevor came down for breakfast in the morning, Mum and Ellen were already seated at the kitchen table. Mum was regaling Ellen with details of her trip to the Milestones Museum yesterday.

'Michael showed me videos of the Ovaltineys on his phone, I never knew that you could do that, he is such a clever man! Our Carol is so lucky to have such a lovely husband. You know that my friend Claire used to be in the Ovaltineys, all that fancy dancing as a child, it did her hip no good in her later years, you know. Oh, hello sleepyhead,' she said as Trevor walked into the kitchen.

'Morning Mum,' he said as he bent down to give her a kiss on her forehead. He said, 'Morning love' to Ellen, as he gently stroked his hand across her shoulders as he moved away from the kitchen table towards the kettle. 'Anyone ready for another cuppa?' he asked, having just spotted that their mugs were both more than half full.

'No, I think that we're fine over here thanks,' said Ellen, with an edge of disdain in her voice. *I can see right through your games, you shifty git,* thought Ellen.

Trevor made himself two slices of toast and marmalade and took them and his tea over to the kitchen table.

'Trevor,' said Mum in a serious tone that caught Ellen and Trevor's attention immediately, 'I didn't sleep well last night; I am so concerned about all the trouble you've got yourself into. Now, I know that it is not my place to interfere between you and Ellen, you also know that I love you both so much and I am so lucky to be able to live with you, but you have to fix this mess you've got yourself into.' As she paused for breath, both Trevor and Ellen reached across the table, each to hold one of her hands. Looking straight at Trevor, she continued, 'You've got to try to make it up to Ellen, it's a terrible thing you've done, you've betrayed her trust, you're lucky that she didn't just walk out on you, or walloped you with her frying pan! That's what I would have done to Les, if he'd been straying from the nest with some floozie!'

Trevor, at that point, really struggled to keep a poker face, but he believed that he carried it off.

'Now, I know you mentioned couples counselling,' his Mum continued, 'so give it a go if you think that it will help patch things up between you, then great, but you will have to make the effort. You have to save what you have. If Ellen is able to forgive you eventually, then that will be perfect, but it won't be an easy path. As President Roosevelt said, nothing worth having comes easy.'

Trevor stood up, moved around the table, leant down and gave his Mum a big hug and a kiss.

'Love you, Mum.' *The inconsistent nature of her dementia symptoms is incredible, maybe the stress of talking about it last night, has given her a focus that she has not had for ages, I hope it lasts,* he thought. He then turned to Ellen, 'I've been such a fool to treat you like I did, I just wasn't thinking straight or considering the consequences of my stupid self-serving actions. You need to know that I do love you so much and I will do whatever I can, to put things right between us darling.' The voice in his head said, *I just hope that sometime in the future you may be able to forgive me.* But he decided that it was too early to say those words out loud.

'Your Mum's right Trevor, I should have hit you with the frying pan!' said Ellen roaring with laughter.

Trevor was completely taken off guard by that burst of levity, not sure how to take it.

'Don't worry, it's not too late,' she continued, the short-lived smile dropping from her face. 'Let's make a start by seeing if we can get someone at one of those couples counselling clinics to help us then Trev, are you up for that?'

Trevor knew that any answer other than a resounding 'YES!' would not suffice, so that was the answer he gave. For good measure, he decided to add, 'Most definitely.' He finished his breakfast, put his crockery and utensils in the dishwasher and said to Ellen and Mum, 'I have to go to report at the Police Station now and I'll find out about a counselling clinic while I'm out.' He gave them both a kiss and headed out of the front door. Walking down his driveway, he took a deep breath. *There is hope,* he thought, *it may just be a little chink of light at the end of the tunnel, but Ellen's use of a bit of double-edged humour gives me hope!*

At the Police Station, he apologised for not attending yesterday, but his excuse was not necessary, as they had put a note in his file last week, when he mentioned that he would be attending his in-laws' funeral on that date. Deciding to take maximum advantage of the visitors parking space outside the Police Station, he went next door to the library to rummage through the rack of leaflets. Sure enough, he found three leaflets advertising couples counselling clinics, so he took those, to use as evidence of him keeping to his side of the bargain. In normal circumstances, he would have called the clinics up straightaway, but he wanted to show them to Ellen first, and let her decide which one to call, to prove just how invested in this joint healing process he was, *should be worth a couple more Brownie Points* he thought.

On Trevor's journey home, Classic FM was playing Rodrigo's guitar *'Concierto de Aranjuez'*, a favourite tune of his. He had first heard of it, when an amazing brass version was used in the film *Brassed Off*. After searching for it online, he found the original guitar version, which seemed to be even more full of sadly, haunting, but peaceful melodies. When he found out that it was inspired by a Spanish palace garden and that it came from a short period of peace between the Spanish Civil War and the Second World War, he was even more drawn to it. It resonated with him right now, as he was facing his own strife the soothing melodies seemed to be trying to ease him through this period. He was so chilled, that he nearly hit the car in front of him, at one of Basingstoke's many roundabouts, where it had stalled while trying to pull out onto the roundabout. *Phew! that was close*, he thought, as he slammed his brakes on, *and I didn't take the opportunity to give that car a blast of my horn, I must be chilled,* he thought, *making the first steps to reconciliation with Ellen must be good for me.* The rest of the journey home went smoothly.

Ellen studied each of the leaflets carefully and finally selected one from Charlotte Evans. 'She looks nice and trustworthy Trevor, don't you think?'

Trevor thought, *Wow! I'm being included in the decision-making process, that must indicate progress!*

'Yes, I agree love, she does look trustworthy,' he said with a suitable amount of sincerity. *All I want is someone to tick a box on Ellen's extensive list of my humiliations and not to blab to the local rag!* he thought. 'Shall

I give her a call, or do you want to love?'

'You do it please Trev, you are much better on the phone than me,' replied Ellen.

Yeah, but you seem to manage OK on the phone to the Shopping Channel thought Trevor. 'OK, will do,' he said breezily.

Trevor was able to book an initial consultation for the following week. This pleased Ellen, *not too near, so it will give me time to prepare my list of grievances and not too far away, so that Trevor thinks he's been let off the hook!* She thought.

'Sorry Ellen,' said Trevor 'I've got some surveys to get on with now, but I should be back in time for dinner.

Ellen gave him one of her *special looks,* 'No hanky-panky now Trevor, remember you're out on bail from the police and Mum and I,' she said it, with a hint of a smile, just enough to let him know that her statement was partially meant as a joke.

Trevor managed to give her a tight smile and nodded, offering, 'Yes dear' without sarcasm.

Trevor slipped into his new normal of *'good Boy Scout mode',* carrying out his surveys, mostly during the day and watching TV with Ellen most evenings. The programmes might not always be to his taste, but to keep the peace, he went along with her choices. On the Friday afternoon he received a call from DC Barnes asking him to come in on the following Tuesday for another interview. That soured his mood, he had known that sooner or later, it was going to happen, but he had put it to the back of his mind. He called Caroline Moore, his solicitor and was rather put out to find that DC Barnes had already called her, to check that she could attend on Tuesday. He was definitely learning his new place in the pecking order now and it was humiliating. *Was it a coincidence,* he wondered, *that the second interview is exactly a month after the first one?*

He had more surveys to carry out over the weekend, so that mostly kept his mind off the coming second interview. On Sunday he had a call from Gareth,

'Hi Trevor, it's Gareth,' the voice said, 'How are you doing then?'

Trevor thought, *I am not about to get into an extended conversation with Gareth.* 'Yes, good thanks Gareth, but I'm with a client right now,' was the best lie that he could come up with, at that moment.

'Oh yeah Trevor,' replied Gareth sarcastically. 'How is that Estate Agent then, still hot to trot then is she?'

Trevor thought, *I wish I could slap Gareth over the phone, but that is impossible and besides I still need his help.* 'Have you heard from Sid then Gareth?' responded Trevor, letting just enough annoyance creep through in his voice, to try to get Gareth back on track.

'Yeah, sure Trevor,' said Gareth, 'he has quoted £1,200 for the redecoration work, including all materials and VAT.'

'That will be fine,' said Trevor, thinking *I'm convinced that Sid doesn't pay VAT, this is probably just Gareth whacking on his 'handling charge.'*

Trevor was well aware that this happened a lot in sub-contracting work, the Main Contractor would pass Sub-Contractors quotes up to the end Client, but with a small percentage added, under the euphemism of M.C.D. or Main Contractor Discount. It had always amused Trevor that an additional charge could be called a discount!

'OK, Trevor,' said Gareth, 'will do. By the way, he wants £500 cash up front, to buy materials.'

£500 of materials thought Trevor, *what on earth is he planning on using Gold Flock wallpaper?* 'Tell him I'll send him a bank transfer, if he texts me his bank details.'

'Oh, he won't do it through the bank Trevor, it's cash only for Sid,' replied Gareth.

I'm definitely smelling a rat, thought Trevor. 'Can I do a bank transfer to you then Gareth, so you could give him the cash? I cannot come down to Frome right now, we're very busy at work.'

'Yeah, that will be OK Trevor, I'll text you my bank details,' replied Gareth, a little bit too quickly for Trevor's liking.

'Thanks Gareth, I'll do it as soon as I get your text,' said Trevor, shutting the call down. *These people are taking me for a real sucker,* thought Trevor, but he knew that he didn't have any other options, which didn't involve multiple trips to Frome.

Tuesday came soon enough for Trevor; he drove to the Police Station and was quite annoyed to find that there were no spare visitor car park spaces. Instead, he parked in the council offices Pay and Display car park. He begrudged that he had to pay to park at the council offices. *I'm already paying these shirkers £200 a month in Council Tax and all they do for me, is collect the rubbish, four times a month, that's £50 a bag! I'd do it myself for half that!* Inside the Police Station, Trevor did his weekly signing on, a day early, *well at least I won't have to come down here again tomorrow.* After a brief wait in the reception area, DC Dorey led Trevor to an interview room, where DC Barnes and Caroline Moore were already seated around the interview table, waiting for him.

DC Dorey announced that they will be recording the interview, loaded the cassette tapes and issued the warnings that Trevor remembered from his last visit to the police station. 'Mr Braithwaite,' DC Dorey began, 'you previously said that you intend to plead guilty in court to the charges of causing, inciting or controlling prostitution for gain, is that still the case?

'Yes,' said Trevor.

'Thank you,' said DC Dorey. 'We just want to review, with you, the evidence that we collected from your flat.'

Trevor had noticed the cardboard boxes stacked up on one side of the room, he had just simply presumed that the interview room was being used for temporary storage. DC Barnes lifted one of the boxes onto the spare chair and pulled out some see-through evidence bags. Trevor could feel his face turning red, as he recognised the contents of the bags to be some of Violetta's specialist equipment that Jingfei asked him to buy.

'Do you recognise these items, Trevor?' said DC Dorey.

'Yes,' said Trevor.

'Did you purchase these items, Trevor?' said DC Dorey.

'Yes,' said Trevor.

'Yes, indeed you did Trevor, we found the receipts on your PC,' said DC Dorey.

Somehow, Trevor had managed to resist the temptation to scratch the back of his neck during these simple questions, it had taken great willpower, but he had done it, he was just annoyed that he couldn't control the colour of his face. *Would it have been easier if there had not been females in the room?* he wondered.

And so, it went on for nearly an hour, they had catalogued everything and cross-referenced a lot of the items to the accounts on his PC. They had also merged messages and calls on his phone to messages and calls on Jingfei's phone, to show how complicit he had been in the running of the flat and of organising the hotel room for the girls. Trevor was pleased that when he evacuated the girls from the Travel Inn, he had told them to switch off their phones and dump the SIM cards, otherwise the police would have entangled the girls in this as well. It was dawning upon him that, even though he had pleaded guilty, they had made a lot of effort to show, not just the breadth of his crime, but also just how deeply involved in it he had been. He could hardly start to back-peddle now, to try to reduce the scale of his involvement; they had shown him, not quite a mountain of evidence, but certainly a large hill. He was now genuinely concerned about the possibility of jail time. All his previous assertions to the contrary, made to Ellen and his daughters, had a very hollow ring to them.

When he got back to his car, he blew his top, as he saw that a parking ticket had been stuck on the car.

'OH FOR F**KS SAKE!' he shouted. It was a combination steam venting, the interview, the real threat of jail time and now a £20 fine; they all joined together to make him explode. He checked the ticket; it had only been issued five minutes earlier and he was only late back by ten minutes. The parking warden must still be nearby. *I'll go and argue this with him*, but despite a quick search of the area, he could not find the parking warden, *typical hit and run merchant!* he thought. His journey back home was less fraught, but Ellen noticed his bad mood as soon as he walked in the door.

'What's up Trev?' she asked.

'I was given a parking ticket, while I was in the police station! I've never had a parking ticket before!' he replied, *I never thought that I would be glad to have the parking ticket, but it was rather handy to cover up my jail time worries.*

'Oh! Don't worry about that Trevor, worse things happen at sea!' Ellen replied, with a level of good humour that surprised Trevor.

Definitely no point in telling her about Plod's hill of evidence, don't want to spoil her good mood unnecessarily!

After making lunch for the three of them, Trevor had surveys to carry out, he said to Ellen, 'I should be back by 7pm love, just leave a plate in the microwave for me, would you?'

'If you ask nicely, I'll put some food on it as well!' replied Ellen.

'Ha, Ha!' said Trevor, genuinely pleased to hear that Ellen was regaining her sense of humour, *This bodes well,* he thought.

Thursday came and they realised that Carol was at work, so not able to look after Mum while they went to their initial consultation with Charlotte Evans. However, Mum said that she would be happy to sit in the lounge, watch an old black and white film on TV and do some knitting, 'I'll be fine, don't you worry about me. You both go off and see if you can patch things up, it's you two that I am worried about.'

Trevor was touched. 'Love you Mum, thanks,' he said as he gave her a kiss on her forehead, before they left. The journey to the counselling clinic only took about 20 minutes, but it was the longest time that they had been together, in such close proximity, without company, since his arrest, and the silence was awkward. Trevor was struggling to think of a safe topic of conversation to fill the void, *this does not augur well for the counselling session,* he thought. Unable to come up with anything, he decided that singing along to the radio was the next best course of action. Unfortunately, he didn't know the words to the songs that were playing, so he decided silence was his least-worst option left.

Charlotte Evans' clinic was in a lovely garden office, on the side of a 1970s bungalow, situated up a gravel road in Viables, on the south side of Basingstoke. Trevor had been up this road before, on his way to carry out a kitchen survey, he was well aware that the houses in this area were not at the cheaper end of the Basingstoke housing market. He parked on the gravel drive and when they got out of the car, he saw that there were two signs on the corner of the bungalow, one on each side. The sign on the front wall of the bungalow, was pointing to the front door and said 'Evans Family'. The sign on the side wall of the bungalow, was pointing to the garden office and said 'Evans Clinic'. Obediently, they crunched their way along the gravel path to the garden office, as they approached it, a lady opened the door and greeted them.

'Hello, is it Mrs and Mr Braithwaite?'

'Yes,' said Trevor. *That's odd to say Mrs and Mr, not the usual Mr and Mrs. Have I been demoted already?*

'Please do come in,' said the lady, as she shook their hands, 'I'm Charlotte, lovely to meet you both, please take a seat.'

She pointed to a three-seater settee, which was situated parallel to a coffee table and at a ninety-degree angle to a single armchair. *Oh, this is the first test,* thought Trevor, *I shall prove my non-dominance by letting Ellen choose where she wants to sit first.*

As Trevor had hoped, Ellen duly sat at the end of the settee, nearest to the single armchair and so Trevor sat next to Ellen in the middle seat of the settee. Charlotte smiled at them both.

Got that right, thought Trevor, *I'm near but not too near, passive not dominant, so far, so good.*

Charlotte was nearly as tall as Trevor, with long flowing auburn hair, she looked like she was in her late forties and carried herself well as she walked the few steps from the door to stand beside her armchair. 'Would you like a cold drink?' she asked, 'I have cans of fizz or bottles of water.'

They both chose water and she pulled three bottles out of a fridge in the corner, distributed them and sat down. 'Mrs Braithwaite, can I call you Ellen?'

'Yes of course,' Ellen replied.

'Thank you,' replied Charlotte, turning to Trevor, 'Can I call you Trevor, Mr Braithwaite?'

'Yes of course,' Trevor replied. Charlotte gave him a quick smile, before turning back to Ellen.

'Ellen,' began Charlotte, 'at this introductory session, we will need to broadly cover the issues that you and Trevor have been having, and see if these are something that I can help you resolve, by having further sessions together, is that OK?'

'Yes, thank you,' Ellen replied.

'Now when Trevor booked this appointment, he mentioned a breach of trust which resulted from his infidelity,' said Charlotte, making Trevor wince a little.

Oh gosh, it makes it sound worse when a stranger puts it like that, he thought.

'But I'd like to hear how you felt Ellen, when he told you that he had been unfaithful.' Charlotte continued.

They continued in this vein for the rest of the hour-long session. Trevor was feeling really glum by the end of it. He really didn't want to face any more of these sessions, but he knew that he had to do whatever he could, to get Ellen back on side and ensure that he would get access to her inheritance, to pay off the Pocahunters. Begrudgingly, he paid Charlotte for the session that they had just had and payment in advance for their next weekly session. *I've got to pay all that money, to be humiliated and have to go through so much bloody soul-searching and introspection, this is going to do my head in, big-time!* he thought.

He was pleased to get back outside, into the fresh air and crunch his way back up the gravel drive to his car. 'We'd best be getting back to see Mum,' he said to Ellen, as they got in the car.

'Trevor,' Ellen said as they pulled away, 'you know that it just won't work, if you are not sincere about wanting to fix things between us.'

That floored Trevor, *Bugger! I really thought that I had come across well during that session,* he thought, *listening to all that psycho-babble, nodding in all the right places, looking suitably guilty, what more do they want!*

'Of course, I'm sincere about it love,' he replied indignantly, 'I screwed up big time and let you down badly. I'm so lucky that you are willing to try to give us another chance and let me make amends to you.'

'You didn't look or sound very sincere, to me, in there just now,' Ellen said with sadness in her voice. 'Don't forget Trevor Braithwaite, that I know you of old, I can sense when you are being slippery or two-faced. You might have pulled the wool over Charlotte's eyes, but it just won't work unless you are being honest and truthful, and you know damn well that you have always struggled with that. Even your mother told me, that you used to try to hide your bad school reports. We know what you are really like under that straitlaced façade you like to put on.'

That truth hurt Trevor deeply, he had been found out. He had always thought that he could carry on with his duplicity towards Ellen without a backlash and he was annoyed that he had become more transparent than he wished. The journey home felt more stilted than the journey to the clinic. One of Trevor's favourite songs, Cher's 'If I Could Turn Back Time', came on the radio. If he had been alone in the car, he would be singing it out loud, but today he decided that internalising his singalong was more appropriate.

Mum was pleased to see them arrive home, she walked right past Trevor in the hallway and went straight up to Ellen in the doorway, grasped both of Ellen's hands with both of her hands and looked into her eyes, 'How did it go Ellen love?'

'OK thanks Mum,' Ellen replied flatly.

'What's wrong, Ellen?' Mum said, clearly less than satisfied with Ellen's unenthusiastic reply.

'Oh, it's nothing Mum.' Ellen tried to fob off her mother-in law again, but Mum gave Ellen one of her special looks, over the top of her glasses, as if to say, *you don't fool me!*

'Well, maybe Trevor will be a bit more truthful at the next session Mum,' said Ellen, 'you know that he doesn't like facing up to the truth. I told him Mum, that unless he is honest, it will just be a waste of time and money.'

Mum looked up at Trevor, it was not easy for her, as they were all

squeezed in the narrow hallway and she couldn't move any further backwards. 'Trevor Braithwaite, you're just not going to help fix this mess you made, if you don't go to those sessions with a good heart.'

Trevor knew that they were both speaking the truth, but that didn't make it any more palatable for him to hear. *Oh, this is bad!* he thought, *Well I guess that I really am going to have to properly engage with those bloody mumbo-jumbo, couples counselling sessions, or I will never get Ellen back onside!* 'Yeah, I know you're both right, I will try to engage more, it's just that I've never liked talking about my feelings, opening up and things like that,' Trevor said, mostly to satisfy them, but partially because the truth was slowly dawning on him.

Over the next couple of weeks, Trevor did indeed keep his promise to engage more with the counselling sessions. *It's a bloody harrowing experience,* he thought, *having to sit there and be attacked from both sides.* On their second visit, Charlotte asked Trevor to sit at the end of the settee nearest her, 'Just so I can communicate better with you,' she said.

That greatly raised Trevor's level of discomfort, *it feels like she can sense every variation of the truth that I feed her,* he thought. During his internal musings, he preferred to use the phrase 'variation of the truth' rather than to think he had lied; it had a much nicer ring to it.

At the same time as he was undergoing this grilling, Trevor was doing his best to keep on top of the refurbishment of his in-laws' house. Judging by the photos that Gareth had emailed him, Sid had done a good job of the redecoration, so Trevor was happy to make the final bank transfer to Gareth. The new carpets and vinyl flooring were looking good and Shelly had produced an excellent brochure for the house, along with prominent adverts on the online house-sales websites. With the May Day holiday coming up, he was hopeful of getting some interest in the house. But on 1st May he received a letter informing him that his court trial date had been set for 2nd July. It came as a bit of a shock to him, to see it in black and white like that, but there it was. In Trevor's mind, 1st May would

always be about watching a TV screen showing a seemingly infinite stream of soldiers, tanks and huge rockets parading in front of a bunch of grumpy looking Russian leaders. It seemed to be saying to any non-Russian, 'Come on then, if you think you're hard enough, have a go!' But here he was, facing his day of judgement on the day that should be celebrating the start of Spring, new beginnings and new growth.

Chapter 15

Up Before The Beak

11th June 2013

Trevor was kept busy in May and June, fitting his surveys around his Wednesday visits to the Police Station and the Thursday Couples Counselling sessions. Even though he, initially, had little faith in the benefit of the sessions, he was now coming round to realising that talking these difficult subjects through with Ellen and Charlotte was helping to improve his relationship with Ellen. Not to the point where he was actually allowed back into the marital bed, but Ellen was definitely thawing a bit. She even agreed that her loss of libido was the catalyst for Trevor's wandering urge, but stated that it certainly did not give him *carte blanche* to open a brothel for his girlfriend. *Well, that's gotta count as a concession,* he thought, *I don't get many of those!* It was in the middle of June Caroline Moore called Trevor in to her office for a pre-trial discussion. They tried to make a list of any mitigating circumstances they could present to the court; but it was a bit of a short list:

1) He is a man of good character, 62 years of age, with no previous convictions.
2) He closed the brothel down when requested by the police.
3) He handed over the cash in his car ASAP to the police.
4) There was no intimidation or coercion of the girls working there.
5) He pleaded guilty, at the first available opportunity.
6) He is looking after his dementia suffering mother, who lives with them.

Caroline thought that she would also mention in court that Trevor and Ellen have been attending Couples Counselling sessions, to try to show

Trevor in a conciliatory light. They also discussed the evidence that the Police had collected; 'that's going to be a tough hill to climb Trevor,' said Caroline.

'Yes, I agree,' replied Trevor, 'I cannot make any excuses for having purchased all those items.'

'Agreed,' said Caroline. 'There would be no point in trying to make excuses, the prosecution will be using the purchases to show the depth of your involvement in the enterprise, in which you have already declared your guilt.'

'Do you think that I will be sent to jail?' asked Trevor.

'It's hard to say Trevor,' Caroline replied. 'Given the length of time that you were involved, yes, you probably will receive a jail term. Then again, the Judge might give consideration to your age and hand you a suspended sentence. I think that if you were younger, you would definitely serve time. It really will be up to the Judge to make that decision. I will make as much as I can of your mitigating circumstances, such as they are, and if the Judge is in a good mood, we might get lucky,' she said, opening her hands wide and shrugging her shoulders. 'Sorry, but that is the best I can offer you.'

'So don't book up any holidays', is what you're saying then, thought Trevor glumly.

He left the office and drove to see Phil, stopping on his way to buy Phil's favourite coffee at ASDA. He knew that he could rely on Phil for a peaceful bit of chat and bonhomie. He wondered if the French word *bonhomie* was derived from a conjugation of *'bon'* meaning good and *'homie'* hinting at man? Trevor thought, *I really owe it to Phil; I should spill the beans about my upcoming trial, he is a good man and he deserves to hear it from me first. It won't be an easy conversation, but it has to be broached before Phil reads about it in the Basingstoke Gazette next month.* When Trevor arrived at *Pandora's Box*, he was pleased to see that the shop was empty, as was the usual case on midweek days during school hours. *I don't know how he stays open,* Trevor thought as he walked in. The *ding* of the doorbell brought Phil out from the back of the shop.

'Hi Trev,' said Phil 'I wasn't expecting to see you so soon after your delivery, last week?'

Trevor waved the pack of ready-ground filter coffee powder at Phil. 'Just popped in for a coffee and a chin wag, if you have time Phil?'

'Well as you see, I'm not exactly rushed off my feet at the moment,' said Phil, a stoic smile on his face.

Trevor walked around the counter and followed Phil into the back of the shop, where Phil had a small worktop with a couple of kitchen stools. Trevor sat on his usual stool and watched Phil load the percolator and put it on the small gas hob to start brewing. He decided to come straight to the point, 'I've got something to tell you Phil, I'm going to be in Court in a couple of weeks' time.'

'You! Going to Court?' exclaimed Phil. 'What on earth for Trev, have you been racking up the speeding points or something?'

'I wish that it was for that Phil,' replied Trevor sullenly. 'No I've been running a brothel and we got busted by Plod!'

'Ha! Ha!' laughed Phil, nearly spilling the coffee he was pouring into Trevor's mug, 'That's a cracker mate!' Suddenly Phil stopped laughing, as he realised from Trevor's face, that he was not joking, 'You're serious? You're not pulling my leg?'

Trevor rolled out his story to Phil, who maintained a high level of incredulity throughout Trevor's revelations. He made the occasional comment 'No!' - 'I can't believe that!' - 'You've been doing that for all that time and you never let on, you kept such a straight face!' - 'You ole dog, fancy that, ole Trev's still got lead in his pencil!' which led into 'I'm sorry mate, I know you need a bit of sympathy, but I really am struggling to keep a straight face here!'

When Trevor told Phil about his earlier meeting with Caroline Moore, Phil's response was, 'Do you think that you might go to jail?'

'It's possible,' said Trevor solemnly. 'My solicitor thinks that there is a chance that the Judge might take pity on me, because of my age, but there is no guarantee.'

'I think that you're gonna be shafted bigtime mate,' said Phil, finally able to keep a straight face. 'Even if you don't get jail time, I'm sure there will be some humiliating Community Service work, plus, when you're done with that, the POCA bean counters will be round to squeeze you dry!'

'Yes, I know,' replied Trevor, 'I'm not looking forward to that either mate. I will do what I can to keep you stocked up with candles before the trial and I'll let you know if they do put me away. You never know, you might read about it first in the local paper!'

'Thanks Trev,' replied Phil, 'I appreciate your concern for my stock levels, but you really need to be focussing on your own troubles and keeping Ellen sweet.'

'You're right Phil, thanks,' said Trevor. 'Talking of which, I should be heading home, thanks for the shoulder to cry on mate.' Trevor and Phil both stood up and hugged each other, and a small tear came to Trevor's eye, *I'm lucky to have a mate like Phil that I can talk openly with, not everyone has that,* he thought.

Back home, Trevor decided that he would not share Caroline's concerns about the potential for jail time, with Ellen. *I know that I am meant to have turned over a new leaf and become all honest and open and all that,* he thought, *but I just know that she will only get herself all worked up over it unnecessarily and give me endless earache between now and the trial.*

'Hi love, how did it go?' Ellen asked when he walked in.

'Yes, OK thanks,' replied Trevor, 'we worked on preparing a list of mitigating circumstances to present to the Judge.'

'Well, that couldn't have taken very long then Trevor,' said Ellen cynically. 'Where on earth have you been for the rest of the time then? You've been gone nearly three hours!'

She's promoted herself to be my bloody probation officer now! thought Trevor. 'Oh, Phil asked me to give him a hand to move some stock around, so I went there and we had a coffee afterwards.' Thinking, *well that is only half a variation of the truth, so that doesn't count really!*

'Well, OK then, just as long as you're not getting up to any of your old hanky-panky,' replied Ellen. 'I've got my eye on you now Trevor Braithwaite, so you make sure that keep your nose clean, I don't want to hear about any more shenanigans from you, you've given me more than enough grief as it is already!'

'You are right love,' said Trevor, *her ability to string so many clichés together in one sentence never fails to amaze me!* 'No, trust me Ellen, I'm keeping to the straight and narrow from now on, I let you down badly and I promise that I won't do it again.'

'Well Trevor, I'll give you the benefit of the doubt right now, but I'm warning you, don't step out of line!' said Ellen, thinking to herself, *I remember that we were taught a Mark Twain saying at school 'Everyone is a moon, and has a dark side which he never shows to anybody.' That certainly sums my bloody Trevor up nicely!*

'I'm going out to the workshop to make some more candles for Phil,' said Trevor, keen to draw a line under the conversation. 'Do you want a tea love? I'm gonna make one for me, before I go out to the workshop,'

'No thanks Trev, I'm alright,' replied Ellen thinking, *I don't want you bloody poisoning me, just because I'm giving you a long overdue grilling!*

Out in the workshop, Trevor was once again master of all he surveyed, his relief was palpable. He put his radio on, Classic FM had just started playing 'Spring' from Vivaldi's *Four Seasons*. This was one of Trevor's long time, favourite pieces, especially the first four minutes, it was a real pick-me-up for him, after the lecture from Ellen. It always made him think of new beginnings, soaring hopes, treasures to come, the eternally positive promise of new growth that spring holds. After his chat with Phil, Trevor had decided that he really should start to make a stock of candles for Phil, just in case he did get a prison sentence. He didn't want to let Phil down again, like he had a few years ago, when his dad was dying. At the time Phil had been very understanding about it, but he had had to buy in alternative candles. Present difficulties aside, Trevor still tried to live by the Scout Law to be trustworthy. He wanted to prepare as many candles now, so that he could to do his best for Phil. Deep down Trevor also found his candle making therapeutic, it was an escape for him, a chance for him to immerse himself in his own thoughts and produce a tangible product without Ellen's supervision and criticisms.

By the end of June, Ellen was still trying to decide if she would attend the trial or not. She wanted to go to see Trevor face his judgement, but she did not want to be there when all the sordid details were read out in public. In the end she decided that she would not attend the trial, in case there were any press in attendance, who might take her photo. She really did not want to see her face alongside Trevor's on the front page of the *Basingstoke Gazette*. Over breakfast, one day, she told Trevor.

'I've decided that I'm not going to the trial Trevor, I really don't want to have my nose rubbed in all your sick goings-on, so I'll stay home and look after Mum, as Carol can't get time off work.'

'OK love,' replied Trevor, 'I quite understand.' *So, I will be there on my own, that will probably be a good thing, the less witnesses to my embarrassment, the better.*

The morning of Tuesday 2nd July could not come quickly enough for Trevor, he was desperate to put this great unknown behind him. He was of course hoping to keep out of jail, but mostly he was hoping for a measure of certainty about his future. He dressed himself in his best suit and tie and stuck his OFC lapel pin in his left-hand lapel, in the hope that it might help his case. He also packed an overnight bag, with two changes of clothes and some toiletries, which he hoped he would not need. The taxi that he had booked arrived dead on the dot of 9am, as he had requested, *Cor! I feel like a prisoner in the Tower of London, making his last journey to the executioner's chopping block,* he thought. Ellen and Mum gave him their best wishes and kissed him goodbye as he left,

It's been a while since I last had a kiss from Ellen, he thought. *How long will it be until the next one?*

Trevor was not in a mood for small talk and it appeared that the taxi driver was also not up for a chat, so the 15-minute drive was passed in silence. Outside the Court, Trevor paid and thanked the driver, to which the taxi driver responded with, 'Good Luck mate!'

WTF! thought Trevor, *how did he guess that I was on trial?*

Once through the entrance security checks, Trevor approached the reception desk. The staff there logged him in and directed him up the staircase to the first floor Waiting Room, where he took a seat. As he looked around the room, he noticed that it seemed to be roughly divided into two groups, some were smartly dressed but looking nervous. The others were dressed on a scale of casual to scruffy whilst slouching in their chairs and giving off a 'devil may care' attitude. Trevor noticed that some of the room's occupants were studying two typed A4 sheets on a noticeboard, so he walked over to see what was on them. It was a list of scheduled times of Trials and Court numbers; he saw that had been scheduled for 11.30am in Courtroom Three. *That's a two-hour wait in these bloody uncomfortable chairs,* he thought, *is this the beginning of my punishment?* Just before 10am, an usher came in and called for those attending Court One to follow her, this was followed by other ushers collecting people for the other courts. This process was repeated several times until, just after 11am, Trevor was called by the usher for Court Three. Trevor followed him up a staircase, along a maze of corridors and through several doors, *I'll never be able to find my way back through this maze without help,* thought Trevor. As he was ushered through a final door, he found himself in the dock, on one side of a surprisingly small, 1980s era, courtroom. Trevor's architects mind estimated that it was only about 8m wide by 5m deep; the Judge's bench was on the longer side of the court to Trevor's left. Caroline Moore, who was seated at her desk, in front of and a bit lower down than Trevor, briefly smiled up at him in acknowledgement. Further across the courtroom from Caroline was another desk, which Trevor correctly presumed was the prosecutor's desk. There were no jury benches in the room, but across the other side of the courtroom from Trevor was the Public Gallery, comprised of a few sparsely populated benches. Trevor recognised Phil and Barry sitting there, but not the five other people. He presumed that at least one of them was from the *Basingstoke Gazette,* as the court was a regular source of easy news gathering for them.

The Court Clerk entered the Court via a door behind the Judge's bench and announced, 'All rise.'

Trevor was already standing, but the rest of the courtroom occupants stood up, as the Judge entered. The Court Clerk announced, 'Her Honour Judge Sarah Morgan, QC, presiding.'

Trevor, out of force of habit, tried to guess how old Judge Morgan was, his quest was made more difficult by her full-bottomed judge's wig, covering most of her apparently light auburn hair. *Gotta be late forties,* he decided, *doesn't look too bad.*

Judge Morgan announced, 'Please be seated.' Then, looking at the prosecutor, she said, 'Mr Harris.'

Martin Harris, the prosecutor, who had remained standing while the others sat, said, 'May it please Your Honour, I appear on behalf of the Crown and my learned friend, Mrs Moore represents Mr Braithwaite.' Trevor looked at the prosecutor, *maybe late thirties perhaps, don't like those glasses, nor that designer stubble!*

'Thank you Mr Harris,' Judge Morgan replied.

Martin Harris spoke, 'Your Honour, there is an unsigned, draft indictment, of an early guilty plea.'

'Okay,' Judge Morgan said.

Martin Harris continued, 'There is an application for the indictment to be signed.'

Judge Morgan looked at Caroline Moore, 'Do you have any observations Mrs Moore?'

Caroline Moore stood up. 'No, Your Honour.'

'Very well,' Judge Morgan stated, 'I direct that the officer of the Court signs the indictment. Can Mr Braithwaite be arraigned today, Mrs Moore?'

'Yes he can, Your Honour.'

Judge Morgan replied, 'Very good, okay.'

The Court Clerk announced, 'Would the defendant please stand.'

Trevor, a bit bewildered by the speed of the process so far, took a second to realise that it was his turn to do something, then he stood up.

The Court Clerk continued, 'Trevor Matthew Braithwaite, you are charged on this indictment with keeping a brothel used for prostitution, that on or before the ninth day of March 2013, you assisted in the management of a brothel, to which people resorted for practices involving prostitution. Do you plead guilty or not guilty?'

Trevor said, 'Guilty, sir.'

'Guilty, thank you, please be seated,' the Court Clerk replied.

Trevor sat down.

Martin Harris began, 'Your Honour, the defendant is a man of good character, 62 years of age, with no previous convictions. I suspect there'll be an application for a pre-sentence report. I do not propose to add to any of the facts unless it's relevant.'

'Okay,' Judge Morgan said, then she turned to Caroline Moore, 'Mrs Moore, there must be a report in this case.'

'Yes, there will be Your Honour.'

'Well then, I'd like to set a convenient date,' the Judge turned to the Court Clerk, 'Robert, do we have something in about five weeks from today?'

'The 6th of August is available Your Honour.' The Court Clerk answered.

Judge Morgan looked to Caroline Moore, 'Mrs Moore, would the 6th of August be convenient for you?'

'Yes, Your Honour, thank you,' she replied.

Judge Morgan then addressed Martin Harris, 'Mr Harris, are you aware of any other orders, applications or financial matters arising?'

'Yes, Your Honour, I believe that this case meets the tests for a Criminal Lifestyle under POCA.' said Martin Harris.

'Yes, I too believe so, there was a large amount of cash uncovered,' Judge Morgan said.

'Yes, Your Honour,' Martin Harris said, 'there might be a view towards a confiscation order.'

Judge Morgan replied, 'Yes, indeed, we can deal with that on the 6th of August. This really is a most unusual case.' Turning to Caroline Moore again she said, 'Mrs Moore, regarding Mr Braithwaite, I am ordering a pre-sentence report, keeping all options open.

'Yes Your Honour,' Caroline Moore replied.

Judge Morgan continued, 'I understand that Mr Braithwaite is reporting weekly to the Probation Service.'

'Yes, Your Honour, he reports every Wednesday at Basingstoke Police Station.'

Judge Morgan replied, 'Okay, that's good.' Then suddenly addressing Trevor she said, 'Mr. Braithwaite...'

At which point Trevor, ever eager to appear compliant, leapt to his feet.

'There is no need to stand Mr Braithwaite.'

Trevor resumed his seat, slightly dejected at having his part curtailed.

Judge Morgan continued, 'I will not be sentencing you today. I want to learn more about you and this unusual case. I will adjourn sentencing until the 6th of August. In the meantime, I want the Probation Service to prepare a pre-sentence report on you. So, I am going to release you now on bail and it will be a condition of your bail that you continue to report weekly to the Probation Service and that you co-operate with them in the preparation of your pre-sentence report. Do you have any plans to change your address between now and the 6th of August?'

Trevor said, 'No Your Honour.'

'Very well, that's it for today then, thank you.' Judge Morgan's tone had an air of finality as she spoke.

The Court Clerk stood up and announced, 'All rise.'

The courtroom occupants rose from their seats and Judge Morgan left via the door behind her bench. Trevor turned around and went to open the door behind him, but the usher was already opening it for him. She led him back down through the three-dimensional maze that was the Court building, to the main reception desk. Trevor was keen to get some fresh air, so he walked outside, carrying his unneeded overnight bag.

Once outside, Trevor sucked in deep lungfuls of the fresh air, glad to be outside, but annoyed that he would have to go through the process all over again in a month's time. He spotted Phil and Barry chatting to each other, on the other side of the road. Deciding that it would be best to satisfy their curiosity now, rather than drag it out over the coming weeks, he crossed the road to chat to them.

'Hi chaps, how we doing?' he asked as breezily as he could manage.

'Yeah, good thanks Trev,' said Phil.

'Sounds like you've had a stay of execution then Trev,' chipped in Barry.

'Yeah,' said Trevor, 'You guys fancy a pint? My shout!'

They both nodded and all three of them walked to few yards to The White Hart. Inside they found a nice quiet corner table where they could nurse their pints and chat. Trevor glanced around, recognising a couple of faces from his time in the waiting room earlier this morning, all were avoiding making direct eye contact with each other.

'So, you've gotta wait another month now then Trev,' said Phil. 'Before you can find out your fate.'

'At least that judge didn't seem too hard on you,' said Barry.

'Yeah, honestly, I was expecting worse treatment today,' replied Trevor, 'but they all seemed quite, er, human in there!'

'Well, it sounds like next time will be the real thing,' said Barry 'let's hope that they will still be 'human' then Trev!' he added with a smile.

Trevor managed to share the joke and Phil had a little chuckle, both careful not to overdo the frivolity as Trevor knew he could still get jail time. After a little while, Phil wanted to have another pint, but Trevor made his excuses to leave, as he knew that Ellen would be waiting anxiously to hear from him. He left Barry and Phil in the bar and went outside. It was short walk to the taxi rank, where Trevor got a taxi to take him home. On the way, he thought that maybe he should have called Ellen instead of going for a drink with the guys. He decided that it would be easier to tell her what had happened in person. *She might even be pleased to see me arrive home.*

Trevor was surprised to see that Ellen greeted him at the front door as he walked up the driveway. She gave him a big hug and a kiss on the lips, 'Oh Trev, I'm so pleased to see they didn't lock you up!'

This was so out of character for her, she never usually bothered to go to the door when guests arrived, that was normally Trevor's job, she preferred to wait in the lounge before greeting them. Trevor believed that she had been taking inspiration from having seen the Queen greet Prime Ministers on TV. The warmth of the welcome also astounded Trevor, *Jeez! It's like I've been resurrected from the dead,* he thought. 'Sorry love,' he said, 'They've just adjourned the trial until 6th August. I've been let out on bail, so they can prepare a report on me in the meantime.'

'Oh Trev!' Ellen wailed despondently, 'I thought that it was all over and they'd let you off!'

'No love,' replied Trevor, 'there's no chance of that happening, because I've pleaded guilty.'

'So now, we've got to wait until then, to find out if you're going to jail or not,' said Ellen, feeling crushed.

'Yes,' replied Trevor. 'It's conditions of my bail that I must keep reporting at the Police Station every Wednesday and work with the Probation Service to prepare what they called a pre-sentence report.' *It sounds to me like I've gotta weave my own noose to hang myself,* he thought.

'Oh God, Trev!' said Ellen, 'I thought that it would be all over today and now we've gotta wait in suspense for another month!'

'Yeah, I know, Ellen,' replied Trevor, 'but there's nothing we can do about it, the Judge wants to read the report before the trial. Let's go have a cuppa.' *Right now, I'll just be glad to get out of this bloody hallway!*

Trevor made tea and sandwiches for himself, Mum and Ellen and they all sat, eating their lunch at the kitchen table, while Trevor revealed the mornings events in court to them. When he had satisfied their interest, he loaded the dishwasher, tidied the kitchen and went upstairs to his study. Something that had been mentioned in court had stuck in his mind and he wanted to research it. He switched his laptop on, thinking, *That's going to be another month before I get my PC and car back! It's so annoying to be left in limbo like this.* Using his favourite online search engine, he searched 'what are the tests for a Criminal Lifestyle under POCA.' *I don't think that I lead a Criminal Lifestyle* he thought, remembering of some of the 'cops and robbers' TV shows he had watched. He was hoping for a 'Get Out Of Jail Free' card. But the more he read, the more despondent he became. He knew that he had been renting the flat for more than six months and the police had collected more than £7,600 from the flat, his car and his study, so that alone surpassed the POCA £5,000 threshold. *If Jingfei hadn't siphoned off some cash and hid it in her Bran Flakes box, I might have been able to get away with that,* he thought. But then he realised that by now the police would have found the spreadsheet on his PC showing his takings over two years from the flat, so there really was no easy way out for him, *Bugger!* he thought, *it was a nice thought, but short lived.*

He didn't have any surveys scheduled for the afternoon; Barry had kept his trial day diary clear. But when he checked his emails, he saw that Barry had now scheduled some for the rest of the week, slotted around his Wednesday visit to the Police Station and the Thursday Couples Counselling session. So, in the absence of being locked up, he decided to head out to his workshop and make some more candles for Phil. He felt good to be busy, but it all seemed a bit like straightening the deckchairs on the Titanic. A crunch was coming and there was nothing that he could do to avoid it, all he could do was to keep himself busy, so as to keep the worry of it, to the back of his mind. The other thing that had Trevor wondering was, *Why was it that it was the Prosecutor who had told the Judge about my mitigating circumstances? Had Caroline Moore given those details to the prosecutor, to cast me in a better light to the Judge? I am surprised that the Prosecutor would want to help my case.* It didn't seem to be like the adversarial process he was used to seeing on TV. In the same vein, Trevor thought; *there definitely was less formality than we see on TV trials, maybe that was due to my guilty plea?*

The rest of the weeks before the trial were filled by his new weekly routine. His first probation visit after the trial was longer than the previous visits. The Probation Officer took him into an interview room and they spent nearly an hour discussing not just Trevor's crimes, but also his physical abilities. *They must be sizing me up for some sort of manual labour, Community Service,* he thought. So, he made sure that his answers minimised his physical strength and maximised his age and he twice repeated that he was looking after his frail, elderly mother, *glad I included that in my list of mitigating circumstances,* he thought.

One morning in the middle of July, as Trevor, Mum and Ellen were having breakfast in the kitchen, Ellen said, 'You know Trev, I am surprised, and pleased of course, to see that there has been no mention of your trial in the *Basingstoke Gazette* so far.'

'That might come after the 6th August trial,' he replied, 'I was just released on bail, not sentenced.'

That did nothing to pacify Ellen. 'Well, in that case, I am definitely not going to that trial Trevor!'

'Okay love, I understand,' replied Trevor. He was about to continue the conversation with Ellen, but was interrupted by his phone ringing, it was Shelly.

'Hello Mr Braithwaite, it's Shelly, your Estate Agent,' she said warmly.

Trevor was certain that his face had turned red.

'Hi Shelly,' he said, 'do you have news for us? I'll just put you on the speaker, so my wife can also hear you.' Trevor did not want Ellen to get suspicious about any phone call he might get from a female. He switched his phone's speaker on and laid the phone on the kitchen table.

'Hello, Mrs Braithwaite, it's Shelly, your Estate Agent,' she said, again. 'Yes, I have good news for you, we have a F.A.P. offer!'

Trevor was momentarily confused. In his Architect days, an F.A.P. was a Fire Alarm Panel, a source of much aggravation to architects and designers. In a second, it clicked for him, that Shelly probably meant a 'Full Asking Price' offer.

'Well, that is good news Shelly,' he said, mouthing 'Full Asking Price' to Ellen.

'Yes,' she said, 'and they are cash buyers, chain free, renting locally, having sold their London house to downsize to the country.'

Trevor imagined Shelly playing Estate Agent 'Lingo Bingo', getting a full line for that sentence. *These people talk like they are cats trying to cross a steam by jumping from rock to rock, and every rock they land on, utters a well-worn phrase, string enough together and you are home and dry on the other side,* he thought. 'That is good news Shelly,' he replied, as Ellen nodded. 'So, I guess that they want to complete as soon as possible?' Trevor continued.

'Yes, that's correct Mr Braithwaite,' Shelly replied. 'Can I tell them that you will accept their offer?'

Trevor used his outstretched, upturned palm to motion to Ellen that she should reply to Shelly. Ellen's eyes widened, she didn't like being thrust, so bluntly, into conversations, but she realised that it was her decision to make, not Trevor's.

'Hi Shelly, it's Ellen,' she said, taking a deep breath. 'Yes, I am happy to accept their offer.'

'Ok,' said Shelly, 'thank you for your acceptance, Mrs Braithwaite, I will set the wheels in motion and get things moving as soon as possible.'

More rocks jumped on, thought Trevor. He knew that when Estate Agents say 'as soon as possible' it probably meant a minimum of three months. The Conveyancing Solicitors, Local Searches and Land Registry all had their rusty old cogs in the machine, ensuring that they could justify their fees by dragging out the process, to make it look as complicated as possible. 'Thanks Shelly,' said Trevor, 'look forward to hearing from you shortly.' He then closed the call down.

'Well, that is good news then,' said Mum, from her side of the table, 'At least that will be one thing off your worry list then Ellen.'

'Thanks Mum,' said Ellen, thinking, *she is so sweet to be thinking of me like that.*

'Yes Mum,' said Trevor, 'that will be good to get that expense out of the way now.'

'What do you mean, 'expense' Trev?' asked Ellen.

'Well, their local council gives no discount off the Council Tax for unoccupied houses,' replied Trevor. 'So, we've been paying that plus the gas, water and electricity bills.'

'But there's been no one in there Trevor, so the utility bills can't be that much,' said Ellen defensively.

'Yeah, very little usage Ellen, that's true,' replied Trevor. 'But, all those companies apply a standing charge every day, occupied or not and that racks up the bills.'

'Oh, I hadn't realised that, Trev,' said Ellen.

No, thought Trevor, *you have no idea about how many bills come with owning a home, even when it is empty. I will expect to get a good slice out of the sales price, to pay me back for all these outgoings, and that will be before I have to pay off the Pocahunters.*

Chapter 16

Judgement Day

6th August 2013

Tuesday 6th August was a beautiful sunny day, Trevor's taxi arrived just before 9am. Trevor, again, had his best suit and tie on and his overnight bag at the ready, but this time, he left his OFC lapel pin off. Ellen and Mum were there to wish him well and to see him off.

'We'll be keeping our fingers crossed for you Trevor,' said Ellen, as she gave him a peck on the cheek.

The traffic was lighter than the usual midweek morning rush hour, because it was the school holidays, so they arrived at the Court earlier than expected. Trevor was in no rush to get inside, he knew that he would just end up sitting in the first-floor Waiting Room. He spotted a suitable place, on the side of the Court car park, to stand and loiter for a couple of minutes. He had chosen well; he was upwind of the smoking area and could see all the comings and goings. He wanted to enjoy a few last minutes of peaceful contemplation, in the fresh air of the summer morning.

If I do get locked up this afternoon, at least I will be able look back on these last few pleasurable moments of freedom, he mused, his mind wandering to the other people loitering around. *He looks like a car thief,* he thought about one swaggering young man going into the Court. *He's probably a junkie,* he thought about another. And after assessing the crimes of a couple of other people going through the Court door, he thought, *I wonder if they could guess what brings me to this place?*

Given that he was more smartly dressed that those he had been casting aspersions on, he decided that he would probably be mistaken for a Court official or an expert witness.

'Alright mate?' came a voice from his left, a young man in baggy, low slung jeans had come up on his blind side, while Trevor had been focussing on playing 'Spot the Crim' looking towards the Court door.

'What?' said Trevor in surprise, as he turned to face the young man.

'Wot you going down for then mate?' enquired the young man.

'Why would you think I'm going down for anything?' Trevor asked.

'You got an overnight bag there mate, that ain't no briefcase, is it now?' replied the astute young man.

Trevor was deflated and annoyed in equal measure, his halcyon pleasure-bubble burst. 'Sorry, I have to go,' he said to his inquisitor, and started walked briskly to the Court door.

He passed through the entrance security checks, walked to the reception desk, where they logged him in and directed him up the staircase to the waiting room. At the foot of the staircase he thought, *At least this will not be like when the French ruling classes, in the late 18th Century, were made to mount the steps to meet their fate with Madame La Guillotine!*

The waiting room was more crowded than it was at his first trial. Standing there in the doorway, it took him an awkward few seconds to spot a suitable empty seat, specifically one which wasn't adjacent to someone who appeared to be an undesirable neighbour. There were no sets of three empty chairs, which would have enabled him to have a space on both sides, so he had to choose the least offensive person to sit next to. Heading for his chosen seat involved stepping over several pairs of the outstretched legs, belonging to slouching ne'er do wells, but when he was finally seated, he was happy with his choice. *Back to a wall, good view of the door, not next to a smelly oik, that's as good as it gets round here.* After about fifteen minutes, the first of the ushers came in to collect their charges and transfer them to a courtroom. After about ten minutes, Trevor's name was called and he followed the usher to Courtroom Two.

The route to Courtroom Two was shorter and less tortuous than the route he had previously taken to Courtroom Three. Trevor was led though a double door which opened onto the main floor of courtroom and then across the left-hand side of the court to the dock. He noticed immediately upon entry that it was a larger courtroom that Court Three, but laid out in a similar manner. This time there were empty jury benches on the opposite side of the court and the Public Gallery was on his right-hand side, behind the Prosecution and Defence benches. He could see Caroline Moore and a colleague seated at the Defence bench. On the Prosecution bench was Martin Harris, the same prosecutor as for his first trial, accompanied by two colleagues. Trevor was surprised to see that the Public Gallery had about 15 people seated there. He recognised Phil and Barry sitting in the front row, but no-one else. *Oh, I've got a better crowd than last time,* he thought, then, *S**t that's not necessarily a good thing for me. Some could be from the Press!*

The Court Clerk entered through a door behind the Judge's bench, in front of Trevor, on his left-hand side and announced, 'All rise.'

All the courtroom occupants stood up, as the Judge entered.

The Court Clerk announced, 'Her Honour Judge Sarah Morgan, QC, presiding.'

Judge Morgan said, 'Please be seated.' Then looking at the prosecutor said, 'Mr Harris.'

Martin Harris had remained standing and said, 'May it please Your Honour, I appear on behalf of the Crown and my learned friend, Mrs Moore represents Mr Braithwaite.'

'Thank you, Mr Harris,' Judge Morgan acknowledged.

Martin Harris continued, 'Your Honour, the defendant pleaded guilty at his first opportunity to the charges against him. Briefly, the facts are that on the ninth day of March 2013, a search warrant was executed at 1002 Alencon Heights. Officers found Mr Braithwaite and a lady called Jingfei Liu present. Also discovered in the flat, were certain items, suggesting that the flat was operating as a brothel.'

'Mr Braithwaite was given a PACE caution, but before the officers arrested him, he made this admission:

"I've rented this flat at 1002 Alencon Heights for two years. I am married, but Jingfei is my mistress and she lives here. Whilst I've rented this flat, I've placed adverts in the papers allowing this flat to be used as a brothel, where prostitutes operate from."

'Mr Braithwaite's admission was recorded in the officer's notebook and signed by Mr Braithwaite. During the search of the premises, £3,290 in cash was found. Mr Braithwaite admitted to the officers that he had more cash in his car, this totalled £2,870. During a subsequent search of his home a further £1,500 in cash was found. The Crown has, at this stage, confiscated £7,660.' Martin Harris stopped for a sip of water.

'Your Honour,' he continued, 'the officers spoke to the neighbours and some complained of men causing a nuisance by buzzing the wrong flat late at night and there being a lot of coming and going from the flat.

'During an interview, following his arrest, Mr Braithwaite stated that after his wife stopped engaging in sexual activities with him, he visited a brothel on the Winchester Road, where he met Miss Liu. They went on to form a relationship, which led to Mr Braithwaite agreeing to establish a brothel for Miss Liu to operate in the flat at 1002 Alencon Heights. Mr Braithwaite paid all the rent, council tax and utility bills for the flat and placed newspaper adverts for it. Miss Liu lived there and arranged for two of her friends to work there each evening.

'Your Honour, the officers have reviewed Mr Braithwaite's accounts for the flat and have concluded that after he had paid all the outgoings, he was left, on average, with £1,100 per month...'

Judge Morgan interjected, 'Are you happy with those figures Mr Harris?'

'Yes, Your Honour, officers have also calculated that the total income from the flat over the two-year period was approximately £146,700...'

'Are you also happy with those figures Mr Harris?'

'Yes Your Honour, there is no financial investigator in Court, but there will be a Proceeds of Crime Application, a Section 18 statement and a proposed timetable sent to the court shortly,' Martin Harris replied.

'Yes, bear with me one moment, I believe that it is here.' Judge Morgan rifled through some papers and found the documents. 'Yes, I have it, the POCA investigator has asked for a hearing after the 5th December. Could we provisionally say the 16th December? Mrs Moore?'

Caroline Moore stood up, 'Yes Your Honour, that would be okay, thank you.'

Judge Morgan looked at Martin Harris, 'Mr Harris?'

'Yes Your Honour, thank you.'

Judge Morgan looked at the Court Clerk, 'Robert, could you fix an hour's hearing for the 16th December?'

The Court Clerk replied, 'Yes Your Honour.'

Judge Morgan nodded her thanks to the Court Clerk, then looked at Martin Harris, 'Please continue Mr Harris.'

'Your Honour, if I may, regarding the sentencing guidelines?'

Judge Morgan replied, 'Yes Mr Harris, please continue.'

'Thank you Your Honour, Mr Braithwaite is a man of previous good character, who was born in 1950, but the guidelines stress that protection of the public must be considered in all cases...'

'Yes, indeed,' Judge Morgan interjected, 'but this is not a dangerousness case though, is it?'

'No Your Honour,' Martin Harris replied.

Judge Morgan continued, 'There is no previous section 15A offence, so it won't be four years or more.'

Trevor's concentration level had slightly dipped during the exchanges, but the mention of 'four years or more' suddenly refocussed his attention. *What! Four years or more! They can't be serious?* His face flushed.

'Correct Your Honour,' Martin Harris replied. 'The Crown would suggest that the maximum category would be the correct starting category, given that Mr Braithwaite was a brothel keeper who made considerable profits in excess of the £5,000 threshold. So that would indicate a starting point of two years, going up to four years.'

Judge Morgan said, 'Thank you Mr Harris.' She turned to Caroline Moore, 'Mrs Moore?'

Caroline Moore stood up again, 'Thank you Your Honour. Has Your Honour had the opportunity to read the pre-sentence report?'

'Yes, I have, thank you Mrs Moore.'

'Thank you Your Honour, I have spoken to the Probation Service to see if an unpaid community probation element could be considered. I wish to make that my suggestion to Your Honour.'

'Yes, noted. Please continue, Mrs Moore.'

'Thank you Your Honour; despite Mr Braithwaite's current good health, his age rules him out of the able-bodied category of community work. Regarding Your Honour's sentencing options, I would like to re-iterate his early guilty plea and his full admissions during his interviews. He handed over large amounts of cash to the police. He has done his best to make the police's job straightforward and indeed no other evidence has been presented. The police reports of disturbances to the neighbours have not been put into statements or presented to the Defence. Mr Braithwaite was aware that his business was potentially anti-social. Following receipt of a letter from the Police, informing him that they had received reports of illegal and anti-social behaviour at his flat, he immediately and voluntarily closed the operation down. Indeed, the day after receipt of the letter, he was in the process of cleaning out the flat when the Police officers arrived to search it. Regarding the financial aspect of the operation, Mr Braithwaite's main reason for setting it up was not for personal financial gain, but to provide accommodation and an income for Miss Liu. A secondary reason was to try to clear Miss Liu's gambling debts, which amounted to some £25,000...'

'Miss Liu owed £25,000? From gambling?' Judge Morgan interjected, seeming startled.

Caroline Moore replied 'Yes, Your Honour, repaying this debt meant that, in the early days after setting the business up, Mr Braithwaite was only receiving sufficient funds to cover the bills from the flat. He was not receiving any personal gain. Certainly, large amounts of cash came into the flat, but after clearing the gambling debt, paying rent and all the bills, the profits were...'

Judge Morgan interrupted, 'That's as maybe, but we are concerned about the turnover, rather than any profits, Mrs Moore.'

'Yes indeed, Your Honour,' Caroline Moore acknowledged, 'all that I wished to convey to the court was that Mr Braithwaite involved himself in this business, so that he was able to provide for Miss Liu and therefore be able to continue their relationship.'

'An affair of the heart then, rather than of the wallet, you believe Mrs Moore?'

Trevor noticed Judge Morgan could not resist a slight smile forming on her lips, as she made her quip.

Caroline Moore continued, 'Yes, Your Honour, he now accepts the criminality of his actions and how wrong it was. He has been a man of good character for many years, with no previous convictions, but the tremendous shame that he has now brought upon himself and his family, will not easily be erased. Additionally, Your Honour, there was no suggestion of any intimidation, exploitation or coercion of the girls working there. Mr Braithwaite and Miss Liu did their utmost to provide a good and safe place of work for them. We do not know, at this stage, what has since become of the girls, but we understand that Border Force agents are progressing the deportation of Miss Liu to China. No action was taken against Miss Liu, before her deportation, but it appears that setting up the brothel was originally her suggestion. It also appears that she profited more from the business than Mr Braithwaite, who was, it seems, largely taken for a ride.'

At which point Trevor could see Phil, across the courtroom, struggling to stifle a snigger.

'One aspect of this case,' Caroline Moore continued, 'which has not yet been discussed, Your Honour, is the effect of Mr Braithwaite's actions on his wife, who was, of course, totally unaware of his affair. It has placed considerable strain on their marriage and I understand that they are now attending couples counselling sessions, to help them to rebuild their marriage...'

Judge Morgan said, 'I see. Please continue.'

'Thank you, Your Honour, yes, it was a relationship that he is deeply ashamed of having and he now has a difficult task to remain with his wife and family, regain their trust and to put things right. He is of course keen to stay in the family home at 6 Loban Close, Chineham, as he is caring for his elderly mother there...'

'His mother lives with his wife and him at 6 Loban Close?'

'Yes, Your Honour,' Caroline Moore answered, 'three years ago, Mr Braithwaite designed an annexe to the family home, for his mother to live in, following the death of his father. His mother suffers from dementia and he and his wife did not want to leave her living alone in Bracknell. Mr and Mrs Braithwaite are happy to be able to look after his mother, while still allowing her to have her own space within the home. In terms of good character, Mr Braithwaite qualified as an architect in 1982 and has designed and worked on many notable projects including bank buildings since then. He has supported charitable events at local schools, church fetes and Girl Guide troops, by donating decorative candles for sale...'

Judge Morgan interjected, 'Did you say candles, Mrs Moore?'

'Yes, Your Honour, Mr Braithwaite has a hobby of making decorative candles and is well known in his local area for donating these to local fund-raising events.'

'I see,' said Judge Morgan. 'Please continue.'

'Thank you, Your Honour. The loss of his good character and excellent reputation in the community, at his age, is something that is deeply troublesome to Mr Braithwaite. It will remain a burden to him and his family for years to come. Your Honour, I would like to suggest that the catalyst for Mr Braithwaite commencing these activities, was not just his wife's loss of libido following the menopause, but also possible depression following his redundancy from his high-flying job as an architect for a major bank in 2008. This loss of status, career and income badly affected him, so much so that he hid it, to this day, from his friends, neighbours and many family members.' Caroline Moore stopped to take a sip of water.

'Your Honour, I don't know if I can be of assistance in terms of offering suggestions, to go along with any potential orders, which might mean that immediate custody could be avoided. But in terms of residence, which could be an option for a suspended sentence. A curfew...'

'I'm sorry, in terms of what?' Judge Morgan interjected.

Caroline Moore took a deep breath and said, 'If Your Honour were minded to pass a non-immediate custodial sentence and because he is not suitable for unpaid community work, perhaps a residence curfew might be imposed?'

Wow! She's got some 'cojones', thought Trevor, *to try to tell the Judge her job!*

Caroline Moore continued, 'Under Probation Service supervision of course, Your Honour. Perhaps with an exclusion order banning him from certain massage parlours, if you think that that might be necessary?'

Judge Morgan replied, 'Thank you for your suggestions, Mrs Moore, I had indeed been considering something along those lines.' She turned to Trevor, 'Mr Braithwaite, please stand.'

Trevor complied.

'You have pleaded guilty, at the first opportunity, to an unusual offence, one of keeping a brothel used for prostitution. It is particularly unusual in your case, in that you are a man of 63 years of age, of previously impeccable character. It seems that you embarked on this course of action to please and assist Miss Liu, your mistress. Now, I understand that you personally received roughly £1,100 per month, but the business itself took in roughly £146,700 over the two years it was in operation. So given that you were operating the business for more than six months and received more than £5,000, this puts you firmly in the Criminal Lifestyle category of the Proceeds of Crime Act and as such specialist investigators will, in due course, report back to the Court how much money they believe you should be ordered to pay back. Failure to comply with that order, may make you subject to an immediate custodial sentence. Do you understand Mr Braithwaite?'

Trevor gulped and replied, 'Yes, Your Honour.'

'I am taking into consideration that you closed the brothel down and pleaded guilty, both at the earliest opportunity. Also, that you gave the Police your cash and made their job quite straightforward. There is no evidence of you controlling, coercing, or threatening the prostitutes working for you. It appears that you were using your legitimacy to facilitate the running of the operation and using the income from it to allow Miss Liu to live there, without having to work as a prostitute, whilst clearing her gambling debts. So, this really is a most extraordinary case, a most unusual one. A case unlike every other case of keeping a brothel used for prostitution. But this is a serious offence which requires a custodial sentence.'

Trevor gulped again.

'Now, I am aware that you are looking after your poorly mother and so I am concerned about the potential detrimental effect on her if I send you to prison. Also, I am reluctant to send a man of your age and previous good character to prison immediately. So, it seems to me that I can, in these special circumstances, properly suspend your sentence, as I believe that there would be no public benefit gained by sending you to prison.'

Trevor breathed a sigh of relief.

'I am therefore going to impose a sentence of eight months imprisonment, suspended for one year, and subject to a number of bail conditions. One is that during that period of one year, you must not commit any offence, anywhere in the United Kingdom. If you were to do so, you would be brought back to this court and almost certainly sent to prison immediately. Additionally, I would have liked to impose an unpaid community work order, due to the anti-social nature of your actions. But due to your age, that is not possible for me to do so. I will however impose a curfew order on you, running four days a week, for a year, starting from this Friday, to be at your house, 6 Loban Close, Chineham. This curfew will operate from 8pm Friday night to 6am Saturday morning; 8pm Saturday night to 6am Sunday morning; 8pm Sunday night to 6am Monday morning. I do not intend to enforce the curfew by means of an electronic tag, as I believe you to be a fundamentally honest man. However, you must comply with the requirements of that curfew and always be there when the Police call at your address, on random occasions, to check that you are present. This will be in place of your present Probation conditions of weekly signing on at the Police Station. As long as you comply with these curfew conditions and commit no other offences, the imprisonment sentence that I have imposed will not be activated. Do you understand?'

Trevor, overcome with emotion, tried to reply, but the words were stuck in his throat. After clearing his throat hard, he managed to say, 'Yes Your Honour.'

Judge Morgan continued, 'Now, Mr Braithwaite, I must warn you that the curfew is a serious matter. If a problem arises and you need travel somewhere during your curfew hours, then you must apply to the court, through your solicitor, for a curfew variation. It should be able to deal with the variation request administratively, rather than having to come to court. But do NOT make the mistake of breaching the curfew, because you think that you have an emergency. Is that understood?'

This time Trevor was able to reply clearly, 'Yes Your Honour.'

Martin Harris said, 'Your Honour, if I may?'

Judge Morgan acknowledged the Prosecutor, 'Yes Mr Harris.'

'Thank you, Your Honour, I have been instructed to ask for costs in this matter of £470,' said Martin Harris.

'£470? Mrs Moore, would you like fourteen days to arrange payment on that with Mr Braithwaite?' Judge Morgan asked.

'Thank you, Your Honour, yes please,' Caroline Moore answered.

'Very well, Prosecution costs of £470, fourteen days payment terms. There being no further business before the Court, I thank you both very much, I am sure that you have other matters to address.' She looked at Trevor, 'Thank you Mr Braithwaite, you are free to go.'

The Court Clerk announced, 'All rise.'

Everyone in the Courtroom stood as Judge Morgan exited via the door behind her bench.

Trevor sat back down, unable to move, quietly sobbing tears of gratitude. *At one point there, I was convinced that I would be going to jail.* But he was now so relieved that he had escaped imprisonment, he could barely control his emotions. He saw the Phil and Barry were giving him the thumbs up on the other side of the court. It took a lot of effort for him to raise his hand to give them a wave of gratitude. *I really need someone to be with me right now, to share my elation, but I have no-one, I'll just go straight home and tell Ellen the good news.*

Caroline Moore came up to him. 'I shall send you the payment details for the Court costs and to settle our account Mr Braithwaite. Additionally, I will send you the details of the curfew and suspended sentence. Is that OK?'

'Yes, thank you for your work,' replied Trevor, as Caroline walked back to her colleague at her bench.

Trevor suddenly realised that a Court Usher was standing beside him, waiting for him to leave. He looked up and smiled at her, she returned a sympathetic smile. *She's clearly seen emotional men before,* he thought.

He stood up, a little shakily at first and followed her out of the dock, back across the courtroom, through the double doors and downstairs to the reception desk. Phil and Barry were standing to the side of the reception desk, waiting for him. They both approached Trevor and congratulated him, taking turns to shake his hand and pat him on the back.

'Phew that was close Trev!' said Barry, 'For a minute there, we thought that you were going down!'

'Yeah,' said Phil, 'She looked pretty pi**ed off that she couldn't even give you Community Service!'

'You must ready for a pint now then Trev!' said Barry.

'Yeah,' said Phil, 'you've gotta celebrate getting off with just a curfew mate!'

'Sorry chaps,' replied Trevor, 'I need to get home right now, to tell Ellen, she'll be worried about me.'

'OK mate,' replied Barry, 'I quite understand. At least your curfew won't stop you doing our surveys Trev. I guess that you are still OK to carry on with them?'

'Yes,' said Trevor, 'thanks, send me the details and I'll crack on with them Barry, cheers!' Trevor gave Barry, then Phil his best attempt at manly hugs, this time without the handshake, to prevent complicating matters.

They said their goodbyes on the pavement outside the Court, Phil and Barry headed across the road to The White Hart. As Trevor walked down the road to the Taxi rank, a photographer ran up to him and took his picture. *S**t* he thought, *I guess that it was inevitable, but Ellen is NOT going to be happy to see that splashed in the local rag!*

Trevor took a taxi home and was pleased to see Ellen and Mum waiting at the front door as he paid the taxi. He walked up the driveway to them and they both hugged and kissed him, like he was returning from a military campaign in a foreign land somewhere.

'Oh Trev! You can't believe just how happy we are to see you!' said Ellen, positively brimming with joy.

Wow, I never expected her to be this pleased to see me, thought Trevor.

'So glad you're home son, we were praying for you and now our prayers have been answered,' said Mum, hugging him tightly.

'Let's go and have a cuppa and you can tell us all about it, Trev,' said Ellen dragging him inside the house.

Trevor dumped his overnight bag, triumphantly, in the hallway and they all made their way to the kitchen, where Ellen made tea, while Trevor and Mum sat at the kitchen table, clasping hands.

'So, come on Trevor, tell us what happened,' begged Ellen as she placed the mugs of tea on the table.

'Well,' began Trevor, 'the judge said she wanted to send me to jail for four years!' *No point in being too pedantic about all the details.*

Ellen and Mum gasped in unison. 'No!' said Ellen.

'You had a woman Judge?' said Mum. 'That's strange.'

'No Mum, there's loads of female Judges nowadays,' said Ellen. 'Anyway, go on Trevor, how come you're out then?'

'Well, she said that because I had confessed quickly and gave them the cash that I had, then she would give me a suspended sentence.'

'That sounds like they were going to hang you, Trevor!' laughed Mum. Ellen and Trevor joined in the joke.

'No,' continued Trevor, 'they've given me a weekend curfew for a year instead of jail, I have to be at home on Friday, Saturday and Sunday nights. If I break the curfew, I will be off to jail. The police are going to come round, at random times on those days, just to and check that I am not breaking the curfew. Also, if I commit any other crimes in the coming year, I will be straight off to jail.'

'Well,' said Ellen, 'that doesn't sound too bad then Trev, does it?'

'Yeah, I think you're right there, love,' replied Trevor. 'It could have been a lot worse! At least I can still get out and do Barry's kitchen surveys, as long as I am home by 8pm.'

Chapter 17

The Truth is Out

14th August 2013

Trevor soon settled into his new routine, only doing evening surveys on mid-week days and spending more time at home with Mum and Ellen on the weekend. The week after the trial, he was annoyed to receive a call from the police's vehicle storage compound.

'Hello Mr Braithwaite, this is Joyce at the vehicle storage compound, can you tell me when you are going to come and collect your car? We've been leaving messages for you for a week now, but we've only just been given your new phone number.'

Oh, brilliant! The left hand doesn't know what the right hand is doing! thought Trevor. 'OK, thanks, I'll pop down and collect it.'

'Yes, this week if you would please, or it will start accruing storage charges,' Joyce replied, as she cut off the call.

WTF! thought Trevor, *Giving me a hard time, when it's the Plod-shop's fault for keeping my old phone and not passing my new number on sooner!*

Trevor told Ellen where he was going and called a taxi to take him to the storage compound. It took them a little while to extricate Trevor's car, having to shuffle several other cars around first to get to it. When it arrived at the Portacabin office, it was absolutely filthy; bird droppings, cobwebs, leaves and tree sap covered it. He took it to a nearby car wash for a premium wash, which cleaned it well, except for the tree sap. *That's good enough,* he decided, *I'm only going to get rid of it anyway as Ellen prefers the Focus.* He drove to the garage on the A30, where he had purchased the Focus from. They only offered him a paltry sum for it, but he just wanted it gone; *Too many memories of Jingfei in there,* he reminisced. The garage salesman drove Trevor home, so that Trevor could hand over the car's documents.

Ellen was surprised to see the car appear then disappear, 'I thought that you would have kept it, Trevor?'

'No love,' he replied, 'I know you prefer the Focus, and anyway, I need the money to pay off my Solicitor's bill.' That was a bit of a lie, as he still had some cash stashed around the house, but he knew that he had to keep reminding Ellen to minimise her spending until the sale of her parents' house came through. 'Oh yes, that reminds me,' he said as innocently as he could, 'I must check with Mr. Hooper and Shelly about the progress of the house sale.'

'Thanks Trev, yes that is a good idea, we haven't heard much from them recently,' Ellen replied, *Don't think for one moment that I don't know what you're up to, you conniving git Trevor Braithwaite!*

Satisfied that he had got his hint across, Trevor said 'I'll give them a call upstairs, I need to prepare some stuff for my surveys this evening.' He gave Ellen a quick kiss on the cheek, before heading to his study. He was happy to hear from Mr Hooper that they were looking at a date at the end of September to exchange contracts on Flo and Edgar's house. *That will be plenty of time to get the money in the bank before the Pocahunters trial.* He thought with a little smile on his face, *now I just need to keep Ellen sweet and put on a brave face at the counselling sessions and we will be home and dry by Christmas!* He didn't bother calling Shelly, he already knew enough for now. Trevor decided that it was time to write his resignation letter to the OFC, he had no intention of going back there, knowing just how much ridicule he would face. Also, the cost saving would show Ellen that he was doing his best to cut their expenses down. He didn't give a reason for his resignation, as he knew that anything other than the truth, would stand out as a lie to them. *They'll just think that I am doing the honourable thing, in light of my conviction.* That thought put a little smile on his face.

Trevor decided that a bit of fresh air was needed, so he went out to post the OFC letter and the Change of Owner document for his car. It was quite a rare occasion for Trevor to be walking his local streets, he usually went everywhere by car. The post box was only round the corner, so it didn't take him long at all. On his way back, as he was approaching his driveway, he saw Jack-next-door, polishing his car. Jack gave him a friendly wave.

Damn, thought Trevor, *I can't avoid him now. Well, I'm gonna have to face the neighbours sooner or later, might as well get it over and done with now.* Trevor diverted onto Jack's driveway 'Hi Jack, how you doing?'

'Good, thanks Trev, what about you?' asked Jack, slightly extending the word 'you'.

'Yeah, good thanks Jack,' replied Trevor, expecting a follow up question or comment about the trial.

'We were surprised to see you in the *Basingstoke Gazette* yesterday, Trev!' said Jack, 'Dolly couldn't believe it, when I showed her!' he added triumphantly.

'Oh, I haven't seen that yet,' Trevor said weakly, *I wasn't exactly about to dash out and buy a copy!*

'Don't worry Trev, you can have ours. Hold on a sec, I'll pop in and get it for you,' Jack replied. He was nearly at his front door before finishing his sentence, giving Trevor no chance to stop him. Jack was soon striding back towards Trevor, brandishing the paper at shoulder height and with Dolly following along in his wake. 'Here you are Trev, look, you made the front page!'

'Hello Trevor,' said Dolly. 'How's poor Ellen?'

Hello Dolly,' replied Trevor, *I think I managed to hide that smirk, I can never resist the chance to say 'Hijack' and 'Hello Dolly'.* 'Oh, she's doing OK, thanks,' said Trevor, turning his attention to the paper that Jack had thrust in his hand. There he was, splashed across the front page, with an awful picture of him, looking grumpy with a glimpse of the court in the background. The headline 'Local Pimp gets Curfew!' nearly made him explode.

'It says that the judge wanted to lock you away for four years Trev,' explained Jack, 'but they let you off with a curfew, coz you're looking after your Mum. That was a bit of a result, weren't it!' Jack was struggling to restrict the size of his smile, as he eagerly awaited Trevor's response.

'Yes, you are right Jack, I too thought that I was going down for a stretch,' replied Trevor 'I suppose that I had better show this to Ellen, before she hears about it second-hand from someone else. Would you excuse me, thanks.' Trevor strode away as quickly as was polite, *I'm glad to escape further embarrassment right now, but I know there will be more to come!*

As Trevor walked off, Dolly and Jack looked despondent that the conversation had been cut so short.

Ellen opened the door for him as he approached it. 'That's unusual to see you chatting with Dolly and Jack?'

'Yes,' replied Trevor, 'They'd seen about the trial in the *Basingstoke Gazette* yesterday, come and sit down first.' He guided her to her seat at the kitchen table. *This is not going to be pretty, time to bite the bullet!*

He unfurled the paper and rotated it, so that it was facing her.

'What the F**K! How can they call you a Pimp! Trev! Everyone is going to see this! They're going to be laughing at us!'

'Don't worry so much love,' said Trevor, trying his best to calm her, 'you know what they say, today's newspaper is tomorrow's chip wrapper! It'll soon blow over and be forgotten.' As Trevor expected, that did not assuage Ellen's angst.

'Trev, this will be in all the local shops now,' she sobbed.

'That's OK love, I'll do the shopping in ASDA for us,' Trevor replied, attempting to be helpful.

'Oh Trev! Don't take the p**s, you know what I mean! This is so embarrassing, just wait till your poor Mum sees it, she'll go spare!'

Right on cue, Trevor's Mum popped her head round the door from her annexe. 'What's the matter Ellen, what's going on?

'It's your Trevor, he's in the *Basingstoke Gazette* again, look!' Ellen turned the paper to face Mum's seat.

'They could have got a better picture of you Trevor, you do look ever so grumpy,' said Mum as she sat down to study the article. 'Ah that's nice, it says that the judge spared you jail, so you can look after me.'

'Yeah, but Mum, they called Trevor a Pimp!' said Ellen, surprised at Mum's low-key response.

'Well, yes, he was, but he's given that up now, hasn't he Ellen love?' Mum looked at Trevor. 'Haven't you Trevor? It's all water under the bridge now, isn't it?'

'Yes Mum,' replied the dutiful son. *My Mum, ever the pragmatist,* he thought.

'We've known for weeks now, that it would all come out, Ellen and that it will soon all blow over, don't you worry,' Mum continued. 'You know, I was a teenager in the war, we used to tear up old newspapers to use as toilet paper, that was the value of them to us then!'

Ellen still had steam to vent, 'Yeah, but Mum, it's embarrassing to see it splashed all over the paper, all the neighbours will know about his evil doings now!'

'No, it will soon be forgotten Ellen, don't worry yourself about it,' replied Mum with an air of finality.

Ellen was only slightly mollified. She stood up. 'I'm going to start doing dinner, Trevor could you peel some spuds for us?'

As Ellen walked to the kitchen sink, mother and son exchanged smiles behind Ellen's back. Trevor went to the pantry to get the potatoes out, *I'm glad to have Mum around to help defuse Ellen.*

It was on the Sunday night, around 9pm that Trevor had his first 'doorstep curfew' check visit from the police. Trevor had expected to get a visit the previous weekend, but it didn't happen. He guessed that that was the nature of the randomness of the visits. Ellen and he had been watching TV in the lounge, when they heard the doorbell ring.

'Who on earth could that be, at this time of night Trev?' asked Ellen as Trevor was standing up.

Trevor resisted the temptation to say, *how the f**k should I know, I can't see through walls!* Instead he said, 'I'll go find out Ellen love,' as he made strides across the lounge.

It was PC 1829, the same PC who previously came to collect Trevor's spare car key. 'Hello Mr Braithwaite, I just came to check that you are here, per your curfew order.'

'Good evening officer,' Trevor replied.

'Would you mind signing my notebook, just there, under where I noted that I have attended your residence, to confirm your presence,' PC 1829 asked, pointing to a blank area in his notebook.

'Yes, of course officer, no problem at all,' said Trevor as he signed where requested.

'Thank you, Mr Braithwaite, good night,' the PC said as he turned to walk back to his car.

Trevor returned to the lounge and reported to Ellen, 'That was my first curfew visit, quite painless really, I just had to sign the PC's notebook.'

'Ah, that's good,' said Ellen, returning her concentration to the TV.

Glad she's a bit more chilled now, thought Trevor.

At the end of September Maria gave birth to a beautiful bouncing baby boy they called Brian, after Simon's dad. A few days later, Trevor, Ellen, and Mum drove over to Bromley to see their new Grandson and Great-Grandson. Ellen made Trevor stop on the way to purchase small baby clothes and nappies, 'With a young baby,' she told Trevor and Mum, 'you can never have enough of these.'

When they arrived, Maria was nursing baby Brian in bed, there was much cooing, *aah*ing, tears of joy and cuddles from her audience. It was such a lovely family bonding moment. After a short while, the visitors moved to the lounge to leave Maria and her baby to rest in the bedroom. Simon made tea for his guests and brought the mugs into the lounge, together with a couple of packets of shop brought cakes, to share around.

After some small talk, Simon said to Trevor, 'So glad to see that you didn't get some jail time Trevor. You must have been so worried about that?'

'Yes, I was,' replied, Trevor, 'at one point during the trial, I thought that I was going down for four years, but the judge back-pedalled and settled on giving me a four nights a week curfew for a year instead. So that was a big relief, as you can imagine.'

'Yes,' said Simon, 'I bet that it was. Will you have to pay a fine or anything?'

'Yes,' Trevor replied, 'I had to pay court costs and there will be another hearing just before Christmas, where they will be looking at clawing back just short of £150K from me!'

Simon was gob-smacked! '£150K, jeez Trevor! How will you be able to pay that back?'

At this point Ellen, who had been following the conversation, announced, 'I've got to sell my parents' house to pay for his misdeeds!'

The room went quiet.

Trevor said to Simon, 'Yes, it's true, I didn't save much of the money I locked what I could, away from prying eyes, in various places and we transferred our house into Ellen's name, so they can't get that either. So, yes, the sad passing of Flo and Edgar means that, when we sell their house, a big chunk of Ellen's inheritance from them will be needed to pay the Proceeds of Crime order.'

'Wow,' said Simon, 'that is tough! Sorry, but I have to ask you Trevor, when you say you locked money away, did you over pay our mortgage? Was that one of your hidey places?'

'Yes, I'm sorry Simon,' confessed Trevor, 'I should have told you, but I thought it would be better if you didn't know...'

'No, it's OK,' Simon filled the slight pause, 'we appreciate your generosity and we're not going to be all "holier than thou" about the source of the money. You are right, we would not have known about it, but we have just started a new fixed term mortgage on this house, and I was surprised to see that the amount of capital owing was quite a bit less than I had calculated, and so the new repayments are now lower than the previous ones.'

I should have known that Simon, the insurance man, would be on the ball with his figures! thought Trevor.

'To be honest Trevor,' continued Simon, 'It really made a pleasant surprise, when I saw on the statement that there had been extra monthly deposits made into the account. We just couldn't figure out where they came from. Maria had her suspicions that it might have been you, when the news of your "sideline" emerged, but we weren't sure. Do you need it back, so that you don't have to sell Nan and Grandad's house?'

'No Simon,' stated Ellen abruptly, 'I know that what Trevor did was wrong on many counts, but I am glad that it has helped you. Now with the baby here, you will need all the money that you can save on your mortgage. I am just glad that we can help you both out. And just so you know, Trevor also did the same thing on Carol and Mike's mortgage so we had better tell them now, as well.'

Trevor got up and walked over to Ellen's seat and gave her a hug and a kiss. 'Thank you love, that means a lot to me.'

'Yes, thank you so much Ellen,' Simon also went over and gave her a kiss and a hug.

Trevor's Mum piped up, 'Ooh, do I get one too?'

So Simon gave her a kiss and a hug also, as Trevor and Ellen chuckled.

'What's all this merriment going on in here?' asked Maria, popping her head round the door, 'I've only just managed to get Brian off to sleep.' she added with feigned indignation.

'Just as you thought darling, it was your parents, overpaying our mortgage!' Simon declared.

'Oh, thank you both so much,' Maria said as she hugged and kissed Ellen and Trevor. 'You don't know how much that means to us; we are so grateful for your help.'

'You're welcome love,' said Ellen. 'It was all Trevor's idea, of course, I didn't know anything about it, until the whole can of worms came out. And as you can imagine, I was moaning at him so much for having an affair, I didn't know that he had actually done something good in all of it!'

This is boding well, thought Trevor. They stayed for another hour of baby chat and then Trevor said, 'It's nearly 3pm, I'd like to head back now so we can miss the M25 rush hour.' They said their goodbyes, got in the car and headed home.

As they were driving along, Mum said, 'Trevor, I didn't understand all that mortgage stuff you and Simon were talking about, but, if like Ellen says, some good has come out of your dreadful behaviour, then I am glad for that at least.'

'Thanks Mum,' said Trevor, *if I wasn't driving, I'd give her a hug.*

Ellen managed a half turn and thrust her hand through the gap between the car seats to stroke Mum's knee. 'Love you, Mum,' she said, blowing her a kiss.

That night Ellen told Trevor that he need not sleep in the spare bedroom any more, 'Unless of course you want to Trev?'

'No, thanks Ellen,' he said, 'I'd love to join you!'

'Mind you, Trevor Braithwaite, there'll be no "cuddles"' she said with a smile.

It was a week later when Ellen received the bank transfer from Mr Hooper for the proceeds of the sale of her parents' house into her account. Even though the house had sold for the £239,000 asking price, by the time the estate agents fees, Probate charges and Mr Hooper's conveyancing charges had been deducted, she was left with just over £229,000.

She showed the letter to Trevor.

'Look Trev, they've taken £10,000 off in charges! Can you believe it?'

'Yes, sorry love, but that looks about right,' he replied, after clicking away on his calculator. 'You can see the breakdown of charges there. They all look like they are in line with their quotes.'

'Yeah, but Trev, £10,000 is a lot of money!' she said indignantly.

'That's true love, but there is nothing we can do about it, even sharks have got to eat you know!' Trevor replied flippantly. *I'm just glad the money has come through before the Pocahunters trial!* 'And besides, you've still got £229,000 clear, so that's more than you would have got, if we had tried to sell it as it was.'

'Yeah, I suppose so Trev,' replied Ellen a bit crestfallen. 'Shall I move £150,000 into our joint account, ready for your confiscation trial then Trevor?'

'No, there's no need to love,' said Trevor, 'we don't get interest in our joint account, like you do in your account, so it's better off where it is.'

That's surprising, thought Ellen, *I presumed he would be rushing to get his hands on it, maybe this leopard is changing his spots?* 'OK then Trev, I'll use some of it to clear off the overdraft in our joint account, that we built up getting Mum and Dad's house ready to sell and I'll leave the rest where it is.'

'Thanks Ellen, that'll be great,' replied Trevor, *it's looking like there is a light at the end of the tunnel! And it's not just the POCA train coming towards me!*

They were rudely awoken at 5am on the Saturday morning, by the ringing of the doorbell and a loud knocking on the front door. Trevor whipped his dressing gown and slippers on and started down the stairs, by which time Ellen had opened the bedroom curtains a bit, 'It's the police Trev!' she called, 'What on earth do they want at this time of the morning?'

Trevor was already at the door by the time she had finished her sentence. He slipped the security chain off the door and unlocked it.

A PC was standing there, 'Are you Trevor Matthew Braithwaite?'

'Yes,' replied Trevor.

'Curfew check,' stated the PC, 'Sign here,' the PC said, pointing to a blank area in his notebook.

'OK,' said Trevor. *This guy clearly missed the charm school lessons,* he thought, as he signed where requested.

'Right, see you next time,' the PC said as he turned to walk back to his car.

Trevor deliberately did not bother to reply to the PC, *Two can play the Prince Grumpyf**k game matey!* he thought as he shut and locked the door.

In the bedroom, Ellen asked, 'What on earth was that about Trev?'

'It's in the terms of my curfew love,' he replied, 'they can come and check that I'm here, anytime between 8pm to 6am!'

'That's outrageous Trev!' Ellen said indignantly, 'It's five in the bloody morning!'

'Yeah, I know love,' said Trevor, 'but it's what I had to agree to, so I could keep out of jail, we'll just have to put up with it until next August!'

'Oh Trev, that's nine months away!' she protested.

'Sorry Ellen, but there is nothing that I can do about it, we have just got to put up with it,' he replied sadly. *I've brought this on her, it's not fair, but it is what it is, we're stuck with it!*

In the middle of October Ellen decided that they did not need to go to any further Couples Counselling sessions with Charlotte Evans. They had already changed from weekly to monthly after the first two months, 'Let's give it a miss Trev, we've been going for six months now and I don't think that we're going to gain anything more from them, apart from lighter wallets.'

'OK,' said Trevor, 'if you're sure love, then I'll let Charlotte know that we are going to cancel them.' *Thank God for that! What a relief, I've had more soul baring than any man should have to put up with!*

At the end of October Trevor received a letter requesting his attendance at Basingstoke Police Station on 6th November, to be interviewed by the police and a POCA investigator. The letter stated that he should bring all his documentation and computer files relating to his financial activities. *They've already got my PC, what more do these people want?* he grumbled inwardly. Trevor gathered the paperwork he needed, but he didn't have any relevant computer files. As he was driving to the Police Station, he noticed lots of dead fireworks littering the roads. *Testament* to the previous night's festivities celebrating the near destruction of our democratic system, four-hundred years ago. *What sort of country would we be in now, if they had succeeded?* Trevor wondered.

When he was shown into the interview room, DC Barnes and Caroline Moore were already seated on opposite sides of the table. Seated next to DC Barnes, was a wiry looking man with a mop of silver hair and half-moon glasses perched low down on his nose. Trevor sat next to Caroline Moore. DC Barnes gave Trevor the usual warning, loaded the tape recorder, switched it on and asked everyone to identify themselves. The new person introduced himself as Roger Wood, a specialist financial investigator.

DC Barnes started the interview by saying, 'Mr Wood has examined the financial records on your computer and has concurred with the £146,700 total turnover figure reported in court on 6th August 2013. So, that is the amount that the Crown believes that you have benefited by, as a result of your criminal actions Mr Braithwaite, is that understood?'

'Yes,' said Trevor sullenly.

'Now, the problem that Mr Wood has encountered, is that we do not believe that you have the means to pay this amount to the Crown,' said DC Barnes, while Mr Wood nodded in agreement, 'Mr Wood reports that your bank accounts show that you are in fact overdrawn by just over £8,600.'

Inside Trevor scoffed, *Ha! these lazy wastrels are not up to date with their intel!*

'So, Mr Braithwaite,' DC Barnes continued, 'if you are unable to pay the forfeiture amount, the Judge may well decide that your immediate imprisonment is the only option open to them, do you understand?' Trevor noticed, from the corner of his eye, that Caroline Moore looked concerned.

'Yes,' said Trevor, 'can I just say that I think that Mr Wood may have only checked my bank account in early October? Since then, my wife has received the proceeds of the sale of her parents' house and has now cleared my overdraft. She is prepared to transfer further funds, when required, to our joint account to cover the demand for the £146,700.' Trevor saw that Caroline Moore looked happier.

Mr Wood leaned in close to DC Barnes and conferred confidentially. Then DC Barnes said to Trevor, 'Do you have proof of those funds Mr Braithwaite?'

Trevor produced Ellen's letter from Mr Hooper and passed it to DC Barnes, who studied it and then passed it to Mr Wood, more conferring ensued.

DC Barnes said, 'We will need to copy this Mr Braithwaite, is that OK?'

'Yes of course,' replied Trevor unable to supress a hint of smugness in his voice.

DC Barnes left the room to copy the letter. He returned, gave the original back to Trevor, and a copy each to Caroline and Mr Wood. DC Barnes put his copy on the table in front of him. He then addressed Trevor, 'Sorry to ask Mr Braithwaite, but do you have confirmation from Mrs Braithwaite, that she will transfer the funds when requested?'

Trevor's smugness evaporated, 'No sorry I don't, I could ask her to write a letter, would that be acceptable?'

Mr Wood and DC Barnes conferred again.

DC Barnes said, 'A phone call confirmation would suffice for now, if you could follow it up with a letter to Mrs Moore. Could you call your wife on speaker phone?'

'OK, will do,' said Trevor, pulling his phone from his jacket pocket. *Ellen will not be at all happy to be put on the spot like this!* He dialled the number and switched the speaker phone on.

Ellen answered after a couple of rings, 'Hi Trev, did it go OK?'

'Hi love,' said Trevor quickly, to try to stop any more words coming from her. *Phew, so glad Ellen didn't mention Pocahunters!* 'Listen Ellen, I've got you on the speaker phone, I'm with the police, my solicitor and the POCA investigator.'

'OK,' said Ellen cautiously and she received three 'Hellos' in response.

'We were discussing your inheritance from your parents,' said Trevor, 'I have shown them your letter from Mr Hooper. I have told them that you cleared our overdraft a couple of weeks ago.' Trevor found it was always more efficient when giving information to Ellen over the phone, if he broke it down into manageable chunks. 'They just wanted to hear from you, if you would be OK to transfer some of your inheritance, to our joint account, so that I can pay off the POCA demand for £146,700?' *Here goes, all fingers and toes crossed,* he thought.

There was a momentary pause. Trevor thought, *I wonder what she is thinking?*

She finally put Trevor's mind at rest, 'Yes, of course I will do that Trevor.'

Hallelujah, thank f**k for that! thought Trevor.

Mr Wood and DC Barnes had another huddled conference.

DC Barnes said, 'Hello Mrs Braithwaite, this is Detective Constable Kevin Barnes, just so that we can be clear at this end, could you possibly state clearly, in your own words, that you will transfer a sufficient amount of your inheritance, to pay off the POCA demand for £146,700?'

There was another pause as Ellen thought what she would say, then likely used the voice inside her head to repeat it to herself, as a rehearsal.

The pause was short, but long enough for Trevor to wonder, *did she hang up, has she left me here to be incarcerated?*

Then Ellen came through loud and clear 'I, Ellen Shelia Braithwaite of 6 Loban Close, Chineham, do solemnly swear that I will transfer sufficient money from my account to the account that I share with my husband,

Trevor Matthew Braithwaite to pay off the POCA demand for £146,700. Was that OK?'

Trevor thought, *if I had an Oscar, I would give it to her for that speech! I know that she didn't find it at all easy. God, I love that woman!*

Mr Wood nodded approval to DC Barnes. DC Barnes said 'Thank you Mrs Braithwaite, that was fine, if you don't mind, we will draft a letter, confirming what you have just stated and give it to Trevor to bring home for you to sign. Would that be OK?'

Ellen, more confidently now, replied, 'Yes, of course, that will be fine.'

DC Barnes used a cut-throat sign to Trevor, to let him know that he could end the call.

Trevor said, as he picked up his phone, 'Thanks Ellen love, I'll see you later, Bye.' And without further ado, he closed the call down.

In the quiet of the kitchen, Ellen laid the silent phone down on the table.

Oh, how I would have just loved to have shouted 'No! F**k him, lock him up and throw away the key!' to all of them, on the other end of the phone.

But I just couldn't. How would it have looked to Shirley, the girls and everyone, that I had the money, and didn't help my own husband – left him to be sent to prison instead? What a way of airing all our dirty linen to the world. It would be a far cry from 'walloping him with the frying pan' as Shirley once suggested.

Even Simon said how much the money that Trevor gave them has helped them, now they have the new baby.

And he has made an effort, of sorts, in those sessions with Charlotte, to admit and understand his errors and how I feel about it. But still, it was really tempting, for a few seconds. At least, she thought, *I sounded confident and official-like, making that statement, telling them that I would give him the money. I hope Trevor thought I came across well.*

In the interview room, DC Barnes said to Mr Wood and Caroline, 'Perhaps you both could agree on the text of the letter for Mrs Braithwaite to sign? Then I'll type it up and get it printed for Mr Braithwaite to take home for his wife to sign.'

Fifteen minutes later, Trevor was back outside in the fresh air, with his letter of salvation, just requiring Ellen's signature to release him from his torment.

When he arrived home, Ellen was eager to hear how the interview went and glowed with pride when Trevor described how well her starring role in it came across. Ellen promptly signed the form and Trevor scanned it into his work laptop.

He then drove to Caroline Moore's office to drop it off for her, just to make sure that she would receive it safely.

Chapter 18

Pocahunters Revenge

16th December 2013

Monday 16th December was a wet and miserable day. For a man who was about to lose an awful lot of money, Trevor found he was in a surprisingly good mood for such a day. Ellen had decided that she would attend the POCA trial to see her money being taken away. Whether his good mood was due to having Ellen accompanying him, the knowledge that he would not be facing jail time, or that his final hurdle was now upon him, he was not sure. *Must be a combination of all three,* he decided.

Trevor was again wearing his best suit and tie, and Ellen had chosen a flattering long dress and combined it with a long double-breasted coat, both of which she had purchased from the Shopping Channel for the occasion. Trevor drove them in the Focus and parked in the Council car park, making sure that he paid for four hours, which should be far more than would be needed. But his previous parking ticket was still a thorn in his side. Trevor guided Ellen through the security checks and she waited for him while he was logged in at reception. They walked over to the noticeboard to see what courtroom they were meant to be in. It was Courtroom Two again and Judge Sarah Morgan would be presiding once more, so Trevor took Ellen up the staircase and led her into Courtroom Two's Public Gallery. There were a couple of people already seated in the public benches, but the rest of the Courtroom was empty, apart from Caroline Moore seated on the defence bench, who looked up as they entered. Trevor pointed Caroline Moore out to Ellen and they exchanged smiles of acknowledgement. Trevor showed Ellen where he would be in the dock, and where the Crown's Prosecutor would be. She figured out for herself where the Judge would sit, he didn't need to explain that to her. She picked a suitable space on the front row bench; he gave her a quick peck on the cheek and left the courtroom to go to the waiting room.

To Trevor's surprise, the waiting room was quite empty, so it was easy for him to locate a seat which met all his requirements, *I just hope I don't get some smelly oik come and sit next to me now!*

Just before 10am, the first of the ushers arrived to start distributing the crims around the court building. Trevor's usher took him the same route as before, along the corridors, through the double door and across the courtroom floor to the dock. As he entered the dock, he gave a quick smile to Ellen and it was reciprocated. Trevor saw that there were two suited men, seated in the row behind the Prosecutor, he recognised one of them as the chatterbox Roger Wood and presumed that the other gent was also a POCA investigator, he had not seen either of them at the previous trials. After a few minutes wait, the Court Clerk entered through a door behind the Judge's bench and announced, 'All rise.'

The courtroom occupants stood up, as the Judge entered. The Court Clerk announced, 'Her Honour Judge Sarah Morgan, QC, presiding.'

Judge Morgan said, 'Please be seated.' Then looking at the prosecutor said, 'Mr Harris.'

Martin Harris had remained standing and said, 'May it please Your Honour, I appear on behalf of the Crown and my learned friend, Mrs Moore represents the defendant.'

'Thank you,' responded Judge Morgan.

'Your Honour, the investigators statement has been carefully prepared by Mr Wood, who is seated behind me. My learned friend and I have studied this document and agree on the figures detailed in Section 13, dated 6th November 2013.'

'Very good,' said Judge Morgan.

Martin Harris continued, 'Your Honour, you will note on page four, the total benefit accrued by the criminal actions of the defendant, is accepted as being, one hundred and forty-six thousand, seven hundred pounds sterling.'

'Yes,' said Judge Morgan.

'Your Honour, you will note that Mr Wood has fundamentally accepted the figures provided by the defendant. Your Honour will see on page six, that the total amount available to the defendant for satisfaction of the order is, two hundred and twenty-one thousand, five hundred and forty-two pounds. These funds are mostly the result of an inheritance paid to the defendant's wife, primarily as the result of the sale of her parents' house, following their deaths earlier this year,' stated Martin Harris.

'I see,' said Judge Morgan. 'Have you received assurances from the defendant's wife that she is freely willing to share her inheritance, with her husband, in this most generous manner?'

'Yes, we have Your Honour, you will see the agreement document, signed by Mrs Braithwaite, in addendum one of Mr Wood's statement,' replied Martin Harris, with the air of a knight who had just pulled a sword from a stone.

'I see,' said Judge Morgan, reading Ellen's letter. 'Mrs Moore, may I ask, is Mrs Braithwaite in court today?'

'Yes, she is Your Honour,' replied Caroline Moore, motioning towards the Public Gallery, with a slightly perplexed look on her face.

Trevor also looked in the direction of the Public Gallery, even from this distance, he could see that Ellen's face was pale and she had folded her arms around her as if she was cold.

'Then I would like to take this opportunity to commend her most highly for her generosity and for the compassion that she has shown towards her shameless philandering husband, so much so that she should see fit to keep him out of prison, rather than see him put away for his crimes. I am quite sure that some women in her position, would have kept their inheritance and let him rot,' pronounced Judge Morgan, to a smattering of approving noises from the thinly populated Public Gallery.

Ellen's face turned red, but there was a smile on her lips.

I don't think the Judge likes me, thought Trevor glumly.

'Please continue Mr Harris,' said Judge Morgan.

'Thank you, Your Honour,' replied Martin Harris. 'Given that Mrs Braithwaite has kindly agreed to share her inheritance with her husband, I therefore ask for an order for one hundred and forty-six thousand, seven hundred pounds sterling to be served on the defendant. That amount has been agreed with my learned friend, who seeks three weeks to pay. Imprisonment upon default of payment of the full amount of the order, would be two to three years according to the schedule.'

'Thank you, Mr Harris,' said Judge Morgan. 'Mrs Moore?'

'Thank you, Your Honour,' replied Caroline Moore, 'The defendant accepts the further punishment on him in connection with this case, which is the shame he feels for having to rely on using his wife's inheritance to settle the order and secure his freedom. He asks Your Honour for three weeks to pay.'

'Thank you, Mrs Moore,' said Judge Morgan, 'Well, I have say that this is a most unusual end to the most unusual case that I have had before me. If there are no further matters that the Prosecution or Defence wish to raise?'

Caroline Moore and Martin Harris shook their heads.

'Very well, in that case I declare that the total benefit to be one hundred and forty-six thousand, seven hundred pounds and the total available amount to be two hundred and twenty-one thousand, five hundred and forty-two pounds. I therefore order that the sum of one hundred and forty-six thousand, seven hundred pounds be paid within three weeks.' She turned to Trevor, 'Mr Braithwaite, I am sure you understand that if you default on this payment, without having first returned to Court to request a variation on the order in the meantime, then you will be liable for a term of imprisonment, that I fix at two years. Is that understood?'

Trevor stood up. 'Yes Your Honour.'

'Very good,' replied Judge Morgan, then looked at the Prosecution and Defence benches, 'Is there anything else?'

'No Your Honour,' said Martin Harris.

'No Your Honour,' said Caroline Moore.

'Very well, thank you both very much,' replied Judge Morgan, gathering her papers.

The Court Clerk announced, 'All rise.' Everyone stood while Judge Morgan and the Court Clerk left via the door behind the Judge's bench.

Caroline Moore came up Trevor. 'I will send you the payment details for the POCA order and my final invoice for settlement Mr Braithwaite.'

'Thank you,' replied Trevor with mixed emotions, *I'm bloody happy that the end of this nightmare is in sight, but so annoyed that it has cost Ellen most of her inheritance. I still cannot believe that that lazy investigator just used my figures. Boy, am I glad that I fudged them, it took a while, but it was worth it!*

Trevor motioned to Ellen that he would meet her outside the Court room. There he strode up to her and hugged her tightly. 'God, I love you so much darling, I'm so glad that it's over!'

'Yes Trev, I'm glad too that it's over,' she replied, 'it's been a weight around our necks for so long now, at least we can have a good Christmas now, without having to worry about it anymore, let's get out of here!'

They made their way downstairs as they were going out through the security area, Ellen saw the reporter from the *Basingstoke Gazette*, waiting outside. She had noticed him scribbling away during the trial, just along the bench from her. He was standing with a photographer. *I don't want to see another awful picture of Trevor on the front page of the Basingstoke Gazette!*

She tugged at Trevor's sleeve. 'Hold on a sec Trev,' she said as she stopped him in his tracks and straightened his tie, brushed some dandruff off his jacket shoulders and gave his silver mane a quick tidy up. 'There! I want you to look your best this time!' She gave her own hair a quick flounce over her ears.

When they stepped outside, the reporter and photographer had gone, so they walked around the corner to the car park. As they approached the entrance to the car park, they noticed that the reporter and photographer were waiting for them. The reporter came up to Ellen, which surprised her, *I presumed they wanted Trevor, not me!*

'Mrs Braithwaite,' the reporter said, 'What did you think of the Judge's comments, that your husband should be rotting in jail instead of being out, free?'

'That is not what she said!' countered Ellen indignantly.

'She called him "a shameless philandering husband." Is he?' The reporter persisted.

'No of course not, that is all behind us now!' Ellen insisted.

'She said that you should have kept the money and run!'

Ellen was struggling to retain her composure. 'I would never do that, he is my husband and I stand by him!' said Ellen firmly.

She did so well not to punch that t**t out, bless her, thought Trevor.

'Could we have a photo of you both?' the reporter asked, stepping to one side to allow the photographer to get a clear shot.

Ellen quickly tried to compose herself, re-flounce her hair and give Trevor's jacket a quick squaring up before the photographer was ready. Trevor put on his best happy, but not too happy, certainly not smug face, *Hope Ellen will be happy with how it comes out.*

The *Basingstoke Gazette* came out on the Thursday and Ellen sent Trevor down to their newsagent to buy a copy. On the plus side, the photo of them both was better than the one they had snatched of him after the previous trial. *What a bloody awful headline!* he thought as he read 'Wife Saves Love Rat Hubby From Jail' *I suppose that 'Love Rat' is better than 'Shameless Philandering Husband', they probably couldn't fit all that in.*

Ellen was almost pleased with the photo, 'She's taken it from a bad angle Trevor, it makes me look fat!'

She took the picture straight on, she didn't have too much choice of angles to take it from, if you want to show two people, side-by-side and have a bit of the Court building in the background for context! Trevor thought. 'I think that you look good in that picture love and it's not too bad of me. But read the story, they have sympathetically reported the Judge's speech to you, it makes you look like Saint Ellen!' They both laughed.

Ellen read it and agreed with Trevor, 'Yes, that's not bad is it Trev. I'm sure that Dolly and Jack would have read it by now. I'll go show it to Mum.'

Trevor went up his study and switched on his laptop. *Hope to get my PC and phone back next year,* he thought, *they promised that they would return them when the POCA order was paid.* He saw that the email from Caroline Moore had arrived, containing the details for her payment as well as the POCA payment. Ellen has previously given him the login details for her account, *'You know that I'm no good at all that online stuff Trev, you do it for me please,'* she had said at the time.

However Trevor decided, *I'm going to get Ellen and show her the transfer being made, I've gotta be all above board now.* Ellen had finished showing Mum the *Basingstoke Gazette* and they were both now in the lounge watching the Shopping Channel.

'Hi love,' he said, 'I've got the details for the POCA transfer now, do you want to come and watch me put it through?'

'Yes, thanks Trev, I'll pop up. Won't be long Mum,' she said as she blew Mum a kiss.

They both went up to Trevor's study. He cleared the pile of books off the spare chair, so she could sit down and witness him making both the POCA payment and paying Caroline Moore's invoice. It was a special moment for both of them. She had never seen how to make bank transfers online before. It is something which is for many people a simple everyday action, something that they might do without a second thought. But for many other people it is a stressful, worrying, task.

After Trevor's guidance, Ellen seemed sure that she could make a bank transfer by herself next time, if needed. While he had Ellen up in his study, he decided to show her some of the Cruise holidays that he had been researching for the New Year.

'How do you fancy going on a New Year cruise love?' he asked, 'Get a bit of winter sun?'

'But who would look after Mum, Trev?' she responded, sounding highly dubious.

'Look, here's a lovely one, a week of Caribbean Sun,' he replied tempting, 'we can fly out on the day after Boxing Day and we get back on the 3rd January. He played his Ace. 'It's all school holiday time, so Carol and Mike will be able to look after Mum!'

'You know that we've got all the family coming to us for Christmas, so it will be a nice break for you afterwards, to be able to rest and get away from it all,' he continued, 'besides we've not had a holiday for ages and after all the stress I've given you this year, it'll do you good to be waited on in luxury.'

'Ooh I do like the sound of that Trev,' she replied thoughtfully, 'and, as you say, it would be good to have a nice break after the year we have had. Shall I give Carol a call to check that they could look after Mum?'

Well, that idea seems to have gone down rather well, Trevor thought, just about supressing a smirk. *Perhaps I might even manage to get a 'little cuddle' from her while we're away.*

The End

Index by Page

165	ECG stands for Electro Cardio Gram
166	NCP stands for National Car Parks
169	POCA stands for the Proceeds of Crime Act, a law that was passed to deprive criminals of their ill-gotten gains.
199	OTT stands for Over The Top
202	CNDP stands for Châteauneuf-du-Pape, a favourite red wine of mine.
213	Trevor and Simon were a British comedy duo popular in the late 1980s
226	Nookie is old slang for having sexual intercourse
232	Hanky-Panky is old slang for unacceptable or dishonest behaviour
242	The Beak is old slang for a Judge
250	QC stood for Queens Counsellor, in the United Kingdom and some Commonwealth countries, a Queen's Counsel is a senior trial lawyer appointed by the monarch of the country as a 'Counsel learned in the law'.
262	Oik is an uncouth or obnoxious person from the lower social orders

Index by Subject

Page	Subject
110	A&E stands for Accident and Emergency department in a hospital
37	ASDA is a UK supermarket chain
78	babber is an affectionate Somerset slang word for baby
76	BDSM stands for bondage and discipline, domination and submission, sadism and masochism
156	BTFO stands for "Thank you for your Input, but it is not Required at this Juncture", AKA Butt the F**k out
41	CAD stands for Computer Aided Design, as in Revit architectural CAD software,
53	CCTV stands for Closed Circuit Tele Vision
14	City (The), refers to the central financial & business area of central London
202	CNDP stands for Châteauneuf-du-Pape, a favourite red wine of mine.
165	ECG stands for Electro Cardio Gram
34	FM stands for Frequency Modulation, a form of free to air Radio Transmission
31	GP stands for General Practitioner, a local doctor
232	Hanky-Panky is old slang for unacceptable or dishonest behaviour
17	MOT is an annual test of vehicle safety etc.
166	NCP stands for National Car Parks
226	Nookie is old slang for having sexual intercourse
16	OFC stands for the Old Farts Club
262	Oik is an uncouth or obnoxious person from the lower social orders
199	OTT stands for Over The Top
165	OTU stands for Orthopaedic Trauma Unit
136	PACE stands for Police and Criminal Evidence Act 1984
49	PC stands for Politically Correct, Personal Computer or Police Constable
122	Plod is slang for Police

169	POCA stands for the Proceeds of Crime Act, a law that was passed to deprive criminals of their ill-gotten gains.
37	PRU Hospital near Bromley, PRU stands for Princess Royal University
250	QC stood for Queens Counsellor, In the United Kingdom and some Commonwealth countries, a Queen's Counsel is a senior trial lawyer appointed by the monarch of the country as a 'Counsel learned in the law'.
25	RIBA stands for Royal Institute of British Architects
112	sarky is slang for sarcastic
242	The Beak is old slang for a Judge
34	Tinnitus is a ringing noise inside the sufferer's ears/head
213	Trevor and Simon were a British comedy duo popular in the late 1980s
17	TSI stands for "Today's Special Issue"
112	UTI stands for Urinary Tract Infection
150	WPC stands for Woman Police Officer
22	YWC stands for Young Wives Club

Soundtrack list

	Page	Music
1	34	*'La Serenissima'* by Rondo Veneziano.
2	45	'Galaxy of Love' by the Crown Heights Affair.
3	61	'Heal the World', by Michael Jackson.
4	108	'A Change is Gonna Come' by Sam Cooke.
5	116	'Moonlight Sonata' by Ludwig van Beethoven.
6	169	'Disco 2000' by Pulp.
7	224	'Think Twice' by Celine Dion.
8	231	'Concierto de Aranjuez' by Joaquin Rodrigo (guitar).
9	240	'If I Could Turn Back Time' by Cher.
10	247	'Spring' from *Four Seasons* by Antonio Vivaldi.